Sweet Violet and a Time for Love:

Book Four of the Sienna St. James Series

Sweet Violet and a Time for Love:

Book Four of the Sienna St. James Series

Leslie J. Sherrod

www.urbanchristianonline.com

Urban Books, LLC
97 N18th Street
Wyandanch, NY 11798

Sweet Violet and a Time for Love: Book Four of the Sienna
St. James Series Copyright © 2015 Leslie J. Sherrod

ISBN 13: 978-1-60162-692-9
ISBN 10: 1-60162-692-4

First Trade Paperback Printing March 2015
Printed in the United States of America

10 9 8 7 6 5 4 3 2 1

*This is a work of fiction. Any references or similarities
to actual events, real people, living or dead, or to real
locales are intended to give the novel a sense of reality.
Any similarity in other names, characters, places, and
incidents is entirely coincidental.*

Distributed by Kensington Publishing Corp.
Submit orders to:
Customer Service
400 Hahn Road
Westminster, MD 21157-4627
Phone: 1-800-733-3000
Fax: 1-800-659-2436

Sweet Violet and a Time for Love:

Book Four of the Sienna St. James Series

by

Leslie J. Sherrod

To everything there is a season, and a time to every
purpose under the heaven:
a time to be born, and a time to die;
a time to plant, and a time to pluck
up that which is planted;
a time to kill, and a time to heal . . .

—Ecclesiastes 3:1–3a

Acknowledgments

This book is dedicated to all the readers and fans of the *Sienna St. James* series. I am grateful for every single e-mail, message, and enthusiastic word you've offered. This character, who entered my imagination while I walked through a parking garage on my way to a social work seminar years ago, has made it through pages and pages of love, loss, and dangerous clients. Knowing that you've stayed along for the ride, have cheered her on, questioned her decisions, and been encouraged and inspired by her trials and triumphs makes writing about her worth it. Hope you enjoy this next chapter in her life and times.

I also want to offer special thanks to my family, friends, fellow church members, and colleagues, who have never stopped encouraging me, praying for me, and supporting my journey with all of its real life twists and turns. I'm grateful.

To my agent, Sha-Shana Crichton: you have helped and encouraged me more than you know. Thank you! To Joylynn Ross and the Urban Christian family: these books would not exist without you. Thanks for continuing to allow a platform for not only my novels, but for the work of many authors of like mind and purpose. I'm grateful.

Finally, I must give a public praise to the One who has kept every personal promise and perfected all that which concerns me. My continual prayer is that you, Lord, get all of the glory. My trust in you is complete.

Thank you and enjoy!

—Leslie

Prologue

Chocolate chip cookies, a geranium-covered arch, and the youth choir from my church singing a cappella and slightly off key. It all seemed fitting for our wedding.

"You look beautiful." Ava Diggs, my lifelong mentor and career/parenting/relationship/everything advisor studied me just before I went down the grassy aisle in her backyard. Leon stood watching me at the end of the aisle, his hands folded in front of him, waiting. Waiting for me to finally come down, put on his ring, become his wife. Waiting for us to finally become one.

We married on a chilly evening in June, the scent of gardenias and lilies and cocoa-dipped cookie bars wafting in the Tuesday night breeze. Ava Diggs hosted the ceremony at her home in East Towson, insisting that my bridal path weave around her well-nurtured garden. The reception was at Leon's bakery by Baltimore's Inner Harbor. We'd reconnected there just a month or so earlier, but saw no need to waste another month or another minute. He proposed within a week of our reunion. With no hesitation, I said yes.

Roman, my son, who'd just finished his first year of college, was Leon's best man. My sister, Yvette, stood beside me as the self-titled "diva of honor." I let her pick her own gown, and, truth be told, in her muted purple chiffon stunner, she did look better than me.

I didn't care.

The only thing that mattered was that Leon Sanderson and I would be husband and wife.

Finally.

Like a June graduation ceremony, I'd finally stopped failing and repeating my life lessons on love and happiness, faith and forgiveness, and had accepted the promotion to my happily ever after. Our signed marriage license was my degree. And that night, after we left the garden and the bakery, after we set down our luggage in a room in a bed and breakfast that overlooked the quiet waterfront of St. Michael's, Maryland, we spent the night embedded in each other's arms, saying little, moving much.

Things I won't forget about our first night together: The light rain that streaked down the windowpanes and shimmered in the moonlight. The sound of water lapping against the piers. The whisper of my name on Leon's lips. The freedom. The weightlessness.

The joy.

Things I soon realized I'd forgotten about my wedding day: The cabbage soup a former client's foster mother bought to the reception. My mother's quick eye roll and long sigh at my first husband's other family when they arrived.

And, most significantly, the old woman who tapped on Leon's bakery window while we ate our wedding cupcakes. I saw her through the glass and she smiled at me before finally scurrying away, a dingy black patent leather purse bouncing off her side.

The soup and my mother's raised eyebrow were harmless. Well, maybe not the soup entirely.

But the old woman . . .

Chapter 1

"I solemnly swear to tell the truth, the whole truth, and nothing but the truth, so help me God." *Yes, please help me, God:* the only coherent thought running through my brain at the moment. *What am I doing here?*

The bumpy leather of the Bible cover beneath my palm felt cold to the touch. As the bailiff took the sacred book away, I felt all eyes boring through me from the courtroom benches, from the other side of TV screens across the nation, from behind computer and phone devices around the world.

Okay, maybe this case wasn't airing around the entire world, but at the moment it had consumed my complete attention, and that of all of Baltimore. This case had been eating away at my appetite and sleep, and, in the immediate moment, had left a pool of sweat on the back of my thighs. There were some TV cameras, I reminded myself as I thought about that pool of sticky sweat on my legs that was certainly seeping through my stockings and staining my clothes. Should have gone with the darker suit. Leon was right; this was not the time to make a cheery fashion statement with my bright yellow blazer and knee-length skirt. I probably looked like a balloon at a little kid's birthday party and not the leading witness for a triple murder trial. I should have listened to him; he had a background in law enforcement. I was a therapist, at the moment specializing only in children's play therapy, having grown weary of the creeps, killers, and terrorists who seemed to be attracted to my practice.

But this case in which I was testifying had nothing to do with the children I served.

The defendant's attorney, a slender black woman who went by the name of Shanay Deen, stood and flipped through some index cards. She frowned at a note passed to her by her assistant and then grinned at me as if she were a tiger and I was a limping gazelle. She even licked her chops, her tongue flicking over her too-red lips as she looked at her notes and then at me again.

I thought about the homemade play dough I kept in a drawer back in my office for my young clients. The cool squishiness of the multicolored flour and water mixture would have been perfect to pound out the nerves quivering inside of me.

She approached the bench, each of her steps carefully watched by the waiting jury. We all seemed to be holding our breath.

"My client, Delmon Frank, has been charged with murder in the first degree, three times over," the defense attorney began. "This charge carries with it the possibility of an entire life spent behind bars, a punishment that would be appropriate for a cold-blooded killer such as the one who viciously took the life of the victims. However, such a punishment would be a catastrophic mistake for an innocent young man barely out of his teens who is just starting to live his own life, who just happened to be at the wrong place at the wrong time, and who had nothing to do with the tragedies that transpired." She gave a solemn look at the twenty-one-year-old male sitting at the defendant's table. In his suit and tie, I barely recognized him.

But those unreadable eyes and curled lips could not be dressed up or disguised.

"You have a son about his age, Ms. St. James." She leaned in close to me. Her voice was a slight whisper, as if we were patrons in an upscale restaurant chatting aimlessly about the menu and not defense attorney and star witness about to enter the opening act of a courtroom drama. "I don't have to remind you of the seriousness of the matter at hand as I ask you to think of how you would feel if your son . . . Roman, right? If Roman was falsely accused of murder. Think of him, Ms. St. James, as I ask you these questions."

Thinking of Roman would not help her cause. She didn't know that. Very few people knew the current state of the relationship I had with my only son. I pushed down the heartache.

"My name is Mrs. Sanderson, no longer Ms. St. James." I glanced at Leon who sat in the back of the courtroom. He winked at me, but I still saw the irritation on his face.

We were supposed to be packing for our first wedding anniversary trip, but here we were, in a courtroom with cameras flashing. *I'm sorry,* I wanted to say to him, but the attorney took my words.

"Yes. I'm sorry about misstating your name, Mrs. Sienna Sanderson St. James." The woman shuffled through her cards as she butchered my name once more. She stopped at one card and her smile returned. "I have just a few questions for you. Are you ready to begin?"

I shut my eyes for a moment, inhaled, searched for a calm space in my head. Listened.

"Hush 'em. Hush 'em."

The memory jolted through me with such vividness, I could almost taste the butter crème icing that dripped off my lips that day, smell the fresh cut flowers that had sat in squat vases at each table.

"Hush 'em. Hush 'em." The old lady held a crooked finger up to her lips and whispered out of a mouth so crusty and smelly it took all I had to not gag in her face. "What do you hear?" She used her other finger to rap on

the glass storefront of Leon's downtown bakery where we were holding our reception. I stood at the doorway, poised to go in, my right palm pressed against the door. They were waiting for me inside.

"What do you hear?" she asked again, her eyes wide with awe. Her wrinkled brown face full of dark freckles was bright with excitement. She wore a stained blue housecoat and blue slippers, and a large black handbag hung off her frail shoulders. I wanted to be polite, but it was my wedding day, my reception, and I wanted to get inside. "What do you hear?" she asked again.

"I hear you tapping on the window." I gave a smile and pressed against the doorway once more.

"Hush 'em, hush 'em." She leaned in closer to me. Her breath stopped me in my tracks, made my eyes water. "I asked 'what do you hear?' Not 'what do you see?'" Her nostrils flared outward. Anger.

"I don't . . . I don't know." I turned away, but her rapping got louder. Leon looked at us from the other side of the window. His boutonniere was a single blue flower. "I hear you tapping on the window," I said again, rushing through my words this time, ready to leave this woman and her stank breath alone.

"No, that's not tapping you hear." The woman's wide smile revealed several missing teeth and many rotting ones. "That's the sound of glass trying not to break. My finger here is force, wind, weight." She stared at her dirty nail as if it were gold. "The glass is shouting against it. Screaming against it." She stopped tapping and narrowed her eyes at me. "You that glass, young lady. You that glass trying so hard not to break under pressure. I can see right through you. Why are you trying so hard?"

"Mrs. St. James Sienna Sanderson?" The attorney brought me back with her continued butchering of my name. "I'm ready to begin. Are you?"

I opened my eyes, looked at the three posters standing by the prosecution's table. Three enlarged pictures of the victims rested on easels, though the TV cameras were only focused on the last victim, his name and local fame enough to build ratings, I guessed.

What was I supposed to say to the coming questions? I looked around the courtroom, peered into the cameras. *The truth, the whole truth, and nothing but the truth, so help me God.* I settled back into my seat. Exhaled.

"Yes. I'm ready."

Leon shifted in his seat. I saw him shake his head. *Don't bring that old woman up,* I knew he was saying.

Chapter 2

Seven months earlier

As if I didn't already have enough to do.

I stared at the pager vibrating on my bathroom sink. 911 STAT, the small digital screen read. It shook and buzzed and clattered on the marble countertop like it was having convulsions. I silenced it with one touch of my index finger.

"Why did I agree to do this?" I asked my reflection in the mirror.

Eleven fifty-three on a Saturday night, and here I was, locked in my bathroom, looking and feeling a hot mess. My stomach was weak, my eyes were red, and my two-day-old press and curl had reverted to nap and kink. My hair had been natural, free of chemical straighteners for nearly two years now, but nights like this made me want to grab a wig or a weave or the biggest jar of hair-taming raw lye I could find. I hope I hadn't looked this bad during the interview taping earlier that evening.

The pager went off a second time.

"All right already." I shut if off again and collapsed down on the edge of my tub. Two 911 pages in less than two minutes: a record. "I don't have time for this," I groaned.

And I didn't.

I had a full-time job. No, a full-time business. A successful full-time business. Not to mention the interviews, the speaking engagements, and the comfortable advance for my not-yet-written memoir *Fearless: How a Therapist Tracked Down a Terrorist,* in which I was supposed to detail how I'd followed my gut instincts to expose the mastermind behind a horrific explosion at BWI Airport in April. This on-call pager gig was only supposed to be a temporary arrangement, an easy way of "giving back to the community." The key word was "temporary."

So much for that.

Another wave of nausea rolled through my stomach and the pager went off a third time.

Okay, so it was definitely a real emergency going on at the other end of the page, but how on earth was I supposed to respond to a crisis when I was dealing with my own situation?

Too much for a Saturday night.

On the bathroom countertop, next to the trembling pager, sat a skinny white stick. My entire life peered down at this stick, waiting to see whether or not two pink lines would appear.

I rocked on the edge of the tub and willed the vomit to stay down as my eyes stayed glued to the third white stick of the evening. The pager, for its part, clattered down into the bowl of the sink.

I was too old to be pregnant.

I mean, twenty-five-year-olds get pregnant. Thirty-one-year-olds carry babies in their bellies. Shoot, sixteen-year-olds who may have jumped the gun way too early are walking around with swollen stomachs.

Not me. Wasn't supposed to be me.

I was turning forty in a few months.

My son was a sophomore in college and my husband had only been my husband for five months.

What kind of foolishness was this?

I scratched my head and looked at the pink lines again. Yup. There were two of them and that was what the manufacturer's box claimed would happen if the test detected babyness in your pee.

There had to be a mistake, a typo, or something extra in that glass of water I had before I went to bed last night for my pee to be telling three different pregnancy tests I was . . . couldn't even get the word out.

Pregnant.

Pregnant?

My cell phone started ringing. I could hear it vibrating from my purse on the tile floor. When I came home an hour ago, I'd marched straight to the bathroom with the bag from Walgreens hidden in my purse, even though nobody was home to witness my mission.

The bag had been filled with five pregnancy tests.

Yes, I was going to use all five of them because there had to be a mistake. One of these tests was bound to get it right. I could not possibly be pregnant.

My cell phone began a second deluge of rings. I rolled my eyes and answered it.

"Hello, KeeKee," I sang into the phone as I greeted the Saturday night emergency department charge nurse at Metropolitan Community Hospital. "Is it a suicidal, homicidal, or drunk customer tonight?"

"It's D: none of the above." KeeKee's raspy voice was lined with irritation. "Sienna, why didn't you answer my page?"

"Aside from the fact that you didn't give me a chance to, I didn't answer because I knew that you would call. Now what exactly does 'none of the above' mean? Is this really a mental health or substance abuse emergency?"

"Just come in, Sienna, we need you now. Stat. This one is major." KeeKee hung up.

Two pink lines and a new husband who had no idea that I had a collection of positive pregnancy tests stored in my side of the bathroom armoire.

And now some kind of urgent matter in the ED at Metro Community that required three pages and two phone calls in less than five minutes.

I was supposed to have the first draft of the first three chapters of my memoir to my agent by Monday morning. I needed to do something with my hair. And, most important to me, I wanted to be home when Leon walked in the door, which I knew would be within the half hour.

But all of these things were on hold.

All because I had agreed to carry that on-call pager. For free.

It was warm for November. Well, at least the Baltimore version of November warm. Though now after midnight, temperatures still flirted with the mid-fifties. As I got into my car and turned west on Boston Street toward the downtown area, I caught notice of the nighttime sky. Cloudless with a million stars that seemed to shimmer like high-quality sequins on a black velvet gown, there was no hint of an earlier rainstorm that had scented the air with wet dead leaves and pavement. Despite the warm air and clear sky, however, an early snow was in the forecast for tomorrow, with temperatures expected to dip all the way down into the twenties.

So had been my life over the past few months: changes I'd never seen coming; twists and turns I hadn't expected; opportunities that came and went like the restless weather. Fortunately, sunshine had largely filled this new season of my life.

Sunshine.

Leon.

Change for the better.

I'd entered Leon's bakery on a Sunday afternoon this past April, on a day when all had finally and for the first time in my life felt right. After helping to unveil a terrorist who'd bombed BWI airport; after turning down a proposal to a man who could never love me the way I deserved; after closing once and for all the chapter of my estranged husband who turned out to be a sham, and forgiving him so that I could move forward: I unwittingly discovered Leon's bakery on Pratt Street and was reunited with his sweet skills and welcoming smile.

It was the smile he gave me when he saw me sitting at one of his tables that let me know he'd returned permanently to my life.

And I was ready for him. A whole woman. No more pieces.

Better than the cookies that were still warm from his brand new ovens was the envelope he showed me sitting on his office desk that fateful day.

Addressed to me, he said he'd written it three months earlier but had just put the stamp on it that morning. While I had been breaking up with Lazarus Tyson and healing over RiChard St. James, God had been working out the details of a love I needed, a love I could receive.

Perfect timing. Predestined reunion. Purposed plan.

I never opened the envelope. Never saw the note he'd written inside of it. I didn't have to. We were together and that was a good enough end to the story for me.

Only I knew it wasn't the end.

A green light and a blaring honk brought me back to the present. "Sorry," I mouthed and waved to the silver Hummer behind me. The driver swerved to pass me and quickly disappeared into the flow of steady traffic on Boston Street. Midnight in Canton. Leon and I moved into the high-end waterfront neighborhood on the far outskirts of Baltimore's Harbor shortly after our hastily planned nuptials.

No more wasting time and a new beginning for both of us. Together.

It had felt right at the time, leaving behind our old lives and dwellings to settle into a home financed by my practice, his business, and the wave of interviews and endorsements that had greeted my instant fame following the terror investigation. We'd purchased a two-bedroom condo that overlooked the waters of the outer harbor. It had a massive master bedroom suite and a spare space for when Roman came home during college breaks.

A two-bedroom condo and now a possible newborn.

"Jesus, is this some kind of joke?" I prayed aloud as I now made my way west on Orleans Street. The neighborhoods, just like Baltimore's fickle weather, had changed and transformed around me, from glitz and glamour to neglect and desperation, a testament to the turbulence of life and the testiness of times. The sudden rumble of nausea in my abdomen informed me there was no joke, no waiting punch line.

My life was about to face major changes once again.

Chapter 3

"It's about time you got here." KeeKee Witherspoon glared at me from behind the nurses' station. Five years my junior, she always looked like she was about to hit the runway instead of the emergency department, or ED, as staff called it. She was the only nurse in the ED who could get away with not wearing scrubs, and few questioned it. Tonight, she wore black skinny jeans, a pale pink top, and a rhinestone-studded headband that held back her long braids and matched a single bangle on her wrist. Despite her fashion-forward wardrobe, she wore little makeup, only lip gloss and eyeliner, and had no qualms about taking off her many rings to get her hands dirty. I'd watched her help clean up a child's diarrheal accident once, and, on another occasion, I witnessed her help carry without hesitation several greasy bags that contained all the worldly goods of a homeless man seeking the warmth and safety of the ED.

"I'll be with you in a moment, slowpoke," she said either to me or a tech who stood nearby. Several charts were in KeeKee's hand, and pagers, phones, and even the intercom system sounded around her in chaotic dissonance.

Twelve-thirty a.m. in Metro Community's emergency department might as well have been twelve-thirty in the afternoon for how busy it was.

The reality of a hospital by the hood.

"Bed two," she barked to an EMT team pushing a new arrival from the ambulance bay. Bright blood trickled from the arm of the young man on the stretcher. Despite having a small stab wound near one of his biceps, a playful smile filled his face as he winked at the young attendant who pushed his IV pole.

"Put your number in my phone, sweetheart." He nodded his head at her, as if they were meeting in the food court of a mall and not on the floors of the ED. She, for her part, ignored him, but I saw the flash of interest in her eyes.

Fiending for love could be more dangerous than craving dope.

"Sienna, I'll be right with you," KeeKee shouted as she darted away and disappeared behind curtain number seven.

What kind of emergency did she page me for? I shook my head and glanced at the time on a nearby phone. 12:36. Leon should be home by now, his bakery closed, pots and pans cleaned, floor swept and glass display counters sparkling. My lips curled into a smile as I thought about the sweetness of his embrace, the faint taste of chocolate frosting on his lips, the warmth of his body that I knew was waiting in the bed we now shared as husband and wife.

12:43. My smile stopped. What emergency did KeeKee have me missing my husband for?

"Right with you!" KeeKee dashed by me again, this time heading for the radiology wing of the bustling ED. I groaned and marched away from the nurses' station deciding to be proactive. Rooms ten and eleven, the stripped-down, sparse units where psych patients were kept while awaiting emergency evaluations, were on the other side of the station. I stopped in my tracks the moment they both came in view.

Empty.

I could see the plastic beds, white walls, and plastic-enclosed televisions in each from where I stood.

Really? They're both empty?

I had agreed to carry the on-call pager for psych evals while a replacement for the vacancy left by the weekend ED social worker's sudden departure was sought. I volunteered after being told it would be three Saturday nights at most with onsite visits only for dire emergencies. The director of social work at the hospital, Mabel Plattsmith, was a good friend of my mentor, Ava Diggs. Ava said she would do it and I said no way. Ava needed to rest and enjoy her retirement. And her cough nagged me.

This was Saturday number six.

After making sure one of the three security officers who covered the ED was within running distance, I stepped into both rooms ten and eleven to make sure that I had not missed someone crouching or weeping in the corners.

They were indeed both empty. Nausea rolled anew through my intestines.

Why would KeeKee call me down here in the middle of the night if there were no patients for me to see? I headed to the waiting room. Maybe I'd missed a drunk sleeping in the dark blue vinyl chairs who needed a referral to a detox unit. *But couldn't that have waited until the morning?* I groaned again as I waved my temporary badge over the box that would open the exit doors that opened to the waiting room.

Mother with sick baby.

Man sounding like he was coughing up a lung, and not covering his mouth.

Teen girl in the corner staring at the space in front of her.

Woman playing a game on her cell phone while a male who loved the "f" word and wore a homemade sling over his arm chatted indiscriminately on his.

Middle-aged man sitting next to a gray-haired woman who smacked her lips over and over as she studied me.

Nobody stood out to me in the waiting room.

I looked back over at the teenage girl. The look on her face. Her crossed arms. Alone. I thought of the pregnancy tests I'd hid in my bathroom drawer and wondered if she was facing a similar dilemma.

No.

Absolutely not. I caught my flawed thinking and corrected it. We were not facing any kind of similar dilemma because I was not pregnant even if she was. Though I didn't need the money, I was certain to get a large payout from that pregnancy test company who was putting out defective merchandise.

I looked again at the girl, her blank stare, mournful eyes.

Maybe she was suicidal. I waved my badge to get access to the triage nurse to see if she had the scoop on the pensive-looking young girl. Maybe she was the reason KeeKee had demanded my presence.

As the doors to triage slid open, a shadow near the main entrance of the waiting room caught my eye. A man in a black puffy jacket with a black baseball cap tucked low over his eyes stood near the rotating doors, just behind a tall, fake plant. I wondered if Mr. Phil, the overnight security guard who sat at a desk not far from the entrance, had even noticed the man standing there. *Is that man trying to stay unnoticed?*

"Who's that, Kelly?" I asked the approaching triage nurse. "Did he check in?" I nodded my head toward the man.

She followed my gaze and shrugged. "I have no idea what you're talking about. Quinisha King? Please come back." Kelly had moved on and apparently so had the man.

There was no sight of him anywhere, but the gust of wind that filled the waiting room meant that the side door had been opened and shut with great force. I looked over at Mr. Phil. A newspaper had his attention. Was I the only one who had noticed the man?

The teenage girl, apparently Quinisha, followed the nurse back to a triage station.

"The flu. I think I have the flu." I overheard her complaints to Kelly.

I groaned, but then shook my head at my ill-directed disappointment that the girl wasn't suicidal. I headed back to the nurses' station. Back at her post, KeeKee gave me a look that had to be as fierce as the one I gave her.

"Where did you disappear to that fast?" Her eyes narrowed.

"KeeKee, please tell me why I am here and not home with my husband."

"Sorry, missus, but that good lovin' gonna have to wait a little while longer. I need you to handle the patient in room twenty-nine."

"Twenty-nine? That's not even one of the psych rooms. Isn't that the last room in the hallway?"

"Yeah, well that's the room the patient wanted to go to, and nobody was willing to force the issue. That's why we needed you here. I need that room free and that patient discharged. Now."

KeeKee must have seen my raised eyebrow because she put down the charts and papers she had in her hand and came from around the desk. "Come on, Sienna. I'll walk down with you. I'm curious to see how you're going to handle this."

Bed twenty-nine was the last room in the emergency department, the last resort on busy nights. It had been used as a storage room, a private counseling area, and even, on at least one occasion that I'd heard of, as a rendezvous spot for two employees who'd wanted to "get to know each other better." As we walked toward it, I noted that the last patient room in use before it was twenty-one.

"So what exactly is going on?" I tried again as we neared the room. KeeKee gave no response as she fooled around with several papers in her hand. The curtain to bed twenty-nine was closed and a shuffling noise echoed from its walls. I noted that a sitter, a hospital staff person assigned to sit with disruptive patients, stood outside the curtain, peeking into the room. She turned around at our approach.

"Thanks, Tiffany." KeeKee nodded at the sitter. "Sienna can take it from here. Just let security know not to go too far in case we need them."

"Security? A sitter? KeeKee, you've got to tell me something here."

"If I knew what was going on, I would not have paged you." KeeKee stopped short of the curtain, looked up from her paperwork, and gave me a smile I could not read.

I pulled back the curtain.

Chapter 4

"Step one, step two, step three and four. Shake it fast, baby, and hit the floor. Ooooh, yeah! Dum dum dum boo dum dum boo dum."

Worn blue slippers, a blue floral housecoat, a silver mass of hair, and a whole lot of shimmying, clapping, and dancing around. I tried to make sense of the scene in front of me but did not know where to begin.

A woman who looked as old as Ava Diggs twirled and spun around the room. Brown as hot cocoa and covered with a smattering of dark freckles and visible dirt, she looked like she'd just stepped out of her bedroom; that is, if her bedroom was a gutter. Her bra-less, large bosom hung limply under her frayed housecoat and her ankles and knobby legs were ashy above her slippers. Her silver hair was thick and matted on the sides and she snapped her fingers with chipped and dirty fingernails. She seemed unaware of her audience, KeeKee and me, as her frail hips bounced and shook under the fluorescent lights.

"Shake it now! We goin' down. Wooo!" Though probably twice my age, the woman's moves were as sharp and skilled as if she were in a *Soul Train* line. The only thing missing was the music, but she bopped her head up and down as if a song played in her head.

"Uh, KeeKee?" I raised an eyebrow and looked over at the charge nurse.

"She was bought in by ambo from the Harbor," KeeKee finally explained. "A group of tourists found her dancing just like this, housecoat and all, in Rash Field and made the call. We put her in one of the psych rooms but some idiot let her off the gurney and she danced her way down to this room. Nobody had the heart to restrain her or pump her with lorazepam to get her quiet and still. Besides, she wasn't hurting anything but them moves, so I made the call to just let her stay here as long as she doesn't get too disruptive. And now you're here to fix it." KeeKee let out a rare chuckle.

"What's her name?" I asked.

"Your guess is as good as mine. She came in with what you see: that robe and those slippers. No ID. No purse. Nothing. Um, I should let you know that it appears she also does not have anything on under that robe. Once you do what you do to stabilize her, I'll send Dr. Levi in to check her out and make sure there's nothing medically wrong with her."

"Once I do what I do? You're expecting a psych eval? We don't even know who she is. Did you call the police?"

KeeKee shrugged. "They said there are no active Silver Alerts, no elderly people reported missing anywhere in the area, and they won't even come look at her unless there are signs of foul play." She turned to leave but then looked back. "They said to call adult protective services, but that's your domain. That's why I paged you. You know what to do with this one, Ms. Social Worker, so I'm leaving her in your hands. I have a gunshot coming in and I'm going to need this room soon since it looks like we're filling up tonight. Thanks for handling this."

Without another word, she broke into a jog and headed back to the action by the main desk. I watched her disappear and then turned my attention back to the dancing woman. Her steps and swirls had eased somewhat and her mouth moved in silence as her head rocked back and forth.

"Ma'am?" I called out gently. She smiled and curtsied but shut her eyes. She opened them and turned to face a corner of the room and began whispering to the wall. I tried to make out her words, but they were indistinguishable. I inhaled, trying to see if I picked up any smell of alcohol or marijuana. Nothing.

"Ma'am?" I called out again. "You must be worn out from all that dancing. You can have a seat if you like, and I can get you some water or some ginger ale. Ma'am?" I took a step toward her. Her whispering seemed to lower in response to my movement.

Leon should be home by now. I imagined him stepping out of the shower, pulling one of his white T-shirts over his head, smelling like Dove soap. He'd probably be wearing his green pajama bottoms. In our bed. Waiting for me to join him. Another rumble of nausea rolled through my stomach. *Oh, God.* I swallowed hard and willed my intestines to cooperate. *I cannot be pregnant.*

"Ma'am?" Even I heard the sharp irritation in my tone. I softened my voice before I continued. "Ma'am, would you like to take a seat and I can bring you something to drink?"

"Oh, I'll take a whiskey sour with extra ice, hold the cherry." She turned to face me. "Whatchu havin', sugar? Let me guess: a Long Island Iced Tea?" Her eyes were as bright and clear as the starlit night, and just as endless in their depth. "No, a martini," she announced after studying me for a moment. "You look like you like them high-siddity drinks. *Bonjour. Au revoir. Comment allez-vous.*" She giggled and curtsied again.

"Actually, I'm not a drinker, but have a seat. Let's talk." I slid a plastic chair over to her and then sat in one myself. I kept the curtain open and nodded at a security guard who watched us from a distance. The woman eyed me with a half smile and then sat down in the seat I offered.

"We've met before, haven't we?" A distant memory nudged my consciousness as I stared at the blue housecoat, the worn, dirty slippers. "My wedding day. You knocked on the window of the bakery where I had my reception."

The woman smiled at me, but then looked away. "Step one, step two, step three, step four," she whispered and bobbed her head and patted her feet to a beat only she heard.

"You are quite a dancer. I don't think I could keep up with you." I smiled back as I thought through every word I said. There were many ways to handle this situation, and many ways it could go off course. I could feel the narrow open window I had at the moment and I could not afford to let it slam shut. "How old are you?" I asked.

"Shhhhh." The woman put a finger to her lips and hushed me.

"How old are you?" I tried again, this time in a whisper.

The woman's eyes narrowed as she scowled. "Didn't your momma teach you not to ask a lady that question?"

I held my breath as she glared at me, but then her eyes relaxed. "You got a cigarette, sugar? It appears that I left my purse at home." She began digging into the pockets of her housecoat then stuck her hand between her breasts, fishing.

"Where's home?" I pushed my chair back a little. No telling what that woman could have hidden in her bosom. I looked over at the security guard. He took the hint and began inching toward us. Dr. Levi, a newer member of the ED team, joined alongside him.

He would be expecting some answers, some info when he got to the room, I knew.

"Ma'am, where do you live?" I tried again.

She folded her hands in her lap and stared at the floor. A look of sorrow flashed through her face. "I ain't got no home to go to no more. What's your name again, sugar?"

"I'm Sienna. What's your name?" I held my breath, waiting, but her eyes narrowed again. Hardened.

"Oh, you ain't from around here none, are you?" Her voice filled with venom. "Everybody here knows who I am. I'll forgive you this one time for asking me my name, but no more, sugar. Don't expect no more favors out of me, young thang."

"Is your name Sugar?" I gave her a broad smile, trying to ease the sudden dark change in her mood. She laughed a deep, full belly laugh that echoed through the room and quickened the security guard's pace toward us. Dr. Levi slowed down.

"You know full well my name ain't no Sugar, sugar." Her voice seemed to lower with each approaching step of the guard. She looked me straight in the eyes just before he came in the room. "My name is Sweet Violet," she whispered, "and I suggest you go on about your way before I put the 'n' in Violet and acquaint you with my bitter side."

"Okay, uh, Miss . . . Violet." I stood and put my chair between the two of us, but my protective actions appeared to be unnecessary as the guard stepped into the room. She seemed giddy again.

"You got my drink, sweetheart? It's about time. Service here is terrible." She smiled up at him, the animosity of the previous moments dissipated. She stood and began dancing again, ignoring even the guard she'd just questioned. I stepped out of the room and yanked the curtain closed behind me.

"Her drink?" Dr. Levi had caught up and he stood with me outside the room. "What does she need, detox?" he inquired.

"Definitely order a tox screen and check her blood alcohol level. With all the dirt on her clothes and in her hair, I'll call around to some of the homeless shelters and see if any of them know who she is." I put a hand to my forehead and thought better of it. "Actually, I'll leave a note for the Sunday on-call social worker to follow up in the morning. I know KeeKee wants this bed available, but this honestly could have waited until the morning."

I turned to leave as a fresh wave of nausea threatened and heightened my irritation that I'd been called out of my home to deal with this. Even if I called shelters and APS, nobody would do anything until daylight tomorrow. Adult protective services probably would just tell the ED to keep her until they were available to visit with her on Monday morning. I knew how these things worked.

"Uh . . ." Dr. Levi looked uncertain, but he could tell by the look on my face that I had already given my "prescription" for the patient, bless her dancing heart. I hurried away from them and was considering using a computer in an alcove near me to type a note and send a message to KeeKee when I heard the curtain of bed twenty-nine open up with a loud screech.

"Now what did y'all do with my clothes?" the woman who called herself Sweet Violet hissed. She stood there with her housecoat unzipped and falling off of her thin shoulders. Way too much of her personal business showed and I wanted to go wash out my eyes with some hand sanitizer, bleach, something.

"Step one, step two, step three and four. Shake it fast, baby, and hit the floor. Ooooh, yeah!" She began her spinning and shaking again.

The doctor and the guard gasped and I groaned. There was no way KeeKee would let me leave a half-naked elderly Jane Doe dancing around the ED. This would not be waiting until the morning, I conceded. I took a step back toward room twenty-nine, but then bolted for a nearby staff restroom. I could no longer hold back the nausea. I ran faster as I lost control of my gag reflexes. The taste of bile filled my throat.

"That's right, young thang, run!" The woman's loud voice screeched and cackled and echoed through the corridor behind me. "Run, run, run before they get you too! Step one, step two, step three and four. Shake it fast, baby, and hit the floor. Ooooh, yeah!"

Chapter 5

"You know I don't like these late nights, Sienna. I looked forward all day to coming home to you."

His voice was calm, deep, clear, and beckoning. I closed my eyes listening to the melody that was my husband's voice, mad that I had to hear it through a telephone and not directly in my ear.

"I promise that I will be home as soon as I can. And I also promise that this is the last time I'm carrying this pager. I don't mind helping, but Ms. Mabel is going to have find someone else to volunteer their time, or stop being cheap and get a temp agency involved." I exhaled.

"Yes, I agree." He sighed. "Please come home as soon as you can."

"You know I will." I blew a kiss to him over the phone before hanging it up and dialing another phone number. I'd called three shelters already and left three identical messages on their voice mail systems. Did anyone know a Sweet Violet? I looked again through the stack of papers and brochures stored in the social work office's resource cabinet to see what other shelters were nearby.

"Oh, yeah, A New Beginning House." I picked up a pamphlet that detailed a rescue mission for women. It was about ten or fifteen blocks away from the Harbor. I dialed the number, hoping, praying, that this would not be another dead end.

"Anything yet?" KeeKee popped her head in the door-way. I shook my head and shooed her away as someone picked up on the other line.

"Bless the Lord. You've reached A New Beginning House. Let today be your turning point. This is Sister Marta. How can I serve you on this early Sunday morning?"

I glanced at the clock. Two-seventeen a.m. Yup, it was early morning and I had not yet been to bed for the night.

"Oh, hello, Sister Marta. I'm a social worker calling from Metro Community Hospital and we have a patient in the ED who we are trying to identify. She calls herself Sweet Violet and she is wearing a blue housecoat and blue slippers. She appears to love dancing because that's all she's been doing. She's an elderly African American woman with bright silver hair and dark freckles all over her face and arms. Does this description sound like anyone who may have crossed the path of your shelter?"

"Oh, bless God. We found her!" The woman, Sister Marta, shouted out to someone on her end before getting back on the line with me. "I don't know about her name being Sweet Violet, but your description sounds just like one of our ladies, Ms. Frankie Jean. She was number seven for the shower line after dinner, but nobody saw her after she grabbed her shower bucket."

"Did you call the police to make a missing persons report?"

"Oh, honey, this is a shelter. Women come and go from here all the time, even in the middle of the night. The ladies can leave anytime they want, though they know that means they are forfeiting their bed when they do."

"So you don't try to find them, even if they are . . . older and frail?"

"Please, child. Ms. Frankie Jean is anything but old and frail. You've seen her dancing, right?" The woman on the other end chuckled.

"I've seen a little more than I wanted to. Is her bed still available?"

"Yeah, I can take Ms. Frankie Jean back but you gonna have to get her here before seven. That's when the big boss comes and if Ms. Frankie Jean ain't sittin' in our Sunday chapel service, dressed and fed, that will be a worse crime than her leaving in the middle of the night, as far as the management is concerned. We are a ministry, a mission. Our residents are required to attend all services. We help them with food, shelter, and clothes, but they got to do their chores and come to church."

"Where is Ms. Frankie Jean from? Does she have any family?"

There was a pause before her answer. "Oh, child, we don't know hardly any of these women's stories, and to be honest with you, Ms. Frankie is pretty new to our residence so we know even less about her. She showed up last week at our front door asking for a bottle of Kahlua and a pack of Virginia Slims. Ain't had much to say since then. All she does is dance and ask for liquor, but she's sweet and harmless. Nobody bothers her and she don't bother nobody."

"You said sweet. You sure she doesn't go by the name Sweet Violet?"

"Naw, honey." Another pause. "She told us clear as day that her name is Frankie Jean. Ain't never heard of no name of Sweet Violet."

"I suggest you go on about your way before I put the 'n' in Violet and acquaint you with my bitter side." I shook my head at the memory of the woman's earlier, confusing words. She needed a full workup, mental, physical, and psychological evals to get her past and secure her future, but the need for a comprehensive exam was not a reason to keep her in the ED tonight. I could get a cab voucher and send her back to the shelter so she wouldn't lose her bed. I'd put in my note that someone could follow up with her later to ensure she was connected to appropriate services.

"All right, Sister Marta," I spoke into the phone, "I'm going to get Ms. Frankie Jean into a cab and send her your way. You'll probably hear from somebody on Monday just to make sure that she gets hooked up to some services."

"Sounds like a plan to me. God bless you. What's your name again?"

"Oh, I never said. My name is Sienna."

"Thanks, Sienna. God bless you."

"Sorry, I can't take her." The cabbie chomped on a piece of gum and stared the two of us up and down.

"But you must," I pleaded again. It was now nearing three-thirty a.m. My eyes burned from exhaustion, my stomach burned from an unknown ailment, which could not possibly be pregnancy, and my nerves burned in sheer agitation, and for two good reasons. The cab had taken over half an hour to come and now that it was here, the driver was refusing to cooperate.

"Miss, I'm sorry, but that woman cannot get into my cab." The gum rolled around on his tongue and I resisted the urge to smack it flat out of his mouth. Instead, I followed his eyes to the woman who had resumed dancing beside me. Whereas before her movements had rhythm, a fast tempo, and soul, now she swung her arms through the air with grace and poise, spinning around on her toes as if she were a ballerina. Her eyes were closed and she hummed a mournful melody.

"It's a safety issue, a risk. I will not be liable. I cannot take her. Absolutely not." He revved up his engine, shifted his gear out of park.

"She just needs to get to a place about ten minutes away from here. They're already expecting her."

"Not my problem, miss."

"The hospital is paying for this service."

"And I will explain to my boss that there was a question of safety and liability."

"She's harmless." I did my best to remain sounding civil, and believable, as the woman now began swinging and spinning in more exaggerated motions. Dressed in a hot pink sweat suit and black tennis shoes I'd managed to find in a storage closet, she suddenly changed her dance routine from ballet to funky chicken and then she sobered and marched to the window beside me.

"Excuse me, kind sir," she whispered down at the driver, "but are you passing by a liquor store?"

Her tox screen had been negative. Somehow, no trace of alcohol was in her system. She had not consented to any type of physical exam; basic tests showed no brain injury, and she'd given no indication of being suicidal or homicidal. Her actions and behaviors, though bizarre, were not enough to keep her in the ED. Follow-up linkages were necessary, but KeeKee was not having the woman stay another minute, especially since a warm bed was being held for her just blocks away.

"I can't do it." He shook his head at me and pushed another stick of gum in his mouth. "Sorry, but you're going to have to back up from my car. I'm leaving."

And he did. Within seconds, I was standing alone with the woman—who was back to the funky chicken—in the roundabout in front of the emergency department.

"What am I going to do with you?" I shook my head as the woman stopped dancing. She stared up at the starlit sky and smiled in silence. I looked back through the ED's main door. She'd already been discharged and I knew KeeKee well enough to know that there would be no further interest from the hospital to figure out what to do. This was my matter to handle.

"All right, I'm going to drop you off at the shelter. My car. Let's go." I turned toward the employee parking garage, grateful that I'd been given a guest permit that allowed me access to spaces on the first level. "Are you coming, Sweet Violet?" I smiled at her.

"Sweet Violet?" The woman froze and frowned at me. "Who said you could call me that? My name is Frankie Jean and don't you forget it. Do you have my bag?"

My only desire was to get this woman to the shelter so I could get home to my husband. No more questions, no more comments. No more agitating mood swings or confusion. I needed to get this woman to the shelter and someone else in the world of human services could pick up her case and concerns on Monday.

"I have your bag right here, Ms. Frankie Jean." I held up the clear plastic bag that contained her housecoat and slippers as we got into my car, and then I tossed it into the back seat.

"Thank you, sugar." She sighed, smiled, and sat back in the passenger seat. We both stayed silent as I turned down the narrow streets that led to the shelter. With no traffic, we got there in seven minutes. A lamppost on the corner cast a dark shadow on the metal bars that locked over the entrance, but a dim light flickered from deep inside.

"We're here, Ms. Frankie Jean."

"Mmm hmm." She stared straight ahead.

Are you going to get out of my car? In my exhaustion, it took all I had not to blurt that question out loud as several seconds passed and she hadn't made any attempt to unbuckle her belt or reach for the door handle.

"Red velvet cupcakes. Mmmm."

"Excuse me?"

"You had on a plain white dress and you were eating red velvet cupcakes. Mmmm."

My wedding day. The reception at Leon's bakery. Her tapping on the glass. She did remember.

"That's right." She nodded as if reading my thoughts. "I never forget." Her eyes were as clear as the nighttime sky.

I sat speechless, startled. A little unnerved. She turned to get out.

"It's a shame, you know, sugar?" she asked as her door swung open.

I didn't want to ask, but I had to. "What's that?"

"Death. Someone always has to die. Okay, sugar. Thank you. Good night." She got out of the car and was inside the shelter before I could make sense of what had just happened.

Huh? Did that woman just issue a threat or simply offer a fact of life? And the queasiness I suddenly felt, was it because of my . . . non-pregnancy issue, or had the woman just given me a bad case of the heebie-jeebies?

I put my car in drive and pushed my foot on the accelerator. Too tired to attempt to understand my night and too sick to care, I almost missed the dark sedan parked several yards past the lamppost.

But I didn't miss the man inside.

Black puffy jacket, black hat pushed down low over his eyes. I thought about the man who I'd seen at the ED, hiding behind the front door plant; the man who'd disappeared before I could ask a question about him or point him out to the triage nurse or front desk security guard.

I hadn't seen the man's face clearly, but I was certain that the driver of that parked car was one and the same.

I kept my head straight, feeling, sensing that I wasn't supposed to see him. And for some inexplicable reason, I prayed that he hadn't seen me.

As I drove through the quiet, narrow city streets back to my condo in Canton, exhausted beyond measure and sick to the pit of my stomach, I could not shake the nagging feeling that this was not my last dealings with Sweet Violet, Ms. Frankie Jean, or whoever she was.

Little did I realize my life would be turned upside down because of her in just a few hours.

Chapter 6

"Turn up the music, Sienna."

Leon's bald head bobbed up and down to the Sunday morning mix programmed into my car's audio system. Part aerobic, somewhat techno, hinting at gospel, and all spiritual, I blasted my mix not just on Sunday mornings, but whenever my spirit needed a lift or my worship needed a workout.

We were on our way to early morning services at Second Zion Worship Center, having now been members there together for the past couple of months. As newlyweds, we both wanted to start our lives together on the same page; being at a new, but familiar, church together made sense to us. I'd grown to appreciate the expansive ministry when dealing with a foster child and her foster parents several years ago. Leon felt strongly about helping out with the youth ministry, and I had been finding a comfortable place helping out with the extensive counseling ministry network of the respected megachurch. Despite the growth by the thousands of the increasingly multiethnic church, the pastor refused to allow his salary to grow past what he initially accepted when the church had just 300 members. The extra monies that had poured in over the years of growth were used strictly for service and ministry. Far from feeling like a corporation, Second Zion maintained an aura of community and served as a rest stop for spiritually weary souls.

"I don't even remember you coming in last night." Leon's head still bopped, but I noticed he'd turned down the music. A light snow fell around us, but immediately melted on the warm ground.

"Yeah, it was pretty late when I got in, but you don't have to worry about late nights like that for me anymore. I'm going to make sure that Mabel gets this pager back first thing tomorrow morning. I'm done with providing free on-call services!"

"You said that two weeks ago," Leon gave me a side glance and smiled. Side note: he had beautiful teeth.

"I mean it this time, especially after last night. You should have seen this woman they called me in for in the emergency room. She—"

Leon held up a hand. "Don't tell me about it. Your stories always alarm me. I'm always afraid that something will happen to you and none of your stories ever make me feel better about my fears."

"Oh, this woman was harmless; a little off, but harmless," I shooed his concern away. "The only time I felt a little unnerved was just as she was getting out of the car. She said—"

"Wait," Leon interrupted, "she was in your car?" His smile dropped immediately. "You drove a patient somewhere? A psych patient was in this car alone with you in the middle of the night?"

"You make it sound worse than it was." He had a point. The way he put it, my decision to drive Frankie Jean, or whoever she was, back to the shelter, did sound a little unwise. But what else could I have done? "She was harmless," I asserted again, to both me and Leon.

He shook his head before turning the music back up. "I'm holding you to your promise to return that pager. No more late Saturday nights. I've been missing my wife."

"I've been missing you." I smiled and ran a palm over his chocolate bald head. He gave me another side glance and I saw the heat in his eyes.

Mmmm. This man was mine. All six feet and two inches. My husband was too fine and if we weren't already pulling into the church parking lot I would have suggested that we go back home and make up for the lost night.

And then the rumbling in my stomach began again. A thick queasiness that made me think of hot, curdled mayonnaise oozed up my esophagus. *Hurry up and park the car!* I wanted to scream as a sour, metallic taste filled my mouth. *I cannot throw up!* How would I explain such a thing to Leon? There was no way I was telling him about the positive pregnancy tests. No need to alarm him over what I was sure was defective merchandise. *I'm going to try a different brand tomorrow.* I swallowed hard, willing the bubbles gurgling at the back of my throat to settle down.

Leon had the car in reverse, repositioning it between an SUV and a minivan. Normally a smooth driver, the car seemed to start and stop in awkward positions as he struggled for a perfect alignment.

His attention seemed elsewhere as he sighed and began straightening out once more.

"Excuse me." I smiled, my words calm and easy, the exact opposite of the unsettledness that rippled just below my collected exterior. "I need to grab something from the back." I was about to blow. I needed a bag, a bucket, an old soft drink cup, something, anything to catch the catastrophe that was four seconds away from emptying out of my raw stomach. Thank God we had used my car. Trash, old tissues, or something was bound to be on the rear floor since I wasn't as fastidious as Leon when it came to keeping a clean vehicle. I prayed and swallowed hard again as I reached behind Leon's chair in search of something that would address my predicament.

My fingers touched cold plastic.

A clear bag with the words METROPOLITAN COMMUNITY HOSPITAL printed on it, a dingy housecoat tucked inside, lay on the floor behind me. Blue slippers.

"Oh no!" I whispered for many reasons. The first being that my sick stomach was not going to be stopped. And the second: I still had Frankie Jean's belongings in my car.

"Leon, I need to get out!" I pushed the car door open just as he cut the ignition, and just in time, too. My stomach emptied right there on the church parking lot. A woman wearing an oversized white feather hat frowned as she passed our car. I pulled myself out of the car and stood, gripping the top of the car door for balance. The snow had stopped falling, and it wasn't piling up anyway. There was nothing to hide or cover up my current situation.

"Sienna, are you okay?" Leon somehow was standing next to me, his broad palm rubbing my back.

"I'm fine." I pulled away from his touch, not wanting him to be too concerned. "That patient left her bag with her stuff in it in the back seat, and it, the bag, and, uh, remembering some things about last night made me gag. You know how weak my stomach is." I wasn't lying, I convinced myself, forcing the memory of her dancing with her open housecoat, with nothing underneath, into my mind. Yeah, that was enough to make anyone gag. "I promise you, I'm fi . . ." The words got caught in my throat as another wave of nausea rolled out of me. Leon did not budge from my side.

"Sienna, you must not be feeling well. Maybe you picked up some type of stomach bug working at the hospital." The worry in his eyes was genuine.

Sick. A stomach virus. Yes. That's what it was. Had to be. Even Leon suspected no less. I nodded as I clutched my stomach tighter.

"Let's get you home, babe." He was already headed back to the driver's side.

"No." I didn't want him worrying over me. "Look, you're in charge of manning the youth ministry booth after service today. Stay here. I'll come back and get you."

"You shouldn't be driving, Sienna. I—"

"I'll be okay. You stay. I'll be back."

He let out a loud sigh, thought for a moment, then swung his door shut without getting in. "I hate leaving you alone sick, but if you think you'll be okay for a couple of hours, I probably do need to uphold my commitment to the ministry. People are signing their kids up for the spring retreat, and I'm the one with all the answers. Sienna, you sure you'll be okay?"

I forced a smile onto my face as my stomach curdled up again. "Don't worry about me. I've spent most of my adult life managing colds and viruses alone. I'm a big girl."

"You're my wife. You're not alone anymore."

It had to be love. Why else would a man look ready to kiss a woman who'd just vomited all over the ground?

"Thank you." I smiled at my husband of five months. "I feel better just knowing you care. Please stay here. I'll be back by the end of service."

He shook his head as he began walking away. "Don't worry about coming back to get me. I'll get myself home. I'm sure Deacon Tony won't mind giving me a ride since he doesn't live too far from us. You just get home and get in the bed. And stay hydrated."

He saw me looking at the clear plastic bag filled with Frankie Jean's dirty belongings. "No, Sienna, don't worry about that right now. Enough."

"I'm taking it back. Dropping it off. That way I'm a hundred percent done with it all. Finished. That will help me rest better."

"No." Leon shook his head. "You are not feeling well. That bag of dirty clothes is not a priority right now. I want you to go home, get in the bed, and get better."

I looked at him.

He looked at me.

I put on a smile.

"Okay." I walked over to him and stood on my tiptoes to peck his cheek. "That's what you want me to do, so that's what I'm doing."

Leon smiled back at me. He put his index finger under my chin and turned my lips to his.

"You can't possibly want to kiss me right now. I'm . . . sick, remember."

"Get some rest, sweetheart. I'll be home to you soon." He planted a deep kiss on my lips and then turned toward the church entrance. "And don't worry. I'll get that mess taken care of." He pointed back to my stomach contents on the ground.

As he entered the church, I got back in the car and glanced over at the plastic bag of that woman's belongings.

"I will go home and rest, but first I'm getting rid of that bag so I don't have to think about it anymore." I figured if I said it out loud, though he was well out of earshot, I would not have just lied to my husband about going home.

Chapter 7

"I'm pregnant." I said that out loud too, letting the full weight of the words rest on me. There was no denying it anymore. The nausea was way too big of a clue. Okay, and so were the three positive pregnancy tests. I exhaled. Wanted to scream. Cry. Laugh.

I did all three as I drove down Belair Road to the heart of East Baltimore. If anyone driving past me had a glimpse of me at the wheel, hopefully they would think I was just getting filled with the Spirit and not losing my marbles. It was Sunday morning, after all, and my gospel music mix still blared out of the speakers.

"I'm pregnant," I said it again as my emotions continued their spin cycle. My hands shook on the steering wheel. I hadn't carried a life in me for twenty years. And, after two decades of immaturity, waiting for a man, my first husband, to come back to his senses and back into my life (yes, I could finally admit my truth), after forgiving his lies and moving past my foolishness, I had just started living my life over again. A smile came to my face. If I had to carry a man's baby, at least it was Leon's.

We were going to have a baby.

My smile dropped and my heart picked up extra beats. I was about to turn forty years old. Leon was already forty-two. How did I tell him that we were about to start a baby registry at Target and research car seats, strollers, and college savings plans. And what were those contraptions called I'd seen mothers putting soiled diapers in?

And organic baby food and baby bath tubs with built-in thermometers and scales and jets and shower heads? What did I know of these things?

I bit my lip. My hands shook harder on the wheel. We'd never talked about children. Well, we talked about Roman and the kids Leon used to mentor back during his officer days at the Police Athletic League, and the at-risk high school students he let intern at his restaurant. Outside of his concerns about the fatherless sons and the daughters of the streets he tried to redirect, we never talked about children.

We were going to have a baby.

Jesus.

I looked back at the plastic bag with Frankie Jean's belongings and knew the real reason I wanted to get this bag back to her. I needed a distraction. Thinking about a baby was just . . . too much. As I turned a corner and neared the women's shelter where I'd dropped her off just hours earlier, I knew that a distraction and then some was just what I was going to get.

Several police cars lined the block where A New Beginning House stood. A crowd of people murmured on the corners, their mouths covered, their heads close together.

Yellow police tape.

"What is going on?" I parked the car about a block away, covered my ears as another siren wailed by, gasped as a couple of marked homicide detectives whisked past me. As I opened the door of my car and stood, heaviness sat down in me.

"What happened?" I approached a man smoking a cigarette. He sat on the cracked and yellowed marble steps of a corner liquor store.

"Shootin' early this morning." He took a deep drag and let the smoke glide over his face. He was a young man but his features had a worn, hard edge to them. Cold, stone.

Tired. His eyes were a light shade of brown. Golden raisins were what I thought of when his orbs pierced mine.

"What . . . Who . . ." I struggled to get out my words as the heaviness that had sat down inside of me had gotten comfortable, kicked off its shoes, and put its feet up. Whatever had transpired on this block wasn't going to shake off of me for a long time; I knew it, felt it.

The man-boy looked me up and down and took another drag. "You a cop?"

"What?" A small laugh escaped from between my lips as I thought about me standing there in my church clothes looking a far cry from a police woman. *He's serious,* I realized as not even a trace of a smile leaked onto his face. He meant his question.

"No, I'm not a cop." I sobered as another emergency vehicle whizzed by. "Do you know what time the shooting happened?"

"I've seen you somewhere before." The man-boy had no interest in answering my question. Despite the chilly November air, he wore only a T-shirt, white. Blue jeans.

"I have had some television interviews over the past few months and been featured in a bunch of articles. Maybe that's where you've seen me." I wasn't boasting, just stating the facts. Since uncovering that terror suspect several months ago, even I had gotten tired of seeing my face plastered all over the media.

I gave the young man a polite smile and resumed walking down the street determined not to get sidetracked from my necessary distraction. The clear plastic bag with the dirty housecoat and worn slippers inside hung from my palm. Despite the yellow police tape circling half of the block, I was determined to rid myself of the last remnants of the weekend gig that was keeping me from spending quality time with my husband.

Yellow tape enclosed an area a couple of doors down from the shelter. I exhaled, realizing that a part of me had been concerned that whatever had transpired was somehow related to A New Beginning House. A uniformed officer eyed me as I neared the gated entrance. Though officials milled about, I wasn't concerned about being stopped as I noted the mix of women, most likely residents of the shelter, mingled in with the investigators. Clearly, nobody was worried about crowds compromising the crime scene.

Or so I thought.

"Ma'am, can I help you?" A woman's stern voice rang out behind me when I was about three steps away from the entrance. I turned around to face an older white woman, her hair tied back in a frizzy auburn ponytail. She wore a dark red turtleneck and a long, floral-print skirt. SISTER AGNES was written on a plastic badge on her chest. A NEW BEGINNING HOUSE was stenciled underneath her name.

"Oh, I just came to drop off the belongings of one of your residents." I found myself whispering, matching the hushed voices around me. The yellow tape was only feet away from me, closing off the area in front of a narrow red brick row house two doors down from the shelter. I was a little surprised that the small group of women could stand so close to the obvious crime scene. The woman, Sister Agnes, for her part, seemed oblivious to the flurry of activity, the sirens, the investigators surrounding us. She stared at the bag and then me, raising an eyebrow, a razor-thin darkly penciled eyebrow.

"I'm a social worker and I helped a lady, again, one of your residents, who was brought to Metro Community ED last night," I explained. "I saw to it that she returned, but she left behind her things." I held up the bag of soiled belongings.

The thin eyebrow rose even higher. "We didn't have any hospitalized guests last night. They are called guests here, not residents. This is a temporary living arrangement, not a long-term solution. As a social worker, I'm sure you can understand our approach."

I ignored her last statement, having no desire to debate the best way to help the homeless. I only wanted to rid myself of Frankie Jean's bag to be done with this assignment once and for all. My bed, and toilet, was waiting for me at home. And I couldn't wait to get there to wait for my husband to come home from church.

"I was assured by, I believe her name was Sister Marta, that our patient, Ms. Frankie Jean, was a resi . . . I mean, guest at your shelter."

"Sister Marta?" The woman's thin lip quivered. I noticed several of the women around me had grown quiet. All eyes were suddenly on me.

"Um, Frankie Jean. Do you know her?" What else was I supposed to say? The quiet, the attention only added to the discomfort of the nausea that pulled at my stomach again.

"I have to start service. We all must go on." The woman, Sister Agnes, turned away and headed for the front door of the row home that sat between the shelter entrance and the cordoned house. Her black clogs and nude stockings were the last I saw of her as she disappeared into the entrance. Loud wails poured out from the other side of the door before it slammed shut. The small group of women who'd surrounded me began walking toward the same doorway.

"Church," one woman whispered as she passed by me. "We still havin' service even after all this." She was a cinnamon-colored woman with high cheekbones and a nervous smile that flitted across her lips. She was my height, but about a quarter of my size. Though she

smiled, her eyes were red and puffy like she'd been crying. Or maybe she was just high. Or sick. I'd been trying
to practice not jumping to conclusions or assumptions
about people I didn't know.

"Is Sister Marta at the service?" I looked down at the
bag in my hands. There was a trashcan at the corner. If
all else failed . . .

"Sister Marta?" The woman's smile dropped and she
looked at me like I had three heads.

"Yes, I talked to her very early this morning about
someone who stays here, Frankie Jean. Do you know
her?"

The woman drew in a deep breath as the crowd who
had once surrounded us had now all disappeared into the
doorway of the house next door to the shelter.

"Sister Marta dead and I don't know no Frankie Jean. I
gotta get to service now. I ain't losing my bed for missing
church." Whatever flighty nervousness had been on the
woman's face seconds earlier had dissipated into a steely
sorrow. She turned and scooted away from me.

"Dead?" The word fell off my lips and landed in the
quiet hush around me. I looked back at the cordoned-off
door two doors down, noticed for the first time the ANBH
Employee Entrance sign. Sighed. Pushed back the heave
that wanted to run right through me. A belch came out
instead. "What happened?" I whispered loud enough for
no one to hear.

Something was not right. I felt it. I'd just spoken to Sister
Marta a few hours ago. Dropped that woman, Frankie Jean,
off right after. And now . . . "Dead?" I asked again, this time
the word was louder. A police officer who'd happened to
step out from the yellow tape glanced at me before joining
another group of investigators with their hands in pockets,
small talk, slight chuckles, and occasional solemn faces to
respect the mood of the mourners.

"Sixty-seven-year-old Marta Jefferson had been a staff member at A New Beginning House for about forty years." A woman in a black suit spoke solemnly into a large padded microphone steps away, a camera aimed at her face. "Ms. Jefferson was leaving through the employee entrance early this morning when she was tragically gunned down. Police believe it was a robbery as her wallet and cell phone are both missing. There are no witnesses, no suspects, and no other leads, though authorities want to interview a group of juveniles who were believed to be in the area at the time of the incident. That's all the information we have for now. This is Laila Kennedy reporting live in East Baltimore. Back to you in the studio, Steve." The reporter stepped away from the camera and put on another coat of berry-colored lip gloss.

Now what? My heart broke that the sweet shelter worker had lost her life to senseless violence. My stomach twisted in nauseating agony. And my hand still clutched Frankie Jean's bag of dirty clothes.

A robbery? Juveniles? My heart pounded heavy within me, but I knew there was nothing else that I could do. *God, help her family.* I looked at the steady stream of women entering the building, knowing that this group, unrelated by blood but connected by the streets, was part of the family who would be grieving for a while.

The bag of dirty clothes.

I looked at it hanging from my hands, knowing there was nothing else for me to do with it but leave it by the door. Sister Agnes, the stern-looking worker who had spoken with me moments earlier, was under the impression that nobody by the name of Frankie Jean was a "guest" at the shelter. I decided to leave the bag by the doorway, in case she was around nonetheless. I was in the process of dropping the bag by the metal gate when a sharp whisper caught my ear.

"Psst. You the lady asking about Frankie Jean?"
The voice came from behind, so I turned around to see
who it was.

Chapter 8

"Psst. You the woman looking for Frankie Jean?" the voice repeated. I jumped as fingers briefly touched my shoulder. I'd just opened my fingers to let go of the bag of clothes when the voice came from behind.

Or so I'd thought.

"Over here." The whisper had a harshness to it that made me wonder if I really wanted to find who it belonged to. The crowd of women who'd surrounded the crime scene just moments earlier had completely dissipated and, I realized, everyone who wasn't part of the investigative team or media stood on the outskirts. The detectives had let the women hang around, I assumed, in a smart effort to keep such a transient group within arm's reach for questioning. They were all inside the shelter's chapel for service.

So who had touched me?

No one stood behind me.

All that was near me was the metal gated door to my left, the yellow police tape in front of me, the street to my right. Nothing behind me. Nothing else.

Wait; there was a short row of bushes next to the gated entrance. "Bushes" was probably too proper of a word for the wild vegetation that grew next to the shelter. Weeds, uncut grass, tossed paper plates, beer cans, and a single flower all cluttered the space by the entryway.

The flower caught my eye, a deep purple bloom, out of place for the winter season, as if someone had come across it in another place, another time, and planted it there as one last chance of beautifying the landscape that was littered with broken glass, cigarette butts, and overgrowth.

The flower had my attention, but then something else grabbed it. Movement in the bushes. *Is that a face?*

As if on cue, a pair of eyes blinked at me. I jumped back, startled, turned toward the street, ready to run if I had to.

"No!" the voice whispered after me. "Please don't leave!"

I looked back, seeing now two hands held up as if in surrender. A torso, legs emerged from the thick evergreen, weeds, trash.

"Don't tell them I'm here. I don't want to have to go to service. Too sad."

A young woman, maybe a girl, really, stood not far from me.

Dark hair wisped down her back in loose ringlets from underneath a faded green knit cap. A gray T-shirt clung to her bony frame. Bony except for the blooming orb of her abdomen. Holes peeked from her black jeans. A frayed blue blanket hung around her shoulders. I'd never seen her before, didn't know her, and wasn't sure that I wanted to. A wild look peered from her eyes.

A wild look and desperation.

I turned to walk away, to get away, but the social worker in me knew better. A young woman on the streets, a pregnant young woman especially, was too vulnerable for me to ignore. I stopped and she began walking toward me. As she neared, I was surprised that despite her ragged appearance, she smelled of peaches. Peaches and cinnamon. I recognized the scent. Roman had given me a gift basket with a lotion, shower gel, and body spray with the same fragrance years before.

The torn, worn clothes spoke to a life lost on the streets. The scent was a clear whiff of pride in the brokenness. "You have my attention," I said in a whisper equal to hers. Though nobody seemed to notice us, or even be in earshot of us, I felt it important to echo the volume she'd initiated, to stay in her comfort zone.

She had wild eyes.

"Why did you call after me?" I asked.

The young girl continued walking toward me and was now almost beside me. She didn't answer, but instead kept walking and passed right by me, her eyes fixated on an unknown in front of her.

"Hey!" I called after her, no longer whispering. "Why did you call me?" I took two steps to catch up with her. The blanket she kept over her shoulders was wrapped tight around her arms.

"Wait!" I called again, not sure why I was intent on getting this girl to talk to me. Clearly she wasn't all there. I guess it was her pregnant stomach that had piqued my determination. "You asked me a question back there." We were nearing the end of the block. My car was the other direction. "Who are you?"

"Get away," she hissed, her head snapping back over her shoulders as she growled at me.

"Huh?"

"I said get away. You ain't who I thought you was."

"You asked me about Frankie Jean."

"I ain't ask you nothing." Her eyes darted back and forth as we crossed an intersection.

"Do you know where she is?"

"Do *you* know where she is?" The girl glared at me and then picked up her pace as we made it to the other side of the street. Several vacant homes lined this block, windows broken, doorways covered by thin sheets of raw lumber. A curtain hung from an upstairs window of one of them, I noticed. Odd detail, odd timing.

"Is she in there?" I pointed.

"No!" The girl nearly hit my hand. "Don't do that. Don't point."

"She's in there, isn't she?"

The girl stopped in her tracks and turned to face me. "You don't know anything, do you?"

"I know that you stay at the shelter."

"No, I absolutely do not. Not anymore. This is my home." She grinned and waved toward the vacant home with the curtain in the upstairs window. She smiled as if she were pointing to a dream home on the HGTV channel. "This is my abandominium, as my boyfriend likes to call it."

"Oh, that's . . . unique. Nice." I nodded and played along with her show of pride. The girl had to have some serious mental issues I decided.

"You know good and well this ain't nice."

Okay, maybe she wasn't mental. Just not in a good place in life. We both stopped smiling.

"I wasn't saying . . . Never mind." I sighed. "Does Frankie Jean live there with you and your boyfriend?"

The girl glared at me, so much so that I took a couple of steps back.

"I don't know no Frankie Jean," she whispered, "and you don't either. Not if you know what's good for you." She turned toward the home, nearly ran toward it. I noticed a basement window facing the street that had no lumber over it.

The entrance.

"What's your name?" I called out to the girl as she bent down. I wondered how she would get all of her arms and legs and swollen belly through such a small hole. She stood back up and looked at me.

"My name is Amber." Her eyes bore into mine as if she was searching, searching. The blanket around her shoulders loosened. There was something on her arm, I noticed. It had been hidden by the frayed blue threads that fought to keep her warm.

I didn't know what she had on her arm. And, I had no good reason for following her. She didn't seem to be looking for help or services. Leon would absolutely go crazy if he knew that I'd done this.

"Take care of yourself, Amber." I turned to leave, took a few steps.

"Wait!" A whine broke through her voice. I turned around to see that she was taking off of her arm whatever it was that had been hidden by the blanket. "If you see her again, can you give this back to her? Tell her I kept it safe just like she asked."

A black handbag.

I recognized it from a distant memory.

My wedding day, the woman tapping on the glass. Sweet Violet, or whatever her name was, had that same bag hanging from her arms.

I didn't want to touch it, but the girl, Amber, held it out to me. I opened the plastic bag of dirty clothes, the housecoat and slippers, and let the girl drop it in.

"Thank you."

Before I could fully understand or make sense of how she did it, she disappeared into the hole in the basement window.

"All I wanted to do was give this woman back her things." I shook my head as I turned back toward my parked car, now two blocks away. In the moments that I had followed the young girl, the street had become abuzz with new activity. The coroner had just arrived and the body of Ms. Marta was being wheeled away. The body bag on the gurney had brought the gawkers back out in full force, I realized as I pushed my way through the crowd that had seemed to grow in seconds.

Where were all these people before? And you mean to tell me that there wasn't a single witness to the crime?

I passed a trashcan on my way to my car, and I set the bag of belongings on top. But that black handbag, and Amber's wild eyes, and desperate plea, and promise to keep it safe . . .

"What am I doing?" I sighed at myself as I picked the bag back up and headed to my car. Too much activity was happening in and around the shelter. I'd come back another day to return it. I'd worked with enough homeless people to know that even the most meager and humble of belongings could be all that matters in the world.

Sweet Violet, or whoever she was, would be back, I was certain. She'd wanted Amber to safeguard her purse, so she'd be back.

I started my car, aware that my stomach had settled down for the first time all day.

Spoke too soon.

As I looked around my car for a bag, a cup, a container, anything I could use as an emergency bucket if need be, something else caught my eye.

The young man I'd first talked to when I came upon the scene.

He was walking the opposite direction away from the crowd, a cigarette still hanging from his lips. I watched as he walked up to a black sedan car, opened the back door, slowly slipped on a black jacket, and thrust a black baseball cap low over his ears, covering his eyes. He walked around to the driver side door.

The entire scene looked familiar.

I thought about the man I'd seen in the emergency room, who'd left before checking in, who'd gone out of sight before I could point him out to anyone else. I thought about the dark car I'd seen about a block away from the shelter when I'd dropped off Frankie Jean, as

Sister Marta had called her, in front of the shelter early that morning.

My gut told me that the young boy I'd talked to, the male in the corner of the ED, the driver of the car, were one and the same. My gut told me this and my gut was rarely wrong.

A million and ten questions jammed my mind as my gut also told me to hurry up and get the heck out of there and never return.

Except that I still had that woman's belongings.

I groaned as I started my car and finally headed back home. Leon wasn't going to like any of this.

My gut was rarely wrong.

Chapter 9

"You can tell a lot about a person by their liquor. What they drink, who they drink it with, when they drink it, if they even drink at all. Says a lot. What you can't always tell is the why. Why would anyone want to throw some burning liquid down their throats just to stumble around like a rag doll or laugh out loud like a fool? I never did understand that."

She leaned in close to me, her hot, rank breath dizzying as we sat together on a bench in the War Memorial Plaza, the expansive grassy area in front of city hall. "As for me, I only drink on two occasions. To toast life. And to mark death. You, of all people, should appreciate the spirituality of my chosen drinking times." She chuckled at my raised eye. "Didn't Jesus have a sip a wine 'fore he went on out to die? Here, I got some Old Grand-Dad. I'll drink. You pray."

She took out a small bottle of bourbon whiskey. I sat there, stunned, confused. And, as always, confounded by what she said and concerned about what would come next. "Oh, don't get upset none, sugar." She opened the flask and poured it out on the ground, letting the brown liquid trickle over a small patch of dead grass.

"Some people get drunk off of liquor. I only get drunk off of love. That's more dangerous, you know. Loving a man can leave you tipsy, walking around like a ragged fool, tripping over your own feet, landing in your own vomit. You're left with the aftertaste of tears once he's *gone and have nothing to show for your high but an empty, empty bottle." She looked at the bottle in her hand, turned it right side up. She held it up to one eye, examining the remaining drops of whiskey running down the sides of the flask. "Bet you don't know nothing about that kind of intoxication, sugar." She burst into laughter, and then quieted into a bitter silence. "Bet you don't know nothing about that."*

"Sienna, wake up. You're due back in court in an hour." His lips nudged my earlobe; his hands ran over my full belly. A kick responded to his touch.

The dreams.

Seemed like all the events of the past seven months replayed over and over again in my dreams, interrupting my sleep now that the court case had finally begun.

You're due. Leon's words hung heavy in my ears. I felt my eyelids flutter against his warm cheek. His toenails accidentally scraped my ankle as he swung his legs out of the bed.

"Is it really seven already? Why are you waking me up so early? I can get ready in fifteen minutes," I groaned, though I counted it a blessing that my husband was allowed to be my alarm clock. The state's attorney willingly agreed to let Leon stay with me in my hotel room by the courthouse. The room was for my protection from the media madhouse and Leon was my protector, in more ways than one.

"She shouldn't be by herself this late in the pregnancy. She's almost into her third trimester and the events of the past few months have been strain enough without her having to worry about staying alone in a barely secured room," he argued when the state's attorney's office agreed to the room. The room across the street from the courthouse was not just for convenience.

The circus over the last few months had been real, cameras flashing nearly everywhere I went. With the court case finally starting, the invasion had become even more out of control. I couldn't wait for another story to take over the news circuit. The triple murder trial, the gory details that accompanied it, and my role as a witness had headlined the local news for weeks.

"Roman said he'll be in town today." Leon stood in front of the dresser mirror, his hand smoothing over his bald head. I could tell he was debating whether to take out his razor. His quick glance at the wall clock told me he was deciding whether he had time.

The little details of being married, the observations, the unspoken routines . . . I never imagined falling in love with the boring nuances.

"Roman called you?" I sat up in the bed, my body afloat in a sea of white, down-filled pillows. As my brain tried to catch up, my heart sank to a lower depth. Roman. I thought of my last real conversation with him and squeezed my eyes shut to keep a tear from falling out of them.

"He would have been here yesterday for the first day of your testimony, he said." Leon's eyes never left the mirror as he now rubbed the slight stubble on his neck. "But he promised that he'll be here this morning."

"Did he say anything else about . . ." My words trailed off and Leon's eyes locked with mine in the mirror, his hand frozen on his neck, behind his ear. I looked away first.

"Alisa wants to meet you in the lobby right at eight." Leon began fussing over his facial and head hair again. "She wants to go over your testimony again."

"I'm going with the black suit this time." I gave him a half smile as I headed to the bathroom to begin getting ready.

"So you are going to listen to your husband for once?" He winked. I rolled my eyes. "Hey," he called to me just before I shut the door. "You did good yesterday. It will all be over soon."

I smiled back at him and then shut the door behind me, listened to the click as it locked shut, leaned against it, and stared at myself in the lighted mirror that hung over the sink.

Forty years old and I still had it.

My hair was crafted in an elaborate updo that took advantage of my natural curls, the occasional strands of gray blending in with the highlights of auburn and light brown, my new experimental look.

My eyebrows were arched at a perfect angle that highlighted my almond-shaped eyes and high cheekbones. Though my stomach poked out due to my pregnancy, my arms and legs still held true to the fit frame I'd worked myself into over the past year.

A lot can happen in a year, a truth that my swollen belly now testified. This time last year I was trapped in a dead-end relationship. I was angry, bitter, and hurt. Missing Leon. Now I was married to the one man I knew loved me for sure, and I was nearly eight months pregnant with his baby.

I looked at my stomach, and though the silvery stretch marks had seemed to multiply across my abdomen overnight like a crude spider web, I promised to love and appreciate each thread.

These marks showed growth in ways that superseded my vocabulary.

And to think I had been initially afraid to tell Leon about our child. *Our child.* The words brought fear, excitement, anxiety, joy all in one nauseating second. I thought about the day I told him that I was pregnant. That day had held all those feelings and some bonus feelings too.

Confusion. Dread.

I'd learned a long time ago to trust my gut. And my gut that day, in addition to being worn out and weary from first-trimester nausea, told me that there was more to Marta Jefferson's tragic murder than the yellow police tape and the crowd of grieving women convening for Sunday chapel service.

A lot can happen in a short amount of time.

The black suit. I held it out in front of me, sighed, and put it on.

A year ago, I would have never imagined that I'd be married, pregnant.

And on the witness stand for a trial I hadn't seen coming.

"Sienna? You done in there?" Leon's voice and knock on the bathroom door hurried me along. Even outside of my dreams, it seemed like I found myself rehashing and replaying many different memories from the past few months as I prepared for the court case.

"I'm coming," I answered, adding one last coat of wine-colored lipstick to my bottom lip. The black suit I wore looked tidy, efficient, and all business. Even my pregnancy looked official. I rubbed my belly, smiled at the kick that was almost eight months strong. Leon had been right. I should have listened to him yesterday and worn this black suit then instead of the bright yellow ditty that had me looking like a pregnant bumblebee.

"Look at my wife." Leon nodded as I stepped out of the bathroom. His chin rested between his thumb and index fingers as his lips curled up into a delicious smile. "Mmmmm. I've never seen a forty-year-old pregnant lady look as good as you."

"We should be packing for our anniversary trip, not dealing with this madness."

"It's okay, baby. We're together and your testimony should be finished today." He smiled and I smiled back, but we both knew that was wishful thinking at best. Seemed like my every word was the heartbeat of the case, for both the prosecutor and the defense teams. No way would I be cleared to leave anytime soon.

"I'm sorry, Leon. I should have listened to you and never gotten involved."

"The past is the past and the present is the present. We'll get through today and we'll get to our trip." He turned from me, looked out a window to the street eight stories below. I wished that I could see his face, read his features. I heard his words, but I could not make out the tone underneath them.

"Hopefully this case won't drag along any longer than necessary and mess with our flight plans. Dr. Baronsen promised to give me a note allowing me to fly as long as I'm not nine months." I realized that I had turned away as well. "Again, I'm sorry. I should have left it alone."

He left the window and began heading toward the door for the trip across the street. I could already see the growing swarm of journalists and onlookers crowding around the courthouse.

How did I let it get this bad?

"Leon?" I didn't bother to hide the angst from my voice. "I'm not convinced that Sweet Violet had nothing to do with the murders. You still don't think I should tell anyone about her?"

"Sienna." He'd stopped walking. His back was to me. "Please, for once, listen to me. Leave it alone. That homeless woman has nothing to do with anything. You've done all you can for her. Now, for your sanity, for me, for us, please leave Sweet Violet alone and out of all this." He turned to face me and I saw the strain in his eyes. "Just stick to your testimony, which is the truth about what you know for sure, and this whole thing will be over soon. Please, I'm asking as your husband. I'm asking as your friend."

I gave a slow nod, stepped toward him, toward his outstretched hands. I let myself fall into his embrace.

"You smell good, baby," I murmured as I pressed my face, my nose into his shoulder. Dressed in an olive green suit and smelling like spice and body wash, I wanted him to know that I had no problems leaning on his shoulder, that I needed him, respected his thoughts, feelings, and, that, like him, I didn't want to delay the current drama by introducing the unknown variables of Sweet Violet. I didn't even know where she was.

Sugar. That's what was missing from his scent.

He hadn't been at his bakery in three weeks, ever since the media firestorm went truly frenetic with the start of the case.

And it was all my fault.

"Thank you for your support with all of this, Leon," was the only thing I could say.

"Of course, Sienna. Of course." He patted my arms and stepped away. "We need to go before that prosecutor, Alisa Billy, calls up here for you, right? Before Alisa the Billy Goat Gruff starts lighting up your cell phone. She's worse than that nurse at Metro Community, KeeKee."

KeeKee. Metro Community. The night when it all began. Why had I agreed to carry that pager?

"Let's go, Leon. I'm ready." I let his arms drop off of me then I picked up my briefcase filled with notes I didn't need and marched to the door. I needed this day, this trial, and this craziness to be over.

Just as I reached for the door handle, a knock sounded, sending me back two steps. Did someone know I was here? I gasped, knowing that housekeeping and room service usually announced themselves along with a knock, just for this reason.

Leon, in one motion, ran to the door ahead of me, set me behind him, and peered out the peephole, a hand reaching under his suit jacket.

Was he carrying a gun?

That realization startled me more than the knock at the door. If the biggest threat was the media, why would he be carrying a gun?

Leon stepped away from the peephole and looked at me, biting his lower lip. He unlocked the door, turned the handle, pulled it open, and stepped away.

"Mom."

"Roman."

We spoke simultaneously and then said nothing at all.

"I'm going to head down now and let Alisa Billy know you'll be down in a little while." Leon left, closing the door behind him.

My husband, my advisor, my protector, and self-proclaimed bodyguard. Even he had enough sense to leave the two of us alone.

As I stared into my son's narrowing eyes, and felt my own eyes narrowing back at him, I knew that we were going to need more than a few moments just to get past hello.

Roman, my Roman. Before there was Leon or social work degrees or anything else, there had just been me and Roman, clinging to each other, surviving pain and devastation from his absent father, confiding, plotting, planning, arguing, and forgiving. We'd had our ups and downs over the twenty-one years of his life. He'd run away once; twice if you counted his decision to go to college on the West Coast to form a relationship with my first husband's "other" family, against my initial wishes.

But we'd made it through all of these storms together, stronger, closer.

Now as we stood facing each other, I knew both of us wondered how we would get past the chasm that had formed over his winter break. It was now spring and we still hadn't mapped a bridge.

Over what was supposed to be Christmas dinner, Leon and I had shared our news of the upcoming birth with him. Roman, for his part, had broken news to us that shattered every perception I had of him; that made me question if he'd gotten a single message I'd tried to instill in him when I labored in the trenches as a single mother; that made me question his sanity.

The reality that he'd missed such a key, pivotal lesson I'd taught him from the time he was born had been a swift kick to my gut. I was still emotionally bowed over, holding my stomach trying to recover.

And his foot had stayed in kick mode. He hadn't called. He wouldn't answer my calls. We'd never been this separated this long.

But he was standing in the doorway, waiting to be let in. Or waiting for me to come join him in the hallway.

A ding sounded in the hallway and I heard an elevator door open and the sharp commands of Alisa Billy spilled out.

"Sienna, we need to go now. This judge does not like any delays."

Roman stepped aside, letting me exit the room and close the door behind me. "I'm only here until six this evening," he said. "I have to be at the airport by eight."

I heard his whisper, but saw the stubbornness in his stance. Why had he even shown up if he knew that we wouldn't get a chance to talk? His actions, his decisions were deliberate. He hadn't come to talk, I realized, just, perhaps, to say good-bye.

For good.

Chapter 10

He sat in the back of the courtroom, squeezed in tightly with the audience, just outside the reach of the television camera's constant focus.

My son.

The fact that he didn't want to talk to me, yet insisted on watching me in this arena, bothered me.

"Ms. Sienna St. James Sanderson, are you ready, or do you need another moment to daydream?" the defense attorney snapped.

I looked back at her and smiled. "I'm ready, Ms. Deen."

The defense attorney had on a black suit similar to the one I wore, except she didn't have the round belly I had. Her waistline looked like it could fit in my pants pocket. *Once I have this baby, I'm going to get my waistline back, no matter how long it takes.*

Yeah, I was clearly distracted and not focused on my task at hand. I knew why, too. My son was watching me make a spectacle of myself and refusing to talk to me about the matter that had us currently separated.

And I didn't want to accidentally bring up my concerns about Sweet Violet. Leon's insistence for me not to made sense to me at the moment. The court, the lawyers, the police, and investigators know nothing about that woman, or my dealings with her. No need to bring more confusion to an already head-spinning case.

I looked over at the defendant, a young man the same age as my son. He glared back. They had him dressed in a black suit too.

We were all in black. I guessed to mourn the victims. Ms. Marta had been the first one.

"Now, Ms. Sanderson St. James Sienna, you stated yesterday that you had no relation to any of the victims. Are you continuing with that assertion today?"

"Of course. I'm under oath and I have no reason to fabricate a story."

"A simple yes or no would suffice," the attorney snapped again. Alisa even looked at me annoyed. "Just stick to the script we practiced," the prosecutor spoke to me with her eyes. I looked back at the defense attorney, Shanay Deen.

"I am sorry. Yes, I am still stating that I have no relationship with any of the unfortunate victims."

Shanay nodded. "None of the victims were clients, friends, relatives, or coworkers of yours, correct?"

"I did not know any of the victims in any capacity." I moved my mouth closer to the microphone. Did the woman not hear okay?

"Thank you. I have no further questions at this time." The defense attorney nodded again, smiled as she turned back to her seat. I looked over at Alisa Billy who sat with the prosecuting team, raised an eyebrow, wondering why after such an intense first day of questioning, I was only asked one question on day two.

"The witness may—" the judge began. He was an older man with a heavily cratered and bumpy face. Reminded me of a bulldog for some reason. I guess that's why I was surprised the defense attorney cut him off midsentence.

"I'm sorry, actually, I do have one more question for you, Ms. St. James Sienna Sanderson." The young lawyer looked excited, was almost breathless as she turned around and walked back toward me. "You stated that you did not know any of the victims, yet we have evidence that you had a phone conversation with the first victim, Ms. Marta Jefferson, just hours before she was found dead at

an entrance of the women's shelter where she worked."
The attorney blinked at me, her face unreadable as the
entire courtroom seemed to suck in a deep breath and
lean closer in toward me.

Suffocating.

That's how I felt at the moment, and that was also the
final autopsy report for Marta Jefferson. Before the single
bullet pierced her head, she had been suffocated by an
unknown object, from behind.

Close. Personal. The prosecution had used those words
to describe the circumstances surrounding her death. I
swallowed hard, the question that had been floating in
my head for months back again at the forefront of my
consciousness.

But Leon didn't think I should bring her up. Sweet
Violet had nothing to do with any of it. She was harmless.
Senile. A lost old woman who loved to dance to the music
only she heard in her head.

"Well?" The attorney tapped a foot. She wore black
heels that soared for days. Didn't her feet hurt in those
things?

My mind seemed determined to stay on anything but
the moment.

"I'm not sure what you're asking me." It was an honest
statement. What was the evidence that I had talked to
Marta? Phone records? A recording? My documented
notes in Sweet Violet aka Frankie Jean's hospital chart?
They'd kept her name "Jane Doe" in the hospital records,
I knew from KeeKee. *Does the hospital staff know about
her?* The questions fired off in my head. Leon said not
to bring her up. It would only complicate matters for an
already complex case where all the evidence pointed to
the man at the defendant's table.

Delmon Frank. Twenty-one years old. The same age as
my son.

Our eyes met.

During my first conversation with him, he'd been smoking a cigarette.

Had asked if I was a cop.

"Ms. St. James, can you please explain why you stated that you did not know any of the victims, yet there is evidence that you spoke to at least one of them mere hours before her untimely demise?"

"I do not know what evidence you have, Ms. Deen, but I am being one hundred percent honest in saying that I did not know any of the victims. I spoke to Ms. Marta during a routine call related to a hospital matter. I called the women's shelter in an effort to assist a patient I was charged with that night."

Even from several benches away, I could see Leon's eyes flutter in agitation. He didn't want me to say anything further. No purpose would be served other than to stir up confusion. The killer, who had piles of evidence against him, was already on trial. No need to throw in a monkey wrench on a case the prosecution fully expected to win.

Last year my gut feelings had helped me uncover a terrorist who wasn't even on the government's radar. I swallowed over the large, heavy lump in my throat.

That was a different situation. My gut was pretty certain. What I felt now was more of a question, and not firm enough of a question to bring up that dancing old woman and my unfounded suspicions about her.

Leon and I had an anniversary trip to take before our baby was born. Today needed to be my last day of testimony so that the case could move forward and I could board our plane to Florida.

"Can you share more about the conversation you had with Ms. Marta? What exactly was said?"

"Objection." Those words sounded sweet coming from Alisa Billy. She was already on her feet at the prosecution desk. "This line of questioning has nothing to do with anything. Our witness, Ms. St. James, is not the one on trial. Delmon Frank is. Whether or not Ms. St. James had any interactions with the victims is irrelevant."

The judge and the jury and the cameras turned back to the defense team.

"Your Honor," Shanay Deen spoke slowly, and with a smile, "if I can establish that Ms. St. James is not fully and/or accurately disclosing her relationship to any of the victims, then all of her testimony, whether as an expert witness or an eyewitness, will need to be questioned. And if questioned, then, I would argue, her testimony would need to be thrown out."

"Your Honor," Alisa was not done, "Ms. St. James is a social worker. Within the normal realm of her tasks and duties, it is very possible that she could have interacted with the victims in the past. All of them have connections to the issues and matters Ms. St. James addresses within her profession."

I felt like I was watching a Ping-Pong match, and was happy to see the lively back and forth between attorneys, until I realized that the ball was now back in my corner.

Seemed like the whole world was looking at me again. Had I missed something?

"Ms. St. James Sienna," Shanay Deen was asking me, "to be clear for the record, is it your testimony that you do not want to disclose whether you may have had any interaction with any of the victims, in or outside of your professional tasks and role?"

"I did not personally know any of the victims." It wasn't a lie. I hadn't known any of them personally, though I had some form of interaction with two of them just before their deaths.

The second victim's face flashed in my memory and I winced. The pain, the desperation, the wild look in her eyes; I owed it to all three murder victims to share whatever information I had to the court, but to offer any testimony about Sweet Violet, a woman whose identity I wasn't fully sure of and whose whereabouts remained continually unknown, would only add confusion. She really may have had nothing to do with the three deaths. To bring her up would be disastrous.

Delmon Frank stared at me from the defense's table.

Past life lessons had taught me not to bring up a matter unless and until I had enough details to keep a story standing.

And I had no details except the broken recollections of a woman who roamed the streets. Oh, and that pocket watch I would later discover.

"I did not know any of the victims," I repeated, deciding, knowing that I would have to leave it at that. To give more information would open a door I wasn't sure how to close. I shut my eyes, wanting to block out the questions I had, the answers I didn't know how to get. I wanted the trial to be over; to hear Delmon pronounced guilty; to go on my trip with Leon; to finish getting ready for the baby.

To talk to my son Roman about the announcement he'd made that had torn my heart apart, ruined our relationship.

Too much happening in my head to be on the stand.

"Ms. St. James, are you still with us?"

I searched my brain, tried to figure out what words to say. The morning of Ms. Marta's death came back into my head.

I remembered coming back home following the first victim's death.

Chapter 11

Seven Months Earlier

"Oh, you're home." I almost jumped when I saw Leon. I'd just left the crime scene at A New Beginning House. I still had on my church clothes from the service I'd never made it to, the one Leon thought I was leaving to go home and rest because of illness.

"And you weren't home," was Leon's reply.

I shut the door behind me as I entered our condo, trying to figure out how to respond to the sight of my husband stretched out across the sofa.

"Thought you were sick, babe, coming home to rest." He said it lovingly, not accusingly as his large legs swung together and he got up from the sofa. "I was too worried about you to sit through service, so I had one of the church van fleet drivers drop me off. Thought you would be here."

"I did too." I dropped the clear plastic bag of Frankie Jean's things next to a large potted plant we kept in the foyer and joined him on the sofa. "I don't even know where to begin to explain." It was the truth. Did I tell him about the crime scene I'd just encountered? Another wave of nausea rolled through my stomach.

I was going to have to tell him about the positive pregnancy tests soon. No way around it.

"I see you still have that patient's bag." He nodded at the bag that had landed on the floor with a loud plop.

I'd put the black handbag that the young girl Amber had given me inside the bag with the housecoat and worn slippers. The fact that the bag was sitting next to our potted plant and not in the garbage somewhere told Leon everything he needed to know about my intentions.

"One thing I love about you is your heart, your passion." He stroked his goatee slowly as he spoke. Back in his green pajama bottoms and a sleeveless white tee, it was obvious that he had planned to come home and rest alongside me. "I admire your desire to help and not to rest on a matter until you see it all the way through. At some point, though, you're going to have to put that same determination into taking care of yourself."

"I am taking care of myself."

"No, you are trying to save the world. Admirable, but impossible."

"Well, I did stop a terrorist." I reminded him of the events of last year. "My determination then saved lives."

"You have a point, but right now, I'm not talking about terrorists attacks. I'm talking about that bag you just dropped on the floor. I know you well enough to know you are about to get involved in a way that is unnecessary, and, for once, I'm asking you not to."

"Why would you not want me to return someone's property? Being homeless doesn't make anyone less worthy of dignity."

"Sienna, it's not going to stop at returning the bag. This is only the beginning, and we both know it. You have a knack for getting too involved and then finding yourself in danger."

"Leon, I think you are overreacting. It's a bag with a housecoat and slippers." *And a purse.* I left that part out. "I'm just going to make sure it gets back to its owner and that is all. No terrorist attacks, danger, threats, or other catastrophes. Just a bag filled with what appears to be all the earthly belongings of an older homeless woman."

Leon jumped to his feet, marched to the foyer, and picked it up.

"What are you doing?" I followed him.

"I got this." He shook his head. "I get that you are not going to stop until you've returned it to her, so I will help. I'll do anything to put an end to your distractions."

"My distractions? What does that exactly mean?"

"It means that for the five months that we've been married, you've been putting more time and energy into complete strangers who you think need help instead of spending time with your husband who needs you."

"Complete strangers? What are you talking about? I've just been working at my practice and have volunteered a few weekends to help at that hospital. These things aren't really any different from what I was doing before we married, so, I'm not understanding what the problem is here."

"It's not just your job, Sienna. I have a business too that requires me to work late and long hours, but you could never question that I strive to keep you first. Time is a precious thing, and I make spending time with you a priority."

"Wait a minute. Are you accusing me of not making you a priority? I get that time is precious, but are you getting how crazy my schedule is? Besides work and volunteering, I still have the occasional interview or appearance, and now I'm supposed to be working on this book. Wait, is that what it is? You don't like the attention I'm getting while you are struggling to keep your bakery open?" Even I felt the sting—no, the hard, echoing slap—that were my words. "I'm sorry, Leon. I didn't mean that. You know I didn't mean that. I'm not feeling like myself these days. My moods . . ." *Oh, Jesus.* I was really pregnant. I could feel the stew of rolling hormones and emotions boiling all through me.

"Sienna, I'm not going to fight with you." Leon sounded defeated. "I'm just letting you know that I need more of your time. We are newlyweds and the days and weeks and minutes we have right now are setting the stage for the rest of our marriage production. I want the happily ever after with you."

"And we are having our happily ever after right now." I reached up to embrace him, praying he wouldn't smell my vomit-tinged breath.

"I know. I just don't want anything to come between us." We both looked down at the plastic bag still in his hand. The bag swung off his wrist and bounced between us, preventing me from fully embracing him.

"Give the bag to me. I'll check to make sure there is nothing that might give a clue to her whereabouts. I promise you, once this is off my hands, I will make a point not to get involved in anything extra again. I'll just stick to the children I'm working with at my practice, finish my memoir for the publisher, and spend the next fifty years loving on you." *And our child.* I pushed down a dry swallow. *Can Leon even handle that news right now?*

"Whatever you say, Sienna." Leon gave me the bag and turned toward our bedroom. "I'm going to change back into my suit and head back to church. I'll catch the next service. Clearly you don't need me here right now."

"Leon, don't talk like that." I started to follow him into the room, but I had the sudden urge to pee. Pregnancy could bring a lot of annoying symptoms, I was remembering. The mood swings, the throwing up, the constant need to stay in the bathroom. And that was just the first trimester.

What am I saying to myself? I shook my head as I entered the bathroom and closed the door shut behind me. I pulled open the vanity drawer, lifted up the towels that were covering the positive tests. "I'll call Dr. Baronsen in the morning." I slid the drawer shut and then reached for my household cleaning supplies under the sink. Snapping a pair of yellow gloves on, I opened the plastic bag and dumped its contents into the bowl of the vanity. After making sure no bugs or other horrors were evident on the purse that had been hidden inside, I studied the outside of it.

It was an old-fashioned handbag, a worn patent leather clutch bag with a broad shoulder strap and tarnished silver clasps. A long shot, I knew, but maybe a wallet, an ID, something would be inside that would let me know where to take it, where to leave it. As crazy as it felt and sounded, I couldn't just throw this stuff away. I needed to get it to where it belonged so I could move on with my life.

Move on with my marriage.

Does pregnancy make you a little crazy?

I looked in the mirror, tried to picture me with a baby bump, and then I looked back at the bag.

I held my breath as the clasp gave way, realizing that I was afraid of what odor could roll out of its hidden bowels, considering how bad her breath had been. But there was no odor. In fact there was nothing at all. I sighed, wondering what to do next? Just throw it away? Keep the bag in my car in case I saw her while driving around Baltimore? Keep it at Leon's bakery to see if she'd come rapping on the glass again? His shop was near the Harbor, as was the shelter where she last reportedly was. She had to be in the area somewhere, though Sister Agnes, the woman who ran the shelter, seemed to have no knowledge of who Frankie Jean or Sweet Violet was.

That fact bothered me.

Maybe that's why I could not let the bag go. Knowing that a vulnerable old woman was walking the streets of Baltimore unknown and unnoticed made the social worker in me want to do something about it, even something as small as ensuring that she got back her belongings. A housecoat, purse, and slippers. She had to have other clothes somewhere. Where could she be? What was her story? What is her right or real name? *Stop it, Sienna! Don't get involved. You can't save everybody.* I wasn't just a social worker anymore. I was a wife who had her own family and needs to attend to.

There was nothing else I could do, I decided, other than keep it in the trunk of my car in case I ran into her in the street. In the trunk, it would be safe, accessible, and out of the sight of Leon. The bag was an eyesore to my marriage, representing my unwillingness to let things go; things that ate away my time with Leon.

What was the Christian thing to do in all of this?

I'd gotten back into the Word lately. Prayed more. Went to church every Sunday, Bible Study when I wasn't busy.

What would Jesus do? I chuckled to myself thinking of the bracelets and bumper stickers with the WWJD acronym that was popular back in the 1990s. I chuckled, but the question felt real to me.

I had a husband who was, despite Leon's perception, my priority. I also felt a pull of compassion for the vulnerable that insisted that I act, a pull that had led me to my career, that had pushed me to my present roles.

Where was the balance?

And what about my time?

Leon had practically accused me of mismanaging my time—no, my priorities—but didn't he realize and respect the demands on my schedule and my attempt to balance it all? He was my husband, not a baby. Was that what he needed? A caretaker?

I could feel the heat rising from the top of my head. I imagined wisps of steam rising from off of me like a cartoon character, asterisks, exclamation marks, symbols and all.

I felt like cussing.

My moods.

This was going to be a long nine months.

I had a husband and I was about to have a baby. How could anyone think I would ever have "time" again?" All I had at the moment was the pressing need to pee again and to throw up. And I also had an empty black handbag from a homeless woman whose name and whereabouts I didn't know.

Empty. I threw the bag down into the bowl of the sink with the other useless items. No, wait, what was that sound? I picked up the bag again and shook it. Something was inside. A distinct rustling noise sounded when I shook the bag with the tips of my gloved fingers.

I opened the clasped bag and stared down into the darkness. Didn't see anything. *Unless* . . . There was a small zippered compartment on one side. I opened it. Nothing. I shook the bag and heard the rustling noise again.

There was definitely something in this bag, but where?

I kept a flashlight in my vanity drawer, in case there was ever a power outage while I was in the bathroom. It was a secret fear of mine, being stuck in the dark in an enclosed space with no way to see, the aftereffect of a traumatic experience I'd had a couple of years ago when I was kidnapped and bound and nearly killed, all because I'd tried to help a secret-filled couple who sought me for premarital counseling.

That's another story.

I grabbed the flashlight, flicked it on, and shone it inside the purse's dark cavity to make sure I had not missed any other compartments.

"That's odd."

A row of bright red thread zigzagged just underneath the zippered pocket, as if there had been a tear in the lining that had been crudely repaired.

A slight lump bulged from the lining. I would have missed it, thought it insignificant if I hadn't seen the thread.

Using a fingernail clipper to cut through one of the threads, I pulled the string out in one single movement. The lining gave way to a hole. I sighed in disappointment as I realized the only thing behind the lining was old, yellowed newspaper. Filler, I figured. I stuffed the paper back into the lining. Took off the gloves.

What had I been expecting to find? Cleary the purse had been torn and someone had taken steps to repair it, though a third grader probably could have done a better job. I was about to toss the purse pack into the plastic bag when I realized I'd missed stuffing some of the newspaper back into the lining. A scrap lay on the floor, balled up, the size of a sausage patty.

It was too early to have cravings, right? Why did I have the sudden urge for a breakfast sandwich? I realized then that I had not yet eaten anything that day.

I'd already taken off the gloves so I picked up a corner of the small balled-up scrap with my fingertips, ready to just toss it into a nearby wastebasket. As the paper went airborne, something gold and shiny slid out and landed with a soft thud inside the wicker trashcan. I grabbed the can and dumped all the contents on the floor, trying to determine what that object that had been tucked inside the newspaper was.

Found it.

A pocket watch.

Looking like it was made from real gold, a man's pocket watch hung from my fingers from a long chain. A faded inscription was on its rear, too faded and worn to make out.

I opened the watch, and, as I expected, it was dead, stopped at the time 5:11. Those numbers meant nothing to me.

At the moment.

I snapped the case of the watch shut, wrapped it up in a piece of the old newspaper I pulled from the lining, and tucked it back into its secret compartment inside the old black purse.

Now, I really felt compelled to get it back to that woman, Frankie Jean, Sweet Violet. That pocket watch looked expensive and personal. She appeared to have few belongings, but she had that watch. It meant something, I was sure of it.

I was finishing up in the bathroom, trying to figure out my next move to return the woman's belongings, when Leon's voice roared and echoed through the condo.

"Sienna, turn on the TV. Channel twelve. Now!"

I'd never heard him yell like that. Ever. In two seconds, I was out of the bathroom and headed toward the living room television where Leon stood, the remote from our bedroom TV still in his hands.

"Can you please explain this to me?" The roar was gone. In its place, a defeated whisper.

I looked at the screen and gasped. I still had the purse with the pocket watch in my hands as I joined Leon in our living room. The bedroom television's remote was in his hand and he kept pounding on the volume button to no avail.

Wrong remote.

The television was on mute but the images on the screen spoke loud and clear making the headline underneath almost unnecessary: WORKER FOUND SHOT TO DEATH IN FRONT OF HOMELESS SHELTER.

Leon was a former cop. He'd probably seen a million and one unfortunate scenes like this one, so I knew his agitation was not over the story. I followed where his hand pointed and gasped.

And I groaned inside.

How do I even begin to explain? Especially since he just lectured me on the way I spent my time and how I ranked my priorities. Especially since he hadn't wanted me anywhere near the patient I'd treated the night before.

Harmless old homeless woman. That's what I'd told him when he expressed concern that I'd had her in my car.

The TV shot was focused on the yellow tape that surrounded the employee entrance of A New Beginning House. I noted for the first time that a single flat black shoe lay sideways on the ground by the doorway, white chalk outlining it.

The shoe was not Leon's concern, I knew. What had his attention was something—rather, someone—in the periphery: a woman in a black-and-white dress walking down the sidewalk away from the tragic scene.

I looked down at the black-and-white dress I had on, knowing there was no way to pretend that woman was someone else.

"Sienna." He glared at me. "Can you please tell me why you were at a murder scene this morning? Never mind the fact that I thought you were at home resting since you are ill. Never mind the fact that I thought you weren't going to get involved in any more of this. What were you doing there?" His voice was a high-pitched whisper and I realized he was trying his best not to yell.

"I just wanted to return that patient's belongings. I had no idea that the shelter had turned into a crime scene." I looked down at the purse in my hands. Leon's eyes followed mine.

He rubbed his temples, sighed. "I thought you only had a bag with a housecoat in it. Where did that purse come from? Why do you keep getting involved in these things?"

"It's just a purse. Calm down. Nobody's getting involved in anything. I tried to return the bag. The woman wasn't there. A young girl, a pregnant young girl, heard me asking around for her and gave me the purse to keep with the rest of her belongings." The word "pregnant" rolled off my tongue and my heart skipped two beats and I started panting.

I need to tell Leon about the pregnancy tests. I will call Dr. Baronsen first. I'm pregnant? I can't be. I'll be forty in January. God, are you kidding me? Really?

We both looked down at the purse in my hand.

Leon reached for it. "I'm throwing this away once and for all."

"Wait." I swiped it out of his reach. "A gold pocket watch is hidden in the lining. I don't feel right about throwing away something that may have sentimental value to somebody else."

"Sentimental value? It's probably broken and forgotten." He snatched the bag out of my hand and found the watch in mere seconds. He pulled it out, examined it for a moment, and let it dangle from his fingers. "Like I said, broken and forgotten." He stuffed it back into the purse and headed toward the kitchen trashcan.

"Wait, it looks expensive. It might really mean something to her."

"To who?" He spun around to face me, the whisper now gone. A full-blown yell now took its place. "Who exactly is this woman that you want to spend *our* time together looking for? What is her name, Sienna? Her address? Where is she right now? What are you going to do? Spend today, our one day of the week together, walking the streets of Baltimore looking for her? Are you going to go back to that shelter where a worker was killed and interrupt the investigation to see if anyone is missing a pocket watch?"

"Leon, I never said I was going anywhere today."

"Exactly. You didn't say today. But you're going." The yell was gone, but his eyes still looked aflame. "You can't figure out when to spend time with me. You can't make it through a church service for us to worship together. You can't get in the bed and let me care for you while you're sick. But you can find time in your schedule to go looking for a woman whose name and mental state you really don't know, just to give her back some purse she probably found in a trashcan. It's a broken and forgotten pocket watch." His bottom lip trembled and I realized a single tear had found its way out of my eyelid.

We'd never fought before.

Well, at least since we'd been married.

"You have a problem, Sienna." Leon shook his head, turned back toward the trashcan. "I don't know what it is, but you do have a problem."

"No, we have a problem." I let out a slight chuckle, trying to lighten the air between us.

The chuckle didn't come out right.

"I mean, you and I." I tried to explain what didn't even make sense to me at the moment. "It's no longer me. It's no longer just me. It's 'we.' So if you think I have a problem, then it's really 'we.' Oneness. We have a problem, right?" I knew my smile was goofy and my words didn't make sense. It was easier to be silly than to take ownership of an issue.

"You know what?" Leon turned to me one final time. "Just take the purse. Do what you want with it. I'm going back to church. I don't have time for jokes and games and search and rescues. It's fitting that the pocket watch is broken. Our quality time together is just like that watch: broken and forgotten."

"I don't think you're right about the watch or our time, and I'm going to prove it to you."

"I'm sure you will, Sienna. You are always trying to prove that you're right. I mean, you're even about to write a whole book about it, how your gut feelings and instincts are always right. Have you ever considered that just once, maybe just one time, you are wrong?" He asked the question but didn't wait for an answer as he pressed the bag back into my arms and then marched back to our bedroom.

I could hear him rummaging through his dresser drawer, flinging things through his closet as he pieced his church outfit back together again. He emerged a few minutes later dressed once again in his black suit and black-and-white paisley tie.

"You always match my Sunday outfit." I tried again to ease the tension. "Just realized that last Sunday we both had on blue and the week before that we both had on shades of pale green."

"Glad you noticed. I'll be at the early afternoon service and then I'm heading to my shop to prep for tomorrow morning."

He left.

No kiss good-bye.

First time that happened.

"What have I done?" I looked down at the purse in my hand and then ran to the bathroom once again. I felt sick to my stomach, a little hurt in the heart, and uncertain about what to do next.

No, I was certain about one thing. I was going to find that woman and be rid of her stuff out of my life once and for all.

Leon was right. I did have a problem; but it was not about "being right." Rather, I struggled with "letting go."

Chapter 12

"Thank you for your testimony. You may step down now and we will adjourn for lunch." The judge pounded his gavel and the courtroom came alive, making the last few hours of quiet but brutal, repetitive testimony seem like a distant dream.

You think you know what dreams are? Humph, you don't even know what sleep is. You livin' life with your eyes closed, thinking you're awake. Sweet Violet's raspy voice jarred my consciousness, her words to me as clear and as puzzling as they had been some weeks ago when we met in the War Memorial Plaza, the grassy area in front of city hall. We'd had several conversations like this over the months. My mind had been occupied with dissecting distant memories for most of the time I'd been up on the witness stand.

"Sienna, let's grab lunch while we can." Leon pulled me close to him as I pressed my way through the courtroom. Joe Koletsky, a young attorney who served as Alisa Billy's assistant, did his best to try to shield me from the throng of reporters and gawkers with smartphone cameras who swamped me from every side.

And Leon actually thought we were going to be able to eat in peace?

If the killer had stopped at Sister Marta, or even the second victim, there would probably be far less interest in this case; but the last victim had been too high profile for the media not to notice. His picture had been plastered to every news story about the trial, much like his image had already been plastered to billboards and press releases in Baltimore over the decades. Add to these facts that I, a recent media darling after last year's terror attack, was the key witness, and the current camera frenzy was inevitable.

"I have a place for us to eat," Leon whispered in my ear, as if reading my thoughts. "It's quiet. We'll be alone."

The three of us, Leon, Joe, and I, continued to press through the sea of reporters, microphones, and flashes, through the hallways of the courthouse, out the front entrance, and down the marble steps. I noted a car waiting at the bottom.

I also noted Roman standing by a light post across the street. He stood out in the crowd as he was the only one standing still and the only one looking off in another direction. His hands were deep in his pockets and an Orioles baseball cap was pushed down low over his eyes.

"Wait." I grabbed Leon's wrist and he pulled his head closer to me. "I need to talk to Roman," I whispered.

"No. It's just going to upset you."

I felt his hand tug mine a little harder as we headed down the steps toward the waiting car.

"Leon, wait."

"No. Sienna. This day is trying enough. This isn't the time. Roman is a grown man, twenty-one, old enough to make his own choices. You can't change that. Can't change his mind. Can't change him. Even if you could, this is not the day to try. Let's go get lunch. I made reservations."

We were at the car, a black sedan, and I recognized the driver. One of Leon's old partners from when he served with the Baltimore police department, Mike Grant. They'd been hanging out more lately.

"Come on, let's get out of here." Leon kept his hold on my hand firm as he opened the back door and gently nudged me, doing his best to get me out of the view of the swarm of cameras and reporters.

I felt like I was in a dream.

But my son was across the street.

"I'm going to talk to Roman. Now." I pushed Leon's hand off of mine and then considered that I may have spoken too loudly. The last thing I needed was for the news outlets and social media platforms to get wind of my family business in the midst of this courtroom spectacle.

"Sienna." Leon's voice was barely a whisper, but might as well have been a yell.

There was a time in my life that I never could imagine Leon yelling, but as of late, I'd known his yells too well.

What's happening to us?

"He is leaving tonight. His plane leaves tonight. I can't let him take off like this." I turned toward the crosswalk intending to cross the street to get to my waiting son.

But Roman had just hailed a cab.

I had taken only two steps away from the car when it happened.

He hadn't just been looking away, I realized. He had been flagging down a ride.

Roman didn't want to talk to me.

Leon was right. Roman was a grown man making his own decisions. And right now, he'd decided that he didn't want to talk to me. The weight of that realization pressed down on me more than the eight-month-old baby sagging down my forty-year-old belly.

I was supposed to have a fortieth birthday party in January. Roman had promised to plan it, take care of all the details. Was even going to send me on a cruise and had taken pride in being able to pay the hefty bill himself, despite my own newfound fortune.

But the party, the cruise didn't happen. All plans went out of the window during his Christmas break.

The dinner that turned disastrous.

"Sienna, you need to eat before court resumes; eat and sit somewhere comfortable." His eyes were on my stomach.

His child.

My child was now a man and he was about to get into a taxicab, on his way to a flight to another life that left in just a few hours.

The new life inside of me gave a hard kick to my ribs and I realized I only had about forty-five minutes left to eat with no idea where Leon had made reservations.

"Okay, I'm ready. Let's go." I turned back to Leon, took his extended hand and sat down next to him in the back of his old friend Mike's car.

Joe Koletsky shut the door for us and walked off, disappearing into the crowd. He was a quiet man who always dressed impeccably in a black suit. His suits matched his black hair, which he kept parted and gelled down.

"Next stop, my dining room." Mike Grant smiled and winked at me in the rearview mirror, and I had a sudden memory of why I'd always felt ambivalent about hanging around him.

"I thought you made reservations, Leon." I didn't even bother whispering now as we sped up Calvert Street. Mike drove like there were lights and sirens going off on his car although we were in his personal vehicle. We were already three blocks away from the chaos.

"We do have reservations. Just had to be creative about it. Mike and Shavona have lunch waiting for both of us. All three of us." He gave a half nod, half smile at my belly. "We don't have much time and I'm trying to give you some kind of peace and privacy."

Peace and privacy?

With Mike and Shavona?

Peace and privacy were the last two words that came to mind when Mike and Shavona Grant were any part of the sentence. I would have said so with my eyes—I'd become an expert with the nonverbal talk since my wedding date—but after our quick spat over my insistence to talk to my son, I decided to let this one go.

I was hungry, and, from the kicking going on inside of me, so was the other person in our party of three.

This was not how I pictured this pregnancy going. I sighed, as Mike pulled his car up in front of a large row home facing Patterson Park. Court case, chaos, continual spats with Leon, Roman leaving, and the nagging feeling that I was missing something important.

You livin' life with your eyes closed, thinking you're awake.

That woman's words held as much potency as her wretched breath. How I had managed to sit next to her the few times I caught her downtown in the War Memorial Plaza would forever remain a mystery.

Lord, I hope Sweet Violet had nothing to do with this series of deaths for which I'm serving as a witness. It was a silent prayer, but one I found myself praying weekly. Actually, now daily, since I hadn't seen her in a while.

She couldn't be involved, I assured myself. I'd gone over everything with Leon: my suspicions, my questions, everything. He used to be a cop, and he'd helped me sort out other nagging mysteries in the past. I trusted his judgment, and he already judged her harmless.

A little reckless, a lot annoying, but harmless, nonetheless.

Maybe I would feel better if I knew her story; but there was no time to dig, and to what end? Time was precious, Leon had told me months ago. I could still see him in his green pajamas that Sunday morning when I first tried to return Sweet Violet's belongings to no avail.

The Sunday I found that pocket watch.

5:11. The time forever frozen on its gold face.

That morning. Forever the turning point in our still-growing marriage.

Time.

I guessed that's what was bothering me, the timing of it all. The murders, the questions, and Sweet Violet's random appearances all began around the same time.

"You're going to love this, Sienna." Mike was talking to me, I realized. I also realized that I was out of the car and walking into the luxurious remodel that was the Grant's three-story row home. He was living pretty well to be a public servant. I noted the high-end everything that was their living and dining areas.

"Leon filled us in about your potato craving, so Shavona and I made a potato feast for you to enjoy before you head back to the courthouse." Mike pointed to a large spread laid out on a table that took up most of their expansive dining room. Theirs was a house for entertaining: holiday meals, cookouts, Saturday night parties. "We've got homemade waffle fries, red bliss potato salad, scalloped potatoes with smoked turkey sausage, and, of course, Shavona's garlic and cheddar mashed potatoes."

"Okay." I plastered a smile onto my face, though everything in my stomach turned at the menu. I'd told Leon that I had cravings for lemons and Cocoa Puffs. Where did potatoes come from? Even Leon looked slightly confused. We both looked at each other and shared a secret smile.

Regardless of everything that was happening around us and between us, we still understood each other.

"Ooh, there she is." I heard the squeal even before she entered the room. "Girl, look at you, still looking good, well, considering." Shavona Grant grabbed me from behind, spun me around to face her and swirled her hands all over my stomach, top to bottom, side to side as she spoke. I decided to let the invasion of her hands slide, but I could not ignore her scent.

For reasons unknown to me, the woman always smelled of pizza. Perfume? Body wash? Couldn't figure it out. The few times we'd met had been at our husbands' social outings: a fishing trip two weeks after Leon and I married; a bowling night in January; a couples night out with some of Leon's other old police buddies. We'd barely talked to each other outside of those meet-ups, and when we did have conversations, we swapped stories mostly about pregnancy and raising kids.

They had none, but I knew they were trying, and had been trying for nearly a decade. "In God's time," was how she started and ended every conversation when the topic came up.

"Girl, I've been watching you on TV, and I must say you sure have been handling yourself well with that smart-mouthed lawyer. I would have slapped her right across the eyebrows by now. Let's say grace." Shavona sat next to me at the table and had already started piling a plate high with all manner of potatoes. She passed the plate to me then bowed her head. Leon and Mike sat across from us, and although they had been engaged in a lively discussion about the Baltimore Ravens, Mike immediately bowed his head when Shavona's head lowered.

"Father, thank you for friends, food, and fellowship. As our dear friends face the ongoing difficulties that are disrupting their lives, I ask that this meal give nourishment and strength, and our home and lives give necessary support and love."

I had my eyes closed for the beginning of Shavona's prayer, but opened them at the word "friends." These were Leon's people, his old work buddy and his work buddy's wife. I knew that Leon was close to Mike, and that he'd known Shavona for years, but I didn't know them that well. I saw them as Leon's acquaintances. I guess that's why the word "friends" jumped out at me. I barely knew them personally.

"Amen." Mike opened his eyes just before she ended the prayer and looked directly at me.

And winked.

Two winks in the past twenty minutes.

I was not comfortable with this at all. Or was I just reading too much into his eye movement?

"Let's eat, Sienna, and then get back to the courthouse. I think, at least I hope, they are all finished questioning you. Alisa Billy said you might just have to hang around for a few more days." Leon spoke between munches of fries. "They think the case will be over by Friday, and then we are off to Florida."

"That's right, your anniversary trip!" Shavona squealed again. "I'm glad you two will be celebrating, but I don't know about you flying all over the country in your state, Sienna. I don't want my godbaby born on no airplane. You are in the news enough already, girlfriend."

Godbaby?

Had I missed a conversation? Again, I barely knew these people.

"Don't worry, Shavona," Leon replied. "Sienna's doctor has promised to grant Sienna permission to fly as long as it's four weeks before her due date. If we are still sitting in that courtroom after next week, I'm going to be delivering your godbaby midair myself because we are going on our trip."

Godbaby. There went that word again. Really, had there been a conversation I wasn't privy to?

Roman didn't have godparents. He was born at a stage in my life when I was on a mission to prove myself completely independent and capable of making it apart from Roman's father, my first husband. Our marriage was pretty much over before Roman was even born and I could not let my wounds show.

Truth was, outside of my family and the shaky bonds to which we clung, I hadn't had much in the way of friendships to even pronounce anyone "godmother" or "godfather." Ava Diggs, my life and career coach and mentor had been my best friend for years, and she was a lot older than my own mother. She entered my life when I was struggling to get through graduate school and stayed around to offer me my first real job at her foster care agency and then cheered me on as I started my private practice. Roman still had his baby fat and high voice when she entered our lives. She was a friend, but our friendship had been built on my needs and her advice. The older he grew, the stronger I became, the less Ava and I talked. With the media frenzy and the baby preparations, I realized that I had not checked in with her in a while.

If anyone would be godmother, it would be either her, or maybe my younger sister.

"Girl, you are due in the middle of summer." Shavona had put her fork down to grab my hand. "I heard that's a tough season to be pregnant in, you know, with all the heat. I will be praying for you." She laughed, but I saw something else in her eyes. I saw it and I knew for that moment I was awake enough to recognize a dream, albeit a broken one. *You livin' life with your eyes closed.*

"Thanks." I smiled back at the pain, the heartache that stared back at me through several coats of brown mascara. She still smiled, but I did not miss the slight quiver of her bottom lip or the fact that she had picked at her plate of potatoes about as much as I had.

Every now and then her eyes landed on my rounded belly and then on her flat one.

Leon's plate was still pretty full as well. Mike was the only one attempting to eat.

I wondered if Roman was also trying to eat lunch somewhere. Thinking of Roman only reminded me that I was losing him.

Maybe had already lost him.

His flight left in a few hours and neither he nor Leon seemed open to me trying to reconnect with him. Why had he bothered to come? Baltimore was a long ways from where he'd come from. He'd come all that way just to tell me he was leaving for the next leg of his journey tonight?

"I never thought I'd have my own child." Leon spoke as we headed to the door several minutes later to return to the courthouse. I couldn't read his face or voice, but the quiet from all of us that filled the foyer said it all.

Shavona had stopped her oohing and aahing, Mike fingered his car keys, and I was trying to figure out what to do with the child I already had.

You think you know what dreams are?

Mike's car jumped to life with Leon and me in the back seat, ready to face yet again the crowds, the journalists, the stares of the judge and jury, the attorneys, the cold, blank stare of the defendant.

You think you know what dreams are? Sweet Violet's words echoed through my brain cells, jumping from synapse to synapse as I tried to figure out how I'd landed in my present nightmare.

A nightmare that was taking a turn for the worse, I realized as we approached the marble steps off of Calvert Street.

"Leon!" I grabbed his shoulder with one hand and he jolted forward in his seat when he saw where I pointed with the other.

Nothing could have prepared me for the scene in front of us.

Nothing.

Chapter 13

Flashing lights and sirens swamped a corner across the street from the courthouse. The crowds of reporters and gawkers who had earlier followed my descent down the courthouse steps now had shifted their attention to whatever had happened across the street. In the commotion, I only noted one thing, and that was the one thing I pointed out to Leon.

A black Orioles cap lying on the ground in the center of a small area cordoned off by yellow tape.

My mind had gone into overdrive as I tried to make sense of the hat that seemed to hold the crowd's attention. I'd seen too many scenes with yellow tape over the past few months so I told myself I was overreacting, jumpy. It was mere coincidence that the hat looked like one Roman had been wearing when I spotted him near that corner just before lunch.

But I watched him hail a cab. That's not his hat. Whatever happened on that corner has nothing to do with him. I said those three sentences over and over again in my head, not comforted by Leon's gaze and fellow interest in the fallen hat.

"Stop the car." I caught myself from jumping out of it as Mike pulled to a stop on the outer edges of the commotion. The moment the car was in park, I got out and pushed my way through the pedestrian congestion to get as close as I could to the hat. Leon was right behind me. My mind was numb as my heart began pounding harder.

Did something happen to my Roman?

It was a common hat, one that was probably on the heads of countless Orioles fans across the city. I knew this on an intellectual level, but my gut told me it was too coincidental that it lay where I'd last seen my son.

"What happened?" I asked, breathless, as I approached an elderly man in a dress shirt and jeans who stood on the outer edges. He had a square head that was bald at the top with a few random dreadlocks clinging to the sides. He gripped a black cane that had a golden eagle's head as a handle grip.

"Yeah, they almost got him, they almost got him," he mumbled, shaking his head.

"Almost got who? What happened?"

The man kept shaking his head, meandered away. Leon nudged me forward and I became aware that no one in the crowd had singled me out. The cameras seemed oblivious to my presence, focused only on the scores of emergency vehicles that filled the intersection.

Alisa Billy.

I saw the prosecutor talking to an officer. Leon must have spotted her too. He was nudging me in her direction. When I was about three feet away she noticed me.

"Roman is okay."

Her prompt assertion, meant to be assuring, alarmed me. She didn't know my Roman, so how would she know about his condition? *Okay from what? Of course, he's okay. I watched him get a taxicab just before I ate lunch, a little over an hour ago,* I wanted to tell her.

"What happened?" I asked for the third time. The officer to whom Alisa had been talking provided an answer.

"He was jumped by a group of street kids, but like Ms. Billy said, he's okay. He was taken to the hospital to treat some minor wounds."

"Jumped? Street kids?" Leon spoke up.

"Wounds?" was all I heard.

"Yeah, some kids up to no good jumped him. Robbery. Stupidity. Some senseless acts don't have a clear explanation."

Robbery.

The word jumped out at me the same way it did the morning I'd learned about Ms. Marta's death. Robbery to me seemed like a catch-all phrase when authorities weren't clear about motive or circumstance.

"Why Roman?" I asked aloud as I considered the size of the crowd that had surrounded the courthouse even before this supposed robbery.

The officer shrugged. "Why not him? Anybody can be a victim of violence."

"How did you know he was my son?" I turned to Alisa. "How did you know his name?"

"He told the responding officers. That's why I came over here and got involved. Anything or anyone that involves you right now will get my attention. But as Officer Howell implied, this attack seemed random."

As opposed to what? This question I didn't ask aloud, but tucked it away in the mental file box I'd been keeping of "coincidences" that had been occurring over the past few months.

"So you really don't think my son was in any way targeted?"

"Remember your son hasn't been in the picture at all since this whole ordeal began. I didn't even know who he was. I doubt that anyone else would either."

"He was in the news some years ago." I shut my eyes, remembering the fear I'd experienced when Roman had disappeared across the country back when he was sixteen years old. "A simple Google search would have revealed that."

"Sienna." Alisa gave me a sympathetic smile. "I stress to you that the authorities believe this was a random attack. No reason to believe otherwise at this point."

"But you have someone with him at the hospital just in case?" Leon asked the officer.

Just in case of what?

"The ambulance left here about fifteen minutes ago. I know officers were going to meet him where they took him. Not because they are concerned about his continued safety, just to get more info from him so they can catch the hoodlums behind the assault."

"But he was getting into a cab when I saw him. I was about to catch up with him when I saw him getting in."

"Yeah, they pulled him out of the cab, just before he shut the door."

"And that was random? All the people out here they could have robbed and beaten, and they chose a man about to drive off in a cab?"

My heart now galloped as my head spun in a nosedive. I was about to crash. Mentally. Emotionally. Completely.

When the officer didn't respond to my question, I only had one other. "Where did they take him?"

"Metro Community," Alisa answered. "Judge Greenberg, I'm sure, will allow you a few moments to go check on him before returning to the court. I do not have any more questions for you, so unless the defense wants to reexamine you, you're done. I mean, you still have to stay around for the rest of the trial in case you're needed back on the stand, but I don't anticipate that happening."

I was already heading back to the car, glad to see that Mike hadn't left and Leon was still behind me. A kick vibrated through my abdomen.

"Don't worry, little one." I rubbed my belly, aware that the knots and worry that were filling my stomach were sharing space with my unborn child. "We're going to go check on your big brother right now." I wasn't waiting for a judge to okay me visiting my child.

And I wasn't convinced as everyone seemed to be that this was a random attack.

Chapter 14

Minor injuries.

Wasn't that what the police officer and Alisa had said to me?

I gasped at the sight of my son on the ED gurney. Fresh stitches lined his forehead; several bandages covered his lower leg. One cheek was noticeably swollen, and several bruises lined his arms and chest.

"It looks worse than it is," a nurse behind me spoke, seeming to read my thoughts.

KeeKee Witherspoon. In the commotion of getting there, I'd forgotten where "there" was. I hadn't been back since the last shift for which I'd volunteered, the night Sweet Violet was a patient, but from the looks of the hustle and bustle that surrounded me, the place hadn't missed a beat.

"I'm sorry this happened to your son," KeeKee continued as she checked his IV and put a bandage over the stitches. "He'll be okay. The only reason he looks unconscious right now is because we gave him a strong painkiller that knocked him right out. He'll be okay."

She left the room, leaving me to my thoughts, my questions.

Leaving me to my son.

"Roman," I whispered, waiting for, wanting him to awaken. I'd left Leon in the waiting room to manage the legal team requests and the now growing interest of the press. I could see the headlines now: SON OF STAR WITNESS

IN DELMON FRANK MURDER TRIAL BEATEN AND ROBBED BY ATTACKERS.

Robbed.

The word jumped out at me again. *Robbed.*

I stood up, rubbed a small patch of Roman's arm that wasn't covered with bandages, and went out into the hallway.

"Excuse me." I approached a police officer who was writing in a notepad a few steps away from the nurses' station. "My son was attacked during a robbery earlier today by the courthouse. Roman St. James. Can you tell me what, if anything, was stolen from him?"

"Oh, Ms. St. James, I mean Mrs. Sanderson." The officer smiled at me. "I've been following you ever since you helped with that terrorist attack last year. I've got to admit that I like the way you operate. You are one savvy woman." He was maybe five or ten years older than me, blond hair, baby blue eyes, the type of man in uniform I guess some women would swoon over, especially the way he was eyeing me.

But I couldn't care less. I had my dream man.

"Thanks," I replied to be polite, "but I'm wondering if you can help me with any more information about my son's attack?"

"Right, Roman St. James. I read some old articles about how he tried to track down his father years ago. I can only imagine how terrified you must have been when he went missing."

Listening to the officer talk reminded me of how much of my life was an open book; not a comforting thought as I tried to reconcile the word "random" with the attack that had left my son in his current bandaged and bruised position.

"Thanks for your concern, and you better believe that I'm glad he's okay, both then and now. I really do have some questions about this latest threat to his safety."

"Yeah, I heard about the courthouse attack. I wish I could provide you with more answers, but truth is, I'm here following another case. I'll see if I can find someone who knows what's going on with that to help you."

"I would appreciate that." I gave him a full smile though I felt like anything but happy. As I returned to Roman's room, more questions flooded my mind. Why would a group of young men initiate such a brazen attack in front of crowds of people, media cameras, and potential witnesses? This wasn't random. I was convinced.

But who?

And why?

I collapsed back into the seat next to Roman and watched him sleep. Breathe in, breathe out. IVs, oxygen.

Too much.

And we hadn't even talked about the wall that had come between us. I think that bothered me most of all.

What if this just hadn't led to Roman bruised and sleeping? The thought both chilled and heated me. Chilled me to consider the alternative. Heated me that someone actually thought they had a right, for whatever reason, to harm my son.

And we hadn't yet had a chance to talk, to reconnect.

"I love you, Roman," I whispered, running a hand through the mounds of black curls that topped his head. He looked like his father. That reality no longer hurt.

I'd come a long way, but the events over Roman's last Christmas break had exposed to all of us how much damage still needed to be repaired in my emotions and expectations.

"Wake up," I whispered again. "We need to talk." What if he didn't wake up, or didn't wake up in his right mind? KeeKee said he would be fine. Just under the effect of a powerful painkiller. I tried to calm myself down and a kick in my belly gave me another reason to do so. Baby didn't need a wave of my anxiety and panic washing over it as well. I considered calling Leon to come back and offer me company, but I didn't want to invite the legalities and technicalities he was handling back into my brain space.

So I sat alone with my son, phone off, no television present, with few interruptions from the hospital staff, thanks, I knew, to KeeKee's insistence that I be left alone.

But one visitor managed to make it through. I heard her footsteps before I even heard the curtain screech open.

Ava Diggs.

My longtime life mentor, old boss, personified tissue box, and human pillow cushion.

She came in the room, pulled the chair that sat on the other side of Roman and dragged it over next to me. Sitting next to me in silence, I heard the slight wheeze in her breath, noticed her ever-loosening skin over what used to be her oversized frame. She coughed a few times, took out a lace handkerchief, wiped her mouth, and then let out a deep sigh.

"You are his honorary godmother," I finally spoke.

"What was that?" Her eyes never left Roman as she examined his bruised body from head to toe.

"I said you are his honorary godmother." I sat back in the chair. "I was just thinking today that I never picked a godmother for him when he was born because I was too angry at his father, my life, my family, everything, to let one more person in." I looked over at her and she looked back at me as I continued. "But you did come in, Ava. You've been helping me manage so much of my life and career over the years, that the benefits I've received from your friendship and mentorship, I'm sure, trickled down to him. God knew I needed you, for both me and him. You are his honorary godmother. Thank you for being here for me, for us."

"And now you have Leon," she said with finality. "God knew you needed him and now he is here for you. And for Roman."

"Yes. I'm grateful. He's a good man."

"Then what is it?" she asked before her body began shaking again in another violent coughing spell.

"Excuse me?" I passed her a handful of paper towels that were within my reach. She took them, wiped her mouth, and then spoke again after regaining her composure.

"What is it that is making it hard for you to settle down into what you have with Leon?"

"What?" I was genuinely confused, taken aback by her question.

"Half the time I see you, seems like you're pushing him away. Why is he not in here with you right now?"

"I asked him to take care of the lawyers and media."

"Isn't that what the prosecutor's assistant is for?" She leaned in toward me. "Yes, I've been following you on TV, and seems like that little man in the black suit following Alisa Billy around is the PR pro."

"You're talking about Joe Koletsky?"

She nodded. "Whoever. Let him take care of those details. I'm sure Leon would much rather be in here with you and Roman. You are a family now. Be a family, especially in trying times."

"It's not like how you say, Ava." I sighed. "I love Leon and he loves me and he gladly helps me out in whatever role I need him in. Right now, I need him to be my guardian, my protector. He's an ex-cop, you know. Before he was baking those cupcakes he was stopping the bad guys. Now he's doing that for me in his own way."

"He's not just your bodyguard, Sienna, is he?"

"Of course not." I could hear the defensiveness in my voice as whatever nerve Ava struck vibrated along with the other mass of emotions running through me. "Though I have to admit, we've been married almost a year, and, to be honest with you, I feel like we were closer when we first married as compared to now."

"It's been a lot happening over the last few months; a lot, especially for newlyweds." Ava eyed me.

"Yes. Definitely a lot. The aftermath of the terror coverage, this book I'm supposed to be writing. Leon's bakery is struggling a little. A lot. Although I've offered to help him out, he's insisting that his bakery fail or succeed on his own merits." I shook my head, realizing how much Leon's pride irritated me. *Why can't he accept my help?* "My therapy practice has grown beyond anything I planned for; and now everything is on pause because of this trial where I'm the main witness. None of this is what I planned. And now Roman." *Should I tell her how he had upset me and that we'd barely talked to each other since Christmas?* "And, of course, there's the baby. We've got only a month to get ready for it, and it's barely coming up in our conversation with all the other things going on." I thought about our lunch with the Grants earlier that day, and the godparent hints. Clearly Leon seemed to be talking about the baby with his friends more than with me. "Neither one of us expected to be coming together as parents at this point in our lives."

"Yes, you have a lot facing you right now, individually and as a couple, but that's all the more reason to draw closer together. This is not the time to be drifting apart."

"We're not drifting." I struggled to put into words what I had never said out loud. "It's just that . . . Leon does not fully understand me. He does not fully get me, the work I do, why I do it. Though he's never expressed it, I think he blames this whole court case and my role in it on me not leaving matters alone. He doesn't get what I do or who I am as a social worker. And, what bothers me the most, he doesn't get that I follow my gut instincts, and I'm usually right about them."

"You've just said a lot. To me. Those are your feelings, and I'm not going to get into whether you are right or wrong. Rather, have you talked about how you feel with Leon, or are you just drifting along, waiting to see what will happen next? Marriage is work, honey. You're only in year one. You both are going to have different ideas, interests, and perspectives. Figuring out how to come together as one is the tricky part."

"I can't compromise who I am, Ava, and I feel like I shouldn't have to, even if it lands me in difficult or uncomfortable situations like the one I'm in now."

"Nobody is saying you have to compromise who you are, but you do need to remember that you are no longer living an independent life. Your world has expanded to include a husband, someone outside of you who has thoughts, feelings, and beliefs that are just as relevant and as important as yours. I didn't mean to get into all of this right now. It just concerned me that you still seem like you are trying to manage your life trials apart from your partner who wants to support you side by side, not just manage calls from strangers in the waiting room."

I tried to let her words settle, but like snow falling on warm cement, I couldn't handle any additional accumulating emotions.

"I hear you, Ava," I said, ready to end the conversation. "For whatever it's worth, I am compromising, well, accommodating Leon on a request he feels pretty strongly about. That woman I told you about a few months back, Sweet Violet, I'm not bringing her up to the lawyers or investigators."

"Sweet Violet? You mean the homeless lady you've been meeting with in the plaza by city hall? What does she have to do with the case?"

"I guess nothing. That's why Leon wants me to leave it and her alone."

"And you should. You have enough on your plate to want to add another serving, especially one that could confuse others looking for clarity and answers in such a complicated trial as this one. Why would you even think she has any relevance to the murders?"

"Timing. That's all."

Ava pursed her lips as if she was about to say something, but then she shook her head. "I'm not even going to ask, Sienna. If Leon the ex-cop says to leave it alone, I'm not going to stir up any more confusion with further questions. Sienna, is Roman going to be okay?"

We both looked over at him. His chest rose and fell in comforting assurance. "That's what they're telling me. They just gave him a pain reliever that has him knocked out cold."

"Good." She reached out and patted his hand, careful not to mess up the bandages.

"Ava." I felt the need to continue clarifying, maybe defending, what I felt. "You know that I've learned to trust my gut and that's the only reason I can't let things go easily."

"Well, just remember your gut is full of a baby right now, and babies are always a game changer."

Change. Everything in my life was changing.

Ava wasn't finished. "You're doing good, Sienna, but don't settle for good. You have a great man so don't just settle for a good marriage. There's no reason for you not to have a great one." She patted my knee, started coughing again. "I need to go. You don't need me here. Leon can warm this seat. I've got an appointment to get to. I'm seeing a pulmonologist for this cough at two-thirty and it's almost two o'clock."

"Yes, Ava. That cough doesn't sound good. I'm glad you're finally getting it checked out. This baby's going to need a godmother around to keep this mother on the right track."

"Honey, I'm old." She chuckled as she moved toward the room's curtain-covered doorway. "I'll gladly be the godgrandma, if your mother's okay with that, but you need to get one of your younger girlfriends to take on the duties of godmother." She must have seen the face I made, because she stopped walking, turned back to face me fully and offered pointed advice. "Stop blocking out the world, Sienna. Stop blocking out Leon. Stop being so stubborn and inflexible. And tell Roman, when he wakes up, that I stopped by. Bye."

I listened to her footsteps disappear down the hallway, a steady, stable beat in the chaos of the emergency room.

And then another pair click-clacked in. Black shoes. Uniform shoes.

"Mrs. Sanderson St. James?"

"Yes?" *Why can't anyone get my name right?* I looked up at the officer staring down at me. I recognized him as the one who had been talking to Alisa back at the scene.

"I understand that you had a question about your son's attack. Please know that we are doing all we can to find the assailants and bring them to justice."

"Thank you. I appreciate your efforts. I just wanted to get more information about the robbery. What exactly was stolen?"

"From what I've learned, a couple of credit cards we found scattered a block away, as well as his ID. Surprisingly, that's all."

"Surprisingly?"

"Well, his phone was still on him as was his cash."

"His phone? And cash? They didn't take his money? That's good. Odd, but good. How much did he have on him?"

"Huh? Oh." The officer had become preoccupied with a message on his phone. "A five dollar bill, a dime, and a penny. Excuse me." He pointed down to the phone. "I have to take this call. Hello, Sergeant Tim?" He stepped out into the hallway, leaving me to wonder why that dollar amount was bugging me.

A five dollar bill, a dime, a penny.

Five dollars and eleven cents.

$5.11.

I picked up my own phone, realized that my hands were shaking.

511. The same number that had been on that broken pocket watch in Sweet Violet's battered purse.

It's all a coincidence, I told myself, as I had been telling myself over and over for the past few months.

"I suggest you go on about your way before I put the 'n' in Violet and acquaint you with my bitter side," were Sweet Violet's words at our meeting back in November, in this very emergency room.

It's all a coincidence. Just the same, my fingers quivered as I dialed a number on my phone. He answered on the first ring.

"Leon, can you come back here? I need you."

See, I listen, I wanted to tell Ava. *I'm going to lean on him, let him be closer to support me.*

But I also trusted my instincts.

There was nothing random about Roman's attack, or coincidental about the numbers involved. I felt it, and the certainty of that conclusion soared to a new height of awareness inside of me.

This attack was a personal declaration of war from an unknown, unseen enemy. I wasn't sure if Sweet Violet had a role in all of this, but I was determined to find out.

Chapter 15

Seven Months Earlier

"She's an old, homeless woman who probably doesn't even know her bag is missing. Why can't you let this go?"

It was the Monday morning after our first big fight.

Leon was heading out the door to get the day started at his bakery when he noticed the bag dangling off of my arms.

"I'm just going to keep it in my trunk in case I run into her somewhere. That's all."

"Really, Sienna? I thought we agreed that you were going to let all the extra stuff go. You have enough on your plate without compromising more of our time together."

"No, I'm not compromising our time. If anything I'm compromising what I would like to do just to keep you happy."

"What do you mean by that?"

"I'm not going to be walking around the streets of downtown looking for her, as you fear. Keeping the bag in my trunk simply allows me to give it to her if I happen to see her as I'm driving around. See, I'll be safe and no harm will be done." I could hear the bite in my tone. "If she gets her bag back, fine. If not, I'll have peace in knowing that I tried.

"That's what you're telling me, but we both know that's not what's going to happen. There's no way you're going to let that bag stay in your car without you making every attempt to find her, and get involved, and rescue her, and spend more time trying to help her instead of focusing on us."

"Leon, you are taking it way too far. It's just a bag of dirty clothes and an old purse and it's going in the trunk of my car." I grabbed my keys and marched out of the door like he had done yesterday.

No kiss good-bye.

What was happening to us? And why?

My usual Monday morning routine of getting up and heading out to my therapy practice felt anything but normal. And why?

I still needed to tell him I was pregnant, but given our unfinished argument, I had no idea how or when to share the news. As I started the engine, I stared over at the bag of belongings—the housecoat, the slippers, the purse with the broken pocket watch hidden inside its lining—and knew on an intellectual level that dealing with it was more trouble than it was worth.

But something in me would not let it go.

The bag of belongings and my mission to find its owner was setting off all kinds of trouble in my home front, but I could not explain the unshakeable feeling I had to pursue the matter. Maybe it was the pocket watch that looked heirloom quality that had me wanting to reconnect it to its owner. Perhaps I was just feeling a bit off from being too close to a crime scene Sunday morning. Maybe the combination of too little sleep and too many hormones had twisted my judgment and soured my mood.

No. It wasn't just my hormones or lack of sleep. I could not shake the nagging feeling that I was missing, or had missed something important, and that is what was bothering me.

"Are you a cop?" the young man with the old eyes and cigarette hanging from his lips had asked me the day before when I attempted to return the belongings of Frankie Jean, Sweet Violet, or whoever she was.

And I was pretty sure that I had seen the same young man in a black car down the street from the shelter the first time I went there, when I dropped the woman off. Maybe my eyes were playing tricks on me, but something in the attire and mannerisms seemed one and the same.

And then there was the man I'd seen near the emergency room entrance when I first showed up to help. He had been mingling near the greenery by the door, seemingly unnoticed by anyone but me. When I tried to point him out, he'd disappeared.

Was that the same young man?

I felt silly thinking of these things and trying to draw conclusions.

My cell phone rang just as I turned right onto President Street, heading toward 83 North.

"Sienna." Leon's voice sounded through my Bluetooth.

"Leon," I answered.

A long pause.

"Let's meet up for lunch." Leon broke the silence with these words followed by a loud sigh.

"Okay," I answered immediately.

Another long pause.

"I'll have Darci change my schedule around and I'll come to your shop to eat." This time I ended the silence.

"Sounds good, Sienna. Okay. I gotta go."

"Love you."

"Love you too, babe."

We both hung up and I hurried my way up 83 to 695 to get to my Dulaney Valley office suite. I knew a full morning of children needing clinical services awaited me.

Play therapy.

After dealing with that client last year who I suspected of being a terrorist, child's play was all I wanted to handle professionally from now on.

I didn't want to manage grownup issues anymore.

Shoot, I was having a hard enough time managing my own grownup issues.

I was typing up case notes for a child who had attachment issues when my longtime office assistant, Darci Dudley, knocked on my door.

"Sorry to interrupt, Sienna." She ran her fingers through her red hair and shook it: a clear sign that a cute man was somewhere nearby. "You have a visitor."

"Send him on back." I smiled and shook my head as she headed back to the waiting area.

A few seconds later, a gentleman with a tan suit, close shave, and a bouquet of lilies, daisies, and roses stood in my doorway. I started running my fingers through my own hair as the fineness in front of me tilted his head to one side, bit his lower lip.

Leon.

"I don't want to fight with you anymore, Sienna, and I couldn't wait for lunchtime to tell you that."

We stared at each other a few heat-filled seconds and then I could hold it in no longer.

"Leon, I think I'm pregnant." Breath held.

I watched his face go through every state of emotion like a radio dial—fear, wonder, anxiety, concern, exasperation—before finally tuning in to a station, a state, of pure joy.

"I'm thrilled, baby. That's the best news I've ever heard in my forty-two years of living."

We looked at each other in awe and silence and I realized I'd never shared a moment like this with any man before.

Ever.

Roman's father had been out of my life before I even missed a period. I'd never been a parent unalone before. I'd never had a pregnancy partner, a labor coach, someone to sit next to me at little league games or recitals who had the same stake in the matter as I did.

I never had it, and I never before realized how much I'd missed it.

"Leon?"

"Yes, wife and mother of my child?" He was licking his lips.

"Shut the door."

Chapter 16

The deluge of memories, of old arguments, of lingering regrets hung over my head as I followed Leon from the emergency department's waiting room at Metro Community. Roman had been moved to an inpatient unit. "Just for observation," the head doctor of the ED said.

"He looks worse than he really is," Leon assured me as we took the elevators to one of the general med/surg floors. "Truth be told, due to the high profile nature of the case and your involvement, the medical staff is probably doing all they can to cover themselves. Roman's fine. He will be fine."

I'd said very little since Ava left. Though I'd called Leon back to the room, and he'd joined me immediately, ginger ale and graham crackers in hand, I couldn't get out any words.

$5.11.

He would think I was crazy, overthinking, if I brought it up, I was sure. And maybe I was overreacting.

I needed Roman to wake up. I needed him to tell me exactly what he remembered.

"They really did this hospital up, didn't they? New furniture, new floors, flat-screen TV. These private rooms rival our hotel suite." We'd beat Roman to the room and were sitting on upholstered chairs by floor-to-ceiling windows offering sweeping views of downtown Baltimore.

"Please, Leon. It's nice, but it ain't no hotel. And the fact that we are comparing our current situation to a hotel room instead of our own home, or better yet, our anniversary suite in Miami, does not help me feel any better."

"Well, I tried."

"What's that supposed to mean?" I glared at him. My attempt at including him in my personal pain was backfiring. Everything and everyone was getting on my nerves right now.

My son was here in the hospital, a victim of a crime I wasn't convinced was random, and any effort to talk about my fears would be dismissed as irrational by Leon, I was sure.

I was angry with him at what he hadn't even done yet and he didn't even know why. I looked away from him, looked out the window.

"I have a delivery," a chipper voice sounded from the doorway. A transport aide with big, graying blonde hair and a raspy voice pushed the bed carrying my son into the room. "I'll let the nurses know he's up here now and they'll be around to speak with you soon." She positioned the bed, set the brakes and turned on the television without us asking.

A black-and-white Western complete with gunshot pops and war cries filled the screen. Roman stirred a little in his sleep. He'd be awake soon. I was encouraged. The aide left the room after setting down a fresh pitcher of ice water.

"What's going on, Sienna?" Leon eyed me from his seat. I felt small in mine, helpless, as I waited for my son to wake up.

"What's going on? My son was viciously robbed and attacked." *And I think there's more to it than the police are aware of,* was what I didn't say. What I couldn't say. I shut my eyes.

"You can't trust everything in front of you. Some things you have to smell first. Sometimes you got to believe the

scent before you believe your eyes." Her words from one of our talks in the plaza.

"Our son."

I opened my eyes. "What did you say?"

Leon swallowed hard. "I said 'our son.' I didn't father him, and I wasn't there to see him take his first step, but you know that I helped with navigating him through the murky steps of his teen years. I was there at his basketball games and I was there taking pictures on your front steps on his prom night. We went to the movies and he told me about all his girlfriends, half of whom you never even knew about." His fingers gripped the bottom of the seat cushion. "He calls me Dad, Sienna, or have you even noticed?"

"And yet you kept me from meeting with him earlier today." I could not keep the bitterness out of my tone. "Perhaps if I had crossed the street right when I initially planned to do so, perhaps if I had just gone to talk to him instead of letting you convince me not to just yet, perhaps we would not be in this hospital hotel suite."

"Sienna—"

"No, you listen. You want to know what's wrong? I'll tell you. Yes, I'm upset about Roman being hurt, but I'm also upset because I think that something else is going on, something more deeper and scarier that I can't even talk to you about because all you will do is try to diminish my fears and knock down my gut feelings and somehow turn this around to make it seem that I'm doing something to or against you."

I hated listening to myself. I hated what I was saying, how I was acting, what I felt. Did pregnancy make a woman go crazy? I hadn't been pregnant in twenty-one years and last time nobody was around to swing along with my moods.

Was it just the pregnancy?

"Sienna—"

"No, I'm still talking!"

"And I didn't want to talk to you."

The weak voice coming from the bed grabbed both of our attentions.

"Roman?" I jumped up from my chair, ran to his bedside.

"I said ... I said ..." He struggled to sit up a little before collapsing his head back down into the firm pillow. "I said I didn't want to talk to you. Leon knew that and I guess he was just trying to spare your feelings. But the truth is, I didn't want to talk to you then and I don't really want to now."

I realized I'd held a single breath when he started speaking. I gasped for air, trying to come from up under the weight of all that was happening in our little hospital hotel room. "Roman, we have to talk," I managed to squeeze out. "Look at you. This could have been worse. Roman, I'm so glad you're okay. I can't even imagine . . . We need to talk."

"No, I need to talk, and you need to listen. You didn't give me a chance to when I came home over Christmas break. I tried, but you . . . you took things too far." He shut his eyes, and though he was a full-grown man, as Leon said it, I could still see the outline of my little boy in the contours of his face. I reached out to stroke his cheek.

He flinched.

Why was he so angry with me? Was our Christmas flare-up that severe?

"I need to talk to Dad. Alone." His eyes were still closed and he grimaced. He probably needed another shot of whatever it was that had knocked him out. "Alone, Ma."

Dad.

I looked over at Leon and he nodded back at me. Tears pooled in the rims of my eyelids as I wondered how

Roman and I would heal the current rift between us. *And when did Leon become his go-to person?*

Roman had spent most of his life dreaming about, looking for his biological father. Now he had what I'd never been able to offer him, what his DNA donor had never been able to give.

A chance to call someone Dad.

It was as if he didn't need me anymore, even now with his body broken and battered. I could not stop the tears from falling. The taste of salt lined my lips. "Okay, I'll go, but please know that I will listen to whatever you have to say when you are ready. It's just that what you are saying, it's hard for me, and I don't want to accept it. I don't know that I will be able to. But I will listen. I promise to hear you out."

I turned toward the door.

"Sienna, wait." Leon stood, walked to me and gently pulled me back over to Roman's bedside. "We are going to pray."

"Hold on," Roman mumbled. The meds seemed to be lulling him back to sleep. I had a glimmer of hope that maybe this whole line of conversation from him was just part of a crazy nightmare. Maybe he had been speaking out of his mind when he'd said he didn't want to talk to me.

But his eyes were open again and there was no denying the anger that overshadowed them. "Hold up, I told you where I stand on so-called spiritual matters now. Remember? I don't need you doing any praying right now." He glared at Leon.

What? Since when did my son speak against prayer? I cut my eyes over at Leon who mouthed to me, "It's okay."

No. I shook my head. No, it wasn't.

What were all these conversations the two of them had that I was not privy to? And why? When had they talked and about what? And why hadn't I been included?

Roman and I had said about three words to each other since he stormed off on Christmas Eve. Clearly, he and Leon had said much more to each other since then.

Why didn't Leon tell me that they had been talking?

A scowl contorted my face as Leon grabbed my hand. He then placed his palm on one of Roman's shoulders. "This will be quick," he said, as if giving both me and Roman a warning.

He raised his head, looked up toward the heavens. "Father, thank you for sparing Roman's life today."

Roman sucked his teeth. Leon held my hand tighter and continued. "We know that all things work together for the good of those who love you and are called according to your purpose. Even when we can't see it, or understand it, you allow trials to happen to bring us closer to you. Father God, as we draw closer to you, it is my prayer that we also draw closer together as a family. All of us. All three of us." He paused. "All four of us. In Jesus' name I humbly ask these things, amen."

I opened my eyes to see Roman glaring off in the direction of the window. I had many questions, needed many answers from him: about his plans, about the attack, about our relationship; but I knew everything was on pause.

"Okay, Sienna, give us a moment." Leon gave me a reassuring nod.

My whole family and life felt dysfunctional. I'd thought getting married, having a husband, would be the final piece I needed to complete the puzzle of my life. Seemed like the puzzle had been broken up and started all over again the day I said, "I do." My family of two had multiplied and obviously there was no consensus on what everyone's role was in our new unit.

I turned toward the doorway of the room, thinking about Leon's prayer. *All things work together.* Roman would not be getting on his flight tonight. A hospital stay was a heavy alternative, but maybe, somehow, someway, all of this, all of this, would turn out for our good and God's glory.

"You don't pray like you should, do you?" A rotten tooth wiggled in her bottom gum line as she spoke, I recalled. *"Oh, you didn't think I knew about such things, did you? But I do. Ain't sayin' that I goes along with all the religion protocols, though. The Good Lord done gave up on saving my soul back when Kennedy was in office, but I know your type. Praying and singing and tapping your feet along to the worship, being all good with God because He got you through a dark spell. But soon as the light starts getting a little dim, you start second guessing that He's got an extra bulb and you start feeling the walls on your own, looking for a switch plate, trying to make the light shine yourself instead of waiting for Him to fix it."*

I sat down in an empty waiting room, a peach and gold area lined with sofas and chairs, magazines, and a couple of wall-mounted TVs. A game show was on and a studio audience roared with laughter and applause.

Of all the things going on in my life, of all the messages and matters I knew were waiting on my turned-off phone, of all the questions I had for Roman, the doubts I had about the case in which I was a witness, the fears I had about me and Leon and the baby, for some reason, all I could focus on at the moment was a distant memory of a conversation I'd had with Sweet Violet.

And then I thought about that Christmas dinner that had spiraled my relationship with my son into complete and utter darkness and chaos, as far as I was concerned. Sitting alone in the waiting room with my eyes closed, I could recall our holiday disaster nearly word for word.

The memories, the images, the sights and smells and sounds rolled through my mind like a video projector.

"Maybe we should wait until I'm twelve weeks before we tell him."

"No, this is the one time he'll be home until spring break, and I think this news should be told in person."

Christmas Eve.

Leon was dressed in a long-sleeved pale green polo shirt, tan khakis, and a red and white hat with a jingle bell attached to the tassel. He'd been smiling all day while helping me to prepare for our Christmas feast. Really, he took over the preparations, stating that he wanted me off my feet. "You're carrying my child. That's enough work for you to do right now," he repeated as I tried to regain control over my kitchen. Truthfully, I didn't mind his insistence on helping. My first trimester nausea had not yet peaked and just the sight of the roasted turkey, mashed potatoes, green beans, and other dishes made me feel like running to the bathroom.

"Roman's been an only child and he turns twenty-one in March. This baby is going to be a shock to him. If something goes wrong with this pregnancy, we would have gotten him all worked up for nothing."

"Roman will be excited and the baby will be fine," Leon spoke as he inspected a piece of fine china. Though it would only be the three of us, we'd decided not to spare any expense or hold off on the good flatware.

Our first Christmas as husband and wife. Our big announcement to my son. Christmas Eve dinner.

If this was not a big enough occasion to break out the good china, I didn't know what was.

"You look beautiful, Sienna." He winked at me.

Wearing a red empire dress with satin trim, I felt beautiful. My hard-earned waistline was about to go through a major upheaval, so I was determined to wear all my favorite outfits while I could still fit in them. I'd found this dress at a thrift store while looking for toys and games for my therapy practice. Though I seldom bought secondhand clothes these days, this dress, which still had the price tag on it, had called to me from the rack.

"Don't touch those cookies." Leon playfully swatted at my hand which was reaching for his signature dessert. "They're for the dinner at your mother's house tomorrow. You know we have to go there with a peace offering since we kept them from coming tonight." We'd decided that Roman should know the news first before bringing in my mother, father, and sister in on the announcement.

"You could make a living off of these." I ignored him and broke off half of one. My words were meant to be encouragement, but I saw the shadow fall over his eyes.

His bakery by the Inner Harbor had hit some bumps in the road. Not as many customers as the summertime, plus a recent snowstorm had forced him to close the shop for nearly a week. Missing a week's worth of sales would hurt any business, especially one as new and unsteady as Leon's.

I'd hated that I had attacked him on that matter the Sunday we first argued about my insistence on finding Sweet Violet. Though I'd since apologized and offered encouragement every chance I could, I still always saw the shadow, the sadness, the hurt in his eyes.

This marriage business was hard.

I'd thought my marriage, or whatever it was, to Roman's father, RiChard, had been difficult, but he hadn't been there. The loneliness, the pain had been what was difficult. The marriage itself was easy because you don't have to go through the difficulty of working through issues with an absent person.

"It will get better," I offered again as Leon mashed—no, pounded—a pan full of peeled and boiled potatoes.

A knock sounded at the door.

"He's here already?" My face wrinkled, not because I wasn't glad to see my son. I'd imagined and rehearsed how the evening would go, how we would tell him, and how he would respond. The early knock was not part of the script.

"Roman." Leon opened the door and greeted him with an elaborate handshake and fist bump.

"Hey, Ma." Roman came over to me and bent down to kiss my cheek. "Something smells good in here. Where's everybody?"

"Everybody?" I walked behind him, reclosing all the pans and containers he began opening while he spoke.

"You know, Grandma, Pop-Pop, Aunt Yvette, and . . ." *Skee-Gee.* I knew his cousin's name was next on his lips, but Skee-Gee still had several months before his release from jail this time. "And my cousins and Uncle Demari?" He finished up to include Yvette's four other children and new husband.

"They're not coming." I looked over at Leon who nodded back with reassurance.

Roman dropped a pan lid to the floor and it clanged and clashed like a bag full of metal bricks. "What do you mean they're not coming? We have Christmas dinner together as a family every year." His eyes darted around the room as if our family members were hiding and were about to step out from behind unseen curtains.

"We haven't seen you all semester and just wanted to share some time with you alone before everyone starts calling for you to come over their homes. It's our first Christmas as a family." I offered a smile, but could tell from Roman's sudden frozen state that he was not pleased. I picked up the lid, trying to understand his angst.

"Aw, man." He shook his head. "I was really hoping to catch everyone so I could give my updates one time."

"Well, you'll be able to share whatever it is you have to share at Grandma's house. Grandma is fixing a Caribbean-themed Christmas dinner for all of us."

"Is she still trying to drop hints to Pop-Pop that she wants to go on a cruise?"

"I think those hints have gone from dropped to pounded. But her hints have paid off. She doesn't know yet, but your grandfather has already booked a ten-day cruise for the two of them to the Bahamas in the spring."

"Good for her. I know I promised to send you on a cruise for your fortieth birthday next month." Roman pulled an ear, looked down. "But it looks like those plans will have to be put on hold for the moment."

"Roman, you are a sophomore in college working a part-time job. I never expected for you to pay for a cruise. That's why I have Leon." I winked at my husband. "Cruises can be a lot of money for a college student."

"It's not about the money." Roman still pulled on his ear, still looked down. Leon raised an eyebrow.

"Okay, not that I'm worried about you giving me a cruise, but, what do you mean?"

"Look, I'd rather talk about it all at Grandma's house. Like I said earlier, I really only want to share my news one time. Get everyone's questions and offer answers at one setting."

"Roman, you said 'updates' before. Now you are saying news. What is going on?" I looked over at Leon, trying to ignore the alarm ringing somewhere in my chest. *What's going on?* Roman seemed to be avoiding eye contact with both of us.

"Ma, I'll go over everything at Grandma's house to-night."

"Her dinner is not until tomorrow. She respected, somewhat, that Leon and I wanted to have Christmas Eve dinner together with just the three of us." I glanced over at Leon again, who had stopped basting the turkey and had his full attention on me and Roman. "She said she would start a new family tradition and have her dinner on Christmas Day now instead of Christmas Eve. So, you're going to have to wait until tomorrow to share with the rest of the family your 'news,' but you can share whatever it is with me and Leon right now." I crossed my arms.

Roman still avoided eye contact. He'd gone from pulling his earlobe to rubbing the back of his head.

And then he dropped his arm, straightened up, and looked me square in the eyes.

"I did not know Grandma's dinner had been changed to tomorrow. I'm going to miss it. I have a flight out first thing in the morning. It was cheaper to fly on Christmas Day."

"Wha . . . Huh?" I felt my head pop backward. "You just got here. I thought your winter break wasn't over until mid-January. Why would you fly all the way from San Diego just to turn around and go back? And on Christmas Day at that?"

"I'm not going back to San Diego." His voice was monotone.

"Where are you going?" This from Leon, who had put the baster down and now joined us in the kitchen nook. His eyes were just as much on me as they were on Roman.

"India." Roman let the word settle in our ears.

"Indawho?" I gasped.

"Bangaluru, India." Roman glared at me like I'd done something to him. "Like I said, my flight leaves first thing in the morning, though it's going to take almost two days to get there. I have connecting flights in Canada and Germany."

"Roman, what the—"

"Whoa, wait a minute."

Leon and I spoke at the same time, though Leon sounded calm and my voice had gone up several octaves. I held up my hand.

"Okay, where do I even begin with this? Roman, what on earth are you talking about? Flying to India? Bangla . . . whatever you just said, India? What the heck?"

My mother had not raised me to be a cussing woman, but, Lord Jesus, I was as close as I had ever been at that moment.

"It's Bangaluru. Bangaluru, India." Roman glared.

"And what exactly is going on there that you have to fly out tomorrow morning?"

"It's not what. It's who." His voice dropped, and so did his eyes.

"Does this involve a girl, Roman?" Leon sounded. Though he was still calm, I could hear a slight elevation in his tone. Slight.

"She's not a girl. She's a woman, a lady. I'm going there to meet her family."

"So, she's Indian. You're traveling to meet her family during your break." Okay, maybe this wasn't going to be that bad. Roman rarely talked to me about girls, excuse me, women. Had to be serious. But, India though?

"Her name is Changuna. It means 'a good woman.' I met her at my school."

It was the way he said it. Like all our questions had been answered. Like he'd just said all we needed to know and everything was now okay.

"So, she's a fellow student and you're spending winter break with her in India." Leon shrugged, turned back to the turkey, baster back in hand.

Like this was really not a big deal.

I didn't know this "Changuna the good" and I knew even less about India.

"How are you paying for this trip?" I hadn't even begun to ask my questions. "Roman, I had to help you out just to get here from California. A roundtrip to Bangladesh has to be what, at least three grand?"

Now, Roman had the nerve to frown up his face even more.

"Not Bangladesh. Bangaluru." His voice began fading away, but not before I heard him utter this last sentence. "And it's not a roundtrip."

A crash sounded from the far side of the kitchen where Leon had retreated. The pan full of mashed potatoes lay upturned on the tile floor with several cooking utensils falling down beside it. Leon seemed oblivious to the mess he'd just created as he marched back to where Roman and I stood in the kitchen nook. "What do you mean it's not roundtrip?"

Roman bit his lip, but then seemed to stand taller, talk stronger.

"It's not a roundtrip because I'm going to be staying there for a while. You're right, Ma. It is an expensive flight, and since the ticket was paid for by someone else, I figured the least I could do is find the cheapest flight; hence the holiday travel and the two-day trek."

"So how and when does this new girlfriend of yours come back to the States to start the spring semester? Whoever bought your ticket didn't see fit to ensure that you resume your studies as well?" Leon drilled him.

"I never said she was a student. You did."

Now, the only reason I had grown quiet was due to the fact that my tongue felt literally locked. Stuck to the roof of my mouth. Cemented. When it did loosen, I knew that it was not going to be pretty.

"You said you met her at school." Leon paused between each word.

"That is correct." Roman nodded. "She was a guest lecturer for one of my technology classes."

"Lecturer? Wait, she's out of school already? How old is she?" Leon inched closer to him.

Roman took a few steps back. "I mean, she's a couple of years older than me, but not anything really noticeable."

"So, I'm assuming that she is the one who bought your ticket," Leon continued.

Roman nodded.

"And her parents are okay with all of this? Do they even know that you are coming, or are you just going to be popping up at their front door?" My husband crossed his arms, his muscles tight, rippling.

"Her parents?" Roman raised an eyebrow.

"Yes, her parents," Leon challenged back. "You said that you were meeting her family."

"Oh, yes, I am, but not her parents. I don't know if I'll ever meet them, nor do I want to."

Leon raised both eyebrows.

"I'm meeting her kids," Roman explained. "At least that's what we're hoping."

"Kids?" Leon looked over at me. My tongue was still locked.

"Yes. She has a seventeen-year-old son and a fifteen-year-old daughter."

My eyes fluttered. I grabbed ahold of a wooden chair, gripped the top to keep myself from falling over.

"Roman, you'll be twenty-one in March, just four years older than her son." Leon kept his poise while my tongue remained under combination lock and key. "Exactly how old is this woman?" he inquired.

"Look." Roman shook his head and sighed. "This isn't how I was going to tell you two. I had planned on telling the entire family all at once so I would not have to repeat answers to the many questions I know all of you will have. Changuna is a United States citizen and has been one for the past thirteen years. She was helped out by a charity that assisted her with running away from a forced marriage to an abusive man thirty years her senior. She was only fourteen when her parents took her out of school and made her marry a wealthy farmer in their rural village. She had her son ten months after marrying, lost a baby, and then had her daughter. She managed to escape, but doing so meant leaving behind her children with an aunt she's since lost contact with.

"Changuna has worked hard to get her education. She earned two degrees from Stanford in computer science and sociology, and an MBA from Harvard. She's a frequent guest speaker and lecturer at business schools across the country and is focused on developing technology to help at-risk girls and women in third-world countries receive education."

"We're still trying to understand what any of this has to do with you having a one-way trip to India." Leon's arms were still crossed. I was glad that Leon said "we." I wasn't alone in this.

"Bangaluru is like India's Silicon Valley. She's starting a tech company there with the hopes of somehow helping girls who may otherwise be subjected to becoming child brides, including her own daughter whom she has not talked to or heard about for over seven years."

"And all of this has to do what with you?" Leon pried again.

"I'm going over there to help her. We're going to be business partners. She's saved up enough to fly both of us over there and pay rent for a few months while we get up and running. She has a lot of investment capital to get us started."

"School," Leon stated flatly. The word echoed through the kitchen as I shut my eyes and recalled being an eighteen-year-old college dropout to follow Roman's father around the world.

Worst mistake of my life.

I opened my eyes and stared at my son who was the spitting image of the man who contributed to his DNA, black curls and all.

"I knew that my not returning to school would concern you." Roman directed this to me although Leon had been doing the questioning. "And although a college degree is not necessarily needed to work in the tech field—look at Bill Gates—I know that is important; so I'm looking into some online programs that will allow me to finish my degree. One day. Changuna is helping me sort through my options."

Eighteen years.

Eighteen years of working, crying, wishing, praying, hoping, ramen noodle nights, evening classes, master's program, part-time this, full-time that, believing, sweating.

Eighteen years.

That was the time span that covered the years between birthing Roman and then enrolling him into college. The sacrifices. The dreams. The expectations. And now? Only one word came to my head; only one word had the power to unloose my tongue.

"RiChard." The name slithered out of my mouth, opening up enough room in my oral cavity for a host of emotions I'd long buried to enter in, get lodged in my throat, and send waves of nausea through my gut.

"I knew you were going to bring RiChard St. James into this." Roman actually looked mad. He glared at me. "I am not my father, and for the record, I am not you, either. I knew you would see this like me doing what you did in dropping out of school to chase someone else around the world, but there are major differences. For one, I know for sure who Changuna is and I know for sure that she has a good heart with good motives and intentions. We've spent longer than a semester together, unlike you and RiChard, who you ran off with barely into your first semester as a freshman. Changuna and I have made our plans mutually. She is not just telling me what to do for me to simply follow her like a lost sheep. Her kids are already halfway grown, so when we find them, I will not be raising any small children while at the same time trying to work or finish school. This is different from you. I'm laying out reasonable and logical plans."

The cement grabbed a hold of my tongue again and trickled down to my chest, down to my stomach. Felt like heavy rocks were settling in my gut.

"You leave tomorrow?" Leon's voice was a whisper.

"Yes," Roman affirmed. "And I didn't tell you sooner because I knew there would be resistance. I'm grown now, and you have to accept my decision, my well thought-out and researched decision. And yes, she may be a little older than me, but remember her teen and young adult years were stolen from her. I think, if anything, my age, my youth compared to hers, helps her gain those years back." He paused for a moment before continuing. "You should know, I'm planning to propose to her so we can get married in India on New Year's Day where, from what she's told me, there will be massive New Year celebrations even bigger than the ones here in the States. I wanted to wait for five, maybe ten years, but it might be easier moving forward with the business if our relationship is a legal entity."

I opened my mouth to say something, but words were not what came out. My stomach swirled. Within seconds, a new mess splattered to the floor. Now there was more than mashed potatoes and utensils to clean.

"Really, Ma? I tell you I'm getting married, and you throw up?"

"Your mother's pregnant," Leon barked. His tone was almost at the level of the Sunday morning yell he'd had when we first argued about Sweet Violet.

Almost.

"Pregnant? You turn forty next month. Why are you starting over with another child? Pregnant? Really? Oh, wait. You're just joking. You gotta be."

"No."

Roman looked from me to Leon and back. Then: "Well, congratulations, I guess. I don't know what else to say. I thought I was going to see everyone tonight, and I still want to. I need to go over Grandma's house. I thought she was having dinner tonight. I wanted to come here first and early so that I could introduce Changuna to you and then explain everything over Grandma's table. I swear, when you meet her, you'll really like her."

"Introduce her?" I repeated the only words that I heard come out of his mouth.

"Yeah." He beckoned toward the door. "She's here, waiting in my car. I told her that I would check things out in here first before I brought her in, and I'm glad I did, because you responded just like I thought you would. But now that you know everything, I might as well bring her in."

"She's here?" Again, the only words I heard.

"Ma, you'll like her. She's just like you."

I saw the hope in his eyes, was aware that he completely glossed over the big announcement that Leon busted.

I knew then that Roman had it bad. His focus was only on this girl, I mean old woman, and not on school, a coming new sibling, or even plain common sense.

This was really happening.

"I'll go get her now." He turned toward the front door, a half smile on his face.

Chapter 17

Christmas had been six months ago. I stared at the flat-screen television in the fourteenth floor waiting room of Metropolitan Community Hospital, wondering what Leon and Roman were discussing just down the hall with the door closed and me way on the other side.

"Erik, you are the father of two-year-old Dinesha." The TV audience roared in cheers and applause. I wanted to shut it off, the nonsense interrupting my thoughts. Instead, I swallowed hard, trying to shut out the memories of our failed holiday dinner.

Changuna.

I shut my eyes again at the mental image of the dark-haired beauty with intelligent eyes who showed up for our Christmas Eve dinner.

"Girl, why you sitting out here? Shouldn't you be in the room praying for my nephew? Oh my God, Sienna, you and yours just can't seem to stay out of trouble."

My sister, Yvette, clopped into the room in neon orange high-heeled sneakers and a yellow and orange sundress. It was almost two-forty but she looked like the high noon sun. Her youngest child, a daughter, trailed behind her crunching through a bag of cheese curls. She was six years old but had the eyes of an old soul and she rarely smiled.

I thought of Delmon Frank, the defendant in the triple murder trial, and recalled the first conversation I'd had with him, the cigarette that he'd flicked between his fingers, the eyes that looked old and young all at once.

"Fiona, sit here," Yvette barked as she pointed to a seat and then she turned back to me with tears in her eyes. "Is Roman okay?"

"He'll be okay," I managed to whisper though I had no idea how she defined "okay." My definition covered ground beyond the physical into the territory of the mental and spiritual. When had my son turned against prayer? I wondered again. I thought again of Changuna and my mood darkened.

"So are we visiting him or not? You don't know what it took for me to get those people at the front desk to allow Fiona past the main lobby."

With her oldest son, my nephew Skee-Gee, currently incarcerated and her other two kids on equally shaky paths, Yvette had taken to keeping her youngest with her at all times.

"Leon's in the room. The two wanted to talk alone."

"You want me to send Demari in there? He's on a mission to find a free parking space, even after I reminded him we are downtown. I can call him so he can hurry up and join the fellows in prayer."

Like me, Yvette was a newlywed, beating me to the altar by just a couple of months. Her husband, Demari, had a past as dark as his future was bright. In addition to starting a landscaping company, he along with several males from his church, my old church, had formed a nonprofit using basketball as an outreach and mentoring program for teen males. He'd wanted to approach Leon about serving on the board, I knew from talks with Yvette, but avoided the topic while Leon focused on turning his business around.

My involvement with this trial was not helping anything.

"No, you don't have to send Demari in to help with prayer," I answered Yvette's question. "Roman is acting funny about it, about prayer, that is."

"Is he still messing around with that girl, I mean woman?"

"I don't know what's going on." It was the truth. Roman and I had barely talked since the morning of Christmas Day. I shut my eyes and inhaled, remembering the disaster that was his sendoff at the airport. I had very little idea of what had happened in his life since then.

When he'd phoned to say he was coming into town for the start of my turn on the witness stand, I'd assumed he was ready to finally talk.

Clearly, I'd been wrong.

"Do you think it was an accident? Do you really think that what happened to Roman was really random?" Yvette spoke out loud the nagging fear that had been eating away at me. I'd never even told her about Sweet Violet. *But Sweet Violet has no ties to any of this,* I assured myself.

"There are a lot of coincidences," was my only reply.

"Yeah, you think?" Yvette shook her head. "You were associated with all three crime scenes, and while we all know that's mostly because of what you were doing professionally as a social worker, it's a wonder nobody's considered you to be a suspect."

"The common theme is Delmon Frank," I reminded Yvette of the prosecutor's oft-repeated phrase, which had been stated throughout the trial. "And you can connect the dots. The first woman, Ms. Marta, was the robbery victim who was killed outside of the shelter; the second was a former shelter resident."

"Frank's pregnant girlfriend, right?"

I thought about the girl, Amber, who had called me from the bushes at the first scene. She'd given me Sweet Violet's purse. Amber's body was discovered in a vacant row home a month after Ms. Marta was killed. The girl had been dead for about that long, the autopsy confirmed.

She was a woman-child with trouble and secrets written all over and in her eyes. I wondered what trouble and secrets she'd carried to her grave. They said she and her unborn baby were buried in a pauper's field, no one claiming her. The only "loved one" she'd had was the boyfriend accused of killing her, Delmon Frank.

Drug addiction.

That's what was believed to be at the heart of the killings: Ms. Marta robbed of her money to fund his drug habit; the young girl Amber robbed of her life by her boyfriend who attacked her in a drug-induced hallucinatory rage. She'd had bite marks on her hands and arms as she'd apparently tried to defend herself against his attack.

"The messed-up thing is that nobody would have given these cases a second look if it had just been that worker and the homeless girl who were killed. It was that last victim who got everyone's attention; that, and the fact that you were involved. You keep getting mixed up in the craziest of cases."

"Believe me, I'm not trying. I would much rather have a quiet life to myself, see my clients, and love on Leon." *And this baby.* I rubbed my belly. Though I felt an occasional kick, the new life entering mine didn't feel all the way real.

Probably because I still have so much in my current life to work out and get through.

"You still don't want to find out what you're having?" Yvette smiled, nodded toward my stomach.

"Maybe I need to. Maybe that would make it all seem real once and for all."

Yvette smoothed down one of Fiona's long braids. "Girl, ain't nothing fake about having these children. They come and they stay, no matter where any of our lives take us."

Where any of our lives take us.

I thought about the last victim, the one whose tragic killing thrust the entire triple murders into the spotlight. Wrong place, wrong time. Now, that murder may have been random, I considered.

But, Roman and the attack he'd endured? Five dollars and eleven cents was all that was left on him.

Or left with him?

The questions nagged me. The potential answers disturbed me more.

"The police seem pretty certain that what happened to Roman today was a robbery. You know everything associated with me is being watched like a hawk by everyone these days. It was a fluke, the assault. Roman hasn't been part of this whole fiasco. He hasn't even been in town. Those boys would have had no idea who he is."

"Are you trying to convince me or you?" Yvette looked at me from the corner of her eyes. "I'm not saying that prosecuting team is not on its job, but I personally would need more than promises of protection from the media in a hotel room that will only last as long as the trial."

"I think Leon carries a gun."

Yvette considered this and settled back in her seat. "Girl, you might need to learn how to use one yourself. That's all I'm saying." She laughed at the horror on my face. "Seriously, Sienna, I'm just kidding. We know that the blood of Jesus will protect you from the plans of the devil. There is power in the blood and in His name."

"Listen to you, all spiritualitized." I shook my head and tried to laugh despite the twisting unsettledness the talk of guns had thrust into my stomach.

"Girl, at this point in my life, Jesus is all I've got. Jesus, Demari, and Fiona." She kissed her daughter's forehead.

"And me." Our eyes locked. "You've got me, Yvette."

She looked away first. "Sienna, you've got enough going on. I just don't want you, or Roman, or any of y'all to end up like that last victim.

Wrong place. Wrong time. Coincidence or not? The
questions I had about my own safety, what happened to
Roman, and Sweet Violet's words and timing continued
to swirl around in my head.

*"Death. Someone always has to die. Okay, sugar.
Thank you. Good night."* Her last words to me when I'd
dropped her off at the shelter a few hours before Ms. Marta
was found there dead. However, she didn't have a weapon
on her when I dropped her off. She'd been naked under
that housecoat she wore to the emergency room, and I had
the bag that held her belongings.

And there was nothing that tied Delmon Frank to her,
I reminded myself. Nothing, that is, except his dead girlfriend, Amber, who was a former resident at the shelter
where Sweet Violet had stayed for just a few weeks.

Ms. Marta had seemed to be the only staff member
familiar with this woman, Sweet Violet, and she knew her
as Frankie Jean. I recalled our single phone conversation.

The lines all felt connected, but that didn't mean they
meant anything. That didn't mean that they formed a
sensible shape. I thought about those connect-the-dots
puzzles I used to help Roman with when he was a toddler.
I used it as a tool to teach him the ABCs, drawing neat
lines between the letters in alphabetical order resulting in
well-defined pictures. No matter how hard I tried, Roman
would inevitably grab a crayon and connect the dots in
whatever way made sense to him.

Out of order. Random shapes.

I had a lot of lines in my life right now. I had to figure
out the order to them and then step back to see what
shape was taking hold. Maybe then it would all make
sense.

"We'll all be okay," I assured Yvette. She held tightly to
Fiona's little hand.

"Sienna," Leon's deep voice echoed through the room
from the doorway. "Roman wants to talk to you."

Chapter 18

Christmas Eve

"You have an incredibly bright, creative, and compassionate son. You should be proud of the young man you have raised."

The woman standing in my living room had hair that would make a weave-addict drool. Long, bone-straight, brown, healthy. I could cut it all off, no, pull it all out by the root, and make a killing with one of Yvette's friends in the underground world of Remy hair extensions.

"And tell us your name again?" I sounded like I'd sucked in helium, my voice was that high.

"Changuna. Changuna Rangan." The words blurred together in a pronounced accent as she stuck out a hand. French manicure. No nail tips. Nothing fake.

I looked at her hand but didn't move. Roman glared at me and Leon stepped in.

"So, Roman has explained to us that you gave him an airplane ticket for him to go with you to India. Tomorrow."

"Yes! I am very excited that he will be assisting me with this next phase of my life. Not only will I be looking for my children and saving my own daughter, I will be saving many daughters." She smiled. Perfect teeth. Whiter than polished marble.

"As a parent," Leon continued, "I'm sure that you could appreciate our concerns and questions about such a drastic decision that Roman is making to . . . assist you on the other side of the world. He still has several years of college left."

"I know." She shook her head. "I have been surprised myself at his willingness to help, but that is how prayers get answered sometimes, in the most unusual, unpredictable ways. I have prayed and God sent an answer." She beamed. "Roman has promised me that he will finish school. There are really good online options available and several programs that will view his work in India as a study abroad or even internship experience. He is carving out his own pathway. You should be very proud, Sienna."

"Mrs. Sanderson," I squeaked out.

"Oh, I'm sorry." Changuna's smile widened. "It is just that we are so close in age that I thought such formality would be a little awkward, and I also wasn't sure what name of yours is correct."

"Legally, I'm Mrs. Sanderson. Professionally, I still go by Sienna St. James." I paused. "I'm sorry, but I must ask. Exactly how old are you?"

"Oh." She looked surprised at my question. "I'll be thirty-two next month, the week after you turn forty."

I realized that I was smiling, that I had been smiling, a wide, toothy grin that covered the entire bottom half of my face. Through my smiling teeth I cut a look at Leon. "Excuse me, but my husband and I have to check on the food."

"I'll help Changuna to a seat at the table," I heard Roman say as Leon and I marched into the kitchen. As soon as we entered, Leon moved the carving knife off of the counter, put it far out of my reach.

"Get that woman out of my house and out of Roman's head," I whispered.

"What are we going to do, Sienna, tell him he can't go to India and tie him down to a chair?"

"Do you have a better idea?"

"We all go through phases where the lessons we learn don't come from someone else teaching them to us. Some lessons we have to learn ourselves."

"This is not about me and RiChard."

"No one said it was, Sienna."

"And even if it was, that was a big enough lesson that I can share with my son to ensure that he doesn't make the same mistakes. I went through nearly two decades of pain, heartache, tests, and trials because of my crazy decision to run off in the world with him."

"Roman is not you though. He has to put on his own shoes and walk in them."

"Whose side are you on, Leon? Do you not get the investments I've made into this boy's life, financially, emotionally, and as a mother?"

"Of course I get it. This is difficult, but what can we do? Screaming and shouting, and from the looks of things, even calmly talking about his choice isn't going to change anything. You've made your investments. Now you will have to trust that all you've done will pay off."

"You're not getting this, Leon." I blinked at him, wondering if this was the same man who helped me look for my son when he was thirteen and searching for a gang of boys who'd stolen a prized possession of his; if this was the same man who stood beside me waiting for Roman's return when he'd run off looking for his father at age sixteen. "I don't know this woman. I don't know where he is going with her, what he is doing, or if he's even in his right mind to be making these types of decisions. Maybe we can get an emergency petition and have him held in the psych ward because clearly he is out of his mind right now."

"Now, Sienna, you know—"

"I'm serious, Leon. There is no way that I am letting Roman go anywhere near a plane to India with a woman who is nearly as old as my younger sister."

"You are not 'letting' me do anything."

When had Roman come into the kitchen? I hadn't seen him enter, but there he was standing in the doorway. "I'm twenty years old. I will be twenty-one in three months. I'm not crazy and I'm not trying to hurt you. I'm just living my life and this is a decision in which I've put in a lot of thought. I'm not rushing into anything. And I'm also not seeking your permission or blessing."

"Roman, I respect that you think you are grown, but you need to understand this is a huge mistake. You do not throw away your education, which I am largely funding, let me remind you, to go halfway across the world with a woman who has kids nearly as old as you to live God knows where doing God knows what. If you are that interested in starting a business, fine. I am willing to give you startup money in whatever you want to start right here in America, but you are going to finish school and you are going to stay away from this woman completely. That is all."

"And that's just it." Roman's face turned red. I didn't know red on him was possible. "Ma, you have your own business, your own book deal, the continual spotlight. You've made your mistakes, gone through whatever you've gone through, lived your life and given me what I need to live mine. Like I said, I'm not trying to hurt you. I have to do this for me. I'm going to finish school one day, but I need to do this my way. I need to live my own life and I need to do this by myself. I appreciate you, and Leon, for your support, but—"

"Hold up, just to clarify," I interrupted, "you're not going out on your own. You're just jumping support systems. Leaving our nest for another nest that already has two other eggs in it with a hen just as old as the one you're running away from."

"I'm not running, Ma."

"Yes, you are. You've been running ever since the day you found out the truth about your father. You ran to San Diego in the name of college to get answers, and now that you have all your answers about him, you're ready to run far away from the family and friends who've done nothing but love you and take care of you."

"Always RiChard." Roman shook his head, scrunched up his lips, looked away. "Contrary to what you believe, everything in my life is not tied to my father. Me going to India does not mean I'm running away or looking for him again. I've accepted that nobody can find him and that he doesn't want to be found. Truth is, I've let it go. The anger, the betrayal, the pain.

"Listen, me going to India doesn't mean that I don't love you and appreciate you for all you've done to raise me. I'm starting my life, *my* life, now. And I need to do it away from here, away from . . . you, everybody. India is where my life begins. And with Changuna. I prayed on it, Ma. I prayed on it and I believe with all my heart that this is what God wants me to do. She said herself, you heard her, that I'm an answer to her prayer. You've taught me to have faith, so that's what I'm doing. I don't have all of the answers to my own questions, but I'm sure that getting on that plane to India tomorrow is where my answers begin."

"Roman, you have lost your mind if you think I'm going to allow you to drop out of school and board a plane to another continent with a complete stranger tomorrow morning."

"Is everything okay?" Changuna entered my kitchen, that smile still sitting on her face, her track-grade hair swung to one side.

"No," I said flatly.

"Don't start, Ma."

Did that boy just threaten me? Did he just stand in my kitchen and tell me not to start? "I'm not starting anything. I'm ending it right now." I stepped forward, ready to explain to the woman exactly what I thought of her plan. It was her plan, for sure, because my son would never come up with such absurdity.

"No, we're leaving." Roman placed a hand on Changuna's shoulder and led her back to the living room where their coats lay on the sofa. "I have to say good-bye to Grandma tonight." He turned to face me just before he walked out the door. "I'm leaving in the morning, Ma. BWI. Gate D-7."

"Roman, what is going on?" I heard Changuna ask him in the hallway. I listened as their footsteps echoed on the tile floors then I shut my eyes as the elevator that would take them to the condo lobby dinged open.

"Sienna." Leon's arms wrapped around me.

The table was still set, the pans still filled with well-seasoned foods. Our Christmas Eve dinner still rested on the stove. I had a gift bag, a golden gift bag with a sonogram picture wrapped inside, sitting on Roman's plate. My good china. A greeting card for the new big brother was nestled in the bag's silver tissue paper.

"Sienna," Leon whispered again. He pressed his arms tighter around me. I loosened from his grip.

"I didn't want to have to do this, but Roman leaves me no choice." I reached for my cell phone, which lay on a kitchen counter, and scrolled through my contacts. "There is no way I'm going to stand by and let Roman ruin his life. He will not be getting on that plane tomorrow morning."

Chapter 19

"Ms St. James, Ms. St. James!" She was panting, breathless as she caught up with me in the hospital corridor. "I've been trying to reach you for the past thirty minutes." Alisa Billy. We were just outside Roman's hospital room.

"I'm here visiting my son." My hand was on the door, ready to push it open. Leon said Roman wanted to talk to me, so everything else was going to have to wait, as far as I was concerned.

"I know, and I'm sorry this happened to Roman, but we need you back in the courtroom. Now."

I shook my head. "No, I am sorry. I can't come right now. The judge will understand. My son was attacked." *And I'm not convinced it was random.*

"Yes, Judge Greenberg has been understanding and you have been allowed a couple of hours to check on the wellbeing of your son. However, our understanding is that your son only sustained minor injuries and is stable with the expectation that he will be discharged soon. We need you back in court as the defense wants to complete a final cross-examination with only one last question, after which time you will be released from the trial as agreed upon by both sides. If anything else comes up, we will just refer to your written and verbal testimony. This is it, Sienna. It's not even three o'clock yet. A few more minutes and then you are done. A car is waiting downstairs."

"I need to talk to my son."

"You'll have plenty of time after your final testimony. We usually keep witnesses around for the entire duration of the trial, but in an effort to honor your current pregnancy state and your desire to travel before your baby comes, I've really pushed for you to be released. Surprisingly, the defense immediately agreed. Then again, I shouldn't be surprised. Usually it takes a long time to even get these types of cases on the docket, but nobody on either side has kept this from being anything but a speedy trial. Again, I'm sorry about Roman, but you are on the fast track to being by his bedside and taking him home within a matter of minutes. Let's go, Sienna." She turned to leave, her high-heeled footsteps like punched staccato on the marble floor.

"Okay, let me at least let Roman know that I'll be right back."

"Wait." She spun back around and grabbed my hand over the doorknob. "He's sleeping. We need to go."

"How do you know he's sleeping?"

"Sienna, we must go. Judge Greenberg has been very generous with your time. Your role in this trial is almost over."

"My husband just told me that Roman wanted to talk with me."

"Roman is sleeping. He may have been awake, but the painkillers have him knocked out again."

"Wait, were you just in the room with him? And how do you know so much about his current condition?"

"Sienna." Alisa had a way of raising her voice without raising her voice. I guess it was one of her abilities that had made her such a powerful attorney for the state's attorney's office. "Stop being paranoid. Everything is okay. Your son is fine. I'm just doing my job to ensure that the bad guy doesn't get away with these murders. Let's go." Her voice was a throaty bark.

I looked at her and then pushed the hospital door open. Roman lay in the bed, his eyes closed. He didn't budge as I rapped on the wooden door and whispered his name. *That was fast.* Leon had just gotten me from the waiting room.

"See, asleep. Let's go," she demanded again. She turned toward the elevator, her high heels back to punching the floor, her long black hair swinging behind her. I shook my head and followed.

We passed the waiting room. Demari had joined Yvette and Fiona, a Bible resting on his knee. He still had on his work uniform, overalls caked with mud on the knees. Work boots. It was a sacrifice for him to be here in the middle of the day. Both of them, I realized. Yvette must have taken Fiona out of school for the day to ensure that she would be able to stay without interruption.

Why had none of these details occurred to me before?

"You know we got you, boo." Yvette smiled, seeming to read my mind.

Our relationship had come a long way.

She'd been the teenage mom and I the high school standout and our family had never let either of us forget our roles. Though I initially dropped out of college to chase RiChard around the world, I eventually reenrolled, working my way up to a master's degree to prove that I was capable of making it. She'd sunk lower into the struggle to survive as a single mom of five children by four absent or dead men, with no diploma, no job, and no desire to let anyone see her sweat, so she too could prove that she was capable of making it.

We spent years in separate corners, glaring at each other, licking our wounds, building our fences. It wasn't until recent years that we'd found common ground again, mutual respect, real love, self-love, no conditions.

Our relationship wasn't by any means perfect, but I don't think either of us expected it to ever be. We had each other's backs and that was enough.

"Hey, Sienna." Demari smiled. His dimples made him look younger than he was. "Leon went to grab something from the cafeteria. He'll be back up soon. Roman okay? What's this I hear about him not wanting to pray?" His mouth tucked into a worry line.

"We have to go, Sienna," Alisa whispered into my back.

"I'll talk to you. They need me back at the courthouse now. Let Leon know that's where I am and if he can to catch up with me."

"No worries. We're here with Roman, and Mom and Dad are on their way. We'll all be here when you get back." Yvette nodded.

"Thanks."

The elevator door opened and Alisa nudged me toward it. Within moments, I was out of the hospital and in the back seat of a black Lincoln Town Car. I didn't recognize this car or the driver.

"Where's Joe?" I asked as the car turned toward the courthouse. I was used to Alisa's assistant being the driver, the protector, the shield, when Leon wasn't around.

"Oh, he's still at the courthouse." Alisa looked unperturbed as she swiped and tapped on her smartphone.

I settled back in my seat and looked out of the tinted windows. The fact that I could see out and nobody could see in gave me a strange sense of comfort as we meandered through the downtown streets. It was a short drive back to the courthouse slowed only by the downtown traffic and the hordes of workers flooding the streets in the bright afternoon sun.

Almost done with all of this. I closed my eyes and exhaled. Leon and I already had our bags packed and a flight booking app waiting to be used on our tablets and phones. This time tomorrow I'd be in Miami, I hoped. Our anniversary trip. The quick three-night getaway we so desperately needed to start over, to reconnect, to heal from the difficulties of the past few months, to move forward and prepare for the little one soon to join our lives. My parents or Yvette would watch over Roman's recuperation, I knew, letting Leon and I have one last fling before baby.

Maybe I should find out what I'm having. I thought about Yvette playing with Fiona's hair, talking about how real these little lives were that come into our families. Now that the nightmare of the past few months was close to ending, the idea that I was ready to let this baby's coming arrival be real to me seemed possible.

And, dared I say, a little exciting?

"We're almost there." Alisa still played with her phone.

I exhaled again, picturing white sand, warm water, my mammoth-sized belly squeezing into the two-piece swimsuit I'd ordered out of a couture maternity catalogue.

I was in a state of complete relaxation as we passed the final intersection before we reached the courthouse steps.

But something caught my eye in the humid summer afternoon.

A woman wearing a long black wool coat holding on to a worn shopping cart filled with plastic bags.

A matted black and gray wig sat atop her head and she stood still in the sea of walkers pouring in and out of the surrounding office buildings. I would have missed her, thought nothing of it, if not for one detail.

She stared directly at our car.

But nobody can see into these windows. I shuddered, though not sure why. Even if she did know I was in the car, why would it matter?

I hadn't seen her in a while. I'd done all I could to help her and she'd pushed away any offer of assistance, insisting that I was the one who needed help those days I'd talked to her in the grassy area in front of city hall.

Sweet Violet.

"Okay, we're here." Alisa Billy scooted out of her seat as the driver came around to open our door.

"Yes, we are," I replied, before realizing that she was talking to someone on the phone.

She nodded at me as we bounded up the steps, pressed on all sides by the waiting journalists and courthouse crowds. Then just before we entered the door, she froze, her phone still cocked to her ear. "What do you mean we're finished for the day? Sienna and I just got here." She paused, looked at me and scratched her head. "I was told that the defense had one last question for our witness. No, I got a text. I don't know. Didn't you send it?" She put her hand over the phone. "Sorry, Sienna, I'm just trying to figure out what's going on. I'm getting mixed messages. I—" She stopped abruptly, midsentence.

"Alisa?"

She reached for my arm, grabbed my elbow as her eyes crossed.

"Alisa!" I did my best to hold on to her as foam began sputtering out of her mouth. As she gasped for air, the crowd that surrounded us on the steps began screaming, shrieking, running.

Chaos.

"Call an ambulance!" I heard myself shout. "Hold on, Alisa." I held on to the young woman as she slid slowly to the ground. I eased down next to her, holding her head upright in my lap. "Hold on, Alisa." I saw the fear in her eyes, the panic, the horror.

And then the unmistakable glaze as her eyes set in place.

Dead.

As journalists and officers and the general masses swarmed, directed, and gawked around me, I only had one chilling, undeniable thought.

Once again, an untimely death had followed a Sweet Violet sighting.

These could not all be coincidences, I was certain of this, no matter what the cause of Alisa's death would turn out to be.

Chapter 20

Christmas Morning

"Sienna, I completely agree that Roman is making a huge mistake, but this is not the way to fix it. You're only going to drive him away."

Five o'clock in the morning and Leon and I had not yet stopped arguing from the night before.

"I'm his mother. I gave birth to him. I know him. And I know that he is out of his mind. This is the only way to stop this foolishness."

"This is not it, Sienna. You're going to lose him. What you are planning to do is not going to do anything but backfire."

Christmas Eve dinner sat cold in the kitchen, uneaten. The plates and utensils remained untouched on the table. Our Christmas tree, our very first Christmas tree, twinkled and blinked in the corner of the living room. White lights were the only things on the branches as trays of glass ornaments, including a specially ordered hand-painted cherub bulb to commemorate our baby announcement, sat on the floor to the side.

Our original plan was to wait for Roman to help us decorate our new family tree.

New traditions.

Big announcements.

Merry Christmas.

"How dare you try to tell me what to do or not do for my son? What kind of mother would I be if I didn't keep him from running off with that woman?"

"Sienna, he has to walk, run, fail, and get back up on his own two feet. You cannot protect him from living life and learning lessons on his own."

"This is too costly of a lesson for him to learn, Leon. Why aren't you on my side right now? I need you!" We'd circled our condo several times, back and forth, yelling, pleading, glaring at each other. "I need my husband to be on my side right now." My voice came out in a whisper, but the pain I felt thundered through me louder than a thousand train engines.

My son had lost his mind.

Was it something I'd done? Something I hadn't done? I shut my eyes, but I could not shut out Leon's nagging, borderline threatening voice.

"Sienna, you are going to lose Roman. If you go forward with this plan, he will not talk to you. For what he is about to do, he needs to be able to talk to you. This is not the time to burn pathways of communication with Roman, and if you make that call, that's exactly what you'll be doing. Burning down to ashes the pathway for him to come back home."

My cell phone was still in hand. I'd already talked to my contact at a mental health hospital. Dr. Mansley, a psychiatrist at the facility where I often referred patients needing medication management, agreed to assist me with obtaining an emergency petition, a seventy-two-hour hold.

Any court would agree, I was certain, that my son was a danger to himself. Out of his mind. Delusional. There was no way he would be getting on that plane to India in two hours, even if it meant that he would be forced into a mental health facility against his will. Based on the little information he'd provided, I'd managed to figure out his flight time and number. Whether Leon joined me or not, I was about to drive down to BWI to meet the officers who would assist with this petition. My car keys were in my other hand. I marched out the door. Leon followed.

No sleep. Still vomiting. Broken and angry at the nerve of my son. Worried and afraid for the safety and sanity of my son.

"It has to be the hormones." Leon threw up his hands as I got in the car. "It has to be. I've never seen you be this irrational. Stop, Sienna, I beg you. Let's . . . let's figure this out. There's got to be another way to deal with this." His voice echoed in the parking garage. His hands held the car door open, preventing me from closing it.

"There is no time. There is no other way. Get off the door, Leon."

He let it go and I slammed it shut, starting the engine. As I pulled out of my parking space, I could see in my rearview mirror that he was heading for his own truck. By the time I'd exited the garage and reached the first stoplight, he'd caught up with me.

On a typical day, the drive from Canton to Baltimore/ Washington International Thurgood Marshall Airport would take about twenty minutes. However, it was five-thirty on Christmas morning. Lights twinkled on every corner, in every window as I shot through the quiet streets and deserted highways. Leon's Pathfinder was the only other vehicle near mine for most of the way. I got there in thirteen minutes.

Leon had called my cell phone five times.

I didn't answer.

I circled around the departure gates and knew where Roman was immediately.

Two police cars. An ambulance. Airport security cars and personnel.

"Ma'am, you cannot leave your car parked here," a TSA officer barked as I shut my engine and jumped out of my sedan. "Ma'am!"

"That's my son." I pointed.

Roman.

In the middle of the lights, the sirens, the Christmas morning chaos, he sat on the curb, his hands handcuffed behind him, his eyes cast down on the street.

"Wait," I yelled, running toward the scene. I slowed down then stopped as I remembered these men and women were armed. Running and hooting and hollering toward them could not possibly have a good outcome. "Wait," I said again to the officers who stood at the perimeter. "That's my son. He's not a criminal. Why is he in handcuffs?"

"Are you the family member who requested an emergency psychiatric evaluation of Roman St. James?"

"Yes, but why is he in handcuffs?" I asked again. Leon joined me, both of our cars left unattended in the departures drop-off lane.

"Precautionary measure, that's all," the officer responded. "He initially showed some resistance when we approached him, but everything is under control right now."

Under control.

I looked at the dizzying flashes of patrol lights, heard the murmurs of arriving passengers who skirted around the scene to enter the terminal; listened to the static-filled radios and handsets of the emergency responders. Saw Changuna standing to the side, eyes wide, arms and fingers shaking.

Saw my son look up. Our eyes met.

Defeat. Anger.

Passionate anger.

I stepped back although he was maybe fifty feet away. I stepped back and landed against Leon's chest. I waited for Leon's arms to wrap around me.

They didn't.

"Ms. St. James?" Another officer approached, shook my hand. "Listen, one of our crisis response units evaluated your son to determine if he is a danger to himself or anyone else. We have no current concerns as he is presenting as fully competent. There are no legal or medical reasons to place a psychiatric hold on him. We're letting him go." He turned to leave and I noticed that the responders on the scene had relaxed. Small talk. Slight chuckles. "Overprotective," "mothers," "crazy." Words I heard tossed around.

Roman was uncuffed, his bags handed to him. I watched as he shook himself off, put on a backpack, picked up a duffel bag, nodded at Changuna, entered the terminal.

He never looked back.

"Our cars . . ." Leon had turned around to face the street, just realizing that our vehicles had been towed.

A shuttle bus circling the loop stopped in front of us and the driver opened the door. "You need a ride to one of the parking lots?" His voice sounded like gravel filled his throat. A gray golf cap sat low on his forehead. I stared at him. Said nothing. Leon looked away and mumbled inaudible words under his breath. The driver shrugged.

"Merry Christmas." He shut the door and resumed his route.

Chapter 21

"Baltimore City police are investigating the sudden death of the lead prosecutor overseeing the Delmon Frank case. She died of unknown causes just before entering the Clarence Mitchell Courthouse late this afternoon. The trial has been temporarily suspended in light of her death. Star witness Sienna St. James Sanderson was by Billy's side and attempted to render first aid before first responders arrived.

"Investigators at this point are not certain whether fifty-four-year-old Alisa Billy's untimely demise was due to natural causes or even overdose. A toxicology report, which will take several weeks, will be completed to rule out foul play, though sources report that several prescription drugs were found on Ms. Billy's person. Stay tuned to First Witness News for an updated report at eleven. This is Simon Joyce, live in front of the courthouse. Back to you in the studio, Don."

I snapped off the television in the waiting room as a bitter taste filled my mouth. *They're not sure that it was foul play?* I shook my head, wondering why I seemed to be the only person on the planet who thought something sinister was going on. *First my son gets attacked. Random robbery. Then Alisa passes on, God rest her soul. Possible drug overdose?* Was I thinking too hard about this? Nobody else was considering that something more was going on here?

Nobody else knew about Sweet Violet.

I made a decision. Whether Leon agreed or not, whether I was simply going crazy or not, I needed to tell someone about her.

And say what? I asked myself. *That I had several bizarre conversations with a homeless woman who frequented the downtown area? That she seemed to surface not long before someone died, or was attacked, or overdosed?* Wait. I didn't see her around when Roman was assaulted. *Listen to me.* I shook my head. I was grasping at straws, trying to make an issue where there was none.

I didn't even know her real name. In my conversations with her, she only answered to Sweet Violet a couple of times, insisting to me at other times that her name was Frankie Jean.

And Frankie Jean what? Without a last name, an address, or a clear indication of her past, I had little to share with anyone, let alone share my suspicions that she, in her seemingly delusional, probably drunken, state, was some kind of mastermind behind unrelated death and destruction.

The possibility seemed silly and farfetched even as I thought it. How many times had Leon accused me of being too paranoid for my own good? And, yet, following my paranoia had helped save lives from further terror attacks last year.

"Sienna, are you okay?" Leon eyed me from a nearby couch. We were right back at the hospital and my entire family sat scattered around the waiting room, waiting for Roman's imminent discharge. "We just want to make sure he doesn't have any additional head swelling," a nurse had explained the delay.

"I'm about as okay as I'm going to be." I rubbed my eyes as the weight of exhaustion mixed with grief settled into my eyelids and dug into my muscles and bones.

Alisa Billy was dead.

I didn't know much about her. I knew that she was a recent divorcee and she had a pet Pomeranian named Daisy that she enjoyed dressing in cheerleading and princess dress costumes. I only knew this because she showed me pictures of her pooch on one of the few occasions she'd let her guard down.

"The stress of the case." Leon still eyed me. "That's probably why she was taking all of those pills."

I started to say something, but what was the point? Leon would not get my concerns. I doubted that anyone would.

"The stress is too much for anyone." My mother nodded from across the room. Sitting next to my father who had his nose buried in a newspaper, I felt like we were sitting in their family room in their home in Randallstown, and not on the fourteenth floor of Metro Community. Yvette had slipped away to a vending machine with Fiona. Demari had returned home to be with their other children. My son was still asleep.

"Have you talked to Roman yet?" My father didn't budge from behind the paper, seeming to read my mind. I was glad he could not see my face.

That was a loaded question.

As angry as Roman had been about the events of Christmas Day, I knew that my parents were plenty upset as well.

At both of us.

We never talked about it.

"He's been asleep for most of the day, Dad. I decided to let him rest so he won't be in too much pain. I'll talk to him once we leave. They are still talking about discharging him this evening."

My father sighed, grumbled, made some inaudible noise in response.

"That cop keeps circling the hallway." My mother pointed to a man in uniform just outside the waiting area.

"He's not a cop. Just hospital security." Leon rubbed his eyes. "And before you think more of it, Sienna, he's most likely posted by us to protect us from the media. Just the media."

"Why do you keep doing that, Leon?"

"Doing what?"

"Talking to me like I'm crazy for thinking that we may need a cop to protect us from more than the media."

"It's called PTSD." My mother beamed at her assertion. "I learned about it watching a YouTube video on mental health diagnoses." This she said as if I didn't have a master's in social work, as if I did not work as a therapist who had knowledge of illnesses, treatments, and theories. "They used to only diagnose soldiers returning from battle with it," she continued, "but now they say anybody who's been through a traumatic situation can be jumpy and on edge. Sienna's been through a lot lately."

"Yeah, most of it brought on by herself."

I raised my eyebrow at Leon as my mother raised an eyebrow at me. My father peeked over the paper at all of us.

For just a second.

Leon rarely let anyone, especially my family, witness the growing tension between us. Tension moved like waves between us, ebbs and flows. Sometimes we were smooth waters. Other times, riptides cut through, almost unseen above the surface.

I searched for something to say to melt the ice that had taken over the room. A loud squeal from the hallway warmed our ears instead.

"Sienna and Leon, I brought some food because you need to eat. It's been a rough day, but we gotta keep that oven at a good temperature for those baking buns. Girl, you look bigger since this afternoon."

Shavona and Mike Grant.

Had it only been a few hours since we'd eaten lunch with them? The two pulled paper plates and food containers out of a large paper bag, started spooning mounds of leftovers onto them and began passing them around.

"They are going to kick us out of this hospital." I nodded at the NO FOOD OR DRINK sign that sat on nearly every side table in the waiting room.

"No, girl, they are going to understand that this has been a long, trying day for you and your family. This is a medical facility. They should understand that stress and hunger ain't good for a pregnant woman."

And being belittled for my worries was not either, I started to add, but my father had just disappeared again behind his paper after peeking out at me and Leon.

No need to re-stir the pot.

"God is still on the throne. Even now, in this confusion and difficulty, He's not lost one ounce of control." Shavona seemed to be talking more to herself than to us.

"Who is that?" my mother mouthed and pointed as Shavona spooned food onto another paper plate and passed it to my father.

I thought about it for a moment and then I answered. No whisper necessary.

"Mom, Dad, this is Mike and Shavona Grant, Leon's . . . our friends. And our child's godparents."

The smiles that accompanied the handshakes, hugs, and greetings were a bright spot in an otherwise dark day.

"Girlfriend," Shavona stopped in front of me after speaking to my parents and Yvette, who'd reentered the room, "forget about all the foolishness going on right now. We've got a lot of planning to do to get ready for this baby."

My life hurt.

I still had not spoken to my son. Alisa Billy was dead. And uncomfortable suspicions about the murders, deaths, and beatings still gnawed at my consciousness.

But at that moment, at a little after 4:00 p.m., standing in the fourteenth floor waiting room at Metropolitan Community Hospital, I felt something that I had not felt the entire near eight months and counting that I had been pregnant.

Reality. And excitement. At the same time.

Leon took his plate from Shavona, a soda can from Mike, and then sat next to me, his knees touching mine. We exchanged glances, then exchanged smiles.

This was as perfect a moment I would get for a while, my gut told me. I sat back and enjoyed it, and took pleasure and comfort in the kicks and flutters that filled my stomach.

My baby.

My baby and my man, my parents and my friends.

My support, my rocks, my prayer partners.

I looked up to the heavens and smiled. I looked back down and stopped.

Mike Grant, Leon's friend, stared directly at me, winking.

Chapter 22

Christmas Evening

He paid to get his own car from the tow lot and left.

Our first Christmas together and all we'd done was argue, watch Roman get manhandled by the police because of me, and then get our cars towed.

Leon paid for his own car and left.

It took me two hours to finally get up from the bench in front of the international departure gate at BWI. Two hours to stop looking up at the sky, guessing which plane had my son. Two hours to stop waiting for Leon to call me, to check to see where I was, if I'd calmed down, if I was okay.

I left him some messages. Rage. Grief. Guilt. Despair.

All in two hours.

"How are you going to leave your pregnant wife at the airport on Christmas morning without making sure she is okay?"

Hang up. Redial. Leave another message.

"My son left, and then you leave me out here too? Don't you even care how I feel? Don't you even want to know where I am?

Hang up. Redial. Leave another message.

I felt horrible. Low. I heard myself. I hated myself. I felt out of control. Could this all be from hormones running amuck through my system from the little tadpole-shaped being the size of a sesame seed planted deep in my womb?

It had to be. I did not recall pregnancy being so emotionally violent, but I prayed that my current with-child state somehow explained my erratic behavior, my ill-advised decisions, and the fact that I kept leaving weep-filled, rant-filled messages on Leon's phone. I'm surprised no one called the police to come pick me up and take me where the white coats roam; but maybe the guards and skycaps knew I was just a mother coming to terms with a broken relationship and a wayward son.

Two hours of sobs and shock and then I finally got up to retrieve my car.

"Sienna St. James." A passerby smiled. "I recognize you from TV. Marvelous work you did with that terrorist last year. Can't wait to read the book I heard you're writing."

I gave a weak smile and hid a groan as I boarded a shuttle to where my car had been towed. I had to get it together. *Lord, please don't let the scene I just caused end up on YouTube.*

I thought of Roman sitting on a plane to some city I couldn't even remember the name of and felt a new wave of crazy come over me.

What could I do?

Nothing.

Christmas morning. I shook my head, eyes filling with tears as I wished for a do-over.

As I started my car, I remembered what I had put in my trunk. That bag with the dirty housecoat and slippers. The purse with the broken pocket watch.

Our first major argument as husband and wife had been over this bag. That had been only a few weeks ago. I'd stuffed the bag in the trunk with the idea that if I ever saw that woman walking the streets of Baltimore I would give her her things. Leon thought I was crazy for caring. Maybe I was.

My Christmas morning took new shape, new meaning as I turned off of 295 into downtown Baltimore. I was going to get rid of the bag once and for all, I decided. The last thought, the last mention I'd had of that woman was standing in the foyer of our condo several Sundays ago, the bag dangling from my hand as Leon slammed his way off to church. We hadn't talked about it or her ever since, and I was certain that woman and that bag were far removed from Leon's mind.

Driving through downtown toward my home in Canton, that woman and that bag were all I could think about. Thinking of her singing and dancing in the hospital emergency room, thinking of Ms. Marta and the residents of the shelter who would be celebrating this day without their beloved worker, I knew I had to get at least one good deed in, do one thing right.

I had not planned on looking for Sweet Violet. Out of respect for my husband's requests and wishes, I was going to leave the whole thing alone.

Except that I wanted to give back the purse to the girl who had given it to me for safekeeping. I wanted to let her deal with finding Sweet Violet, or whoever she was.

That's how I found Amber's body.

Looking for the young girl.

To be free of Sweet Violet.

Before I went home that Christmas morning, I turned toward the women's shelter where remnants of yellow tape still stuck to the surrounding overgrown greenery. I drove the block beyond the shelter, remembering precisely the "abandominium" Amber had walked into. I rapped on the basement window and waited for a response while the plastic bag of belongings hung from one hand. I had a fifty dollar bill squeezed tight in my other palm.

"Merry Christmas," I shouted through a small crack, determined to give the girl back the purse and to also give her money.

A horrid smell wafted out of the window, seeped through the scarf I'd wrapped around my nose and mouth, burned my eyes. Perhaps a dead stray or rat, I considered as my eyes watered. I bent down farther, looked through the dirty pane.

The sight scarred me.

A blue frayed blanket wrapped around decaying flesh.

I called the police. I called Leon. He still didn't answer. The bag with the purse went back in my trunk and after pointing out the scene to the cops, I went home. I was a social worker there trying to help a pregnant and homeless young girl who had been staying in the vacant home.

It was Christmas. The cops never questioned my story so there was no need to mention the old woman and her bag of dirty clothes.

When I got home, I threw up in the bathroom, and then got in my bed. Leon heated up a plate of the uneaten leftovers from Christmas Eve, served it on a tray with a single rose, rubbed my shoulders, and massaged my feet.

But we never talked about any of it, anything.

A therapist. I called myself one and even had degrees and letters behind my name and a pretty office space where I met with young clients to address trauma and pain, brokenness, anger, and sorrow.

And yet talking to my husband had been anything but child's play for me.

I was failing as a wife, and apparently as a mother, and I didn't know how to stop the nosedive.

"Mom, I have to ask you something." Roman's voice was barely above a whisper as our family troop took over the hallways of Metro Community. It was just a little after 4:00 p.m. and he'd finally been given the green light for discharge. Despite his bandages, swollen cheeks, and scattered bruises, he was finally awake, moving, ready to go home.

"What is it, Roman?" I held my breath as he walked down the hallway next to me. My mother, father, sister, and niece straggled behind us, chatting and laughing along with Shavona. Leon and Mike were farther ahead, which was fine with me; I didn't want to be anywhere near that winking eye.

Roman got quiet again and I didn't push. These were the first words in ages he'd directed toward me that didn't have a harsh tone or a hurt look.

I didn't want to ruin the moment even though I felt a little unnerved that Roman seemed intent on talking so quietly to me.

His question could be about anything. I braced myself.

We were stepping out of the garage elevator when he finally spoke again.

"Mom, I don't want you to think I'm crazy for asking this."

"What is it, Roman?"

A sudden screech of tires squealed right by us as we walked away from the elevator and began walking in the underground parking facility.

"Watch out." Roman nudged me back as a black car with tinted windows sped by.

Looked familiar.

My heart skipped a beat.

Leon and Mike, who were still ahead of us, both paused, both looked back. I could feel that my eyes were as big as my belly.

"It's nothing, Sienna. Probably someone from the media trying to get a picture. See?" Leon pointed to a group of uniformed police officers who stood near an exit. They had parted to let the car zoom past them. Didn't look the least bit concerned.

It bothered me, feeling like I'd just seen something familiar and not figuring out exactly what it was.

"Dad thinks you're being paranoid." Roman's tone was matter-of-fact, an observation. "I won't bother you with my question." He pulled away from me just as we neared Leon's car. My parents' car was parked nearby; they would drop Yvette and Fiona home. I had no idea where the Grants were parked.

I also had no idea what Roman's last statement meant. *Paranoid? Question?*

"What question?" I tried to catch up with him before he reached for the back door handle. "Is this about that girl . . . woman?" I couldn't hold back any longer.

Roman's hand froze for a second on the car door handle. Then he pulled it up and swung the door open with enough force to nearly hit the car beside us. I had to take two steps back to get out of the way.

"I'm not talking to you about that." His voice reeked of pain. I took another step back, my heart breaking at the sorrow that pierced his vocals.

"What is your question?" I pleaded. Leon looked at both of us as he finished shaking hands with Mike and headed toward the driver's side.

"I'm not going to add to your paranoia. I trust Leon's judgment. Let's just go, please." He got in, shut the door behind him.

There was that word again. Paranoia. *What is that supposed to mean?* Did Roman have something to ask me that Leon had told him not to? And if it wasn't about Changuna, then was it related to the events of the day? To the case? To what happened to him? To Alisa?

I was in a near panic as I got into the passenger's seat. My heart raced, my head felt dizzy. Why did I feel so afraid all of a sudden? Was I really just being paranoid?

That car.

That car that sped by had aroused a distant memory, I conceded, but I couldn't put my finger on what it was for sure, or why it bothered me.

"Where are we going?" I asked as Leon turned toward an exit for 83 North, the opposite direction of our condo in Canton.

"Roman wanted me to drop him off somewhere."

"Your flight," I remembered, turning to face my son in the back seat. "You are going to miss your flight. Are you still . . . planning to leave town? You aren't in any shape to be flying off somewhere."

"I'm not leaving. Not yet."

I exhaled. I still had questions, fears; but "not yet" was good enough. I didn't think any airline would be comfortable with him getting on covered with so many bandages, anyway.

"I'm dropping Roman off, and then we are going out, Mrs. Sanderson." Leon looked over at me. "It's been a tough day. I know you are tired, but we're going to go out and eat something nice. You deserve it. You're a trooper."

I gave him a smile, reached for his hand. He let me squeeze it before returning his attention back to the steering wheel.

"I'll go anywhere with you tonight, Mr. Sanderson, as long as it doesn't involve potatoes." We both chuckled. "I mean, really, Leon, you told the Grants I've been craving potatoes?"

Leon shook his head. "I never said such a thing. I have no idea where they got that idea from."

Moments like this.

Why couldn't we have more of them?

We continued to laugh. Roman looked preoccupied in the back seat, his head turned toward the window. "Not yet" was good enough, I reminded myself, feeling a bit of ease that I should have another chance to talk to my son before he disappeared God only knew where again.

He took me to his bakery.

After dropping Roman off at an unfamiliar row home in Charles Village, Leon hopped back on 83 and headed back south to downtown, to his bake shop near the Inner Harbor. I kept myself from asking any questions about where we'd just dropped off my son; it was enough just having him near me, alive, and reasonably well. We'd talk later. I was sure of it.

My heart sank at the CLOSED sign that hung just above the deadbolt on Leon's shop door. The trial and his determination to shield me from the media frenzy had necessitated him to leave his bakery closed for several weeks. With no reliable, consistent help or crew to keep things running, the extended closure could not have come at a worse time as he had been struggling as it was.

The striped shades were down and the lights were off, but when he flicked them on, I gasped. The entire interior had been filled with flower petals. Pastel shades of blue, pink, yellow, and purple petals covered the red booths, white tables, tiled floor. A single table in the center of the room was set with porcelain plates, cloth napkins, and sterling silver forks and a slender candle served as the centerpiece. Leon lit the candle and dimmed the lights. After pulling out one of the two chairs at the table for me to sit in, he disappeared into the kitchen and then brought out a raspberry chocolate mint Bundt cake.

"Shavona and Mike were kind enough to serve us dinner at the hospital. I've got dessert." He sat in the chair across from me. "I made a cake especially for you, to celebrate our first anniversary. I've had it ready all day as I thought we'd be done with the trial and free to do nothing but love on each other. I had planned that we would eat our cake and then grab the suitcases that I've got hidden in the back of the kitchen. I had a limo on standby to take us straight to the airport. Looks like all of that won't be happening, but we can still eat our cake, my love."

"I'm so sorry, Leon."

"No, no. I didn't tell you all of that to make you feel bad. I just wanted you to know my extensive plan and efforts to earn bonus points with you. I'm trying to cash all my points in for a jackpot tonight, wherever we end up spending it."

I looked at his brown face, smiled at the flame that flickered in his eyes. "So you have no problems spending the night with an eight-month pregnant woman? I'm almost fifty pounds heavier than I was this time last year."

"And a hundred times more beautiful." Leon's lips curled. "It's been a bumpy first year, we both know that, but I could not imagine us not being together. I waited a long time to get you, Sienna St. James. I've got you now, and I ain't letting go."

He slid the cake pan to the side, moved the candle over, and reached his palm to my face. "About the only thing sweeter than this cake here is that we made it through our first year, and we made a baby. I don't know what the future holds, Sienna, but I know we're in it together. I'm one hundred percent committed to you and our family."

I closed my eyes as he stroked my cheeks, breathed a little heavier as he moved his chair closer to mine. His lips brushed over my face, landed on my neck.

"I love you, Sienna." His whisper sent warm chills over my body.

Intoxicated.

That's what his love, his touch made me feel.

I turned my chair to more fully feel his kisses, to add mine to the moment.

And then there was a loud rap on the glass storefront window.

I jumped in my seat, but Leon's body remained loose, relaxed; his kisses, his warm, massaging hands, didn't stop what they were doing.

The pounding sounded again. I sat upright in my seat, while his hand fingered my hair.

"Someone's out there."

"They can see the closed sign." He came back in for another kiss, landed it near my mouth.

The rapping sounded for a third time. The blinds were down. There was no way to see who was knocking. A chill of a different kind wiggled through my stomach and tapped on my spine.

"What if it's someone up to no good? Didn't you say there were some break-ins at a few stores down the street?" My entire body had tensed up again. "I'm going to peek out the window."

"No, Sienna." Leon blew out a loud sigh, let his hand swing down away from my body before using it to rub his forehead. "No. Let it go. Nothing is going to happen. I just want to enjoy you, enjoy our time together. You realize this is the first time in a while nobody has known where we are? It's been a terrible day in many ways. I just want to make the most of this moment and enjoy what we've got together. I don't know when we are going on our trip. Let's enjoy this moment. Please stop worrying, Sienna." He reached out his hand to my hair again, pleaded with his eyes for my lips.

But then the sound of shattering glass echoed through the room. A medium-sized smooth white rock slid across the floor.

"Get down." Leon pushed me under the table, stood, and pulled out a gun, all in one motion. "Crawl back to the kitchen," he demanded as he neared the front door. I was too frozen to move. A short scream escaped from my lips as I watched him move closer to the door from my perch under the table.

The gun was cocked, outstretched in his hands as he stood to the side of the blinds. He used nimble fingers to gently pry a single slat slightly open.

I watched as his shoulders dropped down, he sighed, lowered the gun. He walked to the front door, unlocked it again, and opened it.

"No one's out there. Probably some punk kids."

I looked up at the wall clock that hung over the register area of the bakery.

5:11. The big and little hands of the painted chef on the clock face were unmistakable.

"You're shaking," Leon whispered.

My teeth clattered together as I tried to make sense of this twist in our evening. And then I saw a beam of red light that suddenly appeared just to the left of Leon's head.

All eight-months pregnant of me jumped from under the table as everything on top smashed down to the floor.

"Leon, watch out!"

Chapter 23

I'd gotten rid of the bag with the dirty housecoat and the old black purse on New Year's Day, three weeks before my fortieth birthday.

I found Sweet Violet.

Or rather she found me.

After the horror of our first Christmas, I was determined to salvage some kind of holiday spirit for me and Leon. The first two murders, Ms. Marta and Amber, had not yet made any ripples in the news, their cases still unsolved at that point. The time Leon and I had together had not yet been interrupted by the coming chaos.

His bakery by the Harbor was still holding on, but barely.

He wanted to keep his shop open for late night revelers. I wanted to watch the fireworks at the Harbor.

It was a win-win for both of us.

We sat in a booth by the front window, confetti-inspired cupcakes in front of us and in front of the many customers who filled his shop that night.

His staff had started dwindling even back then. While a socially conscious and respectable thing to do, hiring late teens and young adults who had been kicked out of schools and programs but who were looking for a second chance had proven too risky.

The call of the streets and fast money was too loud and impossible to ignore for many of them.

Some of them did make it. I heard later that one of the young ladies had enrolled in a culinary arts program and another young man applied and was accepted to college.

But that night, he was understaffed with several of his employees calling off at the last minute. He needed an extra hand to help pass out his mini cupcake samples just outside the front door. With tens of trays filled with cherry, vanilla, and blueberry cupcakes and a heavy investment in postcard-sized coupons, I didn't wait for him to ask for help after we finished our own cupcakes. I just grabbed a tray of the mini cakes, a stack of the coupons and stood outside the doorway while he went back to taking and fulfilling orders, checking on the ovens, and redirecting the staff that had come in.

I saw her in the crowd, a long wool coat draped around her thin frame.

She stood out to me, a quiet, unmoving figure in the sea of walkers filling the streets and sidewalks as the fireworks had just ended. She was maybe a hundred feet away, her face still pointed upward as her eyes searched the skies, perhaps waiting to see if another firework would go off. She was smiling.

I watched as she pulled out a large bottle of liquor from deep in her coat. She toasted it with a sapling struggling to stand in a patch of dirt and litter. Instead of then taking a swig of the dark liquid, she poured it onto the ground where the small tree was planted.

"Here." I pushed the tray I was holding into the free hand of one of Leon's young workers who'd just come outside to join me. She held a thick stack of the postcard coupons in her other hand and frowned at me as I stepped away.

"They got me doing everything in this shop. Double time ain't enough. I better be getting triple time for all this trouble I'm going through standing out here on a holiday," the girl hissed as I stepped away. I ignored her expressed discontent, determined to catch up with the elderly woman.

Her things were still in the trunk of my car.

The New Year's crowd thickened as spectators headed back to their cars and bus stops. Surrounded by whines and cries from children and slurred words and loud laughter from adults, I became dizzy, hot, and nauseous as I pushed my way to where I had first spotted the long wool coat.

I reached the tree.

She wasn't there. I squinted my eyes, searching the dense area lit by streetlights. No sight of a black coat or wild gray hair.

"Can you please walk or get out of the way?" a woman pushing a stroller shouted from behind me.

"Sorry." I stepped aside, but not before peering down into the stroller where a baby wrapped in a pink crocheted blanket lay sleeping.

I was having one of those. The shock of my midlife pregnancy still new, I rubbed my stomach, forgetting for a moment what I was doing out there, who I was looking for.

Out of the main walkway, I scanned the streets again. No sight of her.

Oh, well.

Leon needed help back at his shop, I conceded, knowing that he needed to get the attention of as many potential customers as possible. His desserts were great. People just needed to taste them, to know about him.

I was about to head back when I realized that I was standing next to the tree that the woman had toasted. I looked down in the dirt, noting a tall bottle of Old Grand-Dad, still full with whiskey, sat upright in the pile of trash and litter that surrounded the base of the small sapling.

Meant to beautify the city street with a manicured plot of greenery, the small patch of dirt and the tree standing in it looked worn out already from the New Year. I shook my head, started to turn away, but something else caught my eye.

Next to the whiskey bottle was a single flower planted in the dry dirt. I thought back to the purple bloom that had been planted in the greenery outside of the shelter the morning Ms. Marta died.

Here was a bright red rose.

I stopped to look down at it. A single red rose sprung up from the ground, its green leaves a sharp contrast from a couple piles of dirty slush left over from a brief snow that had fallen days before.

"A rose in the middle of winter?" I whispered to myself. I bent down farther to investigate, but a voice from behind me made me jump.

"Flowers can't tell lies. If you keep the sun off of them, dry up their waterbeds, and throw in weeds to choke 'em out, ain't no way or reason for them to bloom."

The stench that rose from her breath, the odor of her coat, reached my pregnant-sensitive nose and made me gag. She seemed oblivious to my nasal suffering as she continued, her eyes glued to the flower below us.

"If a rose is in full bloom when you know it's only been kept in darkness, and the ground it's planted in is cracked and cold, don't stop to smell that rose. There's a trap somewhere in those tempting dark red petals. There's deceit. Maybe even death. Run from that flowerbed. You don't want to get buried in that soil."

"Sweet Violet," I called her, noticing that her hair looked more unruly than it had in the emergency room, her skin dry and cracked, her eyes more worn.

She looked up from the misplaced rose, narrowed her eyes at me. "Who told you that was my name?"

"You did."

She frowned, pulled on a chin hair, and then clasped her hands together. "Yes, I remember you."

"The hospital. I gave you a ride back to a shelter where you were staying," I reminded her.

She kept smiling, said nothing.

"And you left your things in my car. Your housecoat, slippers. And I have your purse."

Her smile dropped and her eyes began darting around. There was a wide space around us as if the smell served as an invisible shield keeping passersby at bay.

"I'll go grab your things from my car, if you can wait here for a moment."

Her smile did not return as she stared at me in silence.

"Um, so you'll be here for a moment? I'll get your things, okay?"

She studied me some more and then smiled. "Roses don't bloom in winter. That's why I had to give it a toast." She leaned her head toward me. "Shhhh. I planted it there on Christmas, and it rebelled long enough to stay alive for me to toast it. What type of flower are you in the winter?"

I raised an eyebrow. "Not sure that I know what you mean. I'm going to get your things. Can I help you with anything else? Do you have any family or friends I can contact for you, Sweet Violet?"

Her smile dropped again. "Who told you that was my name?" She began backing up.

"Wait, Frankie Jean?" I tried the name that Ms. Marta had used to identify her.

Her eyes widened again and she turned away from me, scuttling away.

"Sweet Violet? Frankie Jean?" I called after her. "Do you want your purse? The pretty watch inside?"

She froze then turned back around. "You can keep it. You keep it. Keep it!" she shrieked, took a turn, and headed toward a darkened alleyway. Disappeared.

"Sienna, what are you doing out here? Are you okay?" Leon approached me from the opposite side, his eyes scanning the immediate area as I stood blinking, confused. "Did something happen? You don't look well."

"I . . . I just ran into that old, homeless woman whose stuff I've been wanting to return."

"Wait a minute. You still have that bag? I thought we were done with that."

"I was. I am." I shrugged my shoulders. "She didn't want it. I guess that watch meant nothing to her after all."

"Melanie just quit," he spoke flatly, referring to the young girl who I'd given the tray of samples to hold. Clearly his attention and time didn't allow for one more word about Sweet Violet, or whoever she was. No point in even talking to him about the confusion around her name, her anger at being identified either way.

"I'll be right in to help. Just have to do one thing."

He shook his head, headed back to his shop. I went to my car parked at a meter around the corner from the bakery. I popped the trunk and waited for a group of spectators heading to the car behind me to leave so I could open it with without hitting anyone. That woman said she didn't want her bag, but I didn't either. It seemed fitting to leave the bag with the housecoat, slippers, and purse with the pocket watch hidden in its seams at the rose she'd planted. I walked back to the sapling, spotted the bottle of whiskey, quickened my step to leave the bag there with the flower and be done with it and her once and for all.

But the rose was gone, an upturned tiny pile of dirt now left in its place. I looked around me, moved my head to try to peer down the alleyway where I'd seen her disappear.

Nothing and nobody but groups of families, couples, and rowdy teenagers were within my view.

I left the bag there anyway, settled it next to the upright bottle of whisky in the dirt surrounding the sapling. I had no use for it, as far as I was concerned. Nothing else for me to do but keep moving. I'd tried to help. She didn't want it. I had to get back to Leon who I knew wanted my assistance.

I was steps away from his entrance when a sharp clap and a collective gasp sounded near me. Parts of the crowd scattered away down the block, the opposite direction from where I'd attempted to engage Sweet Violet.

I looked all around me, searching to see what had brought the late night New Year's revelers to a standstill.

Victim three.

I saw the black loafers lying on the ground before I saw the rest of the body sprawled across the pavement.

The crowd's gasps turned to screams as recognition of the victim grew.

Julian Morgan.

Councilman. Philanthropist. Actor. Activist. TV personality. A man who was both a Baltimore legend and a national treasure due to his varied and storied career path that intersected the arts, politics, and entertainment. At nearly eighty-five years old and a pillar of the community, his death hit a deep low in the bass notes of Baltimore.

The weeping began immediately as the crowds that had come out to bring in the New Year realized that a man so tied to the Baltimore landscape and the metropolitan scene had been viciously murdered, shot down in what appeared to be an accident.

He had not been the intended target, the investigators would later conclude.

Surveillance video would reveal a scuffle between two other men. A gun was drawn and a shot fired and the bullet landed by chance in the chest of Julian Morgan. Those details would come out later. What was immediately

observed that night, at least what I observed, was a young
man in a black jacket and a black hat running off to a dark
car and speeding off toward President Street. The only
thing that had been missing from that baby-faced man
was a cigarette. I recognized the probable shooter and
killer of the famed Julian Morgan as the young man who
I'd spoken to the morning Ms. Marta had been killed.

Are you a cop? The question he'd had for me.

What I wasn't 100 percent certain of was whether he
was the same man lurking by the front entrance of the
emergency room at Metro Community the night I assisted
Sweet Violet, or whether that was him and the same black
car parked near the shelter when I dropped her off.

I wasn't sure though my gut wanted to believe so.

"Sienna, they caught the man you saw and have tied
him to all three murders. You've shared what you know
for sure, so the other details are not necessary," Leon
pleaded with me when I shared my concerns later, after
filling the police in with what I'd observed for certain.
I'd been able to place Delmon Frank at two of the crime
scenes, Ms. Marta's and Julian Morgan's. No one ever
was able to identify or capture the other young man he
was arguing with the night the stray bullet landed in
Morgan's chest.

"I am proud of you for doing your civic duty, but I
don't want you involved more than necessary. They have
enough information. They have the man. Leave it at that,
and leave that woman you're so worried about out of it.
Don't complicate matters," Leon continually told me.

A grand jury found that there was enough evidence
to indict Frank based on the New Year's downtown
surveillance video and my testimony, which linked him
to the first crime scene. The bullets and other key forensic
evidence at Ms. Marta's and Morgan's scenes matched.
Once Frank was tied to Ms. Marta's murder, shelter resi-

dents identified him as Amber's boyfriend. Though it was too late to look for any of her bite marks on his body, his DNA was in her fingernail scrapings, tests would prove. It all fit together neatly, soundly, allowing prosecutors to go after him quickly.

The death of Julian Morgan demanded swift justice. The other two victims' justice benefited from Morgan's fame.

The only person who seemed to have any questions or doubts was me.

Nobody else knew about Sweet Violet.

And the apparent unrelated coincidences were my observations to keep.

"Sienna, what more needs to be done? They have Delmon Frank and have tied him to all three murders. What else needs to be done?" Leon's sentiments when I brought the topic up over the next few months leading up to the case and my testimony in it. "I hate that you are involved in this. Just share what you've shared from day one and let the rest go. I want to move on with our lives, get past the case, be free of the trial."

His arguments had been valid, his pleas logical, and my worries unnecessary.

Until now.

Chapter 24

"Leon, are you okay?" I sat frozen, all eight-months pregnant of me curled up in a ball, after I'd crawled behind the massive register stand on the far side of his bakery. Four minutes had passed since I'd dialed 911 on my cell phone. I could hear sirens wailing in the distance. Maybe that's what had triggered my memories of New Year's Day.

"Don't worry about me," Leon crawled over to join me. "Are you okay?"

A sound somewhere between a whimper and a moan escaped my lips. These were the four longest minutes of my life as I waited to see if the shots would resume, if someone would then enter, if a red laser beam would find us in our temporary barricade behind the register.

As Leon nursed some wounds on his arms from the shattered glass, I counted at least eleven shell casings scattered about the bakery shop floor.

"Don't touch anything," Leon mumbled as he wrapped a dishcloth around his lower arm. "Evidence."

Evidence.

How many times had I heard that word over the past few months? This time it applied to us, to our circumstances.

We could have been killed.

A shooter aimed indiscriminately at us from the outside of Leon's bakery, and we could have been killed.

But why?

The threats up to now had been media-related, privacy issues. Though I'd had my worries, my doubts, my fears, I never imagined that I'd be cowering behind a metal register stand, my face pushed into Leon's side. I never imagined that he would be bleeding. I pressed my entire body closer to him, aware that every limb on me was shaking.

"It's okay, Sienna," Leon assured me, though I noted the tautness in his own body. One of his arms held me, the other was extended, gun pointed toward the broken front windows, his old police training and instincts at work.

The front window was almost completely gone and the striped curtains that covered the storefront had gaping holes, were shred to pieces. From what I could see, a small crowd had gathered on the periphery. I could hear their mumbles, their expressions of disbelief. That gave me a slight comfort, a small sense of safety. If people felt safe enough to begin gathering outside the shop, then maybe the danger was gone, the shooter moved on.

But did the shooter think we were dead? If that was the intention, then we were nowhere near safe.

I thought of Roman, wanted him close to me. Wished we had finally spoken and cleared the heavy air between us.

"Leon." My voice came out in a mournful whisper, matching the wail of the sirens that sounded seconds away.

His arm around me tightened and he planted his lips on my forehead for a quick kiss. "It's okay, baby. I am not going to let anything happen to you, to either of you."

My God, the baby. I rubbed a hand over my belly and felt a fear and an anger that I'd never felt in my life. What if something had happened to my baby? What kind of animal targets a pregnant woman?

I thought of Amber and knew that my question was already too late. Her belly was obviously full with child and it had not stopped her killer from taking both her and her unborn baby's lives.

But that had been a drug-induced attack, and the alleged perpetrator, Delmon Frank, was behind bars awaiting the completion of his trial.

"That first rock came through the window at five-eleven, the same time that was on that broken pocket watch. Leon, all of this . . . This has to involve Sweet Violet, right?"

He didn't answer immediately. The seconds before he spoke seemed like an eternity, but he was just thinking, considering my question, I realized.

"The time doesn't tell me that Sweet Violet is involved, Sienna," he finally spoke. "It's probably just a coincidence. I think someone is watching you, watching us. Maybe because of the trial, maybe because of something else. I don't know."

Police cars skidded to a stop in front of the shop. I heard heavy boots, shouts, orders. "Move back, move back." Guns raised, glass crunching. I realized that I'd never mentioned the $5.11 that had been left on Roman after the assault. Did he know? My voice was locked in my throat as my heart tried to calm down.

"I wish you had never gotten involved with any of this, Sienna. This is exactly why." His voice was low, not fussing, but the point was taken.

As what looked like a SWAT team stormed into the bakery, Leon nudged me, beckoned me to raise my arms. He let his gun drop to the floor beside us and we both emerged slowly from behind the register; careful movements, so as not to spook any of the armed and shielded officers. When we both had fully come from behind the register, arms still raised, the officers rushed us, one grabbing Leon, another grabbing me.

"Ma'am, are you okay? We got a report of a hostage situation here. Is this man harming you?"

"Leon, be still," I shouted over to my husband, noticing for the first time the rough nature of the officers and Leon's natural reaction to shield himself. The way he moved his arms and twisted his legs, in these fast blurred moments, his actions could be misinterpreted as resistance, I realized. *These guys think Leon is the culprit here.* "No, no, no," I spoke quickly as I realized they were not letting Leon get in a word as they frisked him, turned him over, attempted to handcuff him. "Please, stop. That's my husband. This is his shop. I never said it was a hostage situation. I don't know where you got that report. Please, this is my husband, Leon Sanderson. We were celebrating our anniversary and someone shot through the front windows."

Too many people in the room.

Too much action.

Too much going on.

Confusion.

My words seemed to evaporate into the air before touching the eardrums of anyone present. Seemed like the only word heard by the tactical team was "shot."

"Here's a gun." I heard someone say as the swarm of officers grew and took over the tiny shop. One of them had picked up the gun Leon had dropped to the floor.

"I'm a former officer with the Baltimore Police Department. My name is Leon Sanderson and this is my place of business," Leon managed to get out as handcuffs tightened over his wrist. "I don't know where you got information that this is a hostage situation. That's simply not true. Someone shot at me and my wife. We were here celebrating our first anniversary."

"Ma'am." Another officer disregarded Leon's words. "Although we'll be taking him with us, it's probably in your best interest to seek a restraining order against your husband. Someone from our domestic violence unit can help you. There's no need for you to try to protect him. If he was bold enough to fire multiple bullets at you, he's bold enough to face the charges."

"That is not what happened here at all!" I screamed, a new level of panic settling over my entire body. "This is my husband! He didn't do anything. Someone shot at us from outside the windows. At five-eleven! This homeless lady—" I realized my words were falling on deaf ears as adrenaline, weapons, and more officers flooded the bakery, some picking up and bagging evidence, others pointing at bullet holes in the walls and furniture.

The place was a ragged mess.

"Is this even a registered gun?" I heard another officer inquire. Leon, though just across the room from me, felt like he was miles away.

"I told you. I'm a former cop. Let me get my ID."

"Do you even have a permit to carry a concealed weapon?"

"I'm on the grounds of my business, and I'm protecting my wife. If you give me a chance . . ." His words began slurring together in my ears as the room collapsed on top of me. I felt like I was inside of a bubble, dizzy, everything looking distorted, air squeezing out of my lungs. I had to tell myself to breathe as another officer forced me down into a seat, seeming to care about my physical wellbeing, telling someone to call an ambulance; something about me going into shock.

"Sienna, it's okay!" Leon stared at me through the sea of officers, the concern on his face telling me that he was more concerned about me than what was going on in his corner of the room with several officers thinking he was a criminal, weapons drawn, pointing at him. "Breathe, baby. It will all work out. Sienna, breathe, baby. I need you and my baby to be okay. Breathe." His was a calm, soothing voice in the midst of the chaos.

I felt my lungs expand under his command. Lightheadedness, dizziness took over me.

"Push her head between her knees," I heard someone say as I felt myself blacking out. I felt heavy hands on my head pushing me inward, but something was in the way. That's right, my stomach. I became aware of a volley of flutters and kicks coming from my abdomen. "Jesus, help us," were the only words I could get out as the room began rotating faster around me.

Then darkness.

Stretcher. Flashing lights.

I felt myself being holstered into the back of an ambulance as I came back to consciousness. How long had I been out? I was outside, in front of the bakery. Pratt Street was closed in both directions. "Wait!" I pushed myself up from the stretcher, slid to the edge. "I don't need the hospital. I need my husband."

"Ma'am, please lie down. You're safe. Your husband is in custody." A woman's voice. Uniform. Bright red hair. Arm full of tattoos. Blurry images. I realized tears were blocking my vision.

"No, no, no. Will someone please listen? My husband and I were eating cake for our anniversary and someone started shooting through the window! They are still out there. They are trying to kill us. Please help! Please listen!" I struggled against the paramedic who was trying to keep me flat on the stretcher. "Don't you know who I am?" I hated to go that route, but was desperate to try anything to make somebody listen. "I've been on all the television stations lately. The terrorist attack last year? The Delmon Frank trial?"

"Ma'am, we all are aware that you are Sienna St. James and I'm sure as a public figure it's embarrassing to have your family business aired. However, it is our job to keep you safe. Your husband was shooting at you. Because a gun was involved, your permission is not needed to press charges."

"Leon absolutely was not shooting at me!"

"No need to keep up the act, Ms. St. James. My understanding is that a reliable eyewitness informed us of the hostage situation and called it in. You can let it go, ma'am."

An eyewitness? Who on earth called the police and said Leon was holding me hostage?

"I'm not going to the hospital, miss. Everything is wrong. You can't force me. I'm fine. I just need to figure out what's going on." I jumped off the stretcher, hopped out of the open door of the ambulance. The paramedic didn't pursue me, just shook her head. I saw pity in her eyes.

But fear was in mine.

Someone just tried to kill me and my husband, and, when that didn't succeed, they framed Leon as an abusive hostage-taker. My husband was in custody, his business and reputation in shambles, and I was a victim of misdirected pity.

An eyewitness? Who? Why?

I didn't know the answers. I didn't even know if I was safe. What I did know was that a rock came crashing through the window at 5:11 p.m. and then all hell broke loose.

Maybe it had nothing to do with Sweet Violet. Maybe it had everything to do with Sweet Violet. I had no idea why we were targeted.

Was Delmon Frank some type of gang member? Did he have ties to the streets and the stop snitching code culture that kept most of the city's crime-solving abilities in gridlock? Was my testimony stepping on too many wrong toes?

My biggest fear before today was that the media would ruin my life, taping every detail of it, releasing every word, every statement.

Today, my family members, those who I loved dearly, were attacked. The lawyer who represented me was dead. Of course all of this was tied to the case, but what of Sweet Violet?

I considered these things as I stepped away from the scene, the confusion. I turned toward the Inner Harbor.

Hot summer evening.

The crowds would hide me while I figured out my next move.

Get to Leon.

Get answers.

Get to safety.

The baby kicked in me. Maybe I should have gone to the hospital just for her or his sake. No. Not until I knew better what was going on. My gut told me the baby was fine and that I had to get some answers for all of our sakes.

I changed my direction, hurried my pace to get to the Charles Street Metro Station to catch the next subway train. Using a map feature on my phone, I planned out my route. I didn't want to drive my car in case I was being followed. For some reason, the idea of public transportation appealed to me.

Safety in numbers?

I decided that I'd catch the next train to Mondawmin Mall then transfer to the number fifty-two. Yvette, along with her husband, had purchased her first home not long ago. She'd left her longtime row home in Park Heights and moved into a five-bedroom single family home in the Ashburton neighborhood.

She was a branch manager of a dollar store. Demari's landscaping business had grown exponentially since he began, like Leon, taking young people on as mentees and employees. Yvette and Demari were both tasting the fruits of their successes.

And they both were familiar with the sour tastes of the streets.

I needed a seat at their table, to fellowship, to commune, to figure out what to do from here.

As I stepped onto the escalator that would drop me down into the belly of the Charles Street Station, a black sedan with tinted windows that had been sitting at a red light suddenly sped off. I thought about the car that had zoomed out of the parking garage at the hospital.

Leon had told me not to overthink then, so I told myself not to overthink now.

There were a lot of black cars in Baltimore, and, unfortunately, some of those drivers ran red lights.

Stop getting spooked by every little thing, I reprimanded myself as I broke into a slight jog, determined to get on the train pulling into the station at that very moment.

As the doors shut behind me and I stumbled into an empty seat, I could not help but wonder if the only reason I was not in a panic over the black car that had suddenly taken off as I entered the subway station was because I had not seen Sweet Violet or anything that belonged to her.

Seemed like the only time someone got hurt or killed was when she was nearby.

I exhaled, sat back in my seat. Tried to ignore the stares of the passengers on the partially filled train until I realized why they were looking at me with eyebrows raised.

Some of Leon's blood had stained my clothes.

Fortunately, his blood was only on my suit jacket. I took it off and crumpled the black jacket onto my lap. The nosy stares turned away.

Chapter 25

"What did you do?" Roman's frown greeted me as I walked up Yvette's manicured walkway at a quarter of eight. He sat on the porch steps, his legs massive pillars on the stone stairway, a baseball cap balanced on his knee. The mug on his face, the glare in his eyes, looked lethal.

He was bandaged and bruised, but still able to make me feel worse than he looked.

I wanted to ask what he was doing here, how he'd gotten there, but his question made me forget the ones I wanted to ask.

"What are you talking about?" I wiped both my eyes with my hands, pulled back on my hair. Sighed loudly.

"It's on all the news stations, even cable. Breaking news. They are trying to say that the man you married and I look up to tried to kill you, took shots at you. I know that is not true. What is true is that you were there and you are good at getting a crowd of police involved in a situation that requires none."

"Roman, you may have turned twenty-one in March, but you are still my child and I am still your mother. Respect that." I turned away, ready to head to the porch, too tired, too everything, to deal with him at the moment. What happened to my son?

Changuna.

I didn't have time for that thought chain either.

"Ma." His voice cracked. "Can you please tell me what's going on? Leon told me that you keep getting involved in dangerous situations. What happened? I know Leon didn't shoot at you. Is this related to that trial he didn't want you getting mixed up with?"

"So Leon is talking to you about our disagreements now?" I paused on my way up the steps. But only for a moment.

"Ma, Leon is a good guy. He's only looking out for you," he called after me.

"You need to focus on making sure that you are taking care of yourself, making good choices." I paused again, looked at his bandages. "And getting better." I sighed. "Roman, I love you, and we still need to talk. Can we please call a truce for the moment, at least until I can figure out how to best help Leon and keep all of us safe? Please, Roman? We need to work together right now. Isn't that what we've always done? Before there was Leon . . . or Changuna." I bit my lip as he cut his eyes away from me. "Before there was anybody else, there was me and you. We've been through worse, Roman. Work with me, not against me."

He didn't respond. I saw a flicker in his eyes and it saddened me even more.

A flicker of pure pain.

This child of mine was hurting and something told me that whatever I'd done or hadn't done didn't even scratch the root of the source of his bitterness.

He looked up at me, knew that I saw the rawness. Shrugged.

"Let's go inside, Roman. Let's work as a family to figure everything out." I held out a hand.

He shook his head. "I'm not going in there."

"Why?"

"Aunt Vet has guests. I got a ride over here looking for answers, but I'm not dealing with those people she has inside."

"What are you talking about?"

"Not my kind of people anymore."

I narrowed my eyes, looked away.

What had happened to my son? I shook my head as I finished climbing the steps. I had a feeling I knew what kind of people had filled my sister's house. I opened the screen door and my suspicions stood correct.

"Father, we know that no weapon formed against us shall prosper. Every plan of the enemy must come down in defeat. We are your people, oh Lord, and you will not abandon us. You hear our cries when we have come to a broken place, and you mend and you heal and give strength when we have lost all power to stand on our own."

Several years ago, I had accidentally stepped into a prayer circle in the pastor's office of the church I now attended. Back then, I had only visited the large edifice while on a fact-finding mission to dig up the truth behind a foster care client's claim of a missing sister. The church at that time was in the middle of a citywide scandal based on lies, but the earthquake of prayer in that room seemed strong enough to topple down the entire deceit-filled scheme.

It was hard to believe that stepping into the cool living room of my sister's home, the one leading a prayer of similar magnitude was her. Yvette's voice roared and whispered, demanded and declared, moved like mist and fire through the room where about fifteen people were assembled.

I recognized some of the faces from my old church, the one I attended for most of my life before Leon and I joined where we were now. Most of the faces were new to me, different ages, both males and females. Some were obvious couples, some singles. Young women. Old men.

Children's laughter and a pile of toys and books poured from the nearby family room. One gray-eyed girl of about five or six years old with two thick plaits peeked out from behind the French doors of the family room before a woman, her mother presumably, shooed her back to play with the other youngsters.

"Glad you are here, Sienna." Yvette had finished her prayer. She sat down in one of the plush white couches that made up her formal living room. The guests in her home all joined in sitting down with her. Chairs from her dining room, some stools from the breakfast bar, a couple of metal folding chairs from the basement, were arranged in a rough circle from the foyer to the stone fireplace in the living room. No television was on, no cell phones out; I realized that they wouldn't know the headlines about my current situation.

"Girl, where did you get that wooden vase from? That's pretty." A woman with a teeny gold afro pointed to a knickknack on the mantle, her small talk confirming my suspicions that they weren't aware of my current situation which Roman said was being publicized on the news. If I put my bloodstained suit jacket back on, I'd get immediate attention, but I felt too frozen to think, too frozen to know what to do next. I needed to have a big talk with my little sister, but I didn't want everybody in my business.

"My mother brought that vase back from her cruise to the Bahamas, and I claimed it." Yvette munched on a plate of Swedish meatballs Demari had brought to her. A plate piled high with fried chicken and collard greens sat on a tray by where he sat.

"Thanks, baby." Yvette smiled at him, a bashful smile.

"Aww, that's cute, the way he got her food for her." Another woman, this one with long hair pinned back into a ponytail, giggled. She nudged the knee of the man next to her. He rolled his eyes.

Everyone in the room had a plate of food on their laps or on trays; red cups full of iced tea, a slice of pound cake, or cherry pie.

"Grab a plate, Sienna." Yvette pointed to her dining room where the feast was spread out on a plastic blue tablecloth. "Or at least grab a seat."

My feet, my mouth stayed frozen, locked as I continued to stand by the front door. As all eyes stayed on me, I slithered into a velvet high-back chair by the foyer's umbrella stand. I didn't want the attention. I just wanted to talk to my sister.

"Okay, so we finished with the formalities." A man about forty years old with square black eyeglasses spoke up from the opposite corner. A Bible sat open on his lap. "Are we ready to move on to tonight's topic? This week we're talking about relationships. Why some work—"

"And why most don't," the man sitting next to the long-haired woman interrupted.

"Charlie!" she squealed and narrowed her eyes at him while everyone else broke into laughter.

Yvette looked up at me between the laughs then held out her hand to silence the room. "Hold on, y'all. My sister looks confused. I need to explain to her what's going on."

"Small group session," Demari chimed in. "Pastor started this thing where we rotate houses to talk about real life, real issues. Can't usually get this type of discussion going during Sunday services, so we meet up once a week to fellowship, debate, chitchat about life and the elements in it, in a safe place. We agree at the outset of each meeting that whatever is talked about stays in the room and that we hold each other accountable—"

"And that we eat," another young man interrupted, holding up his red cup for a toast.

"Yeah, that too." Demari chuckled. "And we focus on building real relationships that aren't church phony or tradition driven. The Bible is our textbook as we come together to talk it out. We keep it real here."

"And you better believe it gets *real* real up in here, especially when Demari and Yvette are the hosts." The woman with the gold afro shook her head slowly. "Your sister a trip, but she speaks the truth."

"I've been through some things," Yvette murmured, her eyes on a distant place.

"We pray together, eat together, laugh, and cry together. And we are all better Christians, better people, because of it." Demari spoke again and rubbed Yvette's back. She looked at him and they both smiled at each other.

I nodded, gave a small smile. *How do I pull Yvette aside to talk to her?*

"So tonight we are talking about relationships." The man with the Bible in his lap spoke up again. "And I wanted to bring to everybody's attention that the wisest man who ever walked the planet, Solomon, devoted an entire book on passion and intimacy. Solomon, the same man who wrote that there is a time for every purpose under the sun, took the time to write an entire book in the Bible about the excitement of love. That man and his bride spend time in graphic detail talking about how they can't wait to get with each other and give very detailed descriptions about what they like about each other. That shows they spent time, energy, and effort to adore each other."

"The key word in what you just said is 'bride,'" another man spoke up. "The kind of passion you talking about was only there because they were newlyweds. They're still fresh and ignorant in their relationship. Show me the

Song of Solomon part two, five years and two kids later, and I bet some of that mushiness will have cooled down. Now that's real talk."

"Charlie," the man's wife hollered again as the room roared with laughter.

"Let me ask you a question, Charlie." Demari leaned forward in his seat. "When does your wife stop being your bride?" The room grew silent. Demari continued. "When do you stop being her groom? Maybe that's the whole point of the book. I don't know. I'm not a Bible scholar; but maybe that's just it. I hope that's it. Maybe a secret to keeping marriage alive is to keep seeing your woman as the bride you were lusting after on your wedding night."

"Ooh, you said 'lust.'" A girl around Roman's age spoke up from one of the breakfast stools in the foyer. She had two long braids, dyed dark red. "Are you trying to tell me that the Bible got a sex manual in it?"

"It's got a marriage manual in it. Sex, passion, intimacy, all those things are so important that an entire book in the Bible is dedicated to talking about it all. Like Deac said, the wisest man who ever lived wrote it and that book made it into the Good Book."

"I read that book, the *Song of Solomon,* girl." Another woman, this one a bit older spoke up. "All those two did was talk about their time together, and when they weren't together, they talked to others about how they wanted to spend their time together."

"More power to them." Charlie shook his head. "Solomon was wise enough to know what kind of woman should take up his time. I'm just kidding, Teresa!" he added quickly as the woman next to him playfully balled up her fist and narrowed her eyes.

"What do you like about your wife?" Demari asked Charlie who was still chuckling. "No, I'm serious. What do you like about your wife? I'm looking at the principles in the book. All Solomon did was talk about the features he liked about his bride. Maybe that's another secret to a healthy, happy, passion-filled marriage. Telling her, telling others what it is that you love about her. Try it, man. What do you like about Teresa?

"Keep it G-rated please," a woman in her fifties spoke by the fireplace, her hands over her ears.

"Speak for yourself, Sister Randy," a woman who could have been around eighty years old directed. "I love to hear a man praise his woman and a woman praise her man. Go ahead, both of you. Share what you like about each other."

Charlie and Teresa both groaned, both shook their heads, but I noticed that they turned to look each other in the eyes. No words were said, at least none that any of us understood, but at the end of their unspoken conversation, they hugged.

"Is this how y'all church services are?" The girl with the red braids looked confused.

"No, baby," Sister Randy answered. "This is how *we* are. And we *are* the church."

"Alive and in person," Yvette joined in. "Ain't that right, Sienna? We're talking the truth in here. Aren't these the same principles you've shared in therapy sessions? The truth is the truth. Whether it's coming from a preacher's mouth or a counselor's self-help book, the principles are still the same. Keeping passion alive. Focusing on your mate's finer qualities. Open, honest, or otherwise naked communication." She chuckled. "I bet Leon would agree. Where is he, anyway?"

"You don't know?" I couldn't hold it in anymore, crowd or not. "Leon's . . . in custody. He was set up to look like he did something crazy, and I think it's because of my role in this trial. I need your help."

"Oh, we got this, honey. We got this." A voice from behind me caught me off guard as the front door opened and closed. I hadn't even seen them come in as I'd finally spilled the beans about my situation.

Shavona and Mike Grant.

"Your brother-in-law told us about this group meeting today when we met at the hospital. From what we just heard you say, I'm glad we came. We got your back with this one, girlfriend." Shavona looked mad as she stormed to the dining room to put down a covered pot that smelled of garlic and basil.

The room sprung into action as the television was flicked on, phones were brought out, new rounds of prayer began. Yvette fixed me a plate of food, threatened to spoon-feed me if I didn't eat it, then pulled up a chair close to me and held my hand.

"Though I have had the experience of seeing a significant other carted off to jail, I know that this situation is a little different, so I won't say that I can fully relate." Yvette sighed. "But this too shall pass, big sis."

The roller coaster in my stomach, the questions that flooded my brain hadn't changed one bit; but knowing that I wasn't alone in this trial did help me feel a little better. Most of the people in the room didn't know me, but they all had stopped what they were doing to send up petitions to heaven on my and Leon's behalf.

Leon's baby inside of me was kicking away; the sign of strength in those little feet gave me enough reason to keep going forward.

Even if my other child was still refusing to enter the house.

"Where's Roman?" I tried to push myself up.

"Oh, he got into a car when we were coming in," Mike answered.

"He was driving?"

"No, he got in the passenger seat. I didn't think much of it at the time, so I couldn't tell you any other details."

I was so confused with my son, what he was up to, how he was getting around. I didn't even know what questions to ask, what questions to avoid. Our relationship was too delicate to mess around asking something that would set him off or shut him up from talking to me again.

I shut my eyes to send up a petition, but then realized that I felt too numb to pray. Good thing I was surrounded by so many others who could put my pleas into words.

When I opened my eyes, I saw that Mike Grant was studying my face. He must have seen my despair.

Is this all because I got involved with Sweet Violet?

"Please don't worry, Sienna." Mike sat down across from me. "I will personally do all I can to make sure this gets resolved quickly. I'll make some calls to my connections in the department. You know I got Leon's back. I won't let things get too out of control. Don't worry. Everything will work out."

His words were meant to comfort me, and for a moment they did.

Until he winked at me.

The fourth time that day.

Chapter 26

Five Months Earlier

"Happy birthday, wife of mine."

I opened my eyes and looked into the dark brown eyes of my soul's love. Tangled in the sheets after a near sleepless night, I tried to straighten myself out and smooth my hair back down under my satin night scarf.

Waking up forty years old for the first time brought a host of mixed emotions.

"You should call out of work today." Leon smiled at me from his pillow. He ran his toes over my legs under the sheets I'd just untangled.

"Can't call out when you are the work." I yawned, then wished I could start over. Those were my first words uttered as a forty-year-old woman.

"Yeah, I understand. I need to get to the bakery myself today." He smiled as he sat up and pulled me up to him with one easy move of his arms. "But you can join me this morning for breakfast. It's waiting on the table." He kissed my lips, stroked my ear.

"Wait, you've already been up?" I forced myself to awaken more fully and realized that the savory aroma of bacon, blueberry pancakes, and hot coffee filled my nostrils.

"Of course I've been up. I had to plan your big day; that is, if you can listen to me and take off. Your clients can reschedule. They've done it before."

"Leon, thanks for breakfast." I stood, stretched. "I don't know if I can get all of my clients moved. Some of them have been waiting for over two months for their appointments. Ever since the news coverage last year, you know my waitlist has boomed." I looked back at him. He still sat on the bed. "Besides, like you said, you have your business to get to."

"Turns out that I made arrangements. Mike is standing in for me today. He's using his day off to make sure that I can cater to you."

"That's sweet." I bent back over the bed to kiss his lips one more time. "Thing is, even if I did cancel all my appointments, I still have to get some work done on that book. I'm surprised they're still offering me a contract for as long as it's taking me to figure out what to write."

"Take some time off today, even half the day, a couple of hours, and I will gladly sit down with you to help you develop your outline." Leon's eyes pleaded. "I just want to spend some time with you. I want to celebrate you today."

"Leon . . ."

"Baby . . ."

We stared at each other.

My eyes followed the veins in his arm muscles, studied the outline of his lips. Everything about him was perfect, and this would be the first birthday I'd be celebrating as a perfect man's wife.

Mmmmm.

A loud buzz vibrated through the room. My cell phone.

"Don't get it," Leon whispered as I reached for it anyway. The caller ID indicated that it was Darci. She never called me this early; this could not be good.

"Sienna," she spoke before I even said hello. "I know it's early, but Monifa who's supposed to be providing morning coverage has a family emergency and there are three clients coming in starting at seven with urgent matters she was supposed to see. Can you come in a couple of hours earlier than your usual to see them? I'm not sure what else to do because Jackie and Soo Yee are booked solid too and these three clients have been waiting for appointments for over six weeks."

"It's my birthday." I kept my eyes on Leon who kept shaking his head no. "I—"

"Oh, that's right. I forgot it is your birthday. Happy b-day, Sienna. Let's see, I will . . ." She paused. I heard papers flipping.

I shut my eyes. Leon would just have to understand. I had a business to run, and, even more importantly, clients who had mental and emotional concerns that could not be ignored.

"I'll be in to see them," I announced. What else could I do?

Leon groaned and collapsed back into the tangled sheets as I hung up and proceeded to get ready for the work day.

"I'm going to have to make my breakfast to go, honey. Thank you. Maybe we can meet for lunch. Definitely dinner." I headed to the master bathroom to shower, but turned back to him just before opening the door. "Leon, I don't know what else to do."

He didn't say anything, just got up and left the room.

"Oh my," I whispered as I stepped into the kitchen a little while later, fully dressed and showered. Flowers, balloons, fruit, and homemade cookies filled the island, the breakfast bar, every corner, shelf, and countertop, in addition to the bacon and blueberry pancakes. A large banner was draped across the cabinets: HAPPY 40TH BIRTHDAY!

"And this is just what I had planned for the morning." Leon gave a weak smile.

I can spare fifteen minutes, I thought as pangs of guilt rippled through me; but he was already piling a paper plate high with his good home cooking, grabbing foil. "Take this with you." He licked some chocolate frosting from one of the cookies off his finger. "But promise me that you will meet up with me for lunch. The birthday girl deserves at least an hour or two off."

"Leon, thank you so much. I am truly touched. You are the best ever. You know I want to stay, but I don't know what to do. I am ethically responsible for the clients at my clinic, and I'm in charge of its operation. I can't just call out."

He shrugged and didn't hide the disappointment from his eyes. "Just meet me for lunch."

"I promise to," I replied, though I knew that there were no guarantees in the workday when it came to mental health and counseling.

So of course the day was nothing but crisis interventions: suicidal patients; one client discovering that her husband had a mistress; an issue with our billing service.

"I promised Leon that I would meet him," I explained to Darci at a quarter to twelve. He wanted us to meet at a halfway point between our jobs at a diner in Charles Village.

"Go ahead, Sienna. I can take care of the billing problem." She waved me off.

But then a walk-in came in, her eyes dripping tears as she screamed uncontrollably. What was I supposed to do?

I'll be there as soon as I can, I texted. He didn't text back.

Over two hours later I entered the pink and purple–painted diner that had velvet-covered benches for seats. A couple of patrons sat chatting in the booths and a single waitress joined in gossip as she floated from table to table.

No Leon.

"Cancel my appointments for the afternoon," I told Darci over the phone. There were only two clients left, old customers who had a history of being no-shows anyway.

I drove downtown to his bakery and saw through the window that he was serving platters of his finest pastries and cakes. A little larger crowd than usual filled the space as what appeared to be a busload of Inner Harbor tourists had discovered his bakery, hooked in by the tray of samples being passed out at the front door.

He couldn't leave work now, I knew.

And I understood. I appreciated what he did, how he had to be present to run his business. Why couldn't he give me the same courtesy without trying to make me feel guilty? I could not stop the question from forming in my head. I could not stop the sudden irritation that jolted through my system.

I took my business seriously and he needed to respect that. There were no easy decisions, even when those decisions had to be made on my birthday.

With an unexpected free afternoon and nobody to share it with, I decided to park my car near a street vendor not far from the courthouse. Hot dog and soda in hand, that's how I ended up in the War Memorial Plaza.

That's how I ended up running into Sweet Violet.

It would be the first of our several run-ins in the wide grassy plaza that sat between Baltimore City Hall and the War Memorial building.

"That ain't much of a lunch right there."

I recognized the voice, the smell, even before I turned around. "It's better than no lunch at all," I mumbled.

Leaning against the gray half wall that bordered the plaza, I looked down at the greasy hot dog I balanced in my hands. *Could have had a sit-down meal with my husband.* I swallowed down the piercing thought with a swig of soda and looked up at the elderly woman who now stood in front of me. Today she had on a familiar outfit: the pink running suit I'd given her to change into the night I drove her from the hospital to the shelter.

"Where are you staying these days?" I asked, taking a bite out of the hot dog, taking a chance with a question.

I had nothing better to do.

The woman didn't answer, just stared at me with an unreadable expression on her face.

"Are you hungry? Have you eaten today? I can get you something if you like," I tried.

Still silent.

"Is your name Frankie Jean or is it Sweet Violet?"

A dark glimmer washed over her eyes.

"Well?" I asked, wiping some mustard from my lips with a tip of a napkin. That one bite was enough to make me feel nauseous. I quickly took another sip of soda with the hopes that it would calm my churning stomach down. Or maybe it was the smell that was making me feel nauseated. The woman smelled worse than spoiled pig's feet on a hot summer day.

She mumbled something I could not make out and turned away.

"Wait," I called after her, tossing the half-eaten hot dog in a nearby receptacle. "I'm just asking your name, but if that upsets you, no worries. Let me get you lunch."

The woman kept mumbling. Her step quickened as she looked over her shoulder at me. I decided not to follow her, went back to my spot on the wall. The woman stopped walking, her back still to me.

Then she turned around and scurried back in front of me. "Why you asking me so many questions? Are you a cop or something?"

You a cop? The question jumped out at me, reminding me of the young boy child with old eyes who'd asked me the same thing the morning Ms. Marta was found shot dead.

"I'm a social worker. Remember we met at Metro Community? I gave you the outfit you're wearing now and dropped you off in front of A New Beginning House shelter."

The woman looked down at her pink outfit, looked back up at me. "I remember you." She smiled. "Forgive my manners. Sometimes I forget things. Life ain't nothing but constant details to remember." She stared off into the sky, shut her eyes, smiled, and started humming. Then frowned.

"What time is it, sugar?"

I checked my phone. "Four-nineteen."

"Less than an hour," she mumbled.

"What's less than an hour?"

"What time is it, sugar?" she asked again.

Alzheimer's? Dementia? Liquor? Drugs? Some kind of game? I wanted to make sense of this woman. Maybe that's why I could not just let this go.

"Do you need a watch? I found your pocket watch, remember? In your purse?"

Her eyes narrowed and I had the sudden urge to take a step backward, but I was already leaning against the wall. Nowhere to go.

"What did you do?" she hissed.

"What did I do? You mean with your purse or the watch?" I took a step to the left, as another dark wave rolled through her eyes. *Mental illness?* There were so many possibilities with this one. "I tried to give it back to you on New Year's Day, remember? You said you didn't want it, so I left it by that rose you planted, by that bottle of Old Grand-Dad you left in the dirt."

She smiled and began humming again. I watched as she closed her eyes and raised her arms as if she was going to start dancing.

"You like music. Did you used to be a singer? A performer?"

She ignored my question as she stepped from side to side, did an exaggerated plié. "Let me give you a tip for life, sugar." Her movement and tone changed instantly as she stood still and glared at me. "Don't ever try to mix business with pleasure. People say that phrase but don't understand what it means."

She began breathing hard, as if smoke would come out of her nostrils, steam out of her ears. I took another small step to the left.

"It won't work. It will leave you. It will just leave you." She shook her head, looked saddened. "There's a time for everything. That's what people don't understand. I learned that the hard way. There's time; and then it's gone. Poof." She clapped her hands and then wiggled her fingers.

I tried to understand her words, tried to find meaning in her statements; but I didn't know what was flashing through her head. I didn't know if she knew what was flashing through her head. She wasn't finished.

"It was a gift." The woman shook her head, sorrow in her voice.

"What was a gift? Time? Business? Pleasure?" I tried to keep up.

"That watch, stupid." She glared at me again, and then smiled. "It wasn't supposed to be, but it was a gift." She lowered her voice. "A very scary gift." She began dancing again.

"Who? Who gave you the watch?"

I knew there would be no answer. I watched as she continued dancing, swaying in the January sun. She swirled and spun, taking broad steps away from me. At one point, she stopped and looked up at the sky and laughed. Then she frowned again and walked away. I watched as she picked up a discarded bag of chips from the grass. She shook it, stuck her fingers in to grab some crumbs, and then went back to dancing.

"I'll look for you whenever I come by here," I called after her. "I'll get you lunch next time." If she heard me, she gave no indication, alternating between dancing and glaring up at the sky. She settled eventually on some wall space across the grassy expanse. I noticed a large plastic bag near where she sat.

Her earthly belongings, I assumed.

Yes, I would come back from time to time to see if she was here, to check on her; at least until I knew that someone else was looking out for her or until she accepted whatever help or resources I could offer her.

I was a social worker. My calling, not my comfort, dictated my actions, my being. Why didn't Leon get that about me? The thought bothered me again. Was I supposed to change who I was to make him happy?

There's a time for everything. I recalled the woman's words. That's all Leon had been asking of me. Time. It seemed so simple, yet had been too complicated. Why couldn't I get this right?

I got home on my birthday at a quarter 'til six. My heart jumped, sped up a little faster when I saw Leon's truck sitting in one of our assigned spaces.

"I'm home," I shouted as I entered the foyer. He was nowhere to be seen. The balloons, the flowers, the banner from the morning, had all been cleaned up, folded, moved to one side of a kitchen counter.

"Leon?" I raised an eyebrow when I entered our bedroom and saw him packing bowling shoes into a bag.

"Oh you're home." He zipped up the duffel.

"Yes, ready to celebrate." My son had promised a cruise for my fortieth birthday, I remembered, but we hadn't talked since Christmas. Random thought, wrong time. I swallowed it all down.

"I was invited to go bowling with Mike Grant, one of my old partners. You remember him?" He looked at me, looked down at his bag. "I figured you'd be working late so I told him I'd come. I had other plans for us, but I already canceled the reservation."

"I'm sorry, Leon."

"No, don't be." He shrugged. "It's your birthday. You should spend it the way you want to."

"I want to spend it with you. I just . . . had a lot to get done today."

"I know." He nodded. "Look, it will be a bunch of guys, but I'll see if any of the wives are coming. Maybe you can come too. We'll hang out. Make it a date."

"Sounds good, Leon. Sounds good."

He looked away, sighed. Shrugged. "Let's go."

As he stepped out of the room, I looked at myself in the mirror. I was just beginning to show, my pregnancy relegated to the prenatal vitamin routine I'd established in the morning and the extra bottle of water I washed down every night. Nothing in my life felt real, settled, or easy.

Though I was finally going to spend time with Leon on my special day, I knew that I had messed everything up. I wanted him and wanted our marriage to work more than anything, but just couldn't seem to get it right.

Old habits, mindsets, fears die hard. I had to work on me, but wasn't fully sure how. Why couldn't I just let this man love me?

I didn't know how to be Mrs. Sienna St. James Sanderson, Sienna Sanderson, Sienna . . .

I didn't even know how to get my own name right.

Chapter 27

Mentally. Physically. Spiritually. Emotionally.
Worn.

Yvette's small group session had been a breath of fresh air, but as I closed the door behind me, though I had walked outside, I felt as if I'd just enclosed myself into an airtight room.

The members of their circle had all said a prayer: a single, one-sentence prayer that kept anyone from taking over, and didn't allow anyone to feel out of place. The simplicity was comforting to me, necessary, as the rest of my life, my day, felt beyond complicated.

It was after ten p.m. now on what had to be the longest day of my life. The beating of my son, the supposed overdose of the attorney I'd been witnessing for, and now the mistaken arrest of my husband; one of these events would have been enough to topple a strong woman over.

And I didn't even feel strong to begin with.

I could hear my grandmother singing in my head, her strong soprano voice belting "Maybe God Is Trying to Tell You Something." I believed it, felt it, knew it, that He was.

But what was He telling me?

About Sweet Violet? Or about myself? Maybe both.

Yvette had given me her car keys after I told her I'd caught the bus to her home. No questions asked, no explanations given. The last time she'd let me hold her car it had broken down in a rural area of Pennsylvania and become part of a crime scene. Leon's truck was back at the bakery. I guessed she understood that I didn't want to drive it around until I was sure we weren't being followed, or something like that. I could hear my own paranoia.

Maybe Leon had a point. Maybe it was time that I stopped chasing my gut feelings all over the place. The only destinations my instincts seemed to bring me to were ones that were lonely and danger-filled. Terrible places to learn lessons.

I'm tired of repeating these tests, Lord. I'm going to get this lesson learned once and for all. I will stop going all over the place with my feelings and my caseload.

I had no idea where Roman was. I didn't know who picked him up, where he went; and my sense was that was what he wanted. After praying, talking, and fellowshipping with the crowd at Yvette's house, I'd been encouraged to get rest. "We have your back on this one," Yvette had told me as she walked me to her front door. "I'll call Skee-Gee's lawyer and see if he can help with anything."

"But before you do that, let me wait to hear back from some people I know at central booking." Mike promised to follow up with his contacts at the department, a small comfort that also disturbed me as he winked again.

Was I supposed to trust this man?

I just wanted my husband back with me. I didn't know what else to do, what could be done.

I went back to the hotel across from the courthouse: my home away from home for the past few weeks leading up to the trial. I'd been worried about the media intruding into my life, but obviously the threat to my person was bigger than just the flash of a camera or an intrusive microphone.

I could be dead right now.

The thought sobered me as I stuck the keycard in the hotel room door. Everything in me wanted to collapse. I wanted nothing more than my bed, my husband's arms, and my son's voice telling me that everything really was okay.

I entered the suite, flicked on the lights, and jumped.

"It's okay, Sienna."

Leon.

Sitting on a couch that faced the door and dressed in a polo shirt, jeans, and tennis shoes, he looked like he was about to go on vacation and not like a man just wrongly arrested for a crime he hadn't committed

"What? How?"

"It's okay, babe." He put his finger to his lips to quiet me. "I was able to finally talk and explain everything to the authorities, but we need to turn the lights back out. We can't afford to let anyone know we are here."

With the exception of the lamp I'd turned on, no other lights were on in the hotel suite. I noticed that even the appliances had been unplugged.

"What's going on? Leon?" I stepped toward him, ready to drop in his lap, cry, hold him, let him hold me.

"Not yet." He gently pushed me away and stood to his feet. "We gotta get out of here. I would have called you, but . . . Listen, we just need to get out of here."

He grabbed the suitcase that sat on the sofa and another bag I had not noticed behind the couch.

"It's clean in here," I noticed just before he turned the lamp back off. The counters on the kitchenette had been wiped down, cleared off. The piles of paper, magazines, and books that had been scattered throughout the living area were gone. I had a feeling that the bathroom counters where I'd put all my toiletries and sundries were all cleared and wiped down as well. But I only saw the two bags Leon reached for. *Where are our things?*

The darkness from the snapped out lamp was only temporary. Leon turned on a penlight and motioned toward an internal door that connected to the suite next to ours.

"What's going on, Leon? You're scaring me." I followed him to the door and we entered the next suite, also in darkness. "Leon, talk to me."

"We just have to get out of here. I'll explain in a moment, but we need to leave quietly." He shut the connecting door behind us, pulling it until its lock clicked. As he led me through the next suite, I noted that he smelled of soap and aftershave.

"You've showered. Where are we going, Leon? Where are our things?"

He shook his head to quiet me again and then he tried another connecting suite door. "Okay, we're going to leave out of this one." We stepped into a hallway, entered a stairwell, and went up a few levels. After emerging from the stairwell, Leon used a keycard to enter another room, this one an expansive penthouse suite that had several bedrooms and living areas. The floor-to-ceiling windows of the corner suite provided enough light from the nighttime cityscape that Leon was able to turn off the penlight. Or, maybe, he was afraid of someone seeing the light from outside the window. What was going on? I felt my heartbeat quicken as Leon led us to a private elevator in the rear of the penthouse.

"Did someone say we need to leave from here?"

Leon remained quiet as the soft whir of the elevator took us downward.

"Leon?"

"Nobody told us to go, but I'm not waiting either. You saw what happened today."

"Sw . . . Sweet Violet?" I whispered her name.

"No, Sienna." He frowned at me as the elevator continued its eleven-story plunge. "Please stop thinking that homeless woman is controlling your life and the people in it."

"Leon, the timing of it."

He didn't say anything.

"Leon, what is going on?" I could feel myself starting to hyperventilate as the elevator neared the ground floor. "You haven't told me where we are going or why. Please, Leon."

"Listen." My husband pulled me close to him. Spearmint was on his breath. He'd been chewing gum. He only chewed gum when he was nervous. I felt more alarmed. "Sienna, listen." He held my shoulders, shook me back to attention. "You are going to have to trust me right now."

"We're in danger, aren't we?"

He didn't answer and instead stared at the elevator buttons.

"What do you know, Leon?"

He still didn't answer.

"If it's not Sweet Violet, than what is it? What is going on? They let you go and told us to get away? Wait, no, you said nobody told us to go. You decided that's what we need to do. Leon, you need to tell me something."

"Why isn't our floor lit?" He still stared at the panel. He pressed G for the ground level again. It lit for a moment and then cut off once more.

"Leon, what—"

The elevator stopped with a sudden thud between levels one and two. The power went out.

"Sienna." He pushed me behind him, reached for something in his pants. Did he have another gun?

"Leon, what's going on?"

I felt sweat pooling through his polo shirt as I pressed close against his back.

"Shhh," he quieted me as the elevator returned to life, the soft whir returning, accompanied this time with a slight clicking sound. We reached the ground floor and the elevator stopped with a shiver and a bounce. The door seemed to hesitate before opening, but it finally did with a loud squeal.

We were in the underground garage of the hotel. A single light bulb flickered on a nearby wall casting shadows on a small parking area that served the private penthouse suite. As we stepped onto the parking pad, Leon kept me behind him, his eyes scanning over every corner of the enclosed parking space. A metal garage door was partially open at the end of a short ramp.

"Stay here," he commanded.

"Leon, you have to tell me something. What's going on? Who's after us and are you positive it has nothing to do with Sweet Violet?"

"We'll go over details later."

"So you're not positive."

"Sienna, please," he begged as he crept along the side of the cement wall. Though he had motioned for me to stay behind, I was right up on his heels.

I was not trying to be left alone anywhere, especially since I didn't know what was going on.

The garage felt humid, clammy. A loud drip echoed through the cavernous space.

"You have to tell me something," I whispered as we neared the partially opened garage door.

"I need you to trust me. Look, nobody said that we were in danger. The incident back at the shop, they think it was a robbery gone wrong. The would-be robbers thought the place was closed and got spooked when they realized that it wasn't. That's what's being investigated."

"Leon, you know that's not the case. It doesn't make sense. They said a reliable source called in a hostage situation. You were set up. How can you not—"

"Sienna, I have a feeling about something and you're going to have to trust me."

"So, we follow your gut feelings and completely ignore mine. I'm just supposed to follow blindly behind you while you shoot down any thoughts or insights I have."

"Sienna, not right now." His whisper was borderline yell.

"I don't know how, and I don't know why, but I firmly believe that all of this, the murders, the court case, the incident with Roman, the shooting, your arrest, all of it is somehow tied to that woman. You know that my instincts are good, so I don't understand why you keep brushing me off, or demanding my silence. I should have just told the authorities from day one about Sweet Violet instead of listening to you telling me not to do so."

Leon stopped in his tracks and turned to face me, the glint of his gun visible in his right hand. "I need you to trust me. Trust me."

I looked in his brown eyes and I saw panic in them.

Rare.

Frightening.

"Leon." I wanted to tell him that I did trust him, but that I needed him to trust me too. We were a partnership, right? We married each other because we valued each other's strengths, abilities, and perspectives, right? This is what I wanted to tell him, but something else took over the situation.

The garage door of the penthouse parking pad, which had already been partially open, began a slow, loud wind upward. The metal rattled and groaned in a sudden jolt. An alleyway was visible through the opening, but what had both silenced me and stiffened Leon's body was the pair of black boots standing on the other side.

Chapter 28

"Should we go back to the elevator?" I could feel my heartbeat in my throat as the door continued to lift. Leon, for his part, though standing taut, looked very much in control, calm. He didn't answer me as he kept his feet planted. The boots on the other side gave way to tan khakis, black gloves. Leon positioned his gun at the opening, both hands ready, cocked.

Just as the door fully extended, Leon jumped forward.

"Police!" he yelled, tackling a man who charged toward us. A streetlight at the end of the narrow alley provided the only source of illumination making the man a mere shadow in the darkness.

"Wait, wait!" the man exclaimed. The two were a jumble of arms, legs, and fists as I stood frozen. I realized I was instinctively both shielding my stomach and stifling a scream. *What do I do?* I panicked.

"Wait, Leon!" the man hollered again. The confrontation was over in seconds, both men now sitting separately on the ground, panting. Leon's gun was still in his hand, and a badge lay next to him by a clump of weeds that had broken through the alleyway pavement.

A badge?

The surprise on my face was echoed on Leon's but for different reasons.

"Mike, what are you doing here?" Leon jumped to his feet, wiping a trail of blood from off his lips. He looked at the red streak left on his palm as the other man, Mike Grant, jumped to his feet as well.

"I was just making sure she was safe, like you asked, man. You need to calm down with the jumpiness, brother." Mike straightened up his shirt, brushed some loose gravel off of his elbows. "I followed her here." He pointed to a black sedan with tinted windows parked behind a large Dumpster. Between the lack of light and its well-conceived hiding place, the dark vehicle was nearly invisible.

"You've been following me?" I stared at the sedan. *That car!* I knew I wasn't crazy. That had to be the one I saw speeding away when I entered the subway station earlier that day. Shavona and Mike had shown up at Yvette's house not long after I did, I recalled. He was helping to keep me safe? I tried to make sense of it all.

But that car . . . I was almost certain it was similar, if not the same one, that I'd seen Delmon Frank using months ago. No, that would not make any sense. Leon saw the confusion on my face, shook his head, and sighed.

"Don't try to figure all of this out, Sienna. I'll explain what I can to you, but we need to get out of here first." He and Mike began jogging toward the sedan.

"Shavona is still at Sienna's sister's house. One of the people there will see her home since I told them I was leaving to help you out." Mike spoke next and both he and Leon glanced back at me.

I caught up with them as my heartbeat tried to settle back down from my throat and resume in my chest. "But . . . but . . ." I pointed to the badge Leon had picked up from the ground. It hung from his fingers. "Leon, are you . . . I don't understand. You're not a cop anymore, so why do you have a badge?"

He and Mike looked at each other.

"I told you I need your trust, Sienna. Things aren't always as they appear." He looked again at Mike, who nodded back at him. "Look, Sienna," Leon continued as he opened the rear door of the sedan for me. I got in, and he followed, sitting next to me in the back as Mike got in to play chauffeur for the second time that day.

"You know that I came back to Baltimore to open my bakery. My heart is there, not only because I get to bake my grandmother's old recipes, but because I can offer a way out for the young people caught in the streets. You know from your social work experience that breaking that cycle is hard. I saw it with my brother, who was shot and killed despite my best attempts to save him. I saw it with my niece." Leon had never said much about his niece in Houston whom he'd gone to help and who he'd left after only a year of assistance.

"The more I've seen and the more I worked with some of those kids at my shop, the more I knew I had to do more than teach them how to bake cookies. I wanted to get to the root of the matter." Though we were moving, Mike had not yet turned on the car lights, I noticed.

"You're a social worker so you go about things your way: counseling, programs, that kind of thing," Leon continued. "I'm a cop by training, so I knew that I had to go about things the way I know: get the bad guys, shut down their operations at the highest levels. Mike told me months ago about a need for an undercover officer to help investigate some matters, and I was in a perfect position to take the job on. The department wouldn't have to train a new recruit, and nobody would suspect anything about my actions since I had the shop."

"So is that why things haven't been taking off at the bakery? Your attention is divided?" I had many questions, many, many questions, and I wasn't sure how I felt about him not telling me any of this. "What exactly are you investigating?"

His and Mike's eyes met in the rearview mirror. "Baby." Leon squeezed my hand. "I can't get into any of that right now, but just know that when I pleaded with you not to get involved in all these cases, I had my reasons." He looked at me. "I couldn't tell you any of this because we couldn't afford to have your perspective or testimony influenced about the cases."

"Drugs," I concluded. The state's attorney's office, the investigators, had all stated that the murders were drug related. If Leon was so passionately against me being involved as it affected whatever he was doing, that was the only type of investigating I could think of that he'd be involved in. It made sense, too; if his concern was reaching kids who were going off track, most of the off-track roads in Baltimore began and ended with the illegal drug industry.

His silence at my assertion confirmed my line of thought.

"Delmon Frank drove a car like this one." I could not ignore the certainty I felt about my memories. He'd gotten into a black sedan with tinted windows the morning Ms. Marta was killed. And, though it had been dark and it had been at a distance, I was pretty certain that same car he drove was the one I'd seen parked near a streetlamp when I dropped Sweet Violet off at the shelter in the dark hours of the morning.

I still had a lot of questions.

"He's undercover too, babe." Leon's eyes looked straight as Mike drove through alleyways and narrow side streets to get out of downtown.

"What? Who? Delmon is a cop?" I did a double take.

"Are you a cop?"

I recalled wanting to laugh when he'd asked me that. Dressed in church clothes and on a social work mission, I knew I looked the furthest thing from a woman in blue when I approached him on that street by the original crime scene. Leon was right: everything was not what it seemed.

"He's undercover, but was in the wrong place at the wrong time, and blowing his cover, even now with the trial, would be fatal to years of investigative work. I can't get into details, Sienna, but we're close."

"That's why the trial was so speedy. I didn't think a triple homicide case would turn around in the court system that quickly. That makes better sense now, but Alisa Billy is dead. What happens next? Did she know? Who else knows? And what would have happened if he was found guilty?"

"I know you have a lot of questions, but I really can't, I really shouldn't, get into it all right now." He looked at me as the car veered onto 83. "Frank's own defense team doesn't know the truth. His lawyer, as I understand it, has no idea that he's really an undercover. It's a sticky, delicate, dangerous situation, with a fine, shaky line dividing the good guys from the bad. That's why I didn't want you getting involved in any of this. That's also why I've been staying close to you."

"Armed and ready."

"Of course; you're my wife and the mother of my soon-to-be-here child." He reached out a hand, patted my stomach. "I will always, always protect you."

"Wait. Alisa Billy is dead, so the case is on indefinite pause. Was that supposed to happen? That wasn't part of the plan to keep Delmon's identity protected, was it?"

"Of course not. Her death was off script and only complicates matters. She didn't even know the danger she was in. Her assistant, Joe Koletsky, was supposed to be protecting her, but that call she got to come back to the courthouse immediately took her out of his reach."

"So, she didn't just overdose on prescription drugs." I wasn't asking. I already knew the answer.

"Of course not." Leon leaned forward as Mike turned onto an exit. "But this is a very public case handling a very private, dangerous affair. For the integrity of the case, the public needs to think no foul play was involved. If they thought otherwise, the media would begin asking too many questions of the wrong people."

I sat quiet for a moment, letting these new details absorb, knowing that my questions and conclusions would only increase as I thought more about it all.

We turned onto Maryland Avenue. It was dark, way past eleven o'clock at night. Traffic was light, the car lights finally on as we zoomed through the neighborhood of Charles Village.

The route looked familiar.

"We came this way earlier today when you dropped off Roman."

"Safe house," Leon answered my unspoken question.

"So Roman knows everything?"

"No. He knows very little. Except what was absolutely necessary for him to know."

"There was something he wanted to ask me," I remembered. I also remembered the five dollars and eleven cents that had been found on his person. "Everything is all related."

"Sienna, I really don't want you worried about this. You have incomplete information and it needs to stay that way for the time being."

"Why were we shot at? Why is Alisa dead? I need some kind of answer, Leon. This is crazy. Obviously, we are in danger. You can tell me only half a story and think I'm going to stay calm about it?"

"Sienna, you are nearly eight months pregnant with our child. This entire pregnancy has been filled with one disaster after another. I need you to stay calm. I need you to know that I am taking care of things. For once in your life, you need to let go of your desire to control things and let me handle this. Please, just trust me."

"So that's it, that's the real reason why you don't want to share more details with me, because I'm pregnant. Yes, I'm pregnant. That doesn't mean that I'm helpless. Maybe you're forgetting that I've spent the last twenty years being a strong, independent woman capable of completing projects, helping clients, starting a business, even helping to capture a person who was a national threat."

"Sienna, of course I know you are a strong, independent woman. I know that being pregnant does not change the essence of who you are; but right now, I'm asking you to accept some dependency, to trust me enough to take care of matters that extend far beyond what you know or think in regard to this case. I'm not asking you to be less of the woman you are; I'm simply asking if you can accept fully the man I am."

"Do we need to turn back around and go to that prayer circle at Yvette's house?" Mike chuckled from the front seat. "Y'all gettin' serious up in here." The car pulled to a stop in front of a towering bow-front row home on Maryland Avenue. From the looks of things, no lights were on. I closed my eyes, tried to breathe. Anger, worry, confusion had all combined to make me feel sick.

"You think we should go around back?" Leon asked. Mike complied, turning the car into a narrow alleyway behind the row of white-painted brick homes. The car's lights were back off. Mike eased to a stop in a parking space partially hidden by a large oak tree and a series of evergreen bushes. At last, he shut the engine.

"Wait." Leon grabbed my shoulder as I reached for the door. A few seconds passed and then a tiny prick of light, like that of a penlight, filtered through some miniblinds covering a basement window.

"Okay." Leon pulled at the car door handle. "Let's go."

I followed Leon and Mike out of the car and down a stairwell that took us to a basement door. Maybe I'd watched too many movies or TV shows, but despite the old home's historic outward façade, I expected to walk into a high-tech room filled with the latest gadgets and all things digital.

Instead, the basement looked and smelled like, well, an old, mildew-filled basement in desperate need of a make-over. The walls were colorless cinderblock, the floor old black linoleum. A concrete wash basin covered with dust sat in a corner next to a washing machine that looked like it had seen better days back in the eighties. A large brown carpet square sat in the middle of the open space and on it was a cheap futon and a desk with a computer, printer, and several closed-circuit TVs.

An older white man with thick black glasses and a dead cigarette butt hanging out the corner of his mouth sat in front of the desk. A stack of papers and a half-eaten club sandwich sat in front of him.

I recognized him immediately.

Detective Sam Fields.

Years ago, I'd gotten mixed up with some twin sisters who had a vindictive and deadly mother. The two had gone into hiding without a trace and the man in front of me was the detective who had made their disappearance possible. I never did fully understand how his one-man operation worked—the business cards he'd given me back then led me to a pizza shop—but he must be good. I realized then that those twins, who at one time had been five o'clock breaking news features, had left the media radar without a trace.

His presence both encouraged and frightened me.

Why is he here?

"All right, the passports are ready and a doctor's note for her to board the plane is in this envelope." He patted the stack of papers. "Happy anniversary."

"Passports?" Leon's face wrinkled. "We don't need passports for Miami."

"Your itinerary has changed. You are indeed flying to Miami as planned so as not to raise any suspicions. However, once you get to MIA, you're going to transfer to a private charter flight to Freeport. You should be happy. Not many newlyweds get to spend their first anniversary in a private villa in the Bahamas."

What?

"Um, Leon, what is he talking about? Are we supposed to be flying to another country when I'm this close to my due date? This seems a little extreme. Is it really necessary? What is going on?"

From the frown on Leon's face, I could tell he had the same reservations.

"I've taken care of everything." Sam Fields had a gravely sounding voice that cut into whatever Leon had been about to say. "The medical forms clear Sienna for both airplane and international travel, and I've got you staying in a villa near a hospital and a private physician on call if needed. The doctor's an expat from Boston who used to head up a labor and delivery unit in one of the major hospitals up there."

"Wait a minute, our trip to Miami was only for three nights." A new swarm of fears and questions flooded me as I tried to make sense of this new information. "My clients, my baby, my life; Leon, all of this is moving too fast and is not making sense. You are going to have to give me something, some information. I need to know what's going on. This plan seems too extreme and unnecessary," I repeated as my head spun.

"Sienna, none of this is what I was expecting myself. This isn't what I had in mind and I can't say I like this either." Leon rubbed his forehead, sighed. "But I promised that I would always take care of you and keep you, and our baby, safe. I know I am asking a lot of you to trust me even when you don't have all the details, but if this is what it takes to ensure your safety, this is what we're going to have to do."

"So let me make sure I understand why the two of you are upset," Mike chimed in. "You are having a baby and you are getting an extended trip to the Bahamas. Those are your horrible problems, right? Am I missing something?" He turned his head to one side and looked back and forth between me and Leon.

I felt like I was going to explode. I threw my hands up in the air, looked at my husband, hoping, wishing, praying that he understood the tumultuous sea of emotions in which I was adrift.

"Mike." Leon's voice was low, calm. "It's been a crazy day for Sienna, for both of us. She's provided testimony for a murder trial, dealt with her son being attacked, witnessed the death of the attorney she was assisting. She's been shot at, traumatized, and just learned that the whole thing is deeper than she realized as far as my involvement."

"And that trip to the Bahamas is sounding worse by the moment." Mike shook his head.

Was I crazy for feeling what I did? I couldn't even name the feeling. Just felt it. All in my stomach, my head, my nerves.

"Roman," I whispered, my voice hoarse as if I'd been yelling for hours. "What about Roman? I may not know what's going on, but I know enough to know that he's in danger. Look at what happened to him today. Maybe, maybe, he does need to go back to India." Had I actually said that? Were things that bad at the moment that I actually wanted him to go running off to another country with some girl, excuse me, woman I barely knew?

I didn't miss that Leon and Sam Fields exchanged glances.

"What's wrong? Is Roman okay?"

"Roman's fine." Leon quickly assured me. "You do need to talk to him. I think he's ready to talk to you now. I know he's ready to talk now."

"Mike said he got into a car in front of Yvette's house. Do you know where he went? Is he okay?" My voice faded into a whisper.

"He's upstairs," Leon spoke barely above a mumble himself. "Mike told me where he was and I sent for him."

"Upstairs?" I looked up at the ceiling as if it were glass, as if I could see through it to wherever my son sat waiting.

I assumed he was waiting, I realized. Leon said Roman was ready to talk, but what if he was wrong?

Trust me, baby. I could hear Leon's voice pleading with my consciousness.

"Remember, this is a safe house. Roman is here and he is safe."

"I'm going to go talk to him." I turned toward the basement staircase, a series of white plaster-covered steps.

"Do that, Sienna, but just know we don't have long. We have to get to the airport."

"Your flight is not until tomorrow evening." Sam Fields was packing up some papers, stuffing them into a briefcase I just noticed he'd had by his foot.

"What?" Leon spun around to face the squat but solid man.

"It's the best I could do on such short notice." Sam finished his club sandwich in two bites.

"Surely there are plenty of flights from Baltimore to Miami before tomorrow evening," Leon countered.

"For the precautions you needed me to take, including looking out for your wife's delicate condition, tomorrow evening is what it is. Your flight leaves at five-thirty; your charter to Freeport is at nine-thirty and you'll arrive at your private beachfront villa at ten-thirty p.m., in the cover of darkness."

"I don't like this." Leon shook his head.

The detective shrugged. "Best I could do. You're safe right here. Just follow protocol. A cab will be around to get the three of you tomorrow between three and three-thirty." He grabbed his briefcase, tossed the sandwich wrapper in a metal trashcan and exited from the same backdoor we'd entered.

"The three of us?" I looked at Leon and the other two men in the room. Was Mike going with us to the Bahamas? I was thoroughly confused. As if reading my mind, Mike answered.

"Roman."

"He's not going back to India?"

"Just talk to him." Leon collapsed onto the futon. "Talk to him. We have plenty of time now. Use this penlight to get around upstairs and stay away from the windows. Don't worry, though. Nobody can see in. I'll meet you upstairs after you talk to him." His voice faded with each word. His eyes began to close.

"And I'll stay guard." Mike sat down at the desk, messed with some knobs on the closed-circuit television, punched some keys of the computer, and brightened the monitor.

"Shavona?" Leon asked as he kicked off his shoes, stretched out completely on the long, narrow futon.

It had been a long, exhausting day for him, for both of us.

"I'll tell her the usual, that I was called in to work an extra shift. Not really a lie, you know." Mike leaned back in the desk chair.

Leon sighed and a half second later I heard a soft snore coming from his full lips. I had always been amazed at his ability to fall asleep instantly, but after getting a peek at his real day job, his nightly exhaustion made sense. I would have passed out permanently from exhaustion if my normal day was half of what today was.

For all the danger and fatigue I now knew he'd been facing, I wished I could go back and hug and hold him even more during our past year's nights together.

I started up the stairs, but not before looking back. Leon was flat on his back. Mike looked up at me.

And winked several times.

I hurried up the stairs.

Roman was asleep in a bedroom on the third level.

Despite the sparse appearance of the basement, the rest of the house was in pristine, designer condition. Updated kitchen with granite countertops and stainless steel appliances. A large foyer painted in shades of bright white and mint green. Airy curtains.

I guessed if a neighbor or misdirected delivery person knocked on the door, nobody would ever suspect that the house served as a sanctuary of sorts. Pictures on the walls and magazines in the foyer spoke to international travel, luxury hotels, and exotic destinations. Looked like the neighbors were led to believe that the owner of the home, who probably "showed up" from time to time, was a world traveler who took frequent trips.

Great way to keep the house undisturbed and well maintained. Great way to prevent suspicions or draw attention.

I found Roman in the master suite of the home, all six feet plus of him curled up in a fetal position in a king-sized canopy bed. Shining the penlight on him, I saw that he still had a few bandages on and the swelling around his eyes looked about the same as it had when we'd left the hospital earlier that evening.

Had it all really been the same day?

I looked at a digital clock on a nightstand. 12:32. Tomorrow was today, I realized, yawning, feeling the weight of fatigue heavy on my eyelids.

"My baby." I pulled at the tight curls that framed his round face "Not my baby anymore." I gave a half smile as a swift kick on the inside landed just under my ribs. That was the strongest kick yet. A mother of a twenty-one-year-old and an infant.

Starting over.

And what a start it was shaping up to be.

I'd had enough excitement for the day and Roman looked content in his sleep, no strain, no anger, no contempt. I wanted him to stay like that so I let him sleep.

We had time.

I could wait until the morning to talk to him, to find out what it was he had to ask me, and, hopefully, understand why his travel plans had changed. Was it just a safety concern? Not that I wanted him to go to India, especially in his bruised and battered state; but something told me that his change in itinerary had little to do with the events of the day.

Both my men were sleeping.

I decided to let the day be over for myself. Roman needed his rest. I needed a clear mind and a fresh start.

We had time.

I retreated to a bedroom I found across the hallway from him, curling my toes on the thick white carpet, and then crashing into a mound of white, down pillows.

Sleep never felt so tortured and so sweet.

Chapter 29

Screeching tires.

I sat straight up in the bed, still wearing the same clothes from the day before, a shoe on one foot, the blankets only partially turned down. I rubbed my eyes, focused them, trying to remember where I was and why.

Oh.

I crashed back down into the soft pillows, wishing the nightmare I was living would revert to a dream and the sweet peace I'd had while sleeping would be my reality.

More screeching tires.

I sat back up.

Though a clock by the bed read 7:39, the room was still heavy in darkness, the shades over the windows obviously some type of extra-duty strength of opaqueness. Nobody most certainly could see into this place, because I most certainly could not see out. The screeching tires belonged to the morning rush hour, I realized.

I fixed my eyes on the doorway, looked across the hall. The door to the room where Roman had been sleeping was closed.

"Roman!"

Remembering my questions, my fears, from the night before, I hopped out of bed, rushed to the bedroom door and knocked.

No answer.

I held my breath, pushed it opened.

The bed was empty.

Though I'd just gotten several hours of sleep, an exhaustion that defied words took over me and I crumpled down to the floor. Alone, confused, anxious, I didn't know what to even think, say, or do next.

"Ma."

The voice came from behind me, the touch on my shoulders gentle then strong as Roman, who emerged from another room, was suddenly standing next to me, helping me up.

"Leon will be back later. I fixed breakfast. Come on, eat."

I followed him to the room he'd just come out of and marveled at its setup. With a computer desk and closed-circuit TVs lining several tables, this "bedroom" looked the way I'd expected the basement to look, and then some. Gadgets, gizmos, and other high-tech devices lined the long tables and folding chairs that were crammed in the all-white space. It was some type of command room, two stories above the front entrance and tucked in what looked like a spare bedroom from the hallway.

"It's just us here, but don't worry. Leon showed me what code to press if something unexpected happens. Help would get here in minutes, he said. Plus, there's a real panic room through the closet." Roman pointed. "It's fireproof, bulletproof, and bombproof with no way for any unwanted intruder to get in."

"Not sure if that makes me feel better, considering the possibilities." We both grinned. Felt like old times.

Except my stomach was heavy with child, we were in a safe house with a panic room, and we were preparing to leave for a trip out of the country in less than twelve hours.

"I'm sorry, Mom." Roman looked down. "I . . . I . . ."

"Roman, I'm sorry too." A long pause. Quiet. Peace. "You said you fixed breakfast?" The time for answers would come. For now, we were dancing cautious baby steps around our reconciliation.

"Downstairs."

I followed him down a narrow rear staircase to a kitchen that made me jealous. Seeing it now with the lights on, I appreciated the workmanship and high-end features of the cabinetry and appliances. *Someone put a lot of money into this place for it to be of occasional use.*

We moved in silence: he putting ceramic plates filled with sausage, eggs, and toast on the kitchen island; me pouring tall glasses of orange juice I found in the well-stocked refrigerator. Our dance was a delicate one.

We hadn't had a real conversation since Christmas, about six months ago. After a few bites of food and more silence, I couldn't take it anymore.

"Roman."

"Ma."

We spoke at the same time. I put my fork down.

"So, you're not going back to India." Was that really where to begin? I watched as Roman's lips tightened. He dragged a forkful of eggs around his plate. I quickly added more. "I'm sorry about what happened to you yesterday, and that it disrupted your plans."

Roman put the fork down and shook his head. "You're not really sorry. You didn't want me to go anyway."

"Roman, I—"

"You would rather I be put in a psych ward than let me live my own life."

"It was a mistake. I was frantic and I didn't want—"

"You didn't want me to make the same mistake you made chasing my father around the world. I get it." He looked up at me for a second and I saw something I hadn't seen in his eyes for years.

Tears.

"I'm sorry, Roman."

"Don't be. You were right. There, I said it. Let's get it over with." His words settled like a wet blanket, heavy, suffocating. On both of us.

"Roman, I want you to be happy. I want you to experience love. This wasn't about me being right or wrong. I just didn't want you to get hurt. You've been through enough. I didn't want you to go through anything else, especially all the way on the other side of the world." I paused. "I know what it's like to wake up on another continent questioning everything you think you know about love, realizing that choices you've made can't be undone. You are a great student, almost halfway through college, and I didn't want your choice to ruin your educational chances and your future."

Roman let out a loud sigh, sat back in his seat.

"How is it there? India." I could not say the girl's name. We both knew this was the closest I'd get to asking at the moment about their relationship.

Roman leaned forward in his seat, picked at his eggs again. "I never went."

"Excuse me?"

He put the fork down, looked me in the face. "I said that I never went. I didn't go."

"Wha . . . Why? What happened?"

"I misinterpreted her intentions. I mean, she misinterpreted mine."

"What do you mean?"

"I . . . We . . . After you had the cops manhandle me at the airport, she asked me if I'd gotten your permission to come with her. I told her, I said, 'I don't need my mother's permission to love you.'" Roman bit his lip before continuing. "She looked at me in horror when I said that. I didn't understand why at first, but then this man, her fiancé, comes up and hugs and kisses her."

"Fiancé?" My mouth dropped open.

"I misunderstood. I thought we were in a relationship, but she just saw me as an employee and an assistant who would help her build her business and look for her kids. She was bringing me to India to work for her since I offered to help and had spent so much time providing her technical support. She . . . We weren't a couple, and I somehow missed that."

"Oh, Roman." I shook my head, not sure how to feel about this new twist. I didn't want him with her, but I hurt for my boy. He blinked back tears.

"It was the most embarrassing moment of my life." He looked back up at me. "That whole morning was the most embarrassing of my life." He shook his head. "I don't understand love anymore. I thought she loved me. I thought my father loved me. And . . ." He paused. "I thought you would never hurt me, but you did."

"I'm sorry, Roman. I didn't handle things right. I'm sure Changuna wasn't trying to hurt you, and your father, well, I'm not really sure what to say about him, but don't give up on love, son."

"I prayed about India, Ma. It's the one time in my life I really prayed about something, even more than when I was looking for my father, for RiChard. I really thought God was guiding my steps. But He left me hanging in the long run. I wasn't supposed to go and He didn't tell me. If I don't know for sure that God is hearing me and guiding me, if I don't know for sure what love is supposed to look like and feel like, how am I supposed to have a relationship with Him? You see? I'm not getting it, Ma, and it hurts too much to figure it out. It's not just you and Dad and Changuna. God hurt me too, Ma."

I started to tell him that God had been screaming at him through his mother not to go, but, no, that was not the way to go.

"Roman, God is bigger than our pain and He uses every detail of our lives to shape us into His purposes. I hear you about not understanding everything. Believe me; I've had a few talks with King Jesus on the very matter. Maybe I haven't been the best example for you in these things, especially when it came to my former bitterness over your father. However, one thing I've learned for sure is that God doesn't expect us to understand everything. He just wants us to trust Him. Trust Him with even how you feel right now, your questions, your confusion, your anger, your pain. He hasn't let you go. When you are praying and seeking Him, sometimes He's simply speaking through the silence."

"All right, Reverend Mother." Roman chuckled.

I laughed along with him. "If you think I sound like a preacher, you should hear your Aunt Yvette. If you are having any questions about God's power to move and change lives, actually come into her house on a small session night."

"A what?"

"Long story. But a powerful one." I rubbed my belly. "God loves us. I can't explain it, or fully define it, but God loves us and His timing for every event in our lives is perfect. His timing has a specific purpose and a perfect plan. Don't worry, Roman. God has a time for everything, even a time for love. You'll meet the right one, and unlike me, I'm sure you won't waste two decades of your life trying to recover from a mistake. You've been able to talk out your feelings and fears right after your heartbreak. It took me your whole life time to finally get to the point where you are now."

"So if you are feeling all better, what's going on with you and Leon?"

"Excuse me?"

"He always looks sad and you always look mad. What happened to your 'time for love,' as you put it?"

I felt my hips shift in the seat. Prickly heat rose off my forehead. *Does this boy think he has the right to question my relationship with my husband?*

Roman shrugged at my unresponsiveness, returned to dragging eggs around his plate. I wanted to get the heat of the spotlight off of me so I turned it back onto him.

"So, is your semester going well since you didn't go to India? Were you able to register for the classes you wanted since your plans changed? There's so much we haven't talked about, Roman. You need to catch me up on everything."

Now he squirmed in his seat.

"What is it?" I asked.

"I didn't go back to school. Yet. I didn't know how to tell you about Changuna and I was too embarrassed."

"So, the campus apartment you were sharing with Croix in San Diego?" I realized I had not even scratched the surface of my questions for him.

"He's still there, and I've been sending him money for the rent every month as promised. Just now instead of coming from a job in India, the funds are coming from my job in Baltimore."

"Baltimore?" My head snapped back. "You mean to tell me that you've been in town all of this time?"

"Yes." His voice was barely above a whisper. "I missed out on the semester, but I can return in the fall, they said. I was going to fly out yesterday evening to take a summer course, but, well, you know that didn't work out. Don't worry, though. I'm going to take classes over the winter break and next summer, and extra credits during the spring and fall. I will still graduate on time. I got this, Ma. I promise you. I got this."

I saw the determination in his eyes, a steely, stubborn, "won't stop 'til it's done" determination I recognized. He had his mother's genes, for better or for worse, that was for sure.

"Plus, Ma," he continued, "I've been working and saving up so you don't even have to worry about supplying any extra money for those extra semesters."

"Wait a minute. Where have you been working? And where have you been staying?"

"I've been living right here in this house. Leon set it all up for me through Mr. Mike."

"Leon knew? And Mike? Leon's been involved this whole time?" A feeling washed through me so quickly I couldn't pinpoint what it was. Anger? Betrayal? Confusion?

"Yeah, he didn't want me to tell you anything, I guess because of the case he's working on, and also because I . . . I wasn't ready to talk to you and he respected that. But you're here now, so I'm telling you everything."

"What have you been doing? Where have you been working?" I couldn't believe what I was hearing.

"I was helping out at the bakery."

"Leon's shop?" I gasped. "I've never seen you there."

"Because you're never there, Ma." He let the words settle. "In the beginning, I was afraid to work there because I thought I'd get found out, but Leon was right. You never come to his shop. You are always caught up in your own business."

"Leon knew? He said . . . I . . ." I could not believe what I was hearing and I truly didn't know how to feel about all of it. Had I been that caught up in my own world that I didn't know my own son was hiding in plain sight? And Leon knew all of this and kept me from knowing the truth?

I could feel steam rising from my head.

"Mom, there's something else I think you should know." He paused, scratched his cheek, as I held my breath. What more could possibly be said? "Leon said it was nothing and not to worry you about it, but I think I've inherited some of your instincts. Something isn't sitting right with me."

"What is it, Roman?" I could feel my heart quicken. Baby must have felt it too 'cause little feet pounded and stomped into my rib cage. I shifted in the seat to settle us both down.

"I was about to get in that cab when that group of guys jumped me, right? Well, I don't know who they were, but I got the sense someone put them up to it."

"Why? Who?" My questions would not end.

"The cab driver. He stopped right in front of me and then those boys jumped me. It was odd the way it happened, like he was pointing me out for those boys to get me. It didn't feel random. I know you've been involved with that court case and all, so I wasn't sure if it was all related. That's what I wanted to ask you about, if you think we're all being targeted."

"Did you talk to the police about your suspicions?"

"No. What was I supposed to say? Everyone knows the cab stopped and then the boys jumped. I can't prove my feelings. I did tell the cops what I heard the driver shout out to the boys."

"What was that?"

"He said, 'Don't kill him.' That doesn't mean anything, necessarily. He could have just been a concerned citizen yelling at those guys before he drove away. Or . . ."

"Or what?"

"He could have been giving them directions. That's what it felt like, as if he was telling them to hurt me but not kill me; but how can I prove anything?" He studied my face, and then apologized. "I'm sorry, Ma, I'm not trying to upset you. Leon didn't want me worrying you. He said that you get worked up over minor details, and he doesn't want all this to affect your pregnancy." Roman stared down at my stomach as if he was seeing it for the first time. His eyes stayed glued on my belly for a moment as I tried to process the mounds of info he'd just shared.

"There's a real person in there, huh?" He leaned forward and squinted his eyes at my belly as if he had some type of X-ray vision. "Am I having a brother or a sister?" He looked up at my face, finally pushing away his plate for good.

I didn't answer him. I couldn't answer him.

I knew Leon was just trying to protect me and the baby, but I had reached my final straw with him deciding what I needed to know or not know. We were talking about major things here: his work as a cop, my son's whereabouts and wellbeing, my feeling that something greater was going on than he wanted to notice or admit.

Sweet Violet.

"Roman," I managed to get out, "have you ever seen an old homeless woman wandering anywhere near you?"

He raised an eyebrow. "Huh?"

"A woman in a long black coat, or maybe a pink sweat suit?" I shut my eyes trying to think of other outfits I'd seen her wearing during our conversations in the War Memorial Plaza.

"No, Ma. I have no idea what you're talking about." He shook his head, stood, and stretched. "I'm going to go wash up." He left the table, leaving me to my thoughts, just as I knew he'd slipped away to process his own.

I'd run into Sweet Violet a few times over the last six months. Her conversations were disjointed, broken memories, random nonsense, with occasional philosophical statements that gave me pause. I thought back to our New Year's conversation.

"Flowers can't tell lies. If you keep the sun off of them, dry up their waterbeds, and throw in weeds to choke 'em out, ain't no way or reason for them to bloom."

That rose she'd admitted to planting had looked so out of place, I recalled, and like everything else that seemed to be happening lately, nothing made sense, nothing seemed to be what it appeared to be.

"If a rose is in full bloom when you know it's only been kept in darkness, and the ground it's planted in is cracked and cold, don't stop to smell that rose. There's a trap somewhere in those tempting dark red petals. There's deceit. Maybe even death. Run from that flower-bed. You don't want to get buried in that soil."

A trap. Deceit. What was I missing? Here I was caught up in a murder trial that had put my life and my family's lives and wellbeing in danger. Now I knew that there was a bigger matter going on: undercover operations, the target of which I was not privy to. My husband, apparently knew more of what was going on than I did, and wanted me to trust him.

And all I was stuck on was Sweet Violet.

Did she have anything to do with my current situation? That was the main question I wanted answered at the moment. She showed up at random times and had been near all three murder scenes in person or via her property. Dropped her off at the shelter then Sister Marta is shot. Her purse was given to me by Amber and then the young girl ends up dead. She toasts a tree on New Year's and a popular respected businessman and philanthropist ends up shot by the bullet of two arguing men.

Leon said the suspect for the murders was really an undercover cop who couldn't have his cover blown just yet. So that meant someone else, the real killer, was involved, right? Leon also downplayed any reference I'd made to Sweet Violet over the months, stating she had nothing to do with any of it.

What if he was just saying that?

"Where's Roman?"

I nearly jumped out of my seat at his voice.

"Leon, I didn't hear you come in." I stared at my husband who'd just emerged from the basement. "There really needs to be some type of camera or security screen on this floor and not just the other levels. You really scared me coming in like that."

"There is a camera." He went to a kitchen cabinet and swung it open. A small black-and-white screen revealed Mike coming in through the basement door. He closed the cabinet and looked back at me. "You talk to Roman?"

"Yes. And he told me everything. Everything." I stared at him. "Leon, why have you kept me in the dark about so many things? You want me to trust you, but how can I, knowing that you were willing to keep my own son's whereabouts from me all this time? How could you?"

"I know you are upset, but please know that everything I've done, every decision I've made over the past few months, has been for your best interest. You are forty and pregnant with the media following you and a heavy trial hanging over your head. The last thing you needed was one more ounce of unnecessary stress."

"But my son, Leon? You hid my son from me?"

"Roman was angry with you and I didn't want him saying something to you that would scar the both of you too much. I didn't want him to say something that he couldn't take back and that you wouldn't get over. He didn't want to talk to you and I wasn't going to force it. When he showed up yesterday, I knew he was on the road back to reconnecting with you, and it sounds like that is what is happening. You and he are talking now, right?"

I shut my eyes, wiped tears from them. "I don't know what to say to you right now." I opened my eyes and glared at him. "Just answer this one question for me, no secrets, no half truths. Sweet Violet. What is her role in all of this?"

Leon shook his head, sighed. "Sienna, as far as I know and as much as I can tell, that woman has absolutely nothing to do with any part of the case."

"Everything in me says she does, Leon."

"Sienna, you do realize that you got sucked up into this whole trial because you wouldn't leave her alone. You are so adamant about proving your gut right, that it never occurs to you that you may be wrong."

"Leon, you want me to trust you, and I do. I need you to trust me too. I know what I feel, and I've got good instincts. I need you to have some faith in me as well."

I looked in his eyes, saw tiredness, exhaustion really. He didn't answer right away. He looked over at one of the suitcases we had packed for our trip.

"Sienna, our plane leaves this evening. If you want to do your own digging for answers about Sweet Violet, that's how much time we have. Please know that I do have trust in you, babe. I just don't want you getting hurt or getting pulled into this foolishness more than you already have been."

"I need to find her, get some real answers."

"You're not going to do anything without me. We're together now."

"Then that's what we need to do: work together. No more secrets. No more arguments. No more hidden plans or agendas."

Leon nodded. He took out his phone and set an alarm. "We have exactly seven hours before the cab comes to take us to the airport."

I nodded. "Where do you want to begin? How do we figure out exactly who Sweet Violet is?"

"I'm following your lead. This is your case. I'm just assisting and protecting. Where does your gut tell you to begin?" He sighed again. "I can't believe I'm going along with this, Sienna."

I thought about it a moment, tried to think rationally, but quickly, while I still had his support.

"The shelter," I decided. "Let's go to the shelter where I dropped her off."

Leon reached down into a holster hidden in his waistband. He pulled out a gun, loaded it, and put it back in its hiding place.

"Just in case," he responded to the alarm on my face. "Let's go."

Chapter 30

"I'm sorry. I wish I could say that I know who she is, but I don't. I'm sorry that I can't help you."

We were sitting in Sister Agnes's office at A New Beginning House. The older lady had her graying blond hair pulled back into a tight bun. We'd just caught her after morning chapel service. Residents, or rather guests, had already been fed their breakfasts and dismissed for the day.

No daytime loitering was the policy here. The women were welcome to return at sunset.

"Sister Marta, the morning she was killed, informed me that the woman's name was Frankie Jean. She said that she had only been coming to the shelter for a short time. I dropped her off here early that morning after she showed up at Metro Community Hospital wearing nothing but a blue housecoat and slippers."

"I know the ladies who come in and out of here on a daily basis, and that description just doesn't sound like anyone I've seen. I can't imagine that Marta would hide anyone from me." Sister Agnes had a stern face, but her eyes lightened for a moment. "You know Marta worked here for nearly four decades? She came here as a guest herself back in the early seventies when my husband and I started this mission. She came here homeless and frightened and desperate and ended up staying here permanently as a staff member, our best staff member ever." A tear washed down her cheek. The grief, the sorrow, looked genuine.

"She kept the ladies here in line, and truthfully the shelter hasn't been the same without her. I don't know what we're going to do." She cleared her throat, reached for a cup of water.

"I'm so sorry about your loss, and I apologize for bringing up her name. I know the pain is still very fresh."

"No need to apologize." Sister Agnes smiled, her lips a tight line. She reached for a photo album that had been sitting on the corner of her desk. "Talking about Sister Marta brings back only good memories. The pages in this album," she said as she flipped through them, "simply show how much of a role she played here at A New Beginning House over the years. Every decade of our service is highlighted in this album, and every decade highlighted has a picture of her." She looked at a few of the photos with a faint smile, and then her face turned to business again.

"Again, I apologize that I can't help you any further. I just am not familiar with a Frankie Jean or a Sweet Violet, whatever you are calling her. I have to prepare for lunch now." She slammed the photo album shut, pushed it back to the side. "Though the ladies are not allowed to linger around during the day—they should be looking for jobs and housing—we do serve a daily hot lunch to make things easier for them. I need to check on the kitchen and make sure that meal preparations are going correctly."

She stood and so did Leon and I. The fact that he had not asked any questions let me know that he was not taking my search for answers seriously.

But at least he had come. At least he was playing along.

"All right, Sienna," he finally spoke as we headed back to the car. Mike was playing chauffeur again. I could see him bopping his head to some music in the front seat.

"Wait," I said, looking up the street at the several blocks of abandoned homes. "Let's walk up there."

Leon raised his eyebrows and sighed, but he followed. I heard Mike start up the car. Leon looked back at him and gave a thumbs-up sign. The engine shut off and the music boomed louder.

"Why are we going here?" Leon asked as we crossed the street and headed for the row of vacant homes. Some changes had happened in the months since Amber's body had been found in one of them, I noted. A couple of them had new windows, polished steps.

Renovations.

Obvious construction had started on several of the row homes in the block, but the one which Amber had termed her abandominium, the one in which her body had been found, still had a crumbling walkway, boarded windows, remnants of yellow tape.

I looked up at the worn, decrepit façade, knowing that the broken home only housed the horrors of a young pregnant girl's broken dreams. Who knew what other untold horror stories it held?

A group of construction workers came out of the house two doors down. Blueprint papers were in their hands and one held a bucket of tools as they bounded down the steps and headed toward a van that held ladders and other supplies.

"Excuse me." I approached one of them. "I see that you are renovating some of the houses on this street."

"Yup." A man with a thick, bushy mustache stopped to talk to me as the others continued to the van. "In a few months most of this block will be transformed into a brand new rental community. We're just the contractors, though, so if you want more information, you'll have to contact the new owners of these properties."

"New owners?"

"Yeah, the city sold some of these vacant homes to a development company who took ownership."

"Why just some of the houses and not others?" I pointed to Amber's "home."

"Well, the city only sold what belonged to them. A few of the homes on this street had a private landlord, a slumlord, if you ask me. I think they can't find the owner to make an offer, but that is the plan." He shook his head as his attention turned to the van into which the other workers had piled. "I sure hope they find the owner of the rest of these homes. It will be a hard sell trying to rent out renovated row homes if there are vacant units interspersed among them, you know? Doesn't make sense to me, but like I said, we're just the contractors. Okay, ma'am." He nodded and headed toward the van.

"Excuse me," I called after him. "All of the other vacant homes on this street have the same missing owner?"

The man nodded as he stepped into the driver's seat of the van. "That's what I've been told," he shouted back. "Have a nice day, ma'am." He closed the door, started the engine, and pulled off.

"Ready?" Leon nudged me from behind as I stood there considering what had just been shared. Aside from Amber's hideaway, about five other homes on the block looked to be in the same dismal state. They were mixed in with the renovated properties.

"That's odd that the city would agree to a renovation project with so many vacant properties in the mix." I shook my head as we turned back toward Mike's car. No black sedan with tinted windows today, just his white Lexus.

"Yes, that's odd," Leon agreed, "but for them to have given the green light, they must be fairly certain they'll catch up with the slumlord and buy him or her out. So," he sighed, "are we finished chasing down this Sweet Violet woman or do you have another stop you want to make?"

I thought for a moment as we got into the car. "First a phone call, then one more stop. Then, if we get no more answers or direction, I promise that I will leave it alone. For good. We leave in a few hours." I bit my lip, avoiding the urge to check the time again. I was determined to keep my promise to him.

Which meant I needed immediate answers.

"Good. I like that promise." Leon nodded while scrolling through his phone. "By this time tomorrow, we'll be lounging on a Caribbean beach counting down the moments to our baby's arrival. Here, use my phone to make your call. Don't want to risk that your calls are being bugged."

It was a scary thought, but a real possibility if he mentioned it.

Chapter 31

"Hello, Mr. Monroe?"

"Ah, Sienna! I haven't talked to you in ages. How are you, dear?" The elderly man on the other end of the line greeted me with genuine warmth. Horace Monroe, a member of Second Zion, had been a longtime foster parent who I'd had dealings with long ago. Dayonna Diamond, the last foster child he and his wife Elsie had taken in, had given me a run for my money as I searched for a sister she claimed to have, yet there was no record of. I stayed in touch with the elderly couple from time to time, just to check in and ensure that all was well with them. Today, however, I was calling for a different purpose.

"I'm well, Mr. Monroe, and I hope everyone in your family is well too."

"Oh, we are all fine. Thanks for all you did to help us."

I smiled, glad to hear that peace had come out of the storm for them. "Look, I didn't want to hold you long, but I was curious if you are still in the home renovating business?"

"Not as much as I used to be. Elsie is ready for me to settle down once and for all and just enjoy the new home I fixed up for us. Why do you ask? Are you looking to update a property? I heard that you are expecting a little one."

"Yes, we are, but that's not why I called. I just wanted to know how you go about finding the owner of a vacant property."

"Oh, usually the city can help with those matters."

"What if the city doesn't know?"

"Well," Horace chuckled, "I have my ways of finding out myself, but that's a trade secret I keep under wraps for when I want to be the first one to grab up a property."

"If I give you an address, do you think you can find out who owns it? I have a reason for looking into it as soon as possible, but I can't get into the details right now."

"I can see what I can do. No promises, though."

"Great." I spelled out the street number and name of the vacant home where Amber's body had been found, the vacant home that stood out with several others in the block of renovations. "There may be other homes on that street under the same ownership if that helps to know."

"Okay. Spell it for me one more time, dear. I found my pen and some paper."

Hearing the frailty in his voice and recalling the danger of my mission, I wondered if I was making a mistake getting him involved; however, Leon hadn't stopped me so I figured all was well.

"Thanks, Mr. Monroe."

"Oh, not a problem. After all you did to help bring healing to my family, I'm honored to have a way to help you out."

We said our good-byes and I handed Leon back his phone.

"Anywhere else?" he asked.

"You need to feed your driver," Mike shouted from the front seat. We all laughed.

"I guess we all need to stop and eat. Where to, Leon?"

"Let's go eat down at the Harbor. That way we can drive past the shop. One last time." His laugh died away. "Mike can run in and get us something from one of the food pavilions, my treat."

Mike nodded, turned toward downtown.

"Leon, you make things sound so final." I shook my head. "We won't be in the Bahamas forever. We'll be back to your shop before you know it and the insurance company will get it back in one piece." I thought about the broken glass, the bullet holes, and shuddered.

"Sienna, my bakery is a wrap. This case, the past few months have taken their toll. The shootout yesterday doesn't help things either."

"Insurance *will* cover that, right?"

"I guess. It's complicated."

"You mean like how you had my son working there for the past few months and never told me complicated?"

We shot each other potent glances.

"If you ever made time to come by, Roman's presence wouldn't have been a secret to you."

I let out a loud sigh. "I don't want to start up anything, no arguing. We said we were past that."

"Then let's be past it. I just want to drive by the shop, let you finish your private investigation mission, and move forward. If you don't have any other stops you want to make, let's just get our food, head back to the safe house and get ready for our trip."

I had nothing else to say as Mike drove toward Pratt Street.

And then: "Wait!" I grabbed Leon's shoulder and he motioned for Mike to stop.

We were passing the corner of Baltimore and President Streets where an escalator descended down to the Shot Tower Metro Station.

"She's heading for the subway." I pointed.

Sweet Violet.

Her long black wool coat stood out in the summertime heat. A brown paper shopping bag hung from one of her hands.

"Sienna, I'm coming with you." Leon followed me as I exited the car.

"I'll circle the block a few times," Mike shouted from the front seat. "Just cross back over to this corner when you're ready and I'll get you."

I was already crossing the street. Sweet Violet had just stepped onto the top escalator stair and was moving down into the station.

"Frankie Jean! Sweet Violet!" I still was not sure what to call her, but I saw her turn her head, look around just as she reached the bottom of the escalator.

A train was pulling into the station. I ran down the rest of the steps. Leon was still caught across the street, not having made the light in time. Cars raced down President Street onto I-83 blocking his way.

"Sweet Violet," I called, out of breath. For being so old and frail, not to mention wearing a heavy coat on a summer day, the woman had some speed in her feet. "Sweet Violet," I called again just as the train came to a screeching halt at the station. I caught up to her just as she shuffled toward the opening doors.

"Sweet Violet, where are you off to so fast?"

"Huh? Oh." She stopped for a moment as a crowd of people scattered off. "I knew you would come see me off. I knew it." She clasped her hands together, the brown shopping bag still hanging off of her thin wrist.

"See you off? Where are you going?" I kept a smile on my face, kept my tone easy.

We had only seconds. Passengers who were getting off had already done so. The door would be closing soon and something in Sweet Violet's hurried pace told me she was not going to miss this train.

"To plant my flowers, of course." She looked at me and frowned. She also pulled her bag closer to her body.

"This is the subway. It only travels back and forth between Owings Mills and Johns Hopkins Hospital. Where are you going to plant them?" I followed along.

She looked to the left, then the right, before whispering to me. "I take the subway to the light rail, the light rail to BWI, and the airport shuttle to the Amtrak station. They gave me the ticket, so I know where to go."

I noticed then she had a train ticket in her other hand.

"Who gave you the ticket?"

Too late.

She was stepping onto the subway car and the doors were beeping to announce their pending closure. Just before the doors slammed shut, she tossed me the brown shopping bag.

"Just plant these somewhere pretty, will you?" I heard her say as the doors squealed shut. The shopping bag landed at my feet and the train screeched back to life, jolting forward on its darkened tunnel route. Through the glass windows, I saw Sweet Violet take a seat, unbutton her wool coat. The pink sweat suit I'd given to her the night she showed up at the emergency room was underneath. With all those layers, I was amazed the woman hadn't passed out from heat stroke.

"Bye, Sweet Violet." I shook my head, looked down at the bag, and opened it.

The only things inside were bouquets of violets. Deep purple violets, several bouquets.

"You missed her?"

Leon.

He'd just come up behind me, his voice soothing to my overwhelmed nerves.

"No, she got on the train, said she was about to plant her flowers, then she tossed this bag to me." I pointed to the shopping bag. He picked it up.

"So." He eyed me carefully. "Anything else?"

"She had a train ticket. She said someone gave it to her."

"Aren't there programs that help homeless people with traveling funds if they need to get somewhere and have a relative waiting?"

"Yeah." I considered, not sure what else to think, what else to say or do. "She's never said anything about relatives." Leon didn't seem concerned.

"Anything else?" he asked. I could tell from his posture, his words, that anything else I could come with up with, he would find a way to explain it away.

"Let's go. Let's pack and wait. I'm done." I shrugged my shoulders, not feeling like I was done with anything, but what else was there for me to do? What else was there for me to research?

We headed out of the station and crossed the street where Mike had just circled around and sat waiting for us. The ride back to the safe house was silent.

Chapter 32

"I'm sorry that I have to come along. You two should be enjoying your anniversary trip in the Bahamas alone as a second honeymoon." Roman munched on a bag of sour cream and onion potato chips. I thought back to our honeymoon in St. Michael's, Maryland. Perfection. I had no idea what this trip would be like. I sighed.

3:23.

Our ride to the airport would be there any moment. We sat in the basement of the safe house, a few pieces of luggage waiting by the door. Leon sat checking the closed-circuit screens from his seat next to me on the futon.

"Considering the circumstances, I'm not sure that I would call this an anniversary trip anyway, Roman." I rubbed both of my hands over my belly. "Besides, not sure how much of the Bahamas I'll be able to enjoy with all this extra luggage." I smiled, weakly, but a smile nonetheless.

"It's a family-moon." Leon's hands joined mine over my stomach. "We probably need this time to just be a family unit. All four of us. We haven't really had time to be so before now."

A phone sitting on the desk in the center of the room rang.

"That's the signal. Our ride is here. Let's go." Leon began shutting everything off while Roman rechecked our paperwork.

Was all of this really necessary? I thought about Leon's shot-out store and Alisa's lifeless body and conceded that the extended trip was indeed one that had to be taken.

At least we were all together.

"Shut the lights," Leon directed Roman as the three of us poured out of the back basement door. Mike had long left us after dropping us off following my failed Sweet Violet discovery mission. I still didn't feel satisfied with the results, or lack thereof, of my mission; but, really, what else was there for me to do? And Leon didn't seem to think it necessary to push for any additional answers.

I guessed she was just a harmless older homeless woman whose presence at so many tragic scenes was mere coincidence. I picked up the shopping bag filled with violets on my way out of the door, determined to plant them wherever we ended up as a sign that I had moved on.

A final task.

Seemed like I always had another "final task" to be rid of this woman once and for all.

Leon shook his head at me as we walked toward the blue cab that waited in the parking pad behind the house. "You have a good heart, Sienna," he said as if he could read my mind, as if he understood my intentions. "You are obsessed with completing a case and leaving no stone unturned."

I tried to smile back at him, but something had caught my eye. Leon saw the change.

"What is it now, Sienna?" He asked as he and Roman loaded the trunk with our bags.

"Nothing," I stammered as I walked toward the cab. What could I say? Leon would think I was crazy, over-thinking if I pointed out the observation that had just disturbed my already shaky sense of peace.

The numbers painted on the side of the cab.

511.

It was the cab's ID number, that's all, I chided myself, forcing myself to ignore the sudden pang of alarm that went off in my stomach.

A coincidence.

Not worth bringing up.

My hands shook as I sat down in the rear seat next to Leon. Roman sat up front. The driver, a middle-aged black man with salt-and-pepper stubble on his face seemed oblivious to my alarm. Leon and Roman joked around about something or other, and I did my best to assure myself that I was being silly, unreasonable for thinking the numbers on the cab were more than a coincidence.

The car backed out of the parking pad, crept through the alley, and then joined the beginning rush-hour traffic out of downtown.

"Not going through the city to get to 295?" Leon spoke up, taking a pause from cracking jokes with Roman. How had I missed how close those two were?

The driver shook his head. "Gotta loop around for a while to make sure we're not being followed. Don't worry; I'll get you to the airport on time." The man had a voice that was both rough and rhythmic; a voice, like one, I imagined, an old jazz singer would have after a lifetime of whiskey and smokes.

Whiskey.

Thinking of that reminded me of Sweet Violet and her Old Grand-Dad offering she left by her planted rose on New Year's Day. What was up with the woman and flowers anyway? I wondered.

The shopping bag of violets was at my feet. Not sure how or why I thought I would get the blooms past security at the airport, or through customs. I looked in the bag. Ran a finger over the dark purple blooms.

Five bouquets.

My heart dropped to my knees as I took out one of the bow-tied bouquets.

Eleven stems each.

Oh, God. What was it with me and this number? I shut my eyes, opened them, noticed that we were traveling farther away in the opposite direction from the airport.

Leon still didn't seem perturbed. Would I sound like a fool if I pointed this out to him? If I showed him the flower count or mentioned the numbers on the side of the cab?

My nerves were getting the better of me. I didn't know how much longer I'd be able to contain them, the synapses in my brain firing away in a desperate effort to make sense of the continuing strands of coincidences that seemed to be leading me away from thinking there was no connection between Sweet Violet and the series of violent events that had comprised the last few months of my life.

"I suggest you go on about your way before I put the 'n' in Violet and acquaint you with my bitter side."

I swallowed hard at the distant memory of her words, a sense of desperation and anxiety taking over me as I struggled to find sense and meaning of it all.

"Sienna, you okay?" Leon was studying my face, his eyebrow raised. The driver's eyes met mine in the rear-view mirror. *I can't let him know that I suspect anything.* Did I sound crazy or what? I wanted to kick myself for my growing paranoia.

"What is it, Sienna?" Leon looked more concerned as I'm sure my face was turning pale.

"Ma?" Roman turned around, stared.

I racked my brain trying to think of an answer that would make sense and that would safely get us out of this cab that I no longer trusted. *Because of painted numbers and a bunch of unplanted flowers.* I heard my own silliness. I thought of what to say, what to do, and only one thing came to mind.

I grabbed my stomach.

"Something's not right. I think I need to get checked out. Now." It was not a total lie, I decided. Something sure didn't feel right, and I needed to make sure, for the sake of my baby, that our current situation did indeed check out.

The immediate concern on Leon's face left me feeling guilty. I watched as he looked from the papers in his hand to the time on the driver's dashboard.

"Make the next right," he directed the driver. "We need to go to the hospital."

In the mirror, I could see the man's eyes narrow and a single bead of sweat form on his forehead. He switched lanes and did a U-turn heading back toward the city.

"There's a closer hospital the other direction." Leon sounded aggravated, worried. Roman shifted in his seat, alarm ringing in his eyes as well.

"We're going to Metro Community," the man said, the sweat now gone from his forehead.

Maybe I was overthinking and overreacting, but my gut told me I'd made the right move.

Chapter 33

"Y'all just can't stay away from here." KeeKee Wither-spoon shook her head as she directed me to a wheelchair. "You might as well have just kept that on-call pager with you, Sienna. At least you would be getting paid for showing up here every few hours."

A patient transporter took over the handles of the wheelchair from KeeKee. I was headed to the triage area of the Labor & Delivery Unit since I'd entered the emergency room with my head bowed and my arms wrapped around my stomach.

Lord, what am I doing?

I'd just wanted out of that cab that seemed to be driving in the wrong direction. I'd left the bag of flowers from Sweet Violet in the rear car seat.

I'd had enough of that woman's property causing me trouble. Shoot, that's really how I ended up in the center of this mess anyway, dealing with her and her things.

"Sienna, I want you and the baby to be okay." Leon walked beside me. Roman was behind us, on the phone with my sister who apparently had my parents on the line as well.

"Yeah, Aunt Vet," I heard Roman say. "We're back at the hospital. Something's wrong with Ma and the baby. Yeah, I know. She's not due for another six weeks, or something like that."

How was I going to explain this to anyone? I swallowed hard as the service elevators whooshed us up to the fifth floor where the L&D unit was. I closed my eyes and tried real hard to feel something, anything that would have warranted me saying I needed to be checked out.

All I felt was the baby kicking away, the normal flutters and nudges.

Please forgive me, everyone. My paranoia had put us in this situation, maybe even endangered us as we were supposed to be heading out of the country for our safety, but were instead back at Metro Community Hospital.

"Hook her up to the monitors and check her vitals," a doctor wearing pink and blue scrubs directed some nursing staff. "Hello, I'm Dr. Flanigan, and I understand that you were sent here from the emergency department with abdominal pain. Can you tell me more about what's going on and what you are feeling?"

The commotion around me did not stop as the nursing staff helped me out of my clothes, wrapped me up in a hospital gown, and began fastening around my stomach belts connected to various machines and monitors.

"Uh . . ." I felt my eyelids flutter as the doctor waited for an answer. Leon, who stood next to the bed where I lay, moved in closer, waiting as well. I knew that Roman was waiting in a family area down the hall. I could still hear his voice in the distance explaining the situation to Yvette and my parents.

Lord knows what he was saying as I didn't even know what to say myself.

"I . . ."

"Hold on, one moment." The doctor looked down at her pager. "I need to check on a patient next door. Our nurses will have you set up in a moment and I'll be back to check on you very quickly." She rushed out the room and I exhaled, though I knew this reprieve in explaining symptoms that weren't there was only temporary.

"I'm sorry, Leon, about everything. I know this is messing up all the carefully laid plans meant to keep us safe." My eyes were shut again and I held the back of my hand against my forehead.

"It's okay, babe, don't worry about the trip or our safety. That's my job. You just focus on staying healthy for the baby's sake."

"Wait." I struggled to sit up as something, or rather, someone, caught my attention from the hospital corridor.

"Why is the cab driver outside the room?" My heart quickened its pace. One of the monitors attached to me echoed my panic.

"Calm down, Sienna." Leon stroked my head, gently nudged me back to the pillow under my head. "Remember, he is part of our security team to get us to safety. As this was an unplanned trip, it makes sense for him to stay nearby to secure our surroundings."

That actually made sense.

I wanted to kick myself. My fear and paranoia had definitely put us in a bad position. And why had I been so distrustful of the driver? Oh yes, 511.

What if it really was a harmless coincidence? How would I ever explain this to Leon?

This was his first child. Why was I messing with his experience? A swift pang of guilt rippled through me as the baby inside of me kicked away.

My cell phone rang.

I could hear its vibrations pulsing from the pile of my clothes on the chair next to me. Both Leon and I reached for it simultaneously.

"You don't need to worry about this right now. I'll take care of everything." Leon grabbed it up first. Instead of answering, he turned it off.

Dr. Flanigan reentered the room before I could react.

"I'm so sorry I had to leave, but where were we? Oh yes, Ms. Sanderson St. James, please tell me what's going on."

There was no avoiding an answer and I didn't want to lie.

"I . . . I wasn't feeling right, that's all." I swallowed.

The doctor frowned, moved closer to the nurse who stood on the other side of the bed, her attention focused on an ongoing printout attached to the belt around my waist. *What else can I say right now?* I tried to swallow again, but my mouth felt as dry as a starched cotton shirt.

"I don't know how to explain what I'm feeling." I could feel myself shaking. I rubbed the sides of my abdomen which felt like it was tightening into a knot.

"Are you feeling anything right now?" The doctor looked up at me from the strip of paper before looking back down at it, smoothing the strip between her fingertips.

"I . . ."

"You're having contractions, three minutes apart," she cut in, her eyes glued to the printout. "They're not excessively strong contractions, but the consistency with which they are coming is concerning. I'm going to have to check your cervix to make sure you're not in premature labor."

"What? Is something wrong?"

Leon seemed oblivious to my sudden new wave of fear and panic. This was only supposed to be an act. Nothing should be showing up on that strip the doctor was studying. I strained my eyes, trying to make sense of the continuing lines that scrolled out on the strip of paper from the monitor that was connected to my belly. One line looked like a series of mountains with evenly spaced valleys.

Contractions.

I realized that the tightening knot I'd been trying to smooth down on the sides of my stomach wasn't just my nerves. The doctor had already snapped on gloves, was checking me, before I could make sense of this new turn of events.

"Okay, you're about half a centimeter. That will only worry me if there are any changes. We're going to give you some meds to hopefully relax those contractions since they are coming so frequently and at regular intervals. We're going to keep you here for a few hours to make sure that there are no changes going on with your cervix. You're not too, too far away from your due date, but let's give that baby a little more time in the oven to finish baking."

The doctor said what she had to say and was disposing of the gloves and exiting the room all before I could fully absorb what was going on.

"Am I okay?" I heard myself whisper. "The baby seems to be kicking around its normal self." I looked up at Leon, but the nurse, who still studied the monitor strip answered.

"We're keeping an eye on everything. The baby's heartbeat is strong, so everything we're seeing is reassuring. I'm going to start an IV to keep you hydrated and the doctor will let us know what meds to give you to slow down those early contractions. You'll probably be out of here in a few hours, but you'll need to take it easy."

"So I guess a trip, a vacation, is out of the question? Our bags are packed."

The nurse looked at me like I was crazy as she began the IV. "Honey, the only trip you'll be making right now is to the comfort of your bed. You need to stay off your feet until you get the all clear."

She left the room, leaving just me and Leon.

"I'm sorry," I pleaded again, knowing he had no idea all that I was apologizing for.

The news from the medical staff was not part of my script.

"Sienna, stop apologizing. I'm glad we came when we did. I hate to think that we could have been airborne with you not even realizing that you were having contractions."

It was a sobering thought, I agreed. I rubbed my stomach, willing my baby to be okay and not come too soon.

"I'm going to go update Roman so he won't be worried."

"Give me my phone, Leon. I want to call my parents," I called out to him just before he disappeared into the hallway. He doubled back and gave me my smartphone without hesitation.

My intention was to call them. I'd had no other motive for wanting my phone; that is, until I saw the number of the missed call from moments earlier.

A New Beginning House.

I held my breath, looked at the doorway to ensure that Leon wasn't there, and pressed DIAL.

"Sienna," Sister Agnes answered on the first ring. "I can't really talk right now, we're preparing for our dinner meal, but I wanted to tell you I came across something interesting." She didn't wait for me to respond, instead gave directions to a kitchen staffer, something about the size of a scoop of mashed potatoes, and then she spoke back into the phone.

"I was going through that photo album with the pictures of Sister Marta through the decades, and I came across a picture I'd forgotten about back from 1972. No, Lilah, one scoop of potatoes, not two!"

I could hear Leon coming back down the hallway. He was asking the doctor questions.

Too much.

All of this.

The knot in my stomach tightened again. Were these contractions getting stronger?

"Sister Agnes?" I managed to get out.

"Yes, I'm sorry. What was I saying?" The woman paused before continuing. "I remember. 1972. That's the year Sister Marta came to our shelter, not as a staff member but a guest. She was a woman of the world back then with one foot on both sides of the fence before she decided to come fully on the side of righteousness."

"What was the picture of?" I tried to hurry her along, knowing that Leon and the doctor would not be pleased to see me stressing over a phone call.

Shoot, I was not pleased. I felt my stomach tighten into a knot once again.

"You asked me if a woman named Frankie Jean stayed at our shelter the night before Sister Marta died. I told you I knew of no such woman, nor did I have any reason to believe that Marta would hide someone from me, but now I'm rethinking both possibilities, though it would make little sense."

"What do you mean?" I looked over at the strip of paper coming out of the contraction monitor. The mountain peaks looked higher, the valleys closer together. I wasn't a medical professional, and I hadn't had a baby in twenty-one years, but something about the strip did not look encouraging.

If I wasn't concerned about our safety, I would have hung up on the shelter director right then and focused solely on deep breathing in an effort to help my active uterus calm down, if such a calming down was possible.

"Like I said, Sister Marta was no saint when she first came to our shelter as a resident. I didn't like the company she kept and I told her that she would have to distance herself from the crowd she was running with if she wanted to stay. I do not tolerate foolishness and trouble."

"What kind of trouble, Sister Agnes?" And what did any of this have to do with Sweet Violet?

"I don't know, but you could tell that the friends she had were up to no good. Party people. I tried to help those girls back then, but in the end Marta was the only one who turned to righteousness."

"Girls? A picture? You said there was a picture or something?" I needed her to get to the point. Immediately. Leon and the doctor had paused out in the hallway. I could hear Dr. Flanigan explaining something to him about the medication she wanted to give me.

"Oh, yes. Marta had a friend who stayed at the shelter for a short time back then. I didn't like her and she didn't like my rules. I guess that's what happened, because she left all of a sudden and I never saw her again. That was, what, about forty years ago? And although Marta had seemed real close to her, she never talked about her even once after the woman up and disappeared."

"Do you remember the woman's name?"

"Of course I do. Francesca Dupree. The other women called her Frankie and I remember everyone seemed to be scared of her. Even Marta trembled a little around her presence, though she called her a friend. I didn't like the woman, her smoking, drinking, and cussing."

"Can you send me the picture?" My heartbeat quickened. Francesca Dupree.

"I guess I can. I'll get my teenage granddaughter to come in here and snap a picture and, I guess, text it to you?"

"That's perfect. Thanks, Sister Agnes. I know Sister Marta was a dear worker, so I want to make sure that her legacy stays intact and justice is served. You sharing this information helps."

"Frankie. Haven't seen that woman in nearly forty years. Had forgotten completely about her until I saw this picture today." Sister Agnes sounded like she was talking more to herself than me. "Marta knew I didn't take a liking to that woman, so I guess it would make sense for her to hide her from me if she had for some reason returned. I don't know why she left, and I don't know why she'd come back, especially after all this time. Listen, I need to go, but I'll send you the picture. Now, I'm curious if it's the same woman you're talking about. Just remember, it's an old picture, so I'm not sure how much good it will do. Bless the Lord, good-bye." She hung up without further conversation.

And just in time.

The nurse returned to the room and added something to my IV.

"Okay, we're going to keep you under observation for a little bit to make sure those contractions are slowing down."

"Are they any better?" Leon came in right after. The doctor had gone on to another room.

"Mmmm, about the same." The nurse studied the strip. "Actually, maybe a little worse. But don't worry. I just gave her the medicine Dr. Flanigan told you about. Hopefully, we'll see a difference soon." She fiddled with the monitoring belts across my belly and then left the room.

Leon eased into a chair beside me.

"It's going to be okay, Leon," I tried to reassure him though my head was spinning with questions beyond capacity.

The cab driver walked past the door.

"You said he's just providing security for us, right?" I tried not to sound nervous. I knew that if Leon knew all that was going on in my mind, he'd be horrified.

I had to stay calm for the baby.

It was several weeks too early for the baby to come.

"We're safe, Sienna. I had you checked in under a different name so the front desk won't be disclosing any unnecessary information."

"Who is it that we are hiding from?"

Leon looked at me and shook his head. "You don't have to worry about any of that at all. I've got it, babe."

"Leon." Roman stood in the doorway, an unreadable expression on his face as he beckoned my husband to come to him. I felt like he was avoiding eye contact with me.

"Is everything okay?" I asked.

"I'll be right back," Leon stated, hopping up and meeting Roman in the hallway. I watched them scurry away, Leon's phone to his ear. They disappeared around the corner.

My phone vibrated.

A text.

I pulled up the message and stared at the attachment, the picture sent from Sister Agnes.

Clearly a Polaroid picture and clearly the seventies, I stared at a much younger version of Marta wearing brown bellbottoms and a bright orange blouse.

And the woman standing next to her.

Though the woman looked to be in her mid-twenties to early-thirties and had a huge afro, knit dress, and moccasins, the smattering of brown freckles and the rich cocoa skin were a dead giveaway.

Sweet Violet.

Chapter 34

She was beautiful back then. I gasped, looking at the attention given to her made-up face, the long slender legs, the hourglass figure. A slight gap between her top two teeth even added a hint of natural, easy beauty to her smiling face.

Ms. Marta knew this woman, Frankie Jean. From the way they stood close to each other in the picture, grinning, it was obvious they had been good friends. I thought about what Sister Agnes said about Marta's friends: up to no good, foolishness, and trouble. She said that this woman, Francesca Dupree, was a smoker, drinker, and cusser, all evil vices from where Sister Agnes came from.

She said that everyone seemed to be a little afraid of this Francesca, too.

Amber had been afraid. I remembered how she alternated between trying to give me information about her and wanting nothing more to do with her.

Why would anyone be afraid of this woman, whether looking like a 1970s supermodel, or wandering the streets homeless, and, well, a little off? And how did she end up in that predicament anyway? And where had she been for the past few decades and why had she suddenly returned? Ms. Marta had said that she'd been there for just a week or so when I called her that first night at the ED.

The more answers I got, the more questions I had, but, I realized, the tightening in my stomach had eased up a little. I looked over at the IV. Whatever that nurse put in me was working.

I was also beginning to feel drowsy. Must be some kind of muscle relaxant, I realized, noting that even the baby's kicks, though still present, had slightly lessened in intensity. I began fighting to stay awake to keep figuring out Sweet Violet's past. I felt my eyes closing despite my best attempt to keep them open, my head nodding though I kept snapping it back into an attentive position. The picture, the questions, the easing contractions became a mixed muddle in my head.

And then a loud, piercing bell.

I jolted up in the hospital bed trying to make sense of what I was hearing.

The fire alarm.

I watched as the heavy door to my room automatically swung shut, sealing me alone in the room.

"Code red," an operator announced over the intercom system. "Fifth floor, rear stairwell. Code red, fifth floor, rear stairwell," the operator repeated, her voice calm, steady over the clanging alarm.

If it's a fire drill, she'll announce that the code red is cancelled in a few moments. If it's a real fire, somebody will come in here and direct me to safety. I settled back in the bed, knowing there was nothing really for me to do but wait.

But nobody came.

I checked the wall clock and six minutes had passed. The alarm had not stopped and no one had come to check on me or offer directions. I pressed the nurse's call button. It seemed dead.

Where are Leon and Roman? I wondered. *They should be here with me.* They'd gotten carried away with a call, I remembered.

I got out of the bed, stared at the IV in my arm. I took a deep breath and pulled it out using a couple of nearby tissues to hold back any bleeding. I guessed volunteering in the ED had done me some good. Any other time in my life, I would have been too afraid to mess with the IV, but I'd seen it removed enough times that I barely hesitated to pull it out myself. I yanked my shirt over my head, making the hospital gown look like a billowing skirt underneath it before slipping on my shoes. I walked over to the closed door, touching it, making sure it wasn't hot.

Lessons learned from fire safety classes back in elementary school.

The door was cool to the touch and I didn't smell smoke. I opened it, peered out into the hallway.

Fire alarms throughout the corridor flashed a brilliant white. That was the only action I saw. Nobody, not a nurse, a tech, a wandering soul was in the hallway.

Odd.

I walked back to the bed, grabbed my phone and then headed out the room to find Leon, somebody.

"Hello?" I called out, my words drowned out by the clanging noise. I headed down the hallway, turned a corner, saw the nurses' station.

Nobody was there either.

I turned back toward the room, but just before I rounded the corner, I saw movement near my room.

The cab driver.

I watched him open the door to the room I'd just vacated. He stepped in, clearly not seeing that I was down the hallway, just beyond the bend.

He was here to protect us; Leon had said. If that was the case, then it made sense that he'd be going into my room.

But what if that's not the case?

I thought of the numbers 511, the flowers, the questions I had, the answers I didn't. What if he had pulled the fire alarm and managed to empty the hallways? What if he wasn't here to watch over us, but to hurt us?

I closed my eyes, hearing in my memory the shots breaking through Leon's bakery window, the rain of glass, the ricochet of bullets.

Someone meant to kill us, the full weight of that realization settling anew on me.

I had to get out of there. I wasn't going to chance that the cab driver was here for my good, especially with Leon and Roman nowhere to be found.

Someone had been calling Leon when he left the room with Roman. Someone had called Alisa Billy when she rushed me out of this very hospital yesterday, only to be met with death.

Murder.

I dialed Leon's number.

No answer.

"Leon, where are you?" I huffed and puffed into his voice mailbox as I ran toward a green exit sign marking a staircase. That cab driver would immediately see that I wasn't in the room, and my gut told me he was going to come looking for me, regardless of whether his intentions were good or evil. I rushed through the door, not knowing if this was the front stairwell, the rear stairwell, if there really was a fire or if it all was a false alarm.

All I knew was that I wanted to get away as fast as I could and find Leon and my son.

I entered the stairwell, and the door shut behind me, locking. That's right, I recalled, the labor and delivery unit had automatic locks on everything to prevent infant theft; only a staff badge would give me access back onto that floor.

I'd stopped volunteering for Metro Community months ago, but I still had a badge, the social work director wanting me to stay on their files in case she was absolutely desperate for coverage, though I'd assured her in no uncertain words that I was never returning to work or volunteer there again.

Now I was wishing I had that badge on me. It was in my purse, back in the room. If that driver was up to no good, he could find it in there and have access to the whole hospital.

Not a comforting thought, and not one that gave me any direction, other than to get moving out of there.

"Jesus, help me," I prayed as I scurried down the steps, the fire alarm an echoing clang through the wide, bright stairwell. I made it down to the next floor, the postpartum unit.

Those doors were locked too as this unit also tended to vulnerable newborns. Thinking of all those babies being disturbed by this loud, menacing alarm, I thought of my own baby, aware now that I was off of the IV, the medicine to stop my contractions no longer being pumped into my system.

I could tell.

The tightening in my stomach was back.

This is ridiculous. "Help me, Jesus," I prayed again.

I wanted to pause, catch my breath, give the tightening in my abdomen a chance to settle down, but I heard a door open somewhere in the stairwell. I had no idea what floor, and I knew that it could be anyone coming up or down; but I was operating in a place beyond logic.

I wasn't taking any chances.

I huffed my way down another landing, dialed Leon's number.

No signal.

I heard footsteps, fast and heavy footsteps, echoing through the stairwell, sounding as if coming from above.

At the next landing, I pushed the door to the main corridor, and it gave. Second floor. An administrative wing under renovation, from the looks of it.

"Hello?" I called out to the row of cubicles and closed office doors. A paint bucket and some scraps of lumber lined the nearest wall. The door to the stairwell had a lock on this side. I locked it and then circled the wing, looking for an exit out. On my way to another doorway, I noted a cubicle with a computer powered on. I checked behind me, didn't hear anything, and logged on with my old staff credentials to gain access to the Internet.

Francesca Dupree.

I typed the name into a search engine box.

No results jumped out at me.

"What am I missing? What can I do?" I tapped my fingers on the keyboard, determined to get answers that I didn't think anyone else was looking for.

I tried dialing Leon's number again. No answer. "Where are you?" I left a message. Hung up. New idea for a search.

"Marta Jefferson." I said the worker's name out loud as I typed it in for a new search. Of course the articles and links that came up were tied to her tragic death, the court case. Heck, even my name made it into some of the articles, I noted as I browsed the summaries.

The *Baltimore Sun* had posted her obituary, I also noted. *Born and raised in Baltimore. Douglass High School. Housekeeper at Provident Hospital before embarking in a short career as a backup singer. Performances at The Sphinx, The Royal Theatre on Pennsylvania Avenue. Began working as a shelter worker in the seventies and never left.*

"What am I missing? What am I missing?" I glanced over the obituary again.

Her name.

Kandace Marta Jefferson, her birth name, was written at the top of the posting. Marta was her middle name, not her first. I did a new search with just her first name and last.

"Okay, now what?" I exhaled, trying to ignore the tightening sensations increasing in my stomach as several links of archived articles from the Baltimore-based *Afro-American* newspaper appeared on the screen. The links were mostly black-and-white pictures of show performances, Kandace Jefferson mentioned as a background singer and/or dancer on nearly all of old Pennsylvania Avenue's night clubs and stages. Picture after picture, costume after costume.

And then a reference to a search warrant.

I stopped at this article, seeing something about a federal investigation. No picture, no mention of Kandace, oddly, I observed as I skimmed the article. *Why would this show up in a search result for her if she's not in the article?* I looked over it again to ensure I hadn't missed anything. The only name that jumped out at me was a man's name, Samuel Otis King. The article was dated November, 1971. I made a mental note of the name and the date and returned to the search results for Kandace Jefferson.

Nothing else looked relevant.

What had happened to Marta? I wondered. From a celebrated performer to a homeless shelter resident in a matter of months based on the time line offered by the articles and Sister Agnes's report.

I did a Google search of Samuel Otis King. Nothing of significance came up. I checked Maryland Case Search as the old *Afro-American* article had mentioned something about an investigation, but again, nothing. His name didn't appear in the database of court cases or trials. I wasn't sure if there was a public record of federal court cases, and I felt like I didn't have time to figure it out.

Francesca Dupree.

I held my breath and pressed search after typing her name again, adding the name Kandace Jefferson in the same search box. I didn't expect anything to come up, and I was right.

Except for the same article referencing Samuel Otis King.

I scrolled through it, but again noted that no mention was made of a Francesca, Frankie, or Sweet Violet. I moved the mouse to exit it, before seeing that the grainy archived copy of the article had something else.

A couple of paragraphs and a picture caption had been blacked out. Maybe their names had been part of the article, the only conclusion I could make.

A sharp, deep, long contraction started from one end of my stomach, circled around my back, came back to my waist, and radiated downward. I doubled over, gasped for air.

What am I doing down here? I became aware of my surroundings again, realized that the fire alarm had stopped, that I was alone in an unfinished part of the hospital, and that my pregnancy was not cooperating with any of it all.

Trying to get information about Sweet Violet had only led to problems in my life, and yet, here I was again, endangering myself, and my child, to prove my gut feelings right.

But what were my gut feelings anyway? What had led me on this tangent? That the cab driver was . . . Was what? I groaned, half out of disgust with myself, half out of pain and fear of why I was having pain.

I logged off, shut down the computer. "I'm sorry, Leon," I whispered as I reached for my phone, trying to figure out what I was even supposed to tell him when we finally connected.

A jiggling sound caught my ear.

The door of the stairwell, which I had locked, was shaking, as if someone was trying it, pulling at it, loosening it from its hinges. I heard a metallic rattling sound. That was no key in the knob, I concluded as the door continued shaking.

And then I heard it open.

Still in the cubicle, I could see an exit sign to another corridor just beyond where I sat, but getting up would mean going out to the main aisle which I knew was visible from the stairwell door. I felt safer in the cubicle where I could at least hide under the desk or next to a file cabinet, though the pains shooting through my belly felt like fire and I wondered how I would even stand up to get to either place.

I heard footsteps, slow, pauses in between, as if the person coming from the stairwell was stopping at each cubicle opening.

Oh, God, what do I do?

I held my breath and then clamored for my phone, which had started vibrating on the metal desk. Leon. I immediately shut it off, but I knew that action would do no good. It had been too loud, the vibrations on the metal.

The footsteps picked up pace, sounded like a run toward me. A new pain rippled through my midsection, but I forced myself up to take cover next to a tall file cabinet.

The footsteps were closer now. I hobbled over to the file cabinet, shut my eyes, and readied myself to scream.

And I did.

Large hands reached for me, grabbed me as I doubled over, unable to stop or shield whatever was happening both inside and out of me.

"Sienna!"

"Leon?" I opened my eyes. The hands holding me were those of my husband. The footsteps I'd heard had been his.

"What are you doing down here?"

I heard the horror in his voice.

"I, uh . . ." I tried to answer, but all I could get out was a low moan. I felt myself falling into his arms.

"Gotta get you back upstairs." He helped me up, half carried, half pulled me to the main hallway. Within seconds, we were in an elevator.

"The fire alarm," was all I could get out as another contraction tore through me.

"There was a small incident, electrical or something, in one of the stairwells, but it's already been addressed." He panted, leaned against the elevator wall, still holding me up. "Roman and I got locked in another stairwell after all the doors automatically shut. Not sure what kind of fire safety plan that is for a hospital, especially since I could not get a clear signal on my phone. I've been trying to call you. Both Roman and I, and even the cab driver, have been looking for you.

"You still think he's security?" I managed to puff out.

Leon looked at me like I was crazy, parted his lips to say something else, but the elevator doors opened to the L&D unit. The only word that could come out of his mouth was, "Help!"

I felt hands on me, bed under me, Leon's whisper that all would be okay.

IV restarted, medicine pumped in my veins, hydration. The pain began to subside. Slightly.

"Mrs. Sanderson, we're going to have to keep you under observation and actually keep you in your bed." Dr. Flanigan stood by my bedside. "Despite the pretty strong contractions you were having, fortunately, there are no cervical changes and the medicine and hydration appears to be working. We're going to hold on to you for a little while longer, though, to make sure nothing else starts back up, including you. Stay in that bed, and if you need something or think there is an emergency, next time, just use the nurses' call button."

"The call button doesn't work," I tried to get out, but I was too worn to argue. I nodded, mumbled something

I didn't understand myself, mentally, physically, emotionally exhausted.

And wondering how all of this would end.

Chapter 35

"The doctor thinks she'll be okay. In fact, now they are talking about discharging her soon."

I could hear Leon talking to someone in the hallway. Had I dozed off? My eyes fluttered open. I tried to focus, tried to make sense of the beeps and swishing noises that filled my ears. Monitors. IV. *That's right, I'm in the hospital.* The last few hours felt like a dream as I recalled the taxi ride that brought us here, the contractions that kept us here, the Web search for answers that led me to more questions.

I looked over at the machine that spit out the paper strip that measured contractions. The line that previously looked like mountains and valleys was now nearly straight with a couple of small bumps indicating minor contractions here and there. Whatever episode I'd had was now over. I exhaled, relieved that my stomach was no longer bunching up into a knot. The baby was still kicking, heartbeat strong, as one of the monitoring noises indicated.

I sat up. 5:37, a wall clock read. The day was almost over. We were still in Baltimore. But were we still in danger?

Leon was talking to more than one person in the hallway, I realized, recognizing my sister's voice and my mother's sighs.

"I'll work on trying to figure out your options now," I heard Mike Grant say. "Her complications make things difficult, but not impossible."

A set of eyes peered into the room. "She's up!" Shavona Grant squealed. "Hey, girlfriend. Why you in here giving us all kinds of heart attacks?" She bounced into the room, followed by the others: Leon, Yvette, my parents, and Mike.

I tried to turn my lips up into a smile.

"She's tired." Leon patted my hand. "We need to let her rest. It's going to be a full night."

"What's going on?" I whispered.

"We still need to get out of here." Leon spoke softly, but I didn't miss the questions on my sister's, my parents' faces.

"Are we still going to the B—"

Both Leon and Mike silenced me. Yvette rolled her eyes. "Okay, y'all need to give us more information. I know you ain't talking about traveling somewhere with Sienna on the verge of having this baby." She glared at Leon. "This is ridiculous. I don't like any of it one bit. I wish I could talk to the police, the authorities, somebody who can give us information."

Leon cut me a look, letting me know that most of the people in the room knew little details of what was going on, or even Leon's role in it all.

"Where's Roman?"

"We were at the max level of visitors for you, so he's in the waiting room."

"Leon." I chose my words carefully, sensing the need for continued secrecy, but feeling the need to reveal my concerns. "When you have a chance, I need to talk to you about a phone conversation I had with Sister Agnes at the shelter and some new information I uncovered."

"What?" Leon's face wrinkled. "Sienna, please, leave it alone. With all that is going on with you and the baby, you need to let it go."

"What's going on, Sienna?" Yvette seemed interested in whatever I had to say. "I know my sister," she directed at Leon. "If something is bothering her, it's best to let her talk it out. We don't need her holding on to any kind of stress, especially in her current condition, so we're just going to have to hear her out. What's going on, sis?" she cooed.

"Wait." Mike held up a hand. "Maybe she just needs to share whatever it is with Leon. Perhaps you and everyone else in here should leave so he can address a situation that really doesn't involve all of us." He looked serious, but I didn't miss the quick wink he directed my way.

"I'm sorry, but who are you again?" Yvette's head tilted to one side and both hands went up on her hips. "I know my husband had a chance to talk with you for a while yesterday, but I was never given the pleasure of a full introduction."

My mother moved closer toward us; my father moved closer to the door.

This was Yvette post-Jesus. Had it been pre-Jesus, we all would have been ducking by now. Leon and I knew that. My parents understood.

But Shavona did not. Her head tilted the other way.

"Oh, I thought we'd already been introduced, especially seeing that we were at your lovely house yesterday evening for your Bible Study. I guess you forgot who we are. I'm sorry. My husband is Mike Ulysses Grant II and I am Shavona Wilnetta Grant. He and I are the godparents of Sienna's baby. Again, I apologize that wasn't made clearer to you as we are all just looking out for your sister's wellbeing."

Yvette looked over at me, as did Leon. My father had a sudden interest in the floor tile. Everyone else had their eyes on my sister.

"Godparents." Yvette's eyelids fluttered. "I see." She smiled, but her teeth were clenched. Several strained seconds passed as I watched her take two really deep breaths before continuing. "Sienna, I think I'm just going to go so you can get your rest."

She turned to leave and I sat up. "Wait, Yvette." She was the one person I did not want to leave. My sister was the one person who recognized that I had concerns that were eating away at me. She understood that I needed someone to help me digest it all before I went crazy. With this baby half ready to pop out of my belly, crazy was not a good state for me to be in. She got that. "Don't leave."

"It might be best, Sienna," Leon chimed in, ignoring the smoldering fire in Yvette's eyes. "I hear what your sister is saying, but I just don't think this is the time to get worked up again over matters that are not important to focus on." He stared at me directly, as if to remind me of the sensitive nature of our situation.

"You know what?" I sighed. "I'm tired of the secrets. I'm tired of tiptoeing around subjects that make you uncomfortable, and, most of all, I'm tired of being told what I can and can't think about, what I can and can't talk about, especially as I'm starting to believe that you don't have all the details and knowledge about the situation you say you're handling."

"Sienna, I am handling things. I just need you to—"

"No, I need you to listen." Maybe because Yvette was standing next to me with her arms crossed and her head nodding, I felt a little more emboldened than usual to have such a conversation with my husband in front of an audience. "Since we've been in this place, I've come across some more information about that woman, Sweet Violet."

My mother's forehead wrinkled as she looked over at my father. He shrugged. I didn't care who did or didn't understand or know what I was talking about.

"I can no longer go with any plan, any escape route, anything, until I know for sure that Sweet Violet has nothing to do with the murders I witnessed, the shooting at your bakery yesterday, the attack on my son."

"Sienna." Leon shook his head. "Let's talk alone. I don't . . . We don't need to get anyone else involved more than necessary. You've seen for yourself how bad things can get when you start stirring up people, places, and things that aren't relevant to our situation."

"You keep talking about 'our situation,' but what really is it, Leon? What other secrets are you hiding from me? What other surprises are you trying to keep me from discovering? You say you are trying to preserve my stress level by keeping me in ignorance, but don't you see that your dismissal of my concerns is having the opposite effect? When my gut tells me something is awry, I can't ignore it, no matter how much you don't take me or my observations seriously."

"Sienna," Mike spoke up and all eyeballs rolled over to him. "As an officer who is standing on the *sidelines* of what you and Leon have endured over the past twenty-four hours, in my professional opinion, I think it's best you let Leon, with his *former* police knowledge and as the man who is most concerned about your stress and wellbeing, be the one digging up information and making safety decisions." I took his emphasis on the words "sidelines" and "former" as his attempt to keep me from blowing any covers more than they already had been blown.

"Mike, I appreciate your concern, and please know that I trust my husband. I just want to make sure that as he is making decisions that affect all of us he has all the information he needs, including info that he hasn't been looking into but which my gut feelings tell me is important.

"Humph," Shavona spoke from the corner, her eyes still on Yvette, but her words directed to me. "I think at this point if I were you, I'd be trusting my former cop husband and not my hormone-fed instincts."

Maybe it was my hormones. Maybe it was my fatigue. Maybe it was my strong will wanting to break through any self-imposed filter. Maybe it was all of these things combined, but I could not keep a lid on what flew out of my mouth next.

"And I think I'd be reevaluating my trust in my husband if I knew he was winking at other women every time I looked away."

"Excuse me?" Shavona's mouth dropped open as all the eyeballs in the room turned back toward me. "Are you trying to say something about my husband?"

Couldn't take it back and I couldn't clean it up, so the only thing left to do was put the dirty spoon out on the table for everyone to be fed.

"Yes, your husband," I said to her, "and your friend," I said to Leon, "has been winking his eyes at me every other moment, with both of you right here in the room."

How had my little hospital room become so hostile?

Once again, the aftereffects of anything Sweet Violet.

"My name is Sweet Violet and I suggest you go on about your way before I put the 'n' in Violet and acquaint you with my bitter side." Her words and stank breath pricked my memory at the most inopportune times.

"Wait," Shavona spoke slowly, "you think that my husband has been winking at your eight-month pregnant self?"

"It's not a thought. See, he's winking at me right now."

And he was. Both eyes in rapid succession.

"Sienna," Leon spoke slowly, as if I needed special help in understanding what he was about to say next. "Nobody ever talks about it, but Mike has a tic disorder. It looks like he winks at everybody, especially when he's overly stressed. The disorder almost kept him off the force."

Mike's eyes were winking and blinking so much at this point, I thought he would have a seizure.

"Well," my mother spoke up, "I can't blame you, Sienna, for misunderstanding his eye movements. I thought he was winking at me when we came in here."

"He sure enough winked at me a few times," Yvette piped up. "I guess that's why I've been a little salty toward you, Mike. I'm sorry. I didn't know."

"And I was about to set you straight, son," my father spoke for the first time since coming into the room, "because after the third wink you sent my way, I was ready to—"

"Okay, okay," I interrupted, whatever boldness I'd had moments earlier deflated like a latex balloon with a hole pricked in its side. "I'm sorry. I didn't know and I didn't mean to embarrass you or upset your wife."

"No harm done." Mike gave me a half smile, the winks and blinks slowing down. "I'm just trying to help my brother here out. Things have gotten complicated and more dangerous than any of us expected."

"Don't worry. My lesson is learned. I will stay in my lane and leave the investigation to the experts. I usually can trust my gut, but, I guess my hormones have me off. I'm sorry, Shavona, for . . . everything. I hope you can forgive me."

"Oh, girlfriend, if we can't get past a simple misunderstanding, then how could we ever come together to raise our child?" Shavona chuckled. "I'm just playing. I'm not going to go too crazy over this baby. I'm just happy for you, and I'm honored to be the godmother. We are all family in here now, and I'm thankful. I ain't mad at you."

Hugs. Back slaps. Smiles and chuckles. Even Yvette's shoulders relaxed, though I didn't miss her blank stare at me at the mention of the word "godmother."

And then Roman came to the doorway, looking alarmed. "Turn on the news."

Chapter 36

"Good evening. We begin tonight's newscast with several breaking stories related to the Delmon Frank triple murder trial." The news anchor, a blond-haired man with clear green eyes, stared solemnly into the camera as it zoomed in. "Officials are reporting that the defendant, accused of killing Baltimore philanthropist Julian Morgan and two other victims, has escaped from jail. Authorities are not releasing any details on how the escape occurred or their current efforts to locate him.

"We are also being told that within the last half hour, some type of incident has occurred at the original murder scene, A New Beginning House. Authorities are responding to the scene and have not released any further details about the nature of the incident, possible victims or injuries.

"You may also recall that just yesterday, in a shocking and tragic twist, we learned that the lead prosecuting attorney for the case, Alisa Billy, died on the courtroom steps of an apparent accidental overdose of prescription drugs. An autopsy confirming the cause of death is pending as other sources are raising the possibility of intentional poisoning. In the meantime, reports are surfacing that the trial's star witness, Sienna St. James, may have fled the country out of an abundance of caution for her safety due to these disturbing developments. This follows reports that her husband, former Officer Leon Sanderson, may have been the instigator in a domestic disturbance yesterday."

"I'm turning this off." Mike reached up and pressed the power button of the hospital room's flat-screen television. "We already know that some of those stories are not true, so there's no need in wasting time following this flawed coverage. We need to get out of here."

"Agreed."

"Are we going back to the safe house?" Roman asked, pacing the length of the room.

"Safe house?" My mother raised an eyebrow. "What on earth is going on?"

"We'll explain what we can later, but no, the safe house is not an option seeing that Sienna's original plans were somehow outed. I do not trust anything or anybody right now." Mike continued. "I think we need to split up to leave the hospital. We're too big of a group to travel together. Yvette, Mr. and Mrs. Davis." He nodded at my parents. "You come with me as I'm sure Leon's going to want to stay with Sienna."

"I'm going to stay with Sienna too," my father spoke up. "I don't know what's going on, Leon, but I'm here for backup. This is my daughter and my grandchild. Roman you stay with your aunt and grandmother."

"But Roman was coming—"

"It's okay, Sienna," Leon interrupted me. "Plans are changing as we speak. I just want to get you out of here. If there is some kind of leak to the media, it will only be a matter of time before everyone knows you are here."

"That killer is on the loose. I think we all need to get out of here." My mother's alarm was apparent as she and Yvette scurried behind Mike. Shavona and Roman took the rear.

"I'll walk you to the elevator, honey." My father caught up and held my mother's hand. "But I'll be back, Sienna."

Just me and Leon.

"Do you know what you're doing?" I asked him as he began disconnecting the wires and belts, unplugging machines, eyeing my IV.

"I got you, babe." He gently removed the IV and helped me back into my street clothes. "I want to get out of here before the doctor comes back. I don't want her to have any additional information about you to give to anyone, including the authorities, if, no, when they come asking."

"You're not trusting anyone right now, either." I thought about Mike's words.

"I fully expected Delmon to 'escape' as that's the only way he could keep his cover and not go to jail, but someone in the department is not keeping quiet on matters that they should, and the fact that there's been another incident of some nature at the shelter—not to mention Alisa's death, well, murder—is really concerning. Come on, Sienna." He helped me slip back into my shoes, grabbed my things, and peeked out into the hallway. "All clear. We're heading to the elevator. Your father is holding the door open. Now."

I followed him, my head swirling. Within seconds, the three of us were inside the closed space, my father breathing heavy as the elevator descended.

"You okay, Alvin?" Leon looked concerned, but my father didn't.

"Yup."

"Is the cab driver waiting for us somewhere?" I asked.

"I told you, I'm not trusting anyone until I find out what's happening at A New Beginning House." We were almost at the bottom floor. I pressed the button for the second floor.

"What are you doing, Sienna?"

"That unfinished space on the second floor. We need to sit down for a moment and figure out what we're doing. I can't be walking around in circles with these contractions just getting under control. Plus," I said, lowering my voice, "I want to share with you the information I learned earlier."

Leon sighed, but he didn't object. We got off the elevator, headed for one of the empty cubicles off of the main corridor. I plopped down in a desk chair. Leon and my father rolled chairs over next to me.

"This is a picture Sister Agnes texted me earlier today." I handed Leon my phone. His eyes narrowed as he zoomed in on the image on the screen.

"Marta Jefferson and—"

"Sweet Violet," I finished for him. Leon looked up at me, a question on his face. "Sister Agnes found this picture in that photo album on her desk. I guess she started reminiscing about Marta after we left and ended up finding this snapshot."

"What year was this taken?"

"I forget what she said." I shook my head. "1971? 1972?"

"What are y'all looking at there?" My father reached for the phone and took it out of Leon's hands. Then he shook his head and chuckled. "Now ain't that something? I haven't seen this woman's face in, what, forty years."

"You know her?" I gasped.

"Of course. I mean, I don't know her, but I know who she is. Anybody who grew up in West Baltimore back in the sixties knows who she is."

"Who is she?" Leon and I asked at the same time.

"Francesca J. Dupree, better known by her pen name, Frankie Jean."

"Pen name? She was a writer?"

"Yeah, she was a columnist for one of the little black newspapers that sprung up around town back then, wrote a bunch of short stories and poems."

"She wrote stories . . . for a paper?" I shook my head, still trying to wrap my head around what my father was saying.

"Yup, well, it was supposed to be stories. Everybody was scared to be around her because rumor was that if you talked to her long enough, your personal business would make the front page of the *Garwyn Oaks Gazette,* the little newsletter she wrote for, disguised as a short story. The theme was supposed to be something about planting seeds of knowledge in the black community, but her stories made that paper more of a place for rumors to take root and blossom. Once those stories became the feature, that paper really took off. Actually, now that I recall, she owned that paper along with her husband. They did really well off of it for a time."

"Husband? She had a husband?" I asked, looking at Leon who was sitting back in his chair, his face scrunched up in deep thought.

"Yeah, sure did. Can't remember his name. He was older than her. Real well-dressed fellow, an old-fashioned man's man." My father smiled. "Always had a hat on, a cigar in his mouth, a tall glass of whiskey in his hand. I know that they was real popular at all those clubs down on Pennsylvania Avenue, back when that area was really something. The Sphinx, the Arch Social Club, all of those. True party people."

"Samuel Otis King," I blurted.

"Who?" my father asked.

"Samuel Otis King. That was her husband's name, right?"

"No, not at all." My father chuckled. "But Silent Sam? Haven't heard that name in a while either. Samuel Otis King." He shook his head.

"Silent Sam?" Leon leaned forward in his seat. "That was a real person? I heard that name every now and then when I was working full time for the department. He was supposedly the ultimate gangster, the man who ran Black Baltimore back in the day."

"Oh, he didn't just run Black Baltimore. He ran all of Baltimore, behind the scenes of course. He was a large funder and loan shark for black businessmen who couldn't get money from the banks. He stayed out of view because his business ventures up and down Pennsylvania Avenue were on both sides of the law: liquors, drugs, women; medical clinics, restaurants, beauty salons. He kept control over it all by keeping a firm grip on Baltimore's powerhouses: politicians and the police."

"So, what was the deal between Frankie Jean and Samuel Otis King? I asked. "What, did she have an affair with him?"

"No. Not at all." My father scratched his head, looked up as if trying to pull together old memories. "She and her husband were too in love for extra hanky-panky, so they said. Everybody knew that Frankie Jean got a bouquet of flowers every day from her husband. She would plant those flowers in community parks to 'share the love' as her columns used to say. I'd say her relationship with Silent Sam was quite the opposite of an affair."

"How so?" Leon leaned forward in his chair.

"Oh, she messed up when she began putting Silent Sam's business into her 'fiction' columns. Like I said, they were socialites who frequented all the spots and would know all the people Silent Sam was doing business with. I guess she wanted her paper to become more than a gossip column and so she decided to make it her mission to enlighten the masses about the illegal activities of a man who was pretty much controlling the city. She tried to frame it as a series of made-up short stories, but everyone knew she was really just revealing all of Silent Sam's operations."

"Sounds like a dangerous business move."

"Oh, it was. After a while, the feds were forced to start investigating him and his connections, which, of course, the powers-that-be who were in on it didn't like. The paper stopped suddenly and after she laid low for a bit, she disappeared altogether following the suspicious but uninvestigated death of her husband."

"Wow. They killed him?"

"Yup. I remember reading how they found his body somewhere on Pratt Street, naked and beaten to a bloody pulp."

"Pratt Street?" Leon asked. His bakery was on Pratt Street. I guessed we both were thinking that's why she hung around that area so much.

My father wasn't finished. "I remember the news saying that someone left a bag with his personal effects at the cemetery on the day of his funeral, and his wife, Frankie Jean, immediately left town at the close of the service. No investigation, no suspects, no other mention of the case after that."

"Guess she had no choice but to leave," I piped up.

"You got that right. Everyone said that if she ever showed up again, heads would start to roll and more bodies drop to make sure the secrets behind Silent Sam's power reign over the city would never be revealed, but that was years ago, decades ago." My father pulled on his chin as he spoke.

"Whatever happened to Silent Sam?" Leon asked quietly.

"Nobody knows. People who didn't do business directly with him don't even know what he looks like. There are no pictures. He was never really investigated, never really apprehended. No mug shots, no indictments. Nobody knows what happened to him."

"I Googled Frankie Jean, and Sam, earlier today." I pointed to a darkened computer screen. "But I didn't get any results."

"No, there wouldn't be. Sounds like there are too many secrets to expose. People in powerful places can make records, names, dates, places disappear without even a virtual trace." Leon mulled.

"Well, Frankie Jean returned and heads have been rolling and bodies dropping, forty years since she was last seen around here. Somebody in power is spooked." My father sat back, satisfied with his story.

"Why do you think she came back? Unfinished business?" I asked.

"Or maybe she's just an old woman who tragically lost her husband and her livelihood, who had enough memory to come back home, but enough brokenness to not be able to pull it all together," Leon answered.

"Somebody doesn't want her memories to awaken. And now, she was given a train ticket to get out of town," I recalled.

"They said officials helped her disappear the first time around to keep their tracks covered. I guess there still must be a lot at stake and officials are helping her disappear again. Nobody wants the covers rolled back or the past revisited," my father added.

"The question is who?" I tried to piece it all together. "Leon, you didn't disagree when I concluded that you were investigating something related to the drug market. You hinted that Delmon Frank was part of that investigation and was deep into it. Well, he was following Frankie Jean around, I'm sure of it, so whoever told him to trail her would have some link between the powers that be back then and right now."

"Back then it was guns and numbers that helped run the underground power system. Now it's drugs. Makes sense that there would be a connection. Same pilots, different planes." Leon bit his lip, scratched his head. "Let me get in touch with Mike and update him. See where they are and what he wants to do."

He dialed but hung up without talking.

"No answer," he explained.

"Do you have Shavona's number?"

"No."

"Well, I'll try Roman."

I dialed Roman's number and his voice mail immediately came on, as if his phone was shut off. Yvette's cell phone had the same response.

"I just tried your mother, and I'm not getting an answer either." My father leaned forward in his seat. The three of us looked at each other.

"They're okay," Leon reassured us. "Mike probably had them all turn off their phones as a safety measure, maybe even had them leave them somewhere to avoid being followed."

"But he would have to stay in touch with you, right?"

"He'll probably call me soon."

"So, are we just supposed to be waiting for him to call? What are we supposed to be doing right now, Leon? What's the plan? Where do we go? Where are they?"

"Stop worrying, Sienna. Everything's okay. Please, Mike is a pro at this. Our loved ones are in good hands."

"Okay, Leon, I guess you're right. There's nothing else we can do until he reestablishes contact with you."

My father stood. "Look, you two stay here. I haven't been in the public eye so nobody should pay me no never mind. I'm going to go down to the lobby and use that cab stand to get a cab for us. Leon, you can figure out where you want it to take us. Sienna, you've worked here before, so tell me where you want the cabbie to meet y'all. I figure you don't want to go out the main entrance where someone is bound to be watching."

I thought about it for a moment. "The loading dock. The receiving department is in the basement of the hospital where very few people travel or have access to.

Get the cab to drive to the loading dock, and Leon and I will meet you out there."

"Okay." My father turned to leave. "I'll scope out the area first and will call you when we're there."

My father left, taking the elevator. Leon and I headed to the stairwell.

"Are you going to be okay with all this walking?" Leon eyed my stomach nervously as we headed to the lower level.

"We'll see." I smiled. Truthfully, I was a little nervous myself. Too much was happening. I'd been in plenty of nerve-racking situations before, but none that involved nearly everyone I loved, my family.

Why hadn't I just thrown that woman's stuff away the first night I'd dealt with her? I understood now why Leon hated for me to get too involved. I was drawn to chaos and danger and the secrets of Sweet Violet were nothing but that.

Chapter 37

The lower level was mostly empty when we stepped off of the elevator. A bin with clean scrubs sat near the elevator door and without speaking about it, both Leon and I slipped on tops and bottoms over our clothes to better blend into the underworld of the hospital. Mostly service workers roamed these halls. Nearly everyone wore uniforms, and most were pushing carts or holding containers.

"The loading dock is this way." I pointed, remembering the one time I'd been down here, accompanying KeeKee during one of my coverage nights as she had to pick up a delivery that was waiting for her.

"It's a little bit of a maze down here," Leon commented as we walked through the dimly lit cinderblock hallways. Pipes hung low from the exposed ceilings. Cables and wires lined some of the walls.

"This level is really more like a tunnel that connects all four buildings of this hospital. It's not a straight shot to receiving, but I'm pretty sure that I remember the main turns to the receiving department."

Leon's cell phone rang.

"It's Mike." Leon answered. "Yeah, man, where are you? No, we're on our way to the loading dock. Sienna's dad went to get a cab. Okay, good. We'll be right there." He hung up, but just before he did so, I saw a quick glimpse of his cell's screen.

"Wait a minute?" I froze. "What's Mike's number?"

"Huh? Oh, 443-555-0511," Leon rattled off.

"511. That number has shown up everywhere."

"I'm sure it's just a coincidence, Sienna. There are certain numbers I see all the time. I'm six feet two inches, my old address started with sixty-two, my old basketball jersey was twenty-six. Well, that wasn't exactly sixty-two, but you get the point."

"I don't think all of these 511s are coincidences, Leon. Remember, that pocket watch was stopped at 5:11. The shooting at the bakery was at 5:11. And, if you didn't know already, the money left on Roman was $5.11 at the time of his assault."

"So what are you trying to say, Sienna?" Leon slowed down as we had finally neared the receiving department. Locked doors and a doorbell. We stopped.

"What I'm saying is why does Mike's number have 511 in it?"

Leon groaned. "It's just his number, his cell phone number. Nothing special."

"But what if it is? How did you get involved with Mike anyway?"

"Sienna, you know that we were on the force together."

"No, I mean this time around. How did you get involved with this case you say you've been operating undercover with him?"

"Through Mike, of course. He told me about the need to have someone who was already trained, but was enough on the outside to be an effective observer."

"What exactly were you supposed to be observing, Leon?"

"Just keeping tabs of people involved in investigating high level drug cases. There've been concerns of corruption. That's all."

"Corruption in high places. Sounds familiar." I thought again about what my father shared about Francesca

Dupree, i.e., Frankie Jean. Sweet Violet. "So to avoid discovery you've only dealt with Mike? You've only talked to him and no one else in the department? It's never once crossed your mind that he could just be using you to cover his own tracks?"

"Okay, Sienna, I see where you're going with this, but before you go off on a misdirected tangent and start making assumptions about Mike and his motives, slow down. Mike is as clean as they come. You don't know him like I do. There are things which you don't know about him at all, like his eye, the blinking, his tics. Remember? You thought one thing, but something else was really going on with him. Don't start this again, Sienna."

"I hear you, Leon, and believe me, I'm not trying to embarrass myself or you again. I just find Mike's number way too coincidental. Can you tell me what exactly you've been finding out in your investigation?"

Leon sighed, shook his head, then: "Like I said: drugs and corruption. Apparently there's a fear that some people in high places, including police officers and possibly a person or persons in the state's attorney's office, are part of the drug network in the city. Heroin, cocaine, pills. Big money. That's why they needed someone who wasn't directly tied to the department to be an observer. Things got sticky when you became involved in the trial." Leon sighed again. "Look, Sienna, to be honest with you, things haven't been making sense to me either. The safe house, the sedans being driven around, I don't know how the department could be funding all of this, while at the same time investigating itself."

"And you only deal with Mike."

"Yeah, no one else."

"What about that detective who planned our trip, Sam Fields? Has he been part of this whole operation?"

"No, I contacted him myself since I knew that he was good at helping people get to safety. I remember how he helped those girls safely disappear when you dealt with their crazy mother and her fiance at your practice a few years ago. Mike was upset that I got Sam Fields involved, but like I told you from the get-go, I will do whatever it takes to keep you safe."

"My stomach is tightening up again." It was a small tug, but enough to let me know I probably needed to get off of my feet.

"Let's keep it moving." Leon rang the doorbell of the receiving department.

"May I help you?" a voice scratched through a box beneath the buzzer.

"Yes, we need to . . . drop something off." Leon looked at me and shrugged. The door opened and we walked in.

"Just so you know, Sienna, I got that detective to help make plans for us. And I also got him to give that train ticket to Sweet Violet."

My head swung over to meet his. "What?"

"I didn't know all that history behind her, but I wanted to get her off the scene so you would stop obsessing over her. I told him to make sure a shelter would receive her and take care of her wherever he sent her. I was going to tell you once things calmed down a bit."

"Can I help you?" a young man wearing a T-shirt and jeans came to meet us at the door.

"We just need to go to the loading dock." I looked over at Leon.

"Are you expecting a delivery?"

"Um . . ." Clearly I had not thought this through very well.

"Wait here." The young man turned toward an office. "I need you to fill something out."

"Let's go." Leon nudged me toward the open gate and ramp on the other side of the room as soon as the young man disappeared into an office. We both hurried to the exit.

"Hello? Where'd they go?" We both heard the young man's voice from inside the building as we jumped down to the ground. Darting between two parked trucks, we stayed out of view until we reached the main street. Rush hour traffic was still clogging the roads, but we could see a bright yellow taxicab in the traffic leaving the main driveway of the hospital, about two blocks away. Leon sighed, looking around. There was nothing else for us to do, nowhere else for us to go; just wait and see and pray that this was the taxi my father was in.

"The cab that was supposed to take us to the airport had the numbers 511 on it," I told Leon as the taxi neared us, now only a block away. "Do you think that was a true coincidence?"

"All right, 511, what would it mean, Sienna? A date, a time, an address? What is it that you think it is, since you're so convinced it's not a coincidence?"

I thought about Mike's phone number. "511, that's the phone number travelers can use to check traffic conditions, right? Like 411 is for information, and 911 is for emergencies, right?"

"Yes, Sienna."

"You said you've been helping to investigate drug trafficking involving people in high places. I know it's a stretch, but what if 511 is some type of code they are using to communicate in their drug trafficking ring? If you're talking about corrupt police officers and attorneys who are intermingled in the system with those who are doing right, maybe using those numbers helps tip the bad guys on what they do, who they prosecute, who not to investigate."

"I'm not following you, Sienna."

"For example, Roman was left with $5.11 when those guys beat him. What if somebody, recognizing that the attack had ties to your investigation, made the call to treat it like a random street robbery and nothing more, to keep investigators and resources from digging into it too deeply? And we were shot at in your bakery at 5:11 and from what I can tell, after the initial confusion, it was chalked up to a botched robbery, which doesn't make sense. It's a stretch, I know, but I can't think of anything else."

"Okay, like you said it is a stretch, but if what you're saying is true, how does any of it apply to Sweet Violet?"

"I don't know." I thought about it as the cab crept closer in the evening commuter traffic. "Maybe it's about what she revealed in her stories. Maybe that's what she uncovered, how corrupt leaders were communicating with each other."

I thought more about it, trying to come up with a scenario that made sense. "I'd be willing to bet . . . that her husband just happened to be killed at 5:11. That pocket watch was probably in his bag of personal effects left at his funeral and that it was intentionally set and broken at 5:11 as a sign to her, a warning for her to get out of town. They didn't want her dead, just not around. Maybe Silent Sam, or whoever, was a little sweet on her. I don't know. Leon, I could speculate for hours and days over this, but who knows."

Leon stared at me, trying to keep up as I continued.

"Maybe, just maybe, the numbers 511 started out as a coincidence, but then stayed around, like I said, as a code for communication. Though she seems to be out of her mind now, her return, her presence has been enough to get someone riled up. I've been thinking all along that whenever she shows up, something bad happens. Maybe

I have it backward. Maybe something bad happens because she showed up and someone else is trying to cover tracks that would reveal the past and its present connection to how communication is happening among those who are part of the trafficking ring."

"So, Sienna, you're thinking that Sweet Violet may have exposed the communication channels of corrupt leaders, and those channels and codes have persisted up to today?"

"In light of what we know, doesn't it seem at least possible? Maybe Delmon Frank is one of the corrupt ones. Like I said, I am certain that he was following her around. Clearly someone who knows what's going on is. You said yourself that Alisa Billy's death wasn't part of the plan. And don't forget, something happened at A New Beginning House just now, according to the news. If something bad did happen there, it's almost as if someone is strategically wiping away any current memories or ties to Frankie Jean, because bringing her story back up may bring back new suspicions and a new investigation about current corruption in high places." I thought some more. "And let me just remind you that Mike was quick to turn off the news, remember?"

"Sienna, stop." Leon finally broke his silence. "Like I said, Mike is as clean as they come and I hate that you even have me questioning his integrity. He's been a good friend to me, one of the best. You were wrong about the winking, and you are very wrong about any role he may have in all of this." He said it with certainty, but I could see the slight question in his eyes.

The idea that he was having doubts only fed my fears more.

"Besides, everything does not tie back to Sweet Violet." Leon mulled as the cab was only on the other side of the light. "I get the tie to the first two murder victims. Marta knew who she was, and Amber must have gotten wind of some of her story to have had her purse and know her name. But the third victim, Julian Morgan, how is Sweet Violet involved? I know you said she was in the area just before he got struck by that stray bullet, but it was a stray bullet, Sienna."

"Maybe we missed something. What if it really wasn't a stray? What if it was an elaborate setup? Remember last night? Your bakery? Anything is possible." I pulled out my phone as the light turned green, and did a quick Google search of Julian Morgan. An article about his tragic death on the first of January was one of the first that popped up. "Oh my goodness, look, Leon." I pointed to my screen.

Leon's eyes narrowed and then blinked rapidly.

"The article was posted on January second, at 5:11 a.m. It can't be a coincidence." I looked up at my husband. "This ring of people must even have someone in the media involved to control what stories get out there, and when." We stared at each other as the cab finally pulled to a stop in front of us.

Mike sat alone in the back seat.

"Where's my father?" I asked through the open window. Leon grabbed my hand. I felt sweat in his palm.

He had questions, doubts. *What if I'm wrong?* A pang of guilt flashed through me as I recalled the embarrassment I'd had about the winking.

"I ran into your dad at the main entrance and I redirected him to the others," Mike explained. "Don't worry, they are all safe. I told him that I would take over the plan along with Leon from here."

"So, where is everyone else?" Leon's voice was barely audible. Neither one of us had reached for the door.

"Are you getting in?" Mike reached over and pushed the door open. "My guys sent a van to meet them and get them to the house on Maryland Avenue."

Leon stood stiff for a moment, and then I watched his chest relax. "Okay, is that where we're going?"

"We'll figure it out once we get in the car. Let's just get out of here. Traffic is waiting behind us. Wait, I'll get up front." Mike hopped out and moved to the front passenger seat. "Yes, let's just go there." As Mike gave the driver the address to the house on Maryland Avenue, Leon looked at me, nodded. "Come on," he directed.

I looked at the driver. He wasn't the same one from earlier. The cab number was 1427.

But then again, my dad had called this cab and he wasn't in it, so I was not entirely comforted that all was well, especially with Mike sitting in the front seat.

What if I'm wrong? Leon still looked like he had a question in his mind, but he opened the door for me and then went around the other side of the car to sit behind the driver.

Chapter 38

"You looking up something on your phone?" Mike saw my screen as I got in.

"Yeah, um, just looking up about the death of Julian Morgan back in January."

"That was tragic." Mike shook his head as the cab began its way toward Charles Village. "The city really took a loss with his death. He was the funder behind so many projects, many of which he didn't even tie his name to. Businesses, buildings. Sienna, as a social worker, you would appreciate his generosity to the underprivileged. He gave to foster care programs, hospitals, even that shelter where the first victim worked."

"He helped fund A New Beginning House?" I gave a quick glance at Leon who was glancing back at me.

"Well, not really. He just owned the building where it's located. Let them stay there rent free."

"Wow. That's something. Whatever happened there today, anyway? Have you heard?" I managed to squeak out, fearful of the possibilities as I pictured Sister Agnes at the desk.

"Someone shot out the front windows. That's all. Thankfully they keep that entrance barred and locked, or it could have been much worse." Mike shook his head.

"Shot out the windows, like what happened to my bakery?"

"Crazy, huh?" Mike shook his head again.

Leon's head tilted to one side. "And you said Mr. Morgan owned that property where A New Beginning House stands?"

"Yes; a lot of people don't realize that he owned a lot of the property and homes on that block."

"That's interesting." Leon looked thoughtful. "Very interesting. We'd heard that the city couldn't get a hold of the owner of some of the vacant homes on that street. They're trying to redevelop it, get rid of some of the blight."

"Well, it's hard to do business with a dead guy, even one who worked so closely with many city officials."

"Seemed like he was a little of a slumlord to me, the way those vacant homes around there looked." I threw in my two cents.

"I said he was a funder. I never said he was a saint."

"You seem to know a lot about him," Leon commented. "You never shared this before."

"Well, your wife was close to the case of the man charged with killing him. I didn't want to taint her testimony in any way, you know. Let justice be done."

"Even though you knew it wasn't a real case." He and Mike exchanged glances. Mike didn't reply.

"So," Leon continued, "Morgan was close to the police department too, I take it, since you seem to have known him so well."

"Yeah, he definitely was close to us. In fact, Mr. Morgan owned the house on Maryland Avenue. He was very dedicated to providing resources to us to help us get our job done, stay a step ahead of the . . . bad guys."

"That's interesting," Leon replied. I saw his eyes narrow a bit. "Let me ask you this: how did he get his money? I knew he was well off, but you don't usually see that many black men in Baltimore with that much wealth, enough to seemingly support half of the city."

"I don't know exactly how he got started," Mike explained, "but I always got the sense that his was a rags-to-riches type of story, pulled up from his own bootstraps, dark past, that kind of thing. He used to tell people that his road to success was proof that a rose could bloom in darkness."

"Flowers can't tell lies. If you keep the sun off of them, dry up their waterbeds, and throw in weeds to choke 'em out, ain't no way or reason for them to bloom. If a rose is in full bloom when you know it's only been kept in darkness, and the ground it's planted in is cracked and cold, don't stop to smell that rose. There's a trap somewhere in those tempting dark red petals. There's deceit. Maybe even death. Run from that flowerbed. You don't want to get buried in that soil."

The words of Sweet Violet, uttered moments before Julian Morgan was shot to death.

A chill went through me that started at my feet and worked its way up to my head. My body felt like a piece of cold, heavy lead, but my fingers thawed out enough to send Leon a text:

I think Julian Morgan is Silent Sam.

Leon's phone chimed and he read my text.

I think ur right, he texted back. And someone must have wanted him out the picture. Too risky with Frankie Jean's return, maybe.

I read Leon's text and then looked up. Through the passenger's side rearview mirror, I saw Mike staring at me. He'd said so much about Julian Morgan just now, I wondered if it was a test, to see how much we knew.

Or maybe I'd watched too many movies and read too many books and my imagination was going wild.

I didn't know what to trust, what to believe anymore.

Trust me, a soft, gentle voice spoke to my consciousness. I shut my eyes, grateful for the sudden feeling of peace that took over my nerves. The last few weeks and months of raging hormones, questions, and fears had almost blinded me to the fact that Someone greater than me was working out the details and securing my safety. I didn't know what to think right now, what to feel, or how to interpret the slew of information that had landed in my lap over the past few hours, but I knew that I was going to have to step outside of my feelings and own understanding, and stand in a realm of faith; faith that all this was working together for a reason, that all this was happening in a season when I was still new to love.

I looked over at Leon and realized that the certainty and peace that I'd seen take over him when he nudged us into the car must have been driven by the same calm voice of assurance that had just spoken to me. He'd felt it, and led me, and I'd followed, now feeling the same confidence that all would be okay.

Maybe, despite the rocky first year of our bumps and squabbles, we really were on the right path toward perfecting our partnership, of becoming one, of leaning on and learning from each other, of melding our strengths and weaknesses to form a new living, breathing organism wrought in love and strengthened by faith. I rubbed my stomach and patted over a flurry of kicks that suddenly fluttered inside of me. I smiled feeling a sense of divine perfection at that moment as a new realization came to mind. Our baby was simply the physical evidence of the deeper spiritual union Leon and I created, were creating. We were joined together, for better or for worse, and this new life was a new thing that had sprung from our vows. Just like our marriage, our teamwork, our unified partnership was a new created thing in and of itself.

I would have thought on these things some more as the car zoomed up 83, but my phone vibrated, letting me know I had another text. I clicked it open to see what message Leon had sent me, but the message wasn't from him.

Horace Monroe. I'd spoken with him earlier that day, asking if he could research the owner of the vacant homes near the shelter.

Mike had already volunteered that information, but the text from Horace was just the confirmation I needed.

> Hi, Sienna. I couldn't find the name of a person, but the corporation that owns that house you asked about is named Fifth and Eleventh, Inc.

I forwarded the text to Leon. He nodded and reached out his hand and took mine. With his fingers softly massaging my palms, I knew that whatever happened next, we would be together and okay.

The driver had turned onto Maryland Avenue and we were just blocks away from the safe house.

"Whoa!" The cabbie slammed on his brakes and we all jolted forward in our seats. The tires squealed as we just missed a police cruiser speeding by.

"What the . . ." Mike leaned forward in his seat and we all saw what had gotten his attention. Several police cars surrounded the towering row home where we were headed. Shavona Grant sat on the front steps, crying, rocking, shaking. Her cries sounded over the multitude of sirens zooming around us as more emergency vehicles skidded to a stop in front of the house.

"Turn the car around," Mike's voice was suddenly gruff, demanding.

"Your wife." Leon reached for the door handle. "What's going on?"

"Don't get out," Mike barked. "Turn the car around and go," he commanded the driver.

The cabbie was wide-eyed, and then he gasped and gripped the wheel with both hands. "Don't shoot!" he screamed.

Chapter 39

A gun.

I saw the metal in Mike's hand. Leon saw it too, and reached for his own weapon and pointed it at Mike.

"Get out the car, Sienna." Leon's voice was a low growl.

"I can't . . . I'm not . . ."

"Get. Out. Of. The. Car."

"Leon, I can't leave you."

"She can't leave, Leon." Mike's eyes had a darkness that I'd never seen before. "You both know too much."

"She's getting out." Leon's voice was calm, firm.

"Leon." My voice was a whisper, breaking. "I am not leaving you."

"Sienna, baby, I told you that I would always keep you safe. That is what I'm doing. Get out of the car and run over to those police officers. You are safe. Do it now."

"Leon—"

"Do it now before I have to kill my best friend." A single tear rolled down his cheek.

I reached for the handle, nobody else moved.

"Now, Sienna. I love you."

I touched the handle, pulled it open, and jumped out. Leon reached over and slammed the door shut. The car roared to life and tore around a corner; the tires left skid marks and smoke in its wake.

"Help! Help!" I found my voice and my legs somehow moved underneath me. I cradled my belly to keep it from bouncing and jostling as I ran the half block or so to where officers surrounded the house. "Help!" I ran up to the nearest officer, a woman with a short blond afro.

"Sienna St. James," she recognized me, "what's wrong?"

"My husband. The cab. They just left. They had guns out at each other." I was out of breath, panting, unable to get my words together. Shavona who had been crying on the steps must have seen me coming because she suddenly had her arms around me, tears and snot dripping all over my blouse.

"There were drugs in this house. I got dropped off here and when I was trying to find some food to fix, I came across all these blocks of cocaine, heroin, all kinds of stuff, and a bunch of fake IDs and badges with his picture were mixed in with it all. I didn't know, I didn't know he was like this. He lied, he lied. What do I do? Oh, my God. Oh, my God." Shavona would not stop weeping. Her head dug into my shoulder, her nails into my shoulder blade. "I don't know where he is. I called 911 because I didn't know what else to do. Am I wrong? Oh, God, I don't know what to do." She moaned.

"They just took off in that cab." I still panted. A new tightening sensation crawled across my stomach.

"In a cab?" An officer heard me.

"1427. That's the cab number." I remembered the number because I had specifically checked it to make sure it wasn't 511. "A Yellow Cab, number 1427. Both our husbands are in it and they both had guns pointing at each other."

"Oh, Jesus," Shavona shrieked and moaned, and then began throwing up.

The officers went into action. Some darting off, some on walkie-talkies and cell phones.

"Where is my family? Shavona, where are they? Inside?" I grabbed her by the shoulders, needing answers.

"No, no, no." She shook her head, gasping for air. "He told them to get in a van when we left out the hospital, said it would take them somewhere safe. Then I got brought here. I didn't think anything of it. Sienna, I'm sorry, I don't know what's going on. I don't know this man. I don't know this man anymore." She began sobbing again.

"Shavona, listen to me." I held her shoulders firmly. "Listen, I know what it's like to marry someone and then discover they are not who you think they are. Roman's father." I shook my head, shaking off the memories. "We'll talk one day. Right now, we need to be strong and get it together. The situation is not over and these police need our help to make sure our husbands are okay."

"Ms. St. James, do you have any idea where they were headed?" The police officer with the blond afro stepped up to me.

"It's Mrs. Sanderson now, and I have no idea." I laid my hand on my belly, watched as another officer wrapped a blue blanket around Shavona. "Wait, I think I do know a place they could be going."

We passed by A New Beginning House on our way there. New yellow crime scene tape surrounded the building as pieces of glass and shell casings lay shattered on the ground. The police cruiser I was in came to a stop.

"Stay here," the officer who let me drive with her commanded. Shavona was slumped over in the rear seat next to me, her sniffles still alternating with quiet moans.

I got out of the car and marched right behind the line of officers approaching the house.

Amber's abandominium.

It had been a crime scene already and was close to an active one, so it made sense to me, for some reason, to believe that Mike would want to head there, perhaps thinking it would be off the authorities' radar as too obvious of a place to check.

A SWAT team ran through the alley behind the home. Nobody stopped me as I ran close behind, watching them attempt to secure the house from the rear.

A Yellow Cab was parked out back.

Shots.

I instinctively ducked and ran the other way as the sound of gunfire peppered the air. A flock of pigeons who'd been squawking and bobbing their heads in the alley flew off.

I held my breath from where I squatted by an overgrown bush.

And then I exhaled.

Leon came walking out the house, a self-assured, confident strut. No fear, no sorrow. He held the hand of my mother, patted the shoulder of my sister. Roman followed, and then my dad. They had remnants of duct tape on their legs, their arms. My sister had a small trail of blood leaving her mouth.

But she was smiling.

After a few moments, Delmon Frank came out of the house, the undercover cop charged with murder, who, in the end, was part of the network of deceit and lies holding the city under hostage, a network complete with corrupt officers and politicians, business owners, and other high and well-placed decision makers. Reports would later reveal that some members of the media were, as I suspected, part of this inner circle that was funded by the drug trade and kept afloat by million dollar payouts.

Alisa Billy's assistant, Joe Koletsky, was in on it too.

And Mike Grant.

He left on a stretcher, Leon forced to shoot him in the arm and leg; nonlethal force to take down a man who'd been bent on getting rid of everyone who had an inkling of the 511 connection, and the elderly, homeless woman who started it all. The only reason she'd been kept alive was to track her steps and see who else knew the secrets she represented, who else needed to be shut down. To kill her would have opened the door to a potential investigation no one in the ring wanted to happen.

Her mind was breaking, not fully gone, but tearing into pieces from old age and dementia.

"She never used that train ticket," Detective Sam Fields would later tell Leon. "Some officers found her in War Memorial Plaza, dancing, singing, and pouring liquor all over the grass."

Turns out her husband had been in the army when she first met him, and he must have been real sharp looking in his uniform as that was a memory she'd held on to. In her mental fogginess, she thought the War Memorial Plaza was a military graveyard and that he was buried there. I found an assisted living facility that housed her for free and Ava let me bring her to her house from time to time to plant new flowers in her garden.

But those were facts and details that would come later.

At that moment, standing by the bushes, watching all my loved ones leave the vacant home in one piece, safe, smiling, the nightmare over, all secrets disempowered, I felt only one thing.

My water break.

Chapter 40

Three months later

"Uh-oh, girl, you really messed up with this one."
Yvette licked the barbecue sauce off of her fingers and
downed another glass of my sparkling limeade. "You do
realize that we're going to have to have our small group
sessions over here all the time now."

We were all sitting in the family room of our Canton
condo, the waters of the outer harbor sparkling through
the windows, boats docked by the pier below, sea gulls
gliding in the horizon of the setting sun.

"I know that's right," the girl with two long braids, dyed
red, jumped in. Her name was Tina. Roman sat next to
her, his eyes drinking her in as they shared a Bible on
their laps. She'd just finished a two-year nursing degree
at a community college and had plans to transfer to a
four-year university. Maybe one out of town. San Diego
was on her short list. Roman had flown all the way back
home from his studies out there for Labor Day weekend,
"to attend the small group session," he said, so I knew
something serious between the two of them was budding.

I liked her for my son.

"Well, if we don't do our sessions here, we at least
should have Sienna do the food." A man joined in from
a folding chair set up by the gas fireplace. "No offense
to your cooking, Yvette, but between these barbecued
chicken wings that your sister made and the cupcakes from

Brother Leon's bakery, I'm almost ready to agree to a vow renewal ceremony, just to have them cater the reception." He leaned forward in his seat. "The key word is 'almost.'"

"Charlie, shut up!" His wife squealed as the room broke out into laughter again. Leon ran his hand up my back, rubbed my shoulder. I could smell the sugar on him from his full day at the bakery.

"Sounds like we need to have another talk about relationships," the man with black glasses said. They called him Deac.

"Oh, Lawd, here we go," Charlie groaned and turned toward another couple. "Go ahead, Demari, say what you got to say."

Yvette's husband's lips were indeed parted as if he was about to speak. Everyone noticed and the roar of laughter began again.

"Seriously, though," Deac spoke over the hoots and giggles, "maybe tonight we can go over First Corinthians thirteen again, the chapter that defines love down to a tee."

"All you young folk ever do is talk about love and relationships." Sister Randy frowned, her eyes looking at us all over her bifocals.

"Oh, hush, Sister Randy." The sixty-something woman sitting next to her waved her hand. "Ain't no different than our phone conversations. What was that minister's name you had your eye on at the church banquet?"

"Sister Randy!" Tina gasped. "You were checking out that young preacher from St. Mount Carmel Ministries? He's about half your age. Ooooh."

After the laughs died down, and the Bible pages stopped turning, after the conversation and tears stopped flowing, after the last guest was walked to the door, and the last dish was washed and rinsed, I patted Leon on the arm. "I need to go check on the baby."

He smiled, followed me to the nursery.

I opened the door. The smell of lavender and the sound of a soft coo greeted me.

"She's up." I smiled. We walked to the crib, but Leon got to her first.

"Ava Grace Sanderson." He picked her up, snuggled his scratchy chin next to her soft one. She flashed her wide, toothless grin and we both smiled back.

"Who would have imagined we'd be standing here like this?" I looked at my daughter and her father.

"Who would have imagined we'd be standing here at all?" Leon smiled at me.

She had her father's dimples, my honey brown skin, and a look in her eyes that told me Roman had only been my warm-up child.

That was okay, though. I'd had forty years to get ready for this one. All I'd been through, all I'd learned, all I'd become, made me ready to mother this girl right here.

I looked up at her name on the wall, a collage made of dried flowers and bits of material: silk, satin, tulle, and lace. Shavona had created it and given it as a gift at the baby's dedication dinner. I'd had no idea that Shavona shared an interest in art like me, an interest I'd rekindled with the new book proposal I'd given my agent. "I'm not a writer, I'm an artist, and I can use my gift to change people, make a difference some kind of way," I explained the change of direction. Instead of retelling my story, the adventures of the past few years with the crazy cases I'd managed, and the near-death situations I'd brought on myself and my family, I would use my art skills to create pictures and portraits of hope, using visual media to cover themes of healing.

The publisher thought my idea was unique enough to be a bestseller, and potent enough to be necessary.

The book would be both art and therapy, the ultimate combination of the best I had to offer.

"For the record, Sienna," Leon's voice whispered in my ear, "I always believed in you. I've always trusted your instincts. I mean, after all, you did marry me." We both chuckled, but then he sobered. "I was going to wait until we finally go on our beach trip in a few months, but who knows what you'll have us into then."

He passed baby Ava to me and then reached for a box stowed on the top of her closet shelf. "I never told you that I saw you leave that woman's bag near the tree by my bakery on New Year's Day. You left it there and then I took it. I never told you that I had it. I took that dirty bag of her things and held on to that pocket watch, Sienna. I want you to know that I have always trusted you, even when you thought I was not paying attention."

He opened a shoebox I hadn't noticed sitting on the shelf. He reached into it and took out a worn black purse. It was the same purse that had been hanging from Sweet Violet's wrist on our wedding day, the day she first showed up in our lives, tapping on the glass window at our reception.

"I'll give her the watch next time I see her." I smiled, feeling like it was the right thing to do. I opened the bag, felt for the small tear in the lining. Pulled out the newspaper that held the broken pocket watch.

Newspaper.

I'd forgotten that the watch had been wrapped in newspaper.

"Hmm." I opened up the yellowed paper, passed Leon the watch, then smoothed down the wrinkled creases. I smiled at the scrap and what it said.

"The *Garwyn Oaks Gazette*," I read the name of the paper, dated August, 1969. "Look, a poem, written by"—I smiled—"by Francesca J. Dupree." I pointed to a short column at the bottom of the scrap of paper.

"Read it out loud." Leon smiled.

"Sweet Violet"

I'm his flower, he said,
I'm his sweet violet bouquet.
And he's the bloom in my life
That brightens my day.
Without him I wilt like an untended bud,
I turn from a sweet violet blossom to a violent
bitter flood
Of broken petals scattered in a loveless wind.
But then he returns and I am planted and rooted
again.
I get drunk in his arms
and lose track of the hours
When he
Waters me,
and shines on me
like I'm the world's only flower.

"Not quite Shakespeare." Leon smiled.

"No, but I can fully relate." I closed my eyes thinking of the days in the past when I didn't have Leon, and now the time of my present that he was there for me to love. I opened my eyes and gave him a smile that started somewhere deep inside of me and ended on the curl of my lips.

"I love you, Leon."

He bent down, moved closer, kissed me, from my neck, to my ear, to my mouth. "And I love you, Sienna. Always." His arms wrapped around me, wrapped around our baby.

She sighed and I realized she'd fallen asleep. I put her down in the crib and then stood back up to face him.

"And now," he murmured, pulling me close to him.

"And now what?" Everything in me felt like hot sugar, a dripping glaze, melting in the heat of his chest, in the warmth of his arms.

"And now," he whispered, "it's our time."

Reading Group Guide

1. Sienna and Leon marry at the outset of the book following a brief reunion. How do you know when it's time to marry someone?
2. As newlyweds, Sienna and Leon have frequent disagreements about how she spends her time. Leon believes that her priorities are misplaced and Sienna believes that he does not respect her responsibilities as a business owner in the human service field. Are either of them correct in their perspectives? Why or why not?
3. Sienna learns that Leon has kept secrets and hid information both about himself and her son. Was he justified in keeping her in the dark? Is it ever okay to keep secrets in a marriage?
4. Sienna insists on finding Sweet Violet to return her personal belongings. She acknowledges that it is difficult for her to "let things go" once she has set her mind on helping someone or getting information. At what point, if ever, is it okay to leave a matter alone? Have you ever faced a situation where your gut wanted to move forward, but your logic told you otherwise? Which part of you won and why? What were the results?
5. Roman believes that God has directed him to make a life-changing decision, but then later questions whether or not he truly heard God's voice. When you are faced with a major decision, how do you know God's will for sure?

6. Sienna comes to terms with the fact that she has been lacking genuine friendships. She has had mentors and close relatives, but no longstanding peer friendships. Why has she experienced such distance in social relationships? What does she need to do to change this area of her life? Do you think Shavona is a good friend for her? Why or why not?

7. Often, a wedding day is seen as the quintessential moment of a romantic relationship, when in reality the wedding day is just the beginning of a brand new lifelong experience. What issues did Leon and Sienna have to work on throughout their first year of marriage that they may or may not have expected? What are common obstacles to oneness that arise when two people join together in marital union?

8. Yvette's church has initiated a way of fellowshipping beyond Sunday morning. What do you think of the small group session? What is its purpose? Are there any potential pitfalls of such a gathering? Are there any potential positive outcomes?

9. Where would you say Sienna is in her walk with the Lord? Is her faith strong or weak? How does her faith guide her actions and decisions, or does it? Is her faith in the background or foreground of her life?

10. Sweet Violet offers Sienna random advice and insights based on her mysterious past. Does she say anything that makes sense? Do any of her observations ring true to you? Why or why not?

11. Take a moment to read Ecclesiastes 3: 1–8, which details times and seasons that occur in life. In what time or season do you see your own life? Are you content in your current season? Why or why not? What's next for you?

Author Bio

Leslie J. Sherrod, the recipient of the SORMAG Readers Choice Award for Christian Author of the Year (2012), has a master's in social work and has worked as a social worker, just like her current protagonist, Sienna St. James. Her novels, *Sacrifices of Joy, Without Faith, Losing Hope, Secret Place,* and *Like Sheep Gone Astray,* have been featured in Baltimore's Enoch Pratt Free Library Writers LIVE! series, as well as local CBS and NBC affiliates, and on AOL's Black Voices. She has received a starred review from Booklist and is a contributor to the bestselling *A Cup of Comfort* devotional series. A graduate of the University of Maryland, Leslie lives in Baltimore, Maryland with her husband and three children.

UC HIS GLORY BOOK CLUB!

www.uchisglorybookclub.net

UC His Glory Book Club is the spirit-inspired brain-child of Joylynn Ross, Author and Acquisitions Editor of Urban Christian, and Kendra Norman-Bellamy, Author for Urban Christian. This is an online book club that hosts authors of Urban Christian. We welcome as members all men and women who have a passion for reading Christian-based fiction.

UC His Glory Book Club pledges our commitment to provide support, positive feedback, encouragement, and a forum whereby members can openly discuss and review the literary works of Urban Christian authors.

There is no membership fee associated with UC His Glory Book Club; however, we do ask that you support the authors through purchasing, encouraging, providing book reviews, and of course, your prayers. We also ask that you respect our beliefs and follow the guidelines of the book club. We hope to receive your valuable input, opinions, and reviews that build up, rather than tear down our authors.

What We Believe:

—We believe that Jesus is the Christ, Son of the Living God.

—We believe the Bible is the true, living Word of God.

—We believe all Urban Christian authors should use their God-given writing abilities to honor God and share the message of the written word God has given to each of them uniquely.

—We believe in supporting Urban Christian authors in their literary endeavors by reading, purchasing and sharing their titles with our online community.

—We believe that in everything we do in our literary arena should be done in a manner that will lead to God being glorified and honored.

We look forward to the online fellowship with you. Please visit us often at *www.uchisglorybookclub.net.*

Many Blessing to You!

Shelia E. Lipsey,
President, UC His Glory Book Club

ORDER FORM
URBAN BOOKS, LLC
97 N18th Street
Wyandanch, NY 11798

Name (please print):_____

Address: _____

City/State: _____

Zip: _____

QTY	TITLES	PRICE

Shipping and handling: add $3.50 for 1st book, then $1.75 for each additional book.
Please send a check payable to:
Urban Books, LLC
Please allow 4-6 weeks for delivery

ORDER FORM
URBAN BOOKS, LLC
97 N18th Street
Wyandanch, NY 11798

Name (please print):_____

Address: _____

City/State: _____

Zip: _____

QTY	TITLES	PRICE
	3:57 A.M Timing Is Everything	$14.95
	A Man's Worth	$14.95
	A Woman's Worth	$14.95
	Abundant Rain	$14.95
	After The Feeling	$14.95
	Amaryllis	$14.95
	An Inconvenient Friend	$14.95
	Battle of Jericho	$14.95
	Be Careful What You Pray For	$14.95
	Beautiful Ugly	$14.95
	Been There Prayed That:	$14.95
	Before Redemption	$14.95

Shipping and handling-add $3.50 for 1st book, then $1.75 for each additional book.
Please send a check payable to:
   Urban Books, LLC
Please allow 4-6 weeks for delivery

ORDER FORM
URBAN BOOKS, LLC
97 N18th Street
Wyandanch, NY 11798

Name(please print):_____

Address: _____

City/State: _____

Zip: _____

QTY	TITLES	PRICE
	By the Grace of God	$14.95
	Confessions Of A Preachers Wife	$14.95
	Dance Into Destiny	$14.95
	Deliver Me From My Enemies	$14.95
	Desperate Decisions	$14.95
	Divorcing the Devil	$14.95
	Faith	$14.95
	First Comes Love	$14.95
	Flaws and All	$14.95
	Forgiven	$14.95
	Former Rain	$14.95
	Humbled	$14.95

Shipping and handling-add $3.50 for 1st book, then $1.75 for each additional book.

Please send a check payable to:

Urban Books, LLC

Please allow 4-6 weeks for delivery

ORDER FORM
URBAN BOOKS, LLC
97 N18th Street
Wyandanch, NY 11798

Name (please print):_____

Address: _____

City/State: _____

Zip: _____

QTY	TITLES	PRICE
	From Sinner To Saint	$14.95
	From The Extreme	$14.95
	God Is In Love With You	$14.95
	God Speaks To Me	$14.95
	Grace And Mercy	$14.95
	Guilty Of Love	$14.95
	Happily Ever Now	$14.95
	Heaven Bound	$14.95
	His Grace His Mercy	$14.95
	His Woman His Wife His Widow	$14.95
	Illusions	$14.95
	In Green Pastures	$14.95

Shipping and handling-add $3.50 for 1st book, then $1.75 for each additional book.
Please send a check payable to:
Urban Books, LLC
Please allow 4-6 weeks for delivery